ILLUSION OF SAFETY

BOOK ONE

AVALON O'CLAIR

Copyright © 2023 by Avalon O'Clair

Knights of Orion Citadel™

All rights reserved.

No part of this publication may be reproduced, distributed, or transmitted in any form or by any means, including photocopying, recording, or other electronic or mechanical methods, without the prior written permission of the publisher, except as permitted by U.S. copyright law. For permission requests, contact Avalonoclair@gmail.com.

The story, all names, characters, and incidents portrayed in this production are fictitious. No identification with actual persons (living or deceased), places, buildings, and products is intended or should be inferred.

For my sons, Anthony and Joseph.

May your lives forever be blessed with honor, purpose, the love of family...

...and a touch of magic.

Acknowledgements

Much gratitude to my fabulous editors at Bookmarten Editorial, Brenna Bailey-Davies and Aubry Bennett, for their invaluable guidance in making Knights of Orion Citadel – Illusion of Safety a book of which I am truly proud.

Visit them at https://www.bookmarteneditorial.com

Thanks to the talented folks at MiblArt book cover design services for the amazing series cover design. Visit them at https://miblart.com

Thank you to all my wonderful beta readers (you know who you are) who helped me tremendously in honing my manuscript. You all rock!

Heartfelt thanks to my dear friend Catherine, for the unfailing encouragement, the long walks, and the long talks. God only knows how many gallons of coffee we've enjoyed together while chatting about everything from aliens, to bigfoot, to bases on the moon, kitchen paint colors, religion and the afterlife, and how the price of every damn thing has gotten way out of hand.

Just not politics.
Because I don't do politics.

Contents

1. Chapter 1 — 1
2. Chapter 2 — 9
3. Chapter 3 — 21
4. Chapter 4 — 33
5. Chapter 5 — 45
6. Chapter 6 — 56
7. Chapter 7 — 68
8. Chapter 8 — 79
9. Chapter 9 — 89
10. Chapter 10 — 99
11. Chapter 11 — 108
12. Chapter 12 — 119
13. Chapter 13 — 130
14. Chapter 14 — 142
15. Chapter 15 — 153
16. Chapter 16 — 165
17. Chapter 17 — 176
18. Chapter 18 — 186
19. Chapter 19 — 198

20.	Chapter 20	208
21.	Chapter 21	217
22.	Chapter 22	225
23.	Chapter 23	235
24.	Chapter 24	246
25.	Chapter 25	253
26.	Chapter 26	263
27.	Chapter 27	276
28.	Chapter 28	289
29.	Chapter 29	297
30.	Chapter 30	307
31.	Chapter 31	316
32.	Chapter 32	324
33.	Chapter 33	333
34.	Chapter 34	342
35.	Chapter 35	352
36.	Chapter 36	362
37.	Chapter 37	373
38.	Chapter 38	386
		398

Chapter One

TEN YEARS AGO - Long Island, NY

THUNDER RUMBLED AS EMMA waved goodbye to the white Mercedes that dropped her off. She stood in the glow of a streetlight as the happy family drove away, her smile melting under tears that blurred her vision and chilled her cheeks in the frigid air.

She imagined Heather tickling her baby brother and chattering nonstop from the backseat about winning a tenth-place ribbon in the karate tournament. She choked back a sob. Heather's parents had sat in the front row, as usual, clapping and cheering for their daughter.

Despite the late hour and threatening weather, she lingered on the sidewalk, watching red taillights grow smaller and smaller as the car cruised down the tree-lined avenue, leaving a swirling wake of crimson and gold leaves before disappearing behind the brick wall of the gated community.

Enough with the self-pity! She squared her shoulders, drew a sharp breath, and scrubbed at the tears with her woolen coat sleeve. She hated her weakness, hated the unwelcome pangs of jealousy and loneliness that pinched her heart.

She flinched as a jagged bolt of lightning illuminated a mountainous bank of thunderheads rolling in over Long Island Sound from Connecticut, accompanied by a deafening clap of thunder. The frosty night was dead calm, but that wouldn't last long. She needed to get inside.

With a groan, she adjusted the book-heavy backpack slung over her shoulders and reached for the trophy that sat on the sidewalk at her feet, but a classic black Corvette parked across the street in front of Dr. Baylor's house caught her eye. She hadn't seen that car before, but the neurosurgeon's hobby was buying and selling pricey collectible cars. Although it was weird that he left it on the street. He always tucked them safely away in his eight-car garage, and his long driveway could hold a dozen tour buses. Why in the world would he leave it—

A gust of wind shattered the stillness and carried a barrage of sleet that stole her breath and stung her face. She whirled away from the icy assault and gripped the enormous first-place trophy in one hand, then reached into her coat pocket for her keys. Under a drizzle of freezing rain, she hurried up the well-lit brick path leading to a Château-style McMansion nestled on two manicured acres overlooking the water.

She trotted to a side door and stuck her key in the lock. The key turned without resistance. It wasn't locked? That had never happened before. Father must have noticed the weather and left it open for her. She burst into the welcome warmth of a chef's dream of a kitchen and shouldered the door closed against a gust of wind that blew a scattering of wet leaves across the threshold. *Whew!* Made it just in time. Drizzle turned into a downpour, and another crack of thunder rattled dishes and glassware and caused the lights to flicker.

With a weary sigh, she glared at the sodden leaves. The heck with it; they could stay where they were until tomorrow. She was too tired to worry about it now. She kicked off her wet shoes by the door, dumped the trophy and backpack, and hung up her wet coat before releasing her hair from the braid that hung to her waist. With a yawn, she untied the black belt of her karate uniform, then dropped onto a chair and massaged her aching scalp.

She yawned again, barely able to keep her eyes open. Her pillow was calling her name. All she wanted was a hot shower and her bed. What a day! Exams in biochemistry and calculus followed by the New York Metro Area District Karate Championships. Months of grueling work, but totally worth it. She'd won first place in the advanced class, fifteen-to-seventeen-year-old age group, and was confident she aced her exams, as usual.

With a sarcastic snort, she pictured herself running into Mario Borello's study, trophy in hand, so she could bask in his fatherly approval and love.

What a joke.

Oh, sure, he'd want her prize displayed in the custom-built trophy case at his Manhattan office for his wealthy accounting clients to admire, just like all her other awards and trophies. But a pat on the back? Not likely. She was simply performing her function, earning her keep.

She was nothing but a burden—as he'd often told her—until she grew up enough to pull her weight, until she became another prize possession for him to show off, to brag about.

A Lamborghini in pink tennis shoes and a ponytail, the so-called gifted child with perfect report cards, the piano prodigy, the girl who excelled at everything she did.

But show her any affection? It's not like she was really his daughter. She might carry Mario's last name, but she carried none of his DNA, and they both knew it.

He didn't know she knew.

Yet.

It was her secret, only recently discovered. A secret that—after the anger and heartbreak at the total lie her life turned out to be—set her free.

Her biological father? Her mother took that secret to the grave before Emma could walk.

If only she'd known sooner! How many times had she cried herself to sleep because her father didn't love her, no matter how hard she tried to make him happy, to make him proud? How many times had she wondered what she'd done wrong? Well, her crime was clear now. She was another man's child.

Who could have imagined that a few strands of hair and a simple high school science fair project in genetics would completely change her life?

She grabbed a bottle of water from the fridge. Good thing she'd gone out to dinner with Heather and her family after the tournament. Not much in the house to make a decent meal. Theresa did the shopping, but she wouldn't be back from visiting her son in Miami for a few more days.

Not that Emma minded. The sour and stubborn old witch didn't like anyone else cooking in *her* kitchen, so the housekeeper's continued absence gave her a chance to practice her skills. She smiled as she thought about the acceptance letter for cooking school hidden under her mattress, away from Theresa's prying eyes.

Her stomach did a little flip. Soon, she'd leave this house for the last time and strike out on her own. She couldn't wait to attend Le Cordon Bleu in Paris after graduating from high school in June. Good thing Mama left her a modest trust fund, because Daddy Dearest would blow a gasket when she told him she intended to pursue her dream of becoming a world-class chef and wouldn't attend Julliard or any of the Ivy League schools vying for her hand.

Doctor, lawyer, or engineer, Father insisted. He would even settle for a concert pianist. He refused to understand that her photographic memory didn't make her smarter than everyone else. Sure, she could write a slew of mathematical formulae from memory, but that didn't mean she understood what any of it meant, any more than a copy machine would.

She wasn't interested in pursuing any of those careers. Well, she might have considered music as a career, but the lifelong, frequent travel required of a concert pianist didn't appeal to her. But Father couldn't care less about what she wanted. He'd disown her for sure, and she'd need that trust fund money for travel and living expenses not included in her full scholarship.

Not that Le Cordon Bleu—one of the top cooking schools in the world—was anything to sneeze at. But Father wanted bragging rights for the likes of Harvard, Princeton, or Yale. Well, he was in for a rude awakening.

He would no longer control every aspect of her life. Now that she could prove he wasn't her biological or adoptive father, she'd talked to a lawyer about declaring herself an emancipated minor. She was graduating high school early, and otherwise, at only fifteen, she needed Mario's permission to go to Paris. God knows, that would never happen.

It was her life!

The ball was in her court, and she intended to knock it all the way to France.

She gave a wistful sigh as a pair of silver-gray eyes appeared in her mind's eye. Would she find him in Paris? A recent memory surged forward. She bit her lip and pressed a hand to her pounding heart as excitement blossomed. Just last night, she had dreamed of him again. He rode a black and white horse, a wide-brimmed cowboy hat shading his eyes from the glaring sun, as he trailed behind a herd of cattle that wandered across a green vista.

A cowboy? That was new. Did he live on a ranch now? Maybe on vacation?

They were only dreams, and Heather teased her, telling her she was certifiably nutzoid and in need of a top-notch shrink. But in Emma's heart, she knew he was real. Someday they'd find each other.

She pictured his handsome face in her mind, and butterflies took flight in her stomach. But she threw a net over them for the moment. She had more pressing matters at hand than mooning over the dream of finding her Prince Charming. There wasn't a doubt in her mind that, when the time was right, he'd show up in her life with a glass slipper. And if he rode up to get her on a paint cow pony instead of a white stallion, she was fine with that.

Tomorrow was Saturday, so she'd go grocery shopping in the morning. Heather would take her; she would love an excuse to show off her shiny new red convertible, a sweet sixteenth birthday gift from her parents two weeks earlier.

She headed for her backpack to get her phone, but she froze as glass shattered. A thud. A groan. It sounded like it came from the other side of the house. Father's study?

Oh, no. Did he overdo the martinis again? She was tired and sore and didn't want to haul him up off the floor. *Again.* She swore under her breath. This time, she'd leave him there to sleep it off.

She made it halfway up the stairs before her conscience overruled her bravado. She sat on a step and moaned as the hated tears pricked her eyes.

What was wrong with her?

Why couldn't she stop loving him? He wasn't her real father and had never treated her with anything other than reluctant tolerance and pride of ownership. He had lied to her since the cradle. Lie after lie after lie for fifteen years! How could she ever forgive that?

Why was she so pathetic to still care?

All the same, she stomped back down the stairs. She had to make sure he was okay.

She walked down the hallway leading to the study, but agitated male voices made her hesitate. Who would be there at this late hour? Father never met with clients at home, and he always socialized at the club. The study door stood ajar—a rare occurrence. She backed up against the wall and tiptoed the rest of the way, then peered through the gap between the door and the wall.

Her breath froze in her lungs. In the study, looking like he went a few rounds with a prizefighter, Father strained against ropes that bound him to his desk chair. Vincent Russo gripped his graying hair in a cruel fist and held a knife to his throat.

Antonio Russo stood to the side, looking bored and scrolling on his iPhone.

Her throat was constricted by a scream she fought to repress, and an uncontrollable, cold shudder swept over her body. She willed herself to move, *to run*, but her limbs refused to obey, her body numb except for her pounding heart. She knew the men—two brothers she met recently at the country club—when they'd approached the table in the dining room where she and Father sat having lunch.

The meeting had been awkward and tense; the introductions were formal, as required by the polite society in which they moved. But the way Antonio, the younger brother, had so boldly leered made her skin crawl, and the cryptic words exchanged between her father and Vincent Russo had dripped with barely veiled menace. But she'd asked no questions. She knew better than to stick her nose into her father's business.

Her stomach roiled as Vincent teased the blade down her father's cheek, leaving a thin, bloody trail as the blade barely scratched the skin.

"Last chance, Mary-oh. We know you hid the money. Offshore accounts, I'll bet. That's what I'd do. Where are the numbers and passwords?"

Father glared his defiance through bloodshot and swollen eyes. "Kiss my fucking ass, Vinny. You're gonna kill me, anyway."

"Smarter than you look. What the hell were you thinking? You shoulda known you couldn't piss off my old man and stay breathing. No worries. We'll find 'em." Vincent turned to his brother. "Teachable moment, bro."

Antonio rolled his eyes. "Seriously, Vin? Cliché much? This is like a cutscene from *Grand Theft Auto*."

"Don't snark me, kid! This is business. Our business, you lazy jerkoff, so put that fucking phone away and listen up!"

Antonio sighed and pocketed his phone. "Fine, but I wanna drive the vette home."

"Not in this weather. Maybe over the weekend. Paying attention now?"

Another eye roll, but Antonio nodded.

"Good. This is the way we handle a problem. Any problem, it's all the same. Step one: analyze. Define the problem. Step two: strategize. Determine the solution. Step three: execute. Carry out the solution." He yanked Father's head back and slashed his throat.

Emma screamed as blood gushed, her father's last breath hissing and bubbling through the red torrent.

Vincent turned to his brother, the bloody knife still in his hand. "Grab her! Don't let her get away!"

Antonio headed for the door, right toward her. The instinct to survive kicked in, and she took off running. Her first thought was to flee out the front door, but he would catch her before she made it off the grounds. She had to get to the panic room upstairs. She raced down the hall, through the foyer, and up the stairs, but Antonio was right behind her, closing fast.

"Wait for me, you hot little piece of ass." Laughing, he lunged forward and grabbed her foot. They both fell, sprawling across the steps. She kicked madly to get free. He yelped and jerked his hand back, one of his fingers bent at an unnatural angle. No longer laughing, he spewed an impressive assortment of four-letter words as she scuttled up the stairs on all fours.

She made it up to the landing and gained her feet, but he was right behind her. His legs were much longer than hers, and exhausted from her long day, she'd never outrun him.

She had to fight.

Ten years of karate lessons took over.

She stopped, whirled to face him, and widened her stance. As he reached for her, she sidestepped, grabbed his arm, twisted her body, and threw him over her shoulder. He hit the oak floor with a solid thud but grabbed hold of her long hair. He yanked hard, pulling her down on top of him. Pain exploded in Emma's scalp, sending her into a rage. Screaming, she kicked and clawed at him, leaving bloody scratches down his cheek.

He head-butted her in the jaw, stunning her just long enough to grab both her wrists and twist viciously. Bones and tendons snapped, searing pain sending her over the edge into primal panic. A surge of intense heat flooded her body; the pain eased, and her mind cleared. *Fight! Fight or die!* She rammed her knee into his crotch as hard as she could, but her knee scraped along his thigh, and it was only a glancing blow. Still, he sucked in a breath and lost his grip on her wrists.

She twisted free and rolled away. Unable to use her broken wrists, she lurched to her feet and staggered down the hall. Only seconds passed before his heavy footfalls pounded the hardwood behind her.

She had only one chance against him.

In a flash of clarity, she understood that *this* was the moment she trained for—the moment her mother warned her about so long ago.

Calm replaced fear.

It seemed to happen in slow motion in her mind; the move was perfectly choreographed and executed. She exploited the element of surprise by running straight at him. With a battle scream meant to shock and distract, she launched herself through the air.

The solid jump-kick to his chest sent Antonio careening backward, arms flailing, into the sturdy oak railing of the cantilevered landing. He tumbled over and plummeted, screaming to the black-and-white marble floor of the foyer.

Emma froze, her gut twisting at the sickening thud as his body hit the floor, the horrifying crack of skull meeting stone. She crept forward on legs that threatened to buckle and peeked over the railing. She gagged as a wave of stinging acid rose into her throat, and a litany played in her shocked brain—*this isn't happening, this isn't happening, this isn't happening...*

In the foyer, Antonio lay face-up, his dark eyes staring at nothing. An expanding puddle of red soaked the marble under his misshapen head, and a trickle of blood seeped from the corner of his mouth.

With a scream of rage, Vincent ran into the foyer and fell to his knees beside the body. He stared at his dead brother before his gaze rose and he found her. The absolute hate contorting his face made her go numb from a wave of icy terror.

"I was gonna do you quick, but now I'm gonna make it slow, you fucking bitch. Peel off your skin, for starters. You'll scream to the end, and they'll never find all the pieces of your body." He lunged to his feet and headed for the stairs.

Sobbing, Emma ran for the panic room in the master bedroom closet. She stumbled into the tiny windowless cubicle, pushed the heavy door closed with her body, and hit the panic button with her elbow. Her legs gave out, and she crumpled to the floor, shaking uncontrollably, cradling her useless hands to her chest, crying so hard that her breath came in harsh, hiccupping spasms.

Vincent pounded on the door, shouting obscenities, the furious banging muffled by the thick, reinforced steel of the safe room. But security alarms shrieked throughout the house, and the pounding quickly ceased. The dispassionate voice of a police dispatcher came over the security intercom. "Nine-one-one, what is your emergency?"

Chapter Two

PRESENT DAY

A LUSH FOREST MEANDERED through the Rocky Mountains of Colorado, alive with birdsong and the excited chatter of squirrels. A bald eagle soared in lazy circles overhead as pine needles rustled and bright-yellow aspen leaves fluttered in the cool September breeze. Although storm clouds gathered on the horizon, the morning sun peeked over the treetops, golden rays illuminating a structure akin to a medieval castle that arose from the mountainside.

Benjamin Kincaid sat at the kitchen table, eating scrambled eggs and fresh blueberries and checking his favorite news feeds on his laptop. He glanced at the clock. Almost ten. Where the heck was Chase? His cousin must be sleeping in, but that wasn't surprising, considering he hadn't come home yet when Ben set his Kindle aside after midnight and turned over to sleep.

A twinge of anxiety pinched. Chase *was* home, wasn't he? As a rule, he never stayed the whole night with a hookup. Ben grabbed his phone and checked Chimera's tracker app. The tension eased; Chase's car was in the garage.

Ben had been up for almost three hours, hit his weights, gone for a five-mile run, showered and shaved, and now searched the internet for anything that might suggest Illuminati activity, or anything grisly, weird, or freaky that could be paranormal. It was a slow news day. Nothing caught his attention.

Was it a sick thing that he was disappointed? Probably. Of course, he was glad nothing huge currently threatened the world, but Ben liked to stay busy. *Needed* to stay busy. Knighthood was his birthright, his destiny—whether he liked it or not. The urge for action stirred his blood, leaving him restless and anxious.

They had nothing going on at present. He could spend yet another mind-numbing day continuing his work on a computerized inventory of the treasure trove of documents, books, and ancient artifacts housed in the citadel. And Chase wanted to add a box truck to Chimera's magical repertoire, so he could download the specs and get started writing the computer code. But, *God Almighty*, he needed to get out for a while.

The run had knocked the sharp edge off his anxiety, but the walls were already closing in on him again. The forest beyond the citadel's gates called to him, as it so often did with whispered promises of crisp mountain air scented with pine and fallen leaves and game trails thickly carpeted with leaf litter—trails he'd walked his entire life and knew like the back of his hand—where the only sounds were the gentle rustle of the breeze through the trees, the occasional bird call, and his own breath.

A long walk was just what the doctor ordered to ease his mind, but the forecast that morning had called for severe thunderstorms throughout the day. As if on cue, thunder rumbled in the distance. *Damn*.

Sometimes he loved nothing better than to get lost in a good book, especially his favorite genre of science fiction. But even the thought of settling into a comfortable chair with the just-released epic space adventure by his favorite author, Oliver Dellaryde, didn't hold any appeal.

Maybe he'd check in with a few of the regional sealgair teams and offer his professional help. The Illuminati were lying low, most likely regrouping and planning their next move after their recent failure in a volatile African nation to install their own hand-picked military dictator.

Although Ben had been thrilled to leave the blazing sun and never-ending dunes of the Sahara behind—he was still finding sand on his bedroom floor—he'd had his fill of rest and relaxation. He wasn't in the mood to sit around waiting for new orders from Michael, which could be months in coming. Right now, he craved *action*, even something as mundane as a wendigo or werewolf hunt.

Or maybe he just needed a woman.

Maybe?

Who was he kidding?

He pushed himself up from the table and poured another cup of coffee. Unfortunately, with his unpredictable, dangerous, and often clandestine lifestyle, he was far more likely to find a werewolf than a woman. He could just picture his online dating profile:

> Evil-battling Templar Knight who enjoys classical music, city views, and long walks on the beach seeks an intelligent, well-read, caring woman who won't ask questions, won't mind living in isolation or me

disappearing for weeks at a time with no contact, and who can dig out bullets and stitch gaping wounds with a smile.

Yeah, that would draw the women in droves.

He took his coffee back to the table, opened a new webpage, and clicked on the browser icon for Facebook. Growling, he clicked out before it could load and slapped the laptop lid closed. He had to put the past behind him! Miranda was a married woman—a locked door.

His gaze landed on the half-eaten birthday cake that sat under a tent of plastic wrap on the island countertop, and he frowned. It touched him that Chase had remembered and thought to buy him a cake and a card, but this year, he'd have preferred just to forget about it.

Thirty.

Thirty?

How the hell did that happen?

He sighed and raked his fingers through his hair. The big three-o. Even if he lived to a ripe old age, like ninety, his life was a third over. That sobering thought made his throat tighten.

Uneasiness building, unable to sit still, he took his coffee and wandered aimlessly through silent hallways that once knew the cries and laughter of children, the melodious feminine tones of their mothers, and the booming baritone voices of their fathers and grandfather.

He found himself in the Great Hall, crossing the room to the fireplace. He picked up the ancient coin that lay on the mantel, held it toward the cold, empty hearth, and muttered an incantation. "Mando ignibus." Flames burst into life and settled down into a steady, gentle blaze, but the magical warmth did little to soothe his anxiety. His gaze rose to the ancient Scottish broadsword that hung in pride of place high above the mantel—the enchanted weapon that was the source of Orion Citadel's magic.

Sunlight sparkled on the ornate basket hilt inset with moonstones and rubies, and on the quillon inlaid with gold filigree. The lethal double-edged blade was razor-sharp and etched with the stars of Orion's belt, the three brightest stars of the constellation Orion. Kincaid Lairds had passed the sword from father to son for countless generations.

It now belonged to Chase.

As he sipped his coffee, his gaze roamed over the family photos gracing the mantel, lingering on each beloved face, so long gone. Photos of Uncle

George were conspicuously absent, tucked away in the back of Chase's closet.

Four years.

When would his cousin forgive himself?

He picked up a silver-framed photo of a laughing woman with flaming-red hair, just like his own abundant mane. His throat tightened with the familiar pain of loss and longing. "Miss you, Mom." What wouldn't he do to see her smile again, to feel her arms wrapped protectively around him, to awaken in the morning—just one more time—to her soft voice and gentle touch on his shoulder? *Time to wake up, sleepyhead.* He kissed his fingertip and pressed it to her glass-covered cheek. "Love you. Always."

Another stab of pain struck as he carefully put the photo back in its place next to a picture of two toddlers, one dressed in blue and one in pink. His twin cousins, Keira and Logan, would have been nineteen in a few months. It seemed impossible that sixteen years had passed since that terrible day.

He tossed back the last of his coffee, shook his head, and blew out a sigh. Uncle George would have said that he was brooding again, that it was a damn waste of time, and would have assigned him something constructive to do. But he couldn't help it. How could a man just turn his thoughts off? If only he could!

He trailed a finger over deep scratches marring the gleaming, dark oak mantel where he and Chase carved their initials one sad, lonely, long-ago night. Crude marks whittled into wood. Was childish vandalism to be his only tangible legacy?

It seemed appropriate at the time to think that the following generations to inhabit Orion Citadel would find their initials carved on the mantel and know the Kincaid cousins had been there. It had seemed so important! Now? It seemed stupid and pathetic.

Maybe he really was getting old. Sometimes he felt far older than his now-thirty years. Was that the reason for his restlessness? He was changing. His priorities were changing.

The years were racing past. *He wanted more.*

He had Chase and their angel friend and guardian, Ashriel. But that was hardly a substitute for the love of a woman and his own children. But what could he offer a modern woman who expected to have it all: a career, friends, and family? Nothing but a life filled with danger and isolation, with the specter of death hanging like the sword of Damocles over their heads.

He was a product of his bloodline; there was no choice, no getting out. He'd tried—and failed—to escape his destiny. A blood oath sealed his fate, at least for now. Five long years. He'd kept his oath and always would until he fulfilled his promise. But for now, those old dreams of a normal life were long dead and buried, and he needed to stop trying to resurrect them.

He returned to the kitchen, but as he lowered himself onto a chair at the long oak table, he puffed out his cheeks and blew out a harsh sigh of frustration. Sometimes—not often, but sometimes—he wished he could be more like his cousin. When Chase wanted sex, he simply went out and got laid. He'd hit a bar, cozy up to a nice pair of breasts, lay on the charm and that Colgate smile, buy her a drink or two, and then BANG. Literally.

But Ben had been truly and deeply in love, and the hit-and-run nature of hookups usually didn't appeal to him. Two people using each other for nothing more than physical pleasure, with no genuine connection, no joining of the heart or mind, just made the loneliness seem worse the next day.

Still, a man has needs, and he needed to hold a warm, soft, willing woman in his arms. He'd take the long drive into Denver, check into a five-star hotel, visit a nice wine bar or two, and see what happened. At any rate, a night away from home would be a welcome respite, alone or with female company. Feeling a little better with his decision made, he turned his attention back to finishing his breakfast.

Chase Kincaid lay asleep in his bed, moaning and thrashing, his face glistening with sweat, lost in the throes of a nightmare as consistent as the sun rising every morning. He woke with a huge gasp, his heart pounding at the terrible scene that lingered in his mind's eye. Overheated, he tossed back the covers, grabbed one of the two plastic water bottles that sat on his nightstand, and guzzled down a generous portion of gin. He fell back against the pillows, waiting for the alcohol to work its calming magic. "Alexa. Stop."

The loud, static-like white noise filling the room stopped as the device turned itself off. But instead of peaceful silence, the ever-present ringing in his left ear—an annoying souvenir from Hell—replaced it.

Again, that fucking nightmare? Four years! Would it *never* stop? Was it a memory or just a dream? He had no way of knowing.

For at least the millionth time, he wished he had refused Hades's unexpected reprieve and stayed there—stayed in the pit—taking the torture of the rack and the whip, the burns and the cuts, and the endless thirst and hunger.

It would have been better, because at least he would have kept his self-respect. A Templar Knight should have been more stoic against the pain.

His father would be ashamed of him.

If only he'd held out a while longer! But how could he have guessed that Ash would have the balls to disobey Michael's orders to leave him there for a full year to atone for his rash actions and stupidity?

I'm sorry, Dad. Hot tears stung his eyes, but he blinked them away as he guzzled the last of the gin. What was done was done, and he couldn't undo it. But he'd be damned if he'd let his mistakes dictate the rest of his life! If he did, Hades would win anyway, and no freakin' way was he going to allow that dick to win.

Today was a new day, another rare day off to boot, and he was gonna milk it for all it was worth. Feeling better with the attitude adjustment, he rolled out of bed, grabbed his phone, his AirPods, and a mouthful of mints to mask the gin. He threw on his robe and headed for the kitchen. He needed coffee, and lots of it.

Ben looked up as his cousin strolled into the kitchen. Wearing a robe and slippers, his raven-black hair rumpled from sleep, Chase bobbed his head to the music blaring from the ever-present wireless AirPods Ben was beginning to suspect were glued to his ears, the music so loud that he could hear the pounding beat.

Chase spotted him sitting at the table, reached in his pocket for his phone, and turned down the music. "Morning, Benji. And what a beautiful morning it is."

"Morning." Ben raised a brow and stared as Chase, yawning and scratching his trim beard, poured a cup of coffee. "What's with you?"

"What d'ya mean?"

"You just rolled out of bed, and you're actually cheerful? Since when do you do anything but grunt and fart before you've had at least two cups of caffeine and checked your email for the dirty joke of the day?"

"Can't I just wake up in a good mood?"

Ben snorted. "Not if history serves."

"Well, I did. And you know why?"

"Got laid last night?"

"Well, yeah." Chase wiggled his eyebrows. "That new bartender, Alicia, at the Black Cat. The Ice Queen. But last night, she melted all over me. Dude, she's got more skills than bartending, lemme tell you."

Ben blew out a sigh and dropped his fork with a clatter. "You sang, didn't you?"

A sheepish grin wreathed his cousin's face.

"Dammit, Chase. What happened to keeping a low profile?"

"Quit worrying, will ya? Same old faces in the crowd. Besides, the house band was off, the Kerwynn Brothers was guest band, and Tyler dragged me up on stage. How could I pass that up? You know how great we harmonize. Almost as good as you and me. Man, we brought down the house! They gave us a standing-O."

Ben pushed away a pang of envy. It seemed like a lifetime since he'd played his six-string and sang to an audience. The Kerwynn Brothers' coverage of classic Southern-rock and country ballads was legendary in their neck of the woods, and right up Chase's alley, with his silky-smooth baritone. "Well, guess no harm done. Sounds like a great night. No wonder you're in such a good mood."

"Yeah, an awesome night. One for the books. But it ain't only that. It's 'cause, for the first time in…hell, seems like forever, we ain't up to our eyeballs in crap. The Illuminati dicks are holed up somewhere licking their wounds, no demons raising hell, no big bad ugly trying to destroy the world. But I'm no fool. I know it ain't gonna last. But right now, we're in the freakin' eye of the hurricane, and for the lousy fifteen minutes while the sun shines and the wind ain't blowing, I'm gonna drag my lawn chair outside and soak up some sunshine."

"Hate to tell you this, but it's raining."

"Not literally, dumbass. I got better plans than that. Today is—mark your calendar—*Chase Kincaid Day*. No orders from Michael. No assignment, no training, no work period. Another whole day devoted entirely to the rest and relaxation of yours truly."

"I'll alert the media."

Chase nodded solemnly. "As well you should."

"Got started already, didn't you? Left early yesterday."

"Yeah, me and Mal headed over to Denver for a bit. Didn't stay but a few hours. Played some pool, got some steaks, hit a couple nightclubs. I must be gettin' old. Clubs are too damn loud. Can't even hear yourself think, much less chat a girl up. And way too many jailbait honeys with fake ID's. So, we find a nice bar, and who walks in but a couple of fucking demons."

Chase snorted a laugh as he grabbed the cream from the fridge. "Sounds like the setup for a bad joke, don't it? A knight, a skinwalker, and two demons walked into a bar. Lucky Mal can sense those bastards. Odds are low, but never know if one of 'em might recognize me, so we lit out and wound up at the Black Cat, anyway."

Annoyance pricked at Ben's temper. *Malachi*. He should have known. He gave his cousin a baleful stare.

Chase slammed the refrigerator door. "What's your damn issue?"

"Who, me? I didn't say anything."

"Didn't have to open your yap. Your face said all kinda shit."

Ben crossed his arms and leaned back in his chair. "I read about some guy in Georgia who found a baby alligator and raised it like a pet. Thing grew to like eight feet long."

"Yeah? So?"

"So, they call that guy Stumpy now."

Chase gave him an exaggerated, sarcastic smile. "Ha, ha, ha. You're a freakin' laugh riot."

"Not trying to be funny. Nature will win out, sooner or later. You're walking a dangerous line with that guy."

Chase's eyes narrowed. "That guy's name is Malachi. And he's my friend."

"Look, I know how hard it is—damn near impossible—for us to have ordinary human friends. Too much we can't explain. Think I still keep in touch with my friends from college? But Malachi's a skinwalker, a damn shapeshifter! How can you trust someone who can appear to be anyone or anything he wants? For all I know, you could be him standing here right now."

That was a troubling thought. Ben's heart sped up, and he looked Chase up and down for anything out of character.

Chase sighed. "Paranoid much? Get a grip, will ya? He's a good guy. And he can't get through the dome unless I take him through, remember?"

That was true. Ben's tense muscles loosened. "Yeah, well, I don't like him."

"Good news. *You* don't have to like him."

Ben changed the subject. At twenty-five, Chase was a grown man and would make his own decisions, regardless of his older—and dare he hope, wiser—cousin's advice. "Don't you think it's weird that we haven't heard from Michael?"

"Cool your jets. He popped into my head last night. Right in the middle of a great dream, too, damn it. Talk about bad timing. Dude, get this: blonde, double-D, bikini-wearing triplets on spring break in Daytona Beach—"

Ben threw up a hand. "Stop! No details, please. Just tell me what Michael said."

Chase shrugged. "Your loss. He said he's busy with Rigel Citadel, infiltrating a dark witch coven in Boston. He said to take some R and R but keep our noses clean, 'cause he could call us up for duty at any moment."

"Michael said *that?*"

"Not those words exactly. I translated from the original pompous and arrogant archangel-speak, but that was the gist."

"Yeah, so what's new? Any moment could be six months from now. Still bugs me, Chase. Don't you feel it? Something's off. Since when does he have a problem juggling multiple operations? Michael loves to micromanage. And leaving us to our own devices with no instructions at all? Not even a training schedule? Doesn't fit the pattern."

Chase rolled his eyes as he added several heaping spoons of sugar to his coffee. "Easy there, Sherlock. Sometimes a cigar is just a cigar."

"That was Sigmund Freud, not Sherlock Holmes."

"Holy shit, you're such a nerd sometimes. Ever occur to you that after our bravo zulu last month in Satan's sandbox, he's just cuttin' us some well-earned slack?"

Ben hadn't thought of that. Unlikely, in his experience, but possible. Their mission had gone off without a hitch: one Illuminati jackal knocked off the gameboard and buried deep within the vast, rippling wasteland of sand that was the Sahara desert, and an ammunitions storage depot blown to smithereens.

Without a hitch, that was, except for Chase's motion sickness after teleporting home. Poor guy had been dizzy and puking for over a week, but stubborn as ever, he'd refused Ash's offer of healing. Ben suspected that might be the real reason Michael was giving them an extended break, but he didn't say that out loud. Chase wouldn't like that one damn bit.

"Whatever the reason, I'm gonna get while the gettin's good." Chase grabbed a box of Eggos from the freezer and a bottle of syrup from a shelf, then filled all six slots of the toaster with waffles. "I'm gonna take my caffeine and this gourmet breakfast to my room, crank up the flatscreen, tuck my sweet ass back into bed, and get my Netflix on."

"Let me guess. *Stranger Things?*"

"Nope."

"*Game of Thrones?*"

"Nope."

"*The Walking Dead?*"

"Nope again. Not in the mood for zombies. Too...real."

Ben grimaced. "Not *Jackass*."

"Bingo! All-day marathon."

"When are you gonna grow up?"

"Hopefully never. It's funny. So sorry, it ain't up to your standards, Professor. But I'd rather laugh my ass off than watch stuffy old British people walk around a stuffy old British mansion, making snide remarks at each other."

Annoyance had Ben shoving his fingers through his hair. What did Chase know about quality entertainment? "For your information, *Downton Abbey* has won tons of awards, including Emmys and—"

Chase stuck his tongue between his lips and made a rude raspberry noise.

"You're hopeless."

"Tell me somethin' I don't know."

"You could try reading a book or taking a class online. Hey, I earned two degrees, mostly online."

Chase snorted and pushed the lever of the toaster down. "What the hell would I do that for? They giving classes on new battle techniques against paranormal assault?"

"To challenge your mind. Improve yourself. It'd be good for your self-esteem."

"Bite me, Brainiac. Like your degrees are doing you any good? May as well wipe your ass with 'em."

"Yeah? Say that next time I add another model to your damn car, you knuckle-dragging ingrate."

Chase burst out laughing and reached for a plate on a shelf as Ben's cellphone rang. He checked the caller ID. "Well, I'll be damned." With a grin, he answered the call. "Pete MacDonald, you old dog! What rock have you been hiding under?"

"Hospital," Pete said, his voice weak. "Got outta surgery a few hours ago."

Ben lost his smile. "What happened? What hospital?"

"Lawton, I think."

At the word *hospital*, Chase's head jerked up, and he hurried to sit across from Ben at the table.

"Hold on, Chase is right here. I'll put you on speaker." He put his phone down on the table and touched the icon for the speaker. "Go ahead."

Pete's gravelly Texas drawl filled the room. "Well, I got bad news, boys. And more bad news. Hope this is gonna make any lick of sense. Drugged up on some heavy shit. Two days back, I think, me and Wyatt was heading to a job when he starts gettin' chest pains. Bad ones. Aborted the mission and headed for the nearest hospital."

Harsh, wet coughing jangled the phone. "All happened so fast. Don't remember clear. Wyatt figured he might be checking out, so he was texting his daughter. Maybe I was pushin' the speed limit, cain't say for sure. All's I could think of was gettin' to the hospital. Then a bull elk came outta nowhere. Swerved and ran my truck off the road and right into a tree. Both legs broke, and a arm and a couple ribs in the bargain. Clonked my head, but good. Think they said I got concussion."

There was a heavy pause before Pete continued. "Wyatt didn't make it, boys. Not sure if it was the ticker or the tree. Maybe both."

Ben winced and shared a sympathetic look with Chase, who slowly shook his head. Losing brothers at arms wasn't an uncommon thing, but it still hit hard. Especially when it was someone they'd known personally and called a good friend, even if it had been years since they'd seen him. "Damn sorry to hear that, man."

"Yeah, thanks. His time was up, is all. Fate's a relentless bitch and you cain't outrun her when your dang number comes up."

Ben nodded. "True. And the other bad news?"

"Well, now, you boys knew Wyatt. Sealgair of the highest order, a consummate professional. We accepted the job, so he wanted it done right. I'd do it myself, but I'm outta commission for a good, long while. Now, I know this is lowly work fit for a sealgair, not a knight, but heard them belly-crawling Illuminati are lying low right now after y'all whooped their asses, so I figure you got some time on your hands—" Pete broke off with a wheeze and another fit of coughing.

Chase dropped his forehead to the table with a thump, muttering under his breath, "Don't say it. *Please*, don't say it."

"Sorry 'bout that, boys. Anyhows, Wyatt always said you two were the sharpest knives he'd ever had the pleasure to hone. On the way to the hospital, before that damn elk, he made me promise to set you boys on the case in our stead. So, I'm gonna honor Wyatt's last request and call in my marker at the same time. I'm askin' you boys to handle that job for me."

Chase thew his hands up and stalked to the other side of the kitchen, still muttering, "And he said it. He fucking said it!"

Ben glared and put his finger to his lips. *Shush!*

"Got word we got us a small den up in Oklahoma City. Two, maybe three vamps. That's where we was headed when the tree jumped in front of me. Heads up, boys. You're gonna have to hit this den at night."

Ben shared a look of astonishment with his cousin.

"You're trippin' balls on morphine, Pete," Chase said. "Hit a vampire den *at night*? You leave some of your brains on that tree?"

"That may well be, but I kid you not, son. They say these freaky vamps hunt during the day. You wanna catch 'em sleeping, gotta go with the flow. Old part of the city's like a rabbit warren, hidey-holes left, right, and center. They snatch a vic, gone in seconds. Take street people, strung-out junkies.

"Easy pickings. Worth a little sunburn, I reckon. Assuming my intel is right, and you boys are currently making fathers with daughters nervous up there in the Rockies, Oklahoma City's a fair hike for y'all, and ya got every right to say no. But I hope you'll do it for Wyatt, to honor his memory."

Ben felt bad for Chase, but duty called, and honestly, he was glad for a reason to get out of there and *do something*. Wyatt had been a good man and an excellent teacher. It was the least they could do.

Chase gave his nod of assent, but he sure didn't look happy about it.

Ben gave his pouting cousin an apologetic look. "Yeah, of course we'll do it. Glad to help, Pete. Feel better. And please give Jenna our condolences about her dad. Send me the deets." He ended the call. "Sorry. Looks like Chase Kincaid Day is going to have to wait."

The waffles in the toaster popped up.

Golden perfection.

Chase glared at them and blew out a sigh. "Well, fuck me."

Without a word, Ben slid the large mason jar that sat in the center of the table toward his cousin. Chase shot him a dark look, but he grabbed his wallet from a cabinet drawer and took out four ten-dollar bills. He took them to the table and picked up the jar, gazing for a moment at the handwritten label that had gone yellow with age, although it was covered with clear packing tape. *Foul language is unbecoming of a knight.* "Sorry, Mom. I try." He stuffed the money into the already-near-full jar.

Chapter Three

THE SUN FLED, AND darkness claimed Oklahoma City. This was the small but ugly underbelly of the vibrant metropolis, with sad lives mired in decay and despair. Once-proud buildings sagged on crumbling foundations, hunched over like frail old men, beaten down by time and neglect. Rectangular eyes stared into the gloom, some hooded by tattered blinds or curtains, thin margins of light glowing around the edges, peering side-eyed at the world with suspicion and fear. Some were blind—opaque and black—and still others wore seedy patches of graffiti-covered plywood.

Those who walked these mean streets during the day in the comfortable illusion of safety, making their way past mounds of trash, broken crack pipes, and the sea foam of cigarette butts accumulated at the base of every wall and curb, knew to seek shelter from the danger that rode in on the back of twilight—the denizens of the shadows, both human and non-human, that preyed upon the weak and the foolish.

Night had fallen hard by the time Emma Borello hurried along the sidewalk, her windbreaker hood concealing her face in shadow. Her breath came in labored huffs, and she stooped under the weight of a loaded hiker's backpack. She shivered, the eerie sensation of being watched raising goosebumps despite the sweltering weather. She cast furtive glances over her shoulders, on the alert for any sign of danger on the deserted street.

Still nothing.

Did she imagine the footfalls she was so sure were trailing her earlier?

Her boot caught on a long-dead tree root that bulged through the broken cement, and she stumbled and nearly fell. She cursed under her breath, but as she turned a corner, she smiled at the glow and hum of green neon emanating from a sputtering vacancy sign hanging askew from stained and cracked stucco.

Although the ramshackle motel was a fleabag dump, it was the closest thing to Heaven she could have imagined at that moment. A September heatwave held the area in its cruel grip, and an army of air conditioners sounded like a mega-swarm of insects hovering over the city.

Sweat dripped down her face and trailed down her back and chest, soaking her armpits and her clothes, making her clammy jeans cling to her legs, and leaving itchy trails that drove her mad. She longed to rip off her jacket, but the anonymity provided by the windbreaker's hood was more important than comfort.

Comfort? She snorted. It wouldn't matter if she was naked and had fans blowing on her from all sides. Her neck, back, and shoulders throbbed from carrying her pack jammed with everything she'd been able to stuff into it, and she'd passed exhausted about three miles back. She now truly understood the meaning of the term *bone-weary*.

For the first time since her car heaved its last metallic gasp hours ago on the interstate, leaving her no choice but to torch the traitorous Subaru, hit the bricks, and hoof it to the relative safety of the city, she took an easy breath. Tears of relief stung her eyes. In only a few minutes, she'd be behind four air-conditioned walls and a locked door.

But just as she reached the motel entrance, footfalls caught her attention—two sets of boots on pavement, moving fast. Her heart pounded as panic zipped through her. Was she under attack? *Damn!* Something really was following her. She ducked behind one of the large cement planter urns flanking the motel door and whirled toward the sound, gun ready in her hand.

Gagging from the stench of moldy cigarette butts soaked in urine and fetid rainwater that filled the urn, she spotted two men on the other side of the street, striding down the crumbling sidewalk in her direction. A jolt of shock sizzled down her spine, and her heart skipped a beat and then took off at a gallop. She gaped and nearly dropped the Glock as her gaze became riveted on one of the men's faces as he passed from the glow of one streetlight to the next. She couldn't believe her eyes!

It was him.

It was really him!

They passed and continued without glancing her way. Without hesitation, she left her hiding place, crossed the street, and followed them.

Chase crouched in an alley behind an abandoned factory, trying to apply his skill with a lockpick to a rust-pocked door. Benji kept watch, his bright hair tucked under a dark knit cap, his machete at the ready.

Chase blew out a harsh sigh. *What a fucking pain in the ass.* Was this Oklahoma City, or was it Hell? Couldn't see shit with blurry, stinging eyes. He yanked up the neckline of his T-shirt to wipe the sweat, then glanced up at his cousin, who was sweating bullets, too. This whole deal bugged the living crap out of him. He wanted to honor Wyatt's memory, and they owed Pete for his out-of-territory surveillance assist on a suspected Illuminati cell a while back. But this crazy thing? This was going *way* above and beyond in his damn book. "Holy shit, it's hot. Still can't believe we're doing this at night. It's freakin' unnatural."

Benji shrugged. "They're vampires. It's all unnatural. Imagine how hot it'd be during the day. Look, I don't like it either, but it's a small den, and people are dying, and we owe Pete and Wyatt. Sure, it's a crap neighborhood, but still. Guess drug dealers are people, too."

"Barely. We ever run outta other stuff to kill, they're next on my list." Chase turned his attention back to the lock. He wanted to get this fool's errand over with, check into a nice hotel for a shower and some Z's, and then get back to the citadel and his well-deserved time off. His stress levels were off the charts. Once a sporadic occurrence, now night after night, no matter what he did, the same nightmare haunted him.

Music worked during the day to distract him and keep the memories at bay, as well as draw his attention from the annoying ringing in his left ear, but nothing worked anymore to give him a peaceful night's rest. Booze, NyQuil, weed, even prescription sleeping pills. He may as well toss back chocolate milk and M&M's for all the damn good it did.

He almost dreaded going to sleep because she was waiting for him: a young woman lying on a bare mattress, looking up at him with terror in her eyes, screaming—God, the screaming—and a knife in his hand, dripping blood. And that damn number, 19024B. Again and again, that fucking number in his head. What the hell did it mean?

Get a grip, Kincaid. Heart pounding, he shook off the images, wiped his eyes again, and redirected his focus to the task at hand. Within a few seconds, the lock clicked open. He stowed the pick set and slipped his machete from inside his jacket. Blinding light slashed across his eyes as the harsh beam of a sodium streetlight reflected off the polished blade, and an itchy prickle stung his armpits as they dampened even more with nervous sweat. He blew out a sigh as his vision cleared. "Okay, let's do this fool thing before I regain what little sanity I had."

They slipped into the building, closing the door behind them as quietly as its rusted hinges allowed. They crept down a narrow, filthy hallway lit only by a sad lineup of dim, dusty bulbs hanging by wires from the saggy, mildewed ceiling. He tasted the odors of mold and dust in the back of his throat, but as they moved down the hall, another smell overpowered the rest.

A smell that raised the hairs on the back of his neck.

The unmistakable stink of vampire.

An enormous rat, beady eyes shining, stared at the intruders, then scurried away. The cool depths of the long hallway were a sharp contrast to the hot, muggy night, and Chase shivered as cool air glided over his sweaty skin, glad now that he'd worn his jacket to conceal his weapon.

In the heavy silence, the near-constant ringing in his left ear sounded like a blaring smoke alarm in his head. He jammed a finger into his ear and drew it out a few times, trying to get it to pop, but it did no good.

He took a deep breath and flexed his neck. What the hell? He'd entered the belly of the beast more times than he could count, and taking out only two or three vamps would be a walk in the park. But for some reason he couldn't figure out, he had a bad feeling about this.

A really bad feeling.

The hall branched off in two directions. Chase motioned with two fingers, signaling his cousin to go right. With a nod, Benji disappeared down the other hall. Alone now, the foreboding that had his heart slamming against his ribs worsened. *Come on, Kincaid, nut up.* He adjusted his sweaty-handed grip on the machete and continued.

The cousins emerged within seconds of each other through tattered plastic door flaps on opposite sides of a large multistory chamber. Moonlight struggled to penetrate grimy, cracked windows set high in concrete block walls. Rusted manufacturing equipment gathered spiderwebs and rat droppings, and a corroded metal staircase rose to catwalks bathed in shadow.

Two male vampires, biker-looking dudes with long, shaggy beards and tattoos, lounged on a landfill sofa, guzzling beer and passing a bong by the light of a single candle.

Moving slowly and silently, keeping to the shadows, Benji made his way over to where he stood.

Chase scanned the room. Good, no one else. He grinned and mouthed to Benji, *Milk run.* Unfortunately, the monsters weren't sleeping, but still, only two vamps under the influence of alcohol and weed? This really would be a freakin' piece of cake. So why the bad vibes? Were his instincts going south on him?

The vampires on the sofa must have caught their scents. They stood and spotted them. Snarling, they bared jagged, razor-sharp fangs dripping with thick saliva.

Chase grinned. Easy-peezy. He could almost taste an ice-cold beer, feel the cool spray of a hotel shower on his skin and clean, smooth sheets under his ass. *Room service, here I come.* He nodded to his cousin, and they strode toward the vampires, machetes raised. But they faltered and froze, their jaws dropping as the catwalks came alive with the undead. Vampires seemed to materialize out of thin air and start down the stairs toward them.

"Chase! This is suicide."

"We live through this, I'm gonna rip off Pete's good arm and beat him to death with it." Nothing to do but make a break for it. He reached into the pocket of his jacket. "Flash-bang. *Go!*" They turned and bolted like hellhounds were on their tails, and he tossed the stun grenade over his shoulder toward the vampires. He squeezed his eyes shut as it went off, the deafening noise and intense flash of light sure to blind and disorient the creatures just long enough for them to get the hell out of there. As they ran, he allowed himself one slightly comforting thought—at least his instincts were still right on the money.

Benji burst out the door and into the alley first, with Chase hot on his heels, but they ran right into the path of two vampires returning to the den. They raised their weapons, but Chase's hopes for escape bit the dust as at least a dozen more vampires poured into the alley and surrounded them. He and Benji moved automatically into a defensive back-to-back stance.

The vampires circled them.

Spitting. Hooting. Hissing. Laughing.

The monsters appeared human except for their corpse-pale skin and yellowed fangs. Vermin crawled in greasy hair that hadn't seen soap and water in years, if not decades. He gagged at the stench of unwashed bodies and clothes crusted with dried blood and rank with putrid armpits. Some carried macabre clubs—human femur bones—they smacked into their palms again and again.

Playing with their food.

Enjoying the game.

He assessed the situation: Outnumbered by at least nine to one. No way out. No time to summon help.

They were dead men.

But they sure as hell wouldn't make it easy for the motherfuckers. They couldn't swing their blades in their back-to-back positioning without hitting each other, so they had to make room. "We break on my mark. See ya on the other side, cuz."

Benji snorted. "Not if I see you first."

Chase laughed. He always figured they'd die young and bloody. But they'd go down swinging and send a few of the fanged bastards to Hell's rectum while they did it. Would he wind up in the penthouse with Benji or back in the pit? *Don't think about it, Kincaid.* He'd know soon enough.

A familiar surge of liquid steel coursed through his body as his Templar blood ignited. Man, he loved a good fight! And what better way to die than to check out during an honorable battle against a hated foe?

"Break." He stepped forward, knowing Benji would do the same, giving them both room to swing the lethal machetes. Then he crouched into a fighting stance, knees slightly bent, legs braced. He hardened his jaw, raised his machete, and locked eyes with the nearest vampire. "Bring it, bitch."

His machete sliced through the air as the vampire attacked.

Concealed behind a dumpster at the mouth of the alley, Emma watched in horror as more than a dozen vampires surrounded the two men she followed. Even from where she stood, at least twenty yards away, her belly roiled at the all-too-familiar stench of the monsters. She swallowed back a wave of nausea. The smell triggered memories—terrible memories she fought hard to push back behind the wall.

Trembling, she forced herself to maintain her position, although every fiber of her being wanted to flee. When the battle began—clearly a death sentence for the two men—she jerked up her chin and took a deep breath. She wouldn't leave anyone to such a terrible fate, least of all *him*.

She unpacked her weapons and prepared to fight. Her heart pounded and her hands shook, but as Indy taught her years before, she latched onto the intense hatred she harbored for vampires and used it to fuel her courage.

Fresh and itching for a good fight, Chase easily beheaded the first two vamps that challenged him, and his machete completed another arc, but the third monster feinted to the right, and the blade missed its target.

Thwack. An arrow pierced through the vampire's shoulder. Chase froze. *What the fuck?* An arrow? From where?

Only a momentary distraction. The monster plucked it out and tossed it away. Chase swung, but the vamp easily dodged the machete again. *Holy shit!* He'd forgotten how quick some of the undead could move. Before he could raise his blade again, the vamp swung a femur club, striking Chase in his lower-right back—an excruciating kidney punch.

He cried out and bent sideways against the searing pain, panting like a hound on a summer day, unable to take a decent breath. Sweat blurred his eyes, and he barely ducked another swing of the femur club aimed at his head. Cursing against the agony, he managed an awkward whirl from that crouched position and swung the machete with all his might, slicing clear through the fang's knees.

The monster crumpled to the ground, blood spurting from its amputated limbs. *Take that, you bastard!* But his momentary jolt of victory vanished as one of the biker dudes from the warehouse broke from the group of vamps leaning against the building's brick wall and sauntered toward him to take the other's place.

Shit. They were playing tag team?

He fought to fill his lungs, but it hurt like a bitch just to stand upright. He felt like he'd been T-boned by a damn truck! No time. The vamp was right on him.

Raising his machete high to attack again, another *thwack* sound made him hesitate. Biker dude took an arrow through the neck and forgot about Chase as he tried to pull it out. The arrowhead must have caught on a vertebra, but instead of pushing it straight through, the idiot yanked on it, sawing it back and forth.

Chase wasn't usually squeamish, but the sight made his gut spasm. He gagged as he swung the machete, slicing through the arrow as he finished the biker dude off.

Thwack. Thwack. Thwack. More arrows rained down on the monsters. Chase couldn't believe it. The stupid vamps hardly noticed they'd been skewered. But where the hell were the arrows coming from? He ran a sleeve over his sweat-blurred eyes, the leather not helping much. He glanced wildly around but saw no archer.

Mistake—a noise behind him! Before he could react, a vamp grabbed him, an arm like a steel band compressing his ribs to the point of cracking, turning his labored breath into a wheeze. The vamp's other hand fisted in his hair and jerked his head to the side, exposing his vulnerable neck.

He shuddered at the foul stench of its hot breath on his neck. He struggled in vain to pry its arm away from his chest and to break the creature's brutal grip on his hair. He braced himself for the pain of sharp fangs piercing his flesh, but it laughed and only licked his neck in a long, slimy, stinky swipe of tongue.

He shuddered again, but rage replaced disgust, and Dad's voice spoke in his head: *If you can't beat 'em, trick 'em.* He went limp, playing possum. The stupid creature loosened its hold. *Dumbass.* Chase twisted free and swung his machete, severing the vamp's head.

Three times, as soon as Ben decapitated a vampire, another immediately took its place. As he dodged, punched, and swung, he noticed that the other vamps stood around, just watching. Why didn't they attack all at once?

In a flash, he understood. The battle that would surely result in his and Chase's deaths was a source of entertainment for the monsters—a night at the fights, a cage match. And they wouldn't want to kill them outright, of course. Vampires needed their victims' hearts pumping to keep the blood fountain flowing when it was time to feed.

Well, the dinner show would soon be over. He was tiring; the muscles in his right arm burned like fire with the effort of swinging the machete, and the sweltering heat was taking a heavy toll. His heart slammed in his chest, and his breath came in harsh pants.

A rustle behind him! A vamp jumped on his back and grabbed him around the neck. Cursing, Ben wobbled and nearly toppled over, barely keeping his grip on the machete. He swung his body from side to side as he struggled to throw off the monster, keep his balance, and stay upright.

If he fell, he'd never get up again.

Thwack. There was that weird sound again. The vamp hissed and stiffened, then let go and dropped to the ground. Ben stared at the body. A crossbow quarrel had slammed into one of its eyes and sunk into its brain.

A surge of hope eased his breath. Did Chase get hold of a crossbow?

He wiped his face with his denim sleeve and quickly surveyed the alley. There were other vampires with arrows sticking out of them, too. Some seemed dazed. A few staggered and then fell to the ground, vomiting and writhing.

Poison arrows!

But who was the archer?

Not Chase.

Across the alley, his cousin battled a vamp under the glow of a streetlight. Chase sliced across the monster's chest with his machete and raised his blade again to swing for its neck, but the vampire blocked his swing with a powerful strike of a femur club to Chase's forearm.

The unmistakable sound of bone breaking made Ben's gut twist as Chase cried out and his machete clattered to the concrete.

Laughing with glee, the vampire grabbed Chase's head and rammed it into its own. Chase's eyes rolled back in his head, and he sank to his knees.

With a shout of victory, fists thrust high into the air, the monster planted a boot on Chase's back and slammed him to the pavement. The few vamps still standing swooped down on him like vultures on roadkill.

Ben's breath froze in his lungs for several seconds. "*Chase!*" He wanted to help him; he *needed* to help him!

He couldn't.

No opening.

He had no choice but to fight as another monster closed in, too close for Ben to swing his blade, so he threw a left-handed punch instead. The vamp dodged Ben's fist and plunged a dagger into his right shoulder. Searing pain shot all the way down to his toes, and he lost his grip on the machete. Teeth clenched tight, he slapped his hand over the wound, hunching against the agony.

The vamp raised the dagger again. Ben raised a defensive elbow, bracing himself for another thrust of the knife into his flesh.

But it never came.

An arrow struck the vamp right between the eyes, slicing clean through its skull and protruding through the back of its head. It fell backward onto the concrete.

A thud, and one vampire sailed through the air and crashed into a brick wall. Another thud and a second vampire barely missed Ben as its headless body landed on top of its den mate.

Ben's throbbing shoulder oozed blood through his fingers, and his breath came in heaving gasps as he searched again for his cousin. His eyes stung like hell, and his vision was blurred by sweat.

But he found him.

On the ground.

As still as death.

An icy deluge of terror washed over him. But someone else fought off the vampires surrounding his cousin. It gave him another surge of hope, although he had no idea who the person was. Their unknown ally wore an empty quiver on his back.

This was the archer? He looked like a kid, but that couldn't be. Could it?

In a blur of motion, the archer swung his machete and decapitated a female vamp, then dropped his blade. He grabbed another vampire by the arm, threw him over his shoulder to the ground, picked up the machete, and swung.

Blood spurted as its head rolled.

Ben scrubbed his blurry eyes with his sleeve and looked again, horrified, as a lone vampire kneeled over Chase, its fangs sinking into his neck.

"*No!*" With his right arm useless, Ben grabbed his machete off the ground with his left hand and staggered across the alley toward his cousin.

The archer stood behind the vampire that fed on Chase, a bloody machete in his hand. He dropped the blade, widened his stance, and seized one of the vamp's boot-clad feet. He gave it a vicious twist; bones cracked.

The vampire released its hold on Chase's neck and raised its head, jagged fangs dripping blood and saliva, mouth open to howl in pain. But the howl morphed into a gurgle as the archer's blade hacked through its neck. Its head tumbled to the ground as the body fell on top of Chase.

Seizing the vampire's jacket with both hands, the archer dragged the body off Chase and motioned to Ben. "Help him!"

Although the archer's voice resounded with rage and purpose, it had a high, lyrical pitch. Just how young was this kid? As he stood, the archer's hood fell back, revealing a fine-featured, feminine face. Their ally was a woman! She moved through the alley, finishing the vamps that writhed in obvious pain and vomited uncontrollably from her poison arrows.

"Chase!" Ben kneeled by his cousin, giddy with relief when Chase groaned and then cursed. He struggled out of his jacket, clenching his jaw against the searing pain in his shoulder, then pressing the jacket against Chase's torn neck. "Easy now, little buddy." He helped him sit up, hoping that elevating his cousin's head would help stem the blood loss. He was concerned about how much blood was flowing from the jagged wound. "Some stitches, a few gallons of blood, and a cast for that arm, and you'll be fine."

"Guess a tourniquet is out of the question," Chase rasped.

"Shut up, idiot."

"Pete's a dead man. How the hell are we even alive?"

"A miracle, that's how. Gotta get out of here. Could be more. Think you can stand?"

"Yeah, gimme a hand."

Ben helped his cousin to his feet and turned to the woman who was walking toward them.

Light shone on her blood-spattered face, and despite the gruesome circumstances, his breath hitched. A jolt of desire shook him as he took in the lovely, delicate features of the woman who had just saved their lives. He smiled at her. "Buffy, I presume? You were amazing. How can we ever thank you?"

But her eyes darted elsewhere.

He followed her gaze and saw it, too. Another vampire emerged from the factory door. A straggler arrived late to the party. Probably because his immense shoulders scraped the hallway walls and impeded his progress. The Hulk meets Dracula. Ben's jaw dropped, and his heart sank. "Are you kidding me?"

"Aww, come on," Chase croaked.

Ben tensed for action, but his cousin was as wobbly as a newborn foal, and he had no choice but to support him or let him drop. He was about to lower him to the ground, but the woman handed him her machete.

"I got this. Bigger they are, harder they fall. On my mark."

To his amazement and horror, she marched right toward the gigantic vampire. She raised a gun as she walked, aiming for its chest. His heart clutched with fear for her, and he shouted, "No, get back!"

Chase whispered hoarsely, "Won't work."

"Told you, guys. I got this."

He and Chase exchanged a look of disbelief as she stopped mere feet from the overgrown vampire. She looked the enormous creature up and down and shook her head. "Nobody ever tell you steroids are bad?" She lowered her aim and shot Hulkula right between the legs.

Ben groaned and cringed, his hand instinctively moving to cover his crotch. Right in the balls! That had to be excruciating, vampire or not.

The oversized vamp's eyes crossed, and it hunched over in obvious agony. She turned to Ben with her arm outstretched. "Now!"

He tossed her the machete.

In one fluid movement, she caught it, spun, and brought the blade down on the vampire's neck. Its head dropped and rolled as the colossal body toppled forward with a thud.

Ben could only stare in disbelief.

Now that the danger was past, the woman seemed to wilt before his eyes. Her machete fell to the pavement with a clatter. Her breath came in huge, ragged gulps as she staggered toward them...

...and walked right past him to Chase.

Smiling, tears welling up in her eyes, she reached up and laid a trembling, bloodstained hand on the side of his cousin's face. Ben bit back on the ridiculous urge to shout *dibs*, like they were kids again. This amazing, beautiful woman had just come into their lives, and she had eyes only for Chase.

"I always knew you were real," she whispered.

His cousin seemed to melt into her palm, raising his own blood-stained, trembling hand and covering hers. He wore an expression of wonder and bliss. "Who are you?"

Too late, Ben spotted the red dot of a laser sight on her back.

Too late, he reached out to grab her.

Too late, he roared, "*No!*"

A barrage of bullets sizzled through the night and slammed into her, each strike making her body jerk and forcing a huff of breath from her lungs. Eyes wide, pupils huge, and a trickle of blood seeping from her gaping mouth, she collapsed into Ben's arms.

Chapter Four

The angel Ashriel awoke in a thick forest illuminated only by starlight and a three-quarter moon. He jumped to his feet. *Where was he? What was happening?* He had no memory of how he came to be there—wherever there was.

A terrifying moment of panic tightened his chest and sent his heart pounding. His angelic power to determine his location anywhere on Earth failed to work. He raised a hand to his neck and gasped. No wonder; his torc was gone! Combined with his current inability to fly, he was stranded and lost. Without his torc, he couldn't even teleport!

He glared at his naked wings, ugly and useless, and renewed his vow to seek revenge against the powerful witch who had mutilated him so heinously. Had Santana now thrust him into this new nightmare?

The panic grew when he noticed his attire. Missing were his sword and anchetoch—the long, leather coat crafted from behemoth hide, impervious to any mundane weapon. He was practically defenseless! But worry about his charges overwhelmed his concern for himself. Were Chase and Ben in danger? What if they needed him?

Pain exploded in his head as a high-pitched whine filled the night. The tone surrounded him and pierced his consciousness. Every thought fled his mind except for the all-consuming urge to follow the beacon wherever it led.

He ran like a madman through the dense woods as dark storm clouds gathered overhead, crying out as branches and thorny bramble tore through his clothing and ripped into his flesh.

No rain fell as the odd storm unleashed its fury. Gusts of wind whipped the trees as jagged lightning pitchforked across the sky and thunder cracked and rumbled. He pushed on, careening around trees and leaping over deadwood, ducking branches and vines as the beacon continued its irresistible call. His boot caught on the branch of a downed pine tree, and he stumbled and slammed to the ground.

Breath coming in shallow, harsh gasps, he staggered to his feet and continued. His chin and palms were dirty and scraped raw, and he bled from countless cuts and scratches, clothes filthy and torn, pale-blond curls plastered to his head with sweat, but still he ran. The high-pitched whine grew louder, drowning out the fierce thunder.

He surged forward with new urgency.

He broke into a wide clearing. Lashed by the ferocious wind, illuminated by flashes of lightning, he turned in circles, searching. For what, he didn't know, but it was *important*. The beacon grew louder and abruptly ceased. Sensing a disturbance beyond the storm, he looked up toward the night sky. A jagged bolt of pure white lightning sizzled down and struck him.

Enveloped in the blinding light, he levitated into the air. His body turned slowly at first, then faster and faster, until he was spinning so quickly that he was a blur. The radiant light intensified and faded, and he came to a sudden, complete stop. His body arched as beams of light shot from his eyes and from his mouth, and the light was everywhere.

The light dissipated, and darkness reclaimed the night. Ashriel stood stock-still on the leaf-strewn grass, head down, in the center of the now-peaceful clearing in the Maine woods. The night sky was dark velvet, twinkling with stars.

His powers were restored, his wounds healed, and his clothing was perfect. The missing torc, anchetoch, and sword had been returned.

He raised his head, his eyes blazing like twin blue flames in the dark. An explosive clap of thunder heralded a blinding flash of lightning that lit up the night.

Ashriel's magnificent new wings cast a mighty shadow against the forest green.

Chase surfed the murky waves between asleep and awake. Voices. Whispered words. Garbled. Tired—so damn tired. *Just five more minutes, Mom.* He tried to sink beneath the waves again, down into the peaceful depths, but more noise intruded. *Ping, ping, ping. Doctor Stevens, please pick up on line two.* Someone in heels walked past. The medicinal odor of disinfectant. Someone coughing up a lung in the distance. Hospital? Had to be.

He tried to open his eyes, but his eyelids wouldn't budge. A small motor hummed. Something tightened on his upper arm, tighter and tighter and *tighter*. His heartbeat pulsed under the merciless band. *Ba-boom, ba-boom, ba-boom, ba-boom, ba-boom.* A few clicks, and the painful pressure was released with a long hiss.

Sweet, blessed silence.

He slipped back under the waves.

Sometime later, he awoke flat on his back. His neck stung like hell in a few spots. He opened blurry eyes, raised a weak, trembling hand, and gingerly probed the turtleneck of bandages around his throat. His left arm throbbed like a bitch, and he swallowed convulsively and painfully. His stomach was sour and twitching like he was gonna puke, and if he didn't know better, he'd have sworn a hatchet was sticking out of his forehead. All in all, he felt like crap on ice and wished he could slip back into oblivion.

Benji's face came into view. "How we doing, little buddy?"

He opened his mouth to speak—to order his cousin to smother him with a pillow—but all he managed was a feeble croak.

"Let's get a little water down those pipes." Benji pressed the button on the control panel to raise the head on the hospital bed. "Let me know if I go up too far. And careful with that left arm. You're sporting a shiny new cast."

Broken? Just fucking perfect. No wonder his arm was killing him. He fought dizziness and a wave of nausea as the bed raised him into an almost-sitting position.

His cousin held a cup of water with a bendy straw up to his mouth. "Just a sip or two to start."

The cold water was heavenly, but it hurt like a sonofabitch to swallow. He tried in vain to lift his cement block head.

"Easy, there. Give it time. The nurse said it would take about an hour to come out of it completely, and you've still got about twenty minutes on the clock." Benji leaned down and spoke into his ear. "You're Agent Morris, FBI. Already called Dempsey at headquarters. We're good to go."

"Gotcha." Jeez, he sounded like an eighty-year-old chain smoker. He'd been about to ask what had happened—a car wreck? He couldn't remember—when a nurse bustled into the room.

"We're fully awake now, I see. I'm Barry. How're you doing?"

Chase glared at the man. "Just shoot me. Right between the eyes."

"That good, huh? Any nausea?"

"Wouldn't come too close."

"Let me check doctor's orders. See if she left the okay for you to have some pain and anti-nausea meds. If not, I'll text her." He logged into the laptop that sat on a rolling cart, checked the electronic chart, and nodded.

"Yep. Hang in there, champ. Have you feeling better in no time. Be right back."

The nurse left but came back quickly with two vials of clear liquid. He injected one liquid directly into the IV line taped to Chase's hand. "How's that feel?"

He sighed as a warm, tingly feeling spread throughout his body. The pain eased a lot, and he got a world-class buzz. "Oh, yeah." He grinned. "Good stuff."

"Yeah, I'm real popular around here." He injected the other serum into the IV bag. "This should kick in pretty quick. Take care of that nausea." He checked Chase's temperature, made a notation on the laptop, and then pressed a wired wand with a button on the end into his hand. "Well, the good news is, everything's looking great. Bad news is, you're gonna sound like a bullfrog with strep throat for a while. Your surgeon will be in shortly. After she gives the okay, I'll get you some food. Hope you like Jell-O. You kick back and rest, and if you need anything, just press the call button. I'll be back in a little while to check on you."

The nurse left. Chase silently praised the inventors of whatever magical drugs were in those vials as the pain stopped and the nausea lessened. He closed his eyes and allowed himself to relax.

Until the general anesthetic wore off a bit more and his memory kicked in.

His eyes flew open, and his heart pounded as a rush of adrenaline surged through his blood. "She okay?" Even before Benji answered, he understood it was bad, as raw anguish replaced the mask of fake normalcy decorating his cousin's face. "Tell me."

"Okay." Benji drew a deep breath and rolled his shoulders.

Chase's heart sank. *No, no, no! Don't tell me she's dead.*

"She's still up in surgery, but it's bad, really bad. I threw my badge around and got the resident doc to go talk to the surgeon and give me an update. The shooter was a real pro. One bullet hit her spine, one punctured a lung, and the third tore up her heart. The surgeon said even if she lives, which is doubtful..." He took a shuddering breath. "Even if she lives, she'll never walk again. I've prayed for Ash over and over and left messages on his cell, but nothing. Looks like he's MIA, just when we need him the most."

Maybe it was the anesthesia lingering in his system, but Chase didn't even try to fight the tears that spilled over and rolled down his face. That brave, beautiful girl was gonna die because she jumped into the fray and saved their asses, giving whoever shot her the opportunity to do it. That girl who—with just the touch of her hand on his cheek—stirred something in him no other woman ever had.

Back in the alley, he'd been dizzy from blood loss, and the pain in his neck and arm had been excruciating, but somehow her touch had sent a wave of pleasure coursing through him. As he'd gazed down into her eyes that glittered with tears in the moonlight, he'd felt something. Something he couldn't name. He'd never experienced anything like it, but it was strong, and it was deep, and it was important, and he'd known, *just known*, that his life would never be the same.

And now she was gonna be taken away from him before they even said hello.

A memory clawed its way into his drug-muddled brain: the demon Thorne's taunting words to him upon learning that the Illuminati murdered the young psychic Kenny Morton while under Chase's protection. *That unfortunate boy trusted you. How many people have to die on your watch before you get the message? You've been to Hell, mon ami. You've been as much a demon as I. Knight or not, you're bad luck now, reborn under an unlucky star. Anyone in your immediate vicinity walks in the shadow of death.*

Chase struggled under a tidal wave of sorrow and guilt. Was Thorne right? Was he bad luck? Was this his fault, too? It couldn't be happening, not again. It had to be a dream—a narcotic-induced dream. No, it was another damn nightmare. Anesthesia nightmare. He'd wake up any minute, and it wouldn't be real.

But in his heart, he knew it was.

Their unnamed savior lay in a hospital bed, covered up to her chin with blankets. A respirator tube protruded from her mouth, the rhythmic *whoosh* of its artificial breath filling the room.

Chase, wearing a robe over a hospital gown, his arm in a cast, and his neck bandaged, sat by her side, holding her hand. Hidden from view under the pillow on his lap were a loaded gun and the Aegis of Solomon, a magical weapon that could kill almost anything. He gazed at her too-pale face, noting the sprinkling of tiny freckles on her cute little nose and the way her eyelashes fanned over the purple smudges under her eyes. Her long, straight hair appeared dark brown until the light hit it and revealed glints of red. Dark auburn, the nurse had called it.

She looked so small, so lost in the bed. He remembered standing next to her in the alley. The top of her head had barely come up to his shoulders. Couldn't be over five-foot-two or three. It was hard for him to believe—even though he'd seen it with his own eyes—that her delicate hands had swung a machete, her slim arms had wielded a crossbow, and she had somehow hurled grown men through the air.

A warrior in the guise of a fairy.

His gaze fell on her hand, resting on the white blanket. In the short time he'd been sitting there, the color of her nail beds had gone white, and her hand had turned even more blue. Cyanosis, the nurse called it. Lack of oxygen in the blood because her heart wasn't pumping right. When he'd asked if someone on a respirator could still die, she told him they could, saying that many people who died in the hospital died while hooked up to a respirator. After all, the machine only provided breath and oxygen. If the heart or other organs failed, the patient would still die.

And she was dying.

Not twenty minutes earlier, the surgeon told him that straight up, after Chase shoved his FBI badge in the man's face and demanded to know her status. *I did everything I could, but the damage to her heart is extensive and irreparable, resulting in terminal heart failure. I'm sorry, agent. There's no hope. She's got hours, maybe a day.* With sadness and defeat in his tired eyes, the older man turned and walked away.

Chase wouldn't waste his time praying to Michael, who was concerned only with warfare and defeating the Illuminati, but for at least the hundredth time, he sent up a silent prayer to Ashriel. *Please, Ash! Help her. Don't let her die. Where are you? We need you!*

The same nurse as earlier, a plump black woman who looked to be in her mid-sixties with short gray hair and compassionate brown eyes, came back into the room. She carried a meal tray. "I thought you might be in here, Agent Morris. I brought you some dinner."

"Thanks, but I ain't hungry."

"I heard this pretty little gal saved your life and your partner's by distracting the man who stabbed you, and then that hateful man shot her. I'm sure you feel terrible, and that's understandable. But it wasn't your fault, son, and you need to eat if you're gonna regain your strength, catch that criminal, and make him pay."

"Don't you worry. He'll pay. I'll find him if it's the last thing I ever do. And he'll pay, all right."

She placed the meal on the tray table. "In case you change your mind." She checked the machines and tubes connected to her patient and paused next to the bed, gazing down at her. "Poor little gal. I have a granddaughter about the same age. Such a shame."

"She ain't in pain, is she? And shouldn't she be in the ICU or something?"

The nurse smoothed a gentle hand over her patient's hair. "She's not in any pain. She's in a deep coma. You're right. Usually, we'd have her in the ICU, but the unit is full, and hospital policy is that priority is given to patients with a chance for survival. But don't worry, we'll take excellent care of her right here."

The nurse—her name tag said Adelaide—reached into the pocket of her cheerful puppy-print scrubs and pulled out a sandwich baggie with an oval gold locket inside. "She was wearing this under her clothes when they brought her in. It looks really old and antique-like. I think it's the kind of locket you can put a picture inside, but I couldn't figure out how to get it open. Maybe you can. The picture might help identify her. If you're able to find out who she is, it should go to her next of kin. But in case you don't, I want you to have it, if the law allows. I feel in my heart that it'll mean something to you."

He gripped the arm of the chair with all his might but was helpless to stop the surge of emotion that constricted his raw throat and brought the embarrassing, hot sting of tears that slipped past his tightly shut eyelids.

"Aww." The nurse reached down and gently peeled his hand off the chair. She held his hand and gave it a firm squeeze. "Darlin' boy, I've been a nurse for almost forty-three years. It's hard to accept when death takes someone so young, especially in such an unexpected and violent way. It's not fair, and it's not right, but it happens every day. I couldn't do this work if I didn't have faith that, in the end, there's a purpose to it. A reason we don't understand. That it's God's will." She pressed the locket into his hand, patted his shoulder, and left the room.

God's will?

Rage welled up inside him. He welcomed it, nurtured it.

Anger gave him strength.

Anger gave him purpose.

He'd learned to hide from painful emotions under a shield of anger, beginning at the tender age of seven when the Illuminati killed his uncle, aunt, and Benji's older brother by forcing their car off the road and into a ravine. The authorities declared it an accident, but it was no accident. His education in pain continued two years later, when the demon Eligos murdered his mother and twin siblings, and his broken father became best friends with Jack, Jim, and Jose.

He raised that impenetrable shield now. It was safer, easier, and more productive than drowning in the pain of regret, loneliness, sadness, or guilt.

Or grief.

He would find the bastard who did this, and he would kill him. Slowly. And painfully. Oh, so painfully. His personal experience with torture techniques while doing his time in Hell would serve him well, and he would relish every moment. But not yet. He wouldn't leave her, not while she still lived. Not while he still had a shred of hope.

He lifted her hand, which was ice cold, despite the thick blankets covering her. He kissed it gently and blew his warm breath into her palm. "Please stay with me, sweetheart. You gotta hold on." He paused, noticing the linear scars running along her wrist. They were straight and neat, clearly surgical. How had she gotten them? He shook his head and tucked her hand under the blanket. It hardly mattered now.

He glared at the ceiling as anxiety and frustration welled up and swamped him. "*Dammit*, Ash! Where in the fucking hell are you?"

Benji walked in, carrying a cup of vending machine coffee. He tossed Chimera's keys on the tray table.

"Anything?" Chase asked.

"Called everyone we know, and they're putting out feelers, but so far, no one has a clue who she is. But consecrated blood on her arrows? She's trained in our ways. A knight's daughter, maybe?"

Chase was scratching at the bandage around his neck, trying to reach a maddening itch, but now his hand froze. He nearly laughed at that question. "Dude, seriously? A sibylline we don't know about? Far as I know, the only one born in the last thirty years was—" He broke off as another rush of emotion constricted his sore throat. *Keira. Sweet little Keira.*

Ben nodded. "I know. Odds are low. And Michael would surely have known and told us. Unless..."

"Unless what?"

"Unless they hid her for some reason."

"No way. Not like that, anyway. Mad skills or not, leaving her out there on the streets, alone and unprotected? That's not hiding her; that's throwing her to the wolves! No Templar family would allow that."

Benji threaded a hand through his hair and grimaced. "Yeah, it sounds ridiculous now that I hear it out loud. Okay, maybe a sealgair's daughter then? But if she is, how can no one know her? I don't get it. Nothing on her prints, either. Checked AFIS, both federal and state databases, and either she never had her prints taken in her life or someone went to a lot of trouble to wipe her off the grid."

"Maybe she was sheep-dipped?"

"If she's a government operative in deep cover or on a kill list, it's possible. And that would explain the skill set and why it looks like she was on the run."

Benji lowered himself onto the visitor's chair, sipped his coffee, cringed, and set the cup down on the dresser. "Oh, and I found her backpack stashed behind a dumpster in the alley. Everything you'd expect, plus a few you wouldn't. A laptop, a half dozen fake IDs, some tools, and some clothes. The laptop's locked, so nothing there until I get it home and run a cryptanalysis program to crack the password. But she's clearly no fool, so I doubt we'll find anything we can use to identify her. On the unexpected side, a big wad of cash, like over eight-grand big, and a couple of those reloadable throwaway debit cards, but no credit cards."

Chase whistled. "Eight thousand bucks? That's a lotta scratch."

"I'll say. She also had four jumbo cans of spray deodorant, a ton of breath mints, incense sticks, and a case of mothballs. Those things reek. What was she doing, hunting Mothra?"

"Ain't it obvious? She was hiding her scent. Don't you remember one summer we trained with Pete, him telling us that putting mothballs in our pockets or shoving them in the car vents would work to hide our scents if we ever needed to? Never used that trick, but I keep a box of them stashed under the back seat, just in case."

"Oh, yeah. Okay, makes sense. So, the question is, what was she running from? Was the shooter a human, a demon, or a monster?"

Chase shrugged, imagining the many techniques he could employ to end that bastard's life, whatever it was. "If she was hiding her scent, most likely a monster. But dead thing walking, either way. Only variable is what I gotta use to kill what's left of the bastard when I'm done."

"Are you sure you don't know her? A hook up you forgot about? She sure seemed to know you."

"No, man. Ain't that big of a dick. I'd remember her. Feel like I should know her, but I'm positive we never met before. Besides, you heard what she said. *I always knew you were real*. No, it's something else."

"Like what?"

"I don't know. But when she touched my face back in the alley? When I touch her now, there's something. A feeling. An amazing feeling. Don't know how to describe it."

Benji's eyes turned to shards of emerald ice. "Like Santana?"

"God, no! Not like that at all. That fucking love potion was like being a strung-out junkie needing a fix so bad you'd kill to get it. This is different. It feels...pure. Clean. I feel...it's like...it's like we're *connected*, Benji. But now she's dying—"

Chase choked up, blinked back the tears, and gave an embarrassed laugh. "Listen to me, would ya, waxing poetic? Must've lost way more blood than we thought. Hey, how's the shoulder, man?"

"Flesh wound. Hurts like a bitch, but no big deal. I can move it. Slapped some duct tape on it until we find Ash. You know how I hate getting stitches."

"Yeah." He rapped his knuckles on the cast. "Tell me about it. Listen, I'm gettin' real worried about Ash. Is he not hearing our prayers? Did he wreck the Porsche, or maybe it's just that it broke down?"

"Still don't get why he insists on driving when the guy can teleport anywhere in minutes."

"Really? I totally get it. Cruising down the road, rockin' out to your favorite tunes?"

Benji raised a brow. "Dude. He listens to opera."

Chase grimaced. "Oh, yeah. Okay, not so much rockin' then, but still. He's been around for how many freakin' centuries? Cars are like a new toy to him. Still hella fun."

"Guess it makes sense when you look at it like that."

"But he still coulda called us back. Unless he lost his cellphone *again*, for like the millionth time. And if the Porsche did crap out, he woulda teleported. I don't get it. At any rate, he's been MIA too long. We gotta find him. For her, yeah, but what if he's in trouble, too? What if he *can't* teleport for some reason?"

Ben half snorted, half chuckled. "Sorry to laugh at a time like this, but I just got a visual of Ash standing on the side of the road with his thumb out, trying to hitch a ride with a crystal sword hanging at his side."

Chase managed a smile. "That's a meme waiting to happen. When you leave here, I want you to do whatever voodoo you do and put a tracer on his cellphone. Get a GPS location so you know where to look."

"Already tried. His GPS setting isn't activated. But I can use his phone's IMEI number and apply cell tower triangulation to find the last towers that handled his signal. Won't give us a dot on the map, but it'll give us a radius to work with."

"Better than nothin'. Can you do that from your laptop at the hotel, or do you gotta go home?"

"Hotel is good. Want me to do it now?"

"Gimme ten. I'm gonna hit the head and then the chapel. Pray for him quick. Maybe the soul-phone will get more bars from holy ground. Sit with her. Talk to her, hold her hand, and don't let go. I want her to know she ain't alone. You packing?"

"Of course. Don't worry; if there's trouble, we're ready."

Chase got up, pocketed his gun, and handed the Aegis of Solomon to his cousin. He leaned over the woman in the bed. "Sweetheart, I gotta go do something. Gonna try to get a friend here to help you, but I'll be right back. Benji's gonna stay with you, so don't worry."

Alone in the hospital chapel, Chase paced back and forth in front of a brass tree of flickering votive prayer candles as he ranted into his phone. "Ash, I've prayed a freakin' litany. I've left you so many messages that I've lost count. This is a matter of life and death, and death is winning, you hear me? I'm worried about you, too! You better get here as fast as you can, you dick, or you better be dead, or I swear, I'm gonna rip off your friggin' halo and shove it so far up your ass you won't—"

With a flutter of wings and a rush of air that extinguished the candles, Ashriel stood nose-to-nose with Chase, who dropped his phone and stumbled backward, coming up against a chair and nearly falling.

"I'm here, Laird."

Chase's mouth opened and closed several times, like a fish's, before he found his voice. "Wings? Dude, you got new feathers? How? When? *Where the hell have you been?* Never mind; tell me later." He snatched up his phone, stuck it in the pocket of his robe, grabbed Ashriel's arm, and pulled him toward the door.

"Chase, wait!"

But he didn't wait; he didn't break stride; he just dragged the angel down the hallway in his wake.

"What's happening? You're injured. Will you please allow me to heal you?"

His first impulse was to refuse, as usual. But he couldn't do shit with a broken arm, and he had to wear the damn cast for at least six weeks. "Yeah, okay. Later, at home. Be kinda hard to explain."

"But where are we going?"

"Hold your horses; we're almost there." He pushed Ashriel into the hospital room and closed the door behind them.

Ben looked up from the visitor's chair arranged near the head of the bed as Chase and Ashriel walked in. He heaved a sigh of relief. *Finally.* "Glad you're okay, Ash."

Chase gave Ashriel a shove toward the bed. "Okay, fly-boy, make with the healing and fast."

"But I don't underst—" Ashriel froze, his eyes widening as his sight settled on the woman in the bed. He did a quick double take between her and Chase. His brows rose, and his jaw gaped. He covered and quickly schooled his features, but not before warning bells clanged in Ben's head. What was that about?

Ash moved to stand by the bed. "Who is she?"

Chase flung out his good arm. "She saved our lives; *that's* who she is. Fix her, dammit!"

"How was she injured?"

"Three slugs to the back. Her heart's all messed up. She's dying, Ash, and it's our fault. You gotta save her."

Ashriel went to the door, raised his hand, and sealed it shut. He moved to the bed and placed his palm on the woman's forehead.

"Whoa!" Chase grabbed Ashriel's arm. "What are ya doing? That's not how you usually heal someone."

"I'm not healing her yet. I'm reading her memories. Please unhand me and be silent."

When Chase stood back, Ashriel worked his angelic mojo for quite a while and then turned to them. The absolute rage contorting the angel's face was like nothing Ben had seen in all his life, even in the heat of battle.

"I will *not* heal her. This woman must die!"

Chapter Five

Two days later, Ben and Chase sat at a reading table in the Great Hall of Orion Citadel, nursing a couple of cold beers and cleaning their handguns. With a growl, Chase launched out of his chair and hurled his beer bottle across the room. It hit the brick wall in an explosion of glass shards and suds that made Ben jump and drop the frame of his pistol.

"I can't fucking take this!" Chase paced the few yards between the table and the fireplace like an agitated tiger. "I'm losing my shit just sittin' here, knowing she's lying on a slab in that morgue, *and we let it happen!*"

"Dammit, Chase!" Ben grabbed the gun frame off the floor and smacked it down on the table. "You were totally on board at the hospital. No one said this would be easy, but we all agreed it was the right thing to do, so stop torturing yourself. And me! I hate this, too. But it has to be this way, and you damn well know it. She's not suffering."

Chase glared at him and gripped the back of a chair like he was strangling the life out of it. "That supposed to make me feel better? Well, it don't!" His face crumpled, and his eyes brimmed. "I watched her take her last breath, and it hurt, Benji. Hurt so damn much. Ripped my heart out."

"I know. It was hard for all of us."

"But you know what would make me feel a lot better? Pay back. Going out there and hunting down the sonofabitch who shot her!"

"Look, I get it. I really do. I feel the same way. And we will, at the right time. But you know we can't yet, so get a damn grip already." He scrubbed his hands over his face and raked his fingers through his hair. "Listen, why don't I go pick up some fast food? Your choice—anything you want. Sugar and preservatives, be damned. Hey, I'll even get Twinkies for dessert."

"Not hungry." Chase stalked out, backhanding a reading lamp off the table as he left. The glass lamp shade shattered as it hit the hardwood floor.

"What a damn mess." Ben took a deep breath and blew it out, hoping to relieve the anxiety that made his chest tighten. *God, give me strength*. He left the room, returned with a broom, mop, and dustpan, and cleaned up.

He couldn't wait for it all to be over.

In a dark and deserted hospital morgue, Ashriel leaned against a wall, arms crossed. He glanced at the clock over the door. A few minutes after eleven in the evening.

Like a statue, he stood in the same position at three in the morning. A noise at the door drew his attention.

A man dressed in blue medical scrubs and a surgical mask slipped inside. He eased the door shut silently behind him, walked right past the invisible angel, and made a beeline for the body refrigerator. He aimed a flashlight at the doors, searching. The flashlight's beam zeroed in on the drawer labeled *Jane Doe*.

Unseen, Ashriel stood next to him.

Silent.

Seething.

The man opened the hatch, pulled the body tray out, and pulled back the sheet, revealing Emma's lifeless, pale-gray face. He snapped a few pictures with a cellphone and pulled a fingerprinting kit from his pocket. He paused while making careful prints of her fingers and gazed at her for a moment. "Babe, I don't really know who or what you were, but I ain't ever seen nothing like what I saw in that alley, and I hope I never do again. Gonna have nightmares. But gotta say, you were a real badass. Seriously, respect. Almost feel bad for wasting you, but five mil is five mil. I'd do my own mama for less."

He finished his work, pulled the sheet back up, and slid the drawer home.

Ashriel's handsome face was an ugly mask of hatred as he allowed the killer to walk away scot-free.

For now.

The coffee maker in the citadel's kitchen gurgled and hissed as the last few drops of Ben's extra-extra-strong brew oozed into the pot. He yawned, rubbed his itchy, tired eyes, took a mug off the shelf, and waited. He'd spent a long, miserable night staring at the ceiling in his room, and this pot would be only the first of the morning.

Chase, also looking bleary-eyed and sleep-deprived, shuffled into the kitchen in his robe and slippers as Ben took his first sip and opened the lid on his laptop. Without a word, Chase poured a cup of coffee and joined him at the table. They sat in silence.

With a flutter of wings, Ashriel appeared, pulled out a chair, and joined them. Chase nodded in greeting, and Ben bobbled his head toward the coffee. "Sorry, Ash. Know you prefer sludge, but it's fresh. Extra strong, though."

"No, thanks. I had coffee from the vending machine at the hospital. It was excellent."

"Bastard show?" Chase asked.

"Yes. It was difficult to restrain myself from smiting him."

"I'll bet." Chase thrust his shoulders back and spread his arms in a stretch, then rubbed his eyes. "Well, I guess that's good. We move on to the next phase."

Ashriel nodded. "When?"

"Thursday afternoon, four o'clock," Ben said.

"Not until Thursday?" Ashriel asked. "Why so long?"

"Standard procedure," Ben said. "She's a murder vic. The state will try to find out her identity, but of course, they won't. Unclaimed bodies are an expense and a nuisance to the state, and either donated to medical schools or cremated. Luckily, the state allows friends, neighbors, or, in our case, good Samaritan FBI agents, to arrange and pay for a proper burial. Even in matters of death, money talks. Already did the paperwork and paid the fees."

No one said anything else until ten minutes later, when Chase tossed back his last gulp and banged his mug down on the table. "We're going to the funeral. He might show, and I wanna see this bastard with my own eyes."

"That a smart idea?" Ben asked. "You're on edge as it is. You don't want to blow it."

Ashriel's eyes narrowed. "What do you mean, on edge?"

"He means, it's taking every ounce of self-control I got to keep myself from going out there and sending that bastard to Hell, where he belongs!"

Ashriel's expression hardened. "Chase, calm yourself. You must be patient."

"Calm? *Patient?* I'm sorry, have you met me?"

In an unusual display of anger, the angel slammed his fist down on the solid oak table, making the stoneware cups jump and clatter. "Events must be allowed to unfold in their own time, or all we have done will be for nothing. Do not interfere! Revenge will come, but it must come last."

With a rush of air, Ashriel was gone.

On Thursday afternoon, Ben and Chase, somber in dark suits, rode in grim silence as they drove from their Oklahoma City hotel to the cemetery for Emma's funeral.

Ashriel appeared in the back seat. "Hello."

"*Fuck!*" Chase swerved the car. Luckily, the traffic was light. "Dammit, Ash!"

"Sorry."

Chase gritted his teeth. That was one thing he hadn't missed in the year while Ash had been grounded. Why couldn't he learn to give them a heads-up before he just popped into the car? "You know, one of these days you're gonna make me run off the friggin' road or into another car. Can't you call or text first? Did you find your damn cellphone?"

"Yes, it was in my car. I'll try to remember to do that in the future."

"Good." Chase rolled his eyes. Yeah, he wouldn't bet money on it. "Okay, now that we got some time and I need a damn distraction, what's the story with the new plumage? Who rang your bell, Ash?"

"I don't know. I woke up in the middle of a forest with no knowledge of how I got there or exactly where I was, and then there was a beacon summoning me, like nothing I've ever heard before. Impossible to resist. The next thing I knew, I was standing in a clearing in the woods in northern Maine, flexing my new wings. It was...I believe you would use the word *awesome*."

Benji twisted in his seat toward Ashriel. "It had to be God, right? I mean, who else would have that kind of juice?"

Ashriel considered it for a moment and shrugged. "Your guess is as good as mine. Was it God? Possible, of course, but highly unlikely. He rarely interferes in such a tangible way, not in thousands of years. And we have no evidence to support that theory. Other than God? I don't know. Not even an archangel has that kind of power. We may be dealing with an unknown entity."

Chase stiffened and met Ashriel's gaze in the rearview mirror. "Oh, great. Perfect. Something more powerful than a friggin' archangel?"

"Hang on, guys," Benji said. "Restoring Ash's wings was a good thing. There's no reason to assume whoever did it has bad intentions."

"No reason to assume it has good intentions either," Chase said. "Could be a Trojan horse."

Ashriel leaned forward, his head tilted. "A Trojan horse. A person or thing intended secretly to undermine or bring about the downfall of an enemy or opponent."

"Very good, Mr. Webster." Chase rolled his shoulders, trying to release some of the tension. The left side of his head throbbed, although he'd downed a few aspirins earlier. The possibility that they had a powerful unknown to contend with made his guts twist into knots. He couldn't take any more, not today. "Know what, guys? Forget I even asked. We're already knee-deep in a steamy pile of crap, so does it matter right now who did the deed or why? Ash is back in the friendly skies, and that's a win no matter how you stack it. Let's not look a gift horse in the mouth just yet. Even a Trojan one."

They rode the rest of the way in silence.

At Pine Creek Cemetery on the outskirts of Oklahoma City, among towering trees and rows of headstones, a simple white coffin awaited burial. At four forty-five in the afternoon, under a leaden sky that promised rain, Chase, Ben, and Ashriel stood in silence, the only mourners in attendance, as a balding and grossly overweight minister, wire-frame glasses perched on the tip of his bulbous nose, conducted the funeral service for the woman who was being laid to rest as a Jane Doe.

As Chase listened to the minister's words, he pressed two fingers against his tie, at the place under his clothes where Emma's gold locket rested against his skin. Although they already knew who she was, out of curiosity, he'd tried to open it, but it wouldn't budge. He didn't want to break the antique-looking jewelry that was likely a treasured family heirloom, so he'd given up trying, and on a whim, he had clasped the locket around his neck. Maybe it was weird, but it comforted him to know that the gold that had once rested against her skin now lay against his.

His line of sight landed on the casket. He tried not to think about her body—cold, stiff, and lifeless—lying in that box. He tried not to think about how they were going to lower that box into the ground and cover it with tons of dirt. Suddenly breathless and trembling, he was overwhelmed with the memory of waking up six feet under in a pine box after being drugged and buried alive by an Illuminati agent.

God, he'd been so fucking stupid! A fake ID and a horny teenage boy—always a bad combination. But even at sixteen, he'd known better than to leave his drink unattended, even for a moment, to play her song request on the jukebox, but that demon bitch lying in wait at the bar had been so damn sexy that his brain had all but shut down under the shadow of his teenage lust.

All too clearly, he remembered the confusion, the panic, and the sheer terror of being trapped in the pitch black, in that tiny space, *buried alive*, and the primal instinct to *get out*, screaming for Ashriel, punching the flesh off his knuckles to break through the pine casket lid, scratching and clawing his way toward the surface, struggling for air, choking on dirt, and mindlessly fighting against Ash's vise-like grip on his wrist as the angel teleported him to safety.

With his heart slamming against his ribs, he shivered in a cold sweat. Benji's hand came down on his shoulder and gave him a firm squeeze. Chase gave his cousin a grateful nod and dragged himself back to the present. He mentally shook himself. She was dead, not alive. Emma wouldn't wake up in that box. She wouldn't. She couldn't.

He took a few deep breaths and forced his attention back to the minister.

"...ashes to ashes, dust to dust. He will wipe away every tear from her eyes, and death shall be no more, neither shall there be mourning, nor crying, nor pain anymore, for the former things have passed away."

The words were comforting, as they were meant to be, and he relaxed. *Dude, from your mouth to God's ears.*

When the service was complete and the minister turned to put down his book of prayers, his glasses slipped off the end of his nose. As he stooped to pick them up—not an easy task with his enormous gut—Chase blinked and found himself standing in a dense group of trees that formed a lush, natural boundary on the far side of the cemetery.

Ashriel's hands covered both his mouth and Benji's. With a headshake and a warning look, Ash removed his hands and pointed toward Emma's gravesite, where her casket awaited burial.

The minister straightened and slid his glasses back onto his face. He looked around, but seeing no one, he crossed himself and hurried away, throwing worried glances over his shoulder as he went. The demon Thorne materialized where the minister had stood. He touched Emma's casket for several seconds, turned, and walked away. He passed behind a tree and was gone.

Chase swallowed hard, battling nausea—motion sickness caused by Ash zapping him from one place to another. "What's that bastard doing at Emma's grave?"

"Thorne is a soultrader demon," Ashriel said. "It's safe to assume he made Russo's deal. He must be confirming Emma's death so he can collect Russo's soul."

Benji groaned. "Thorne? *God Almighty.* Can't we ever catch a break?"

Ash touched them again, and they immediately appeared in the car. Chase moaned as he fell into a dizzying pit of misery. "Gimme a fucking break!" He gagged as his stomach spasmed and his head spun. "Gonna spew." He flung open the car door and tumbled out and onto his knees just in time before he started heaving. Ashriel appeared at his side and touched his arm. "I can help if—"

He shoved the angel's hand away.

After he emptied his stomach and the vomiting stopped, he spit a few times to clear his mouth. He sighed with relief as his gut settled and the world stopped spinning. He then rolled away from the mess and into a sitting position. "Better, but I need a coke. Better yet, a beer."

Ashriel disappeared, but he was back in seconds and handed Chase a ginger ale. "I'm sorry for making you sick, but Thorne could have come back, and although he can't detect me when I choose to remain cloaked, he would certainly recognize you. We can't take any unnecessary chances. I will remain here. I'll see you at the appointed time."

"Okay, but when—" Too late. Ash was gone. Chase took a mouthful of ginger ale, swished it around, and spit it out. "Angels and demons. Honest to God, sometimes don't know which is worse."

Later that evening, a cold, misty rain enshrouded the cemetery as Ashriel watched Octavio Russo make his way along the sidewalk to Emma's grave. He was sixty-seven years old, but he looked more like ninety-seven. Jaundiced parchment skin tented over jutting cheekbones and sagged over hollow cheeks. A web of broken capillaries reddened a hawk-like nose; thin lips, dry and cracked, were seemingly frozen in a perpetual sneer; and sunken brown eyes, yellowed and bloodshot, glared from under the brim of a coal-black Borsalino fedora.

He shuffled along, wheezing as he went, bent over a four-footed cane, likely the best money could buy, and the hand that gripped it was claw-like and blue-veined. He wore an Armani suit, a matching black overcoat, and

Ferragamo shoes. Diamonds winked at his cuffs, ridiculously at odds with the green portable oxygen apparatus strapped to his back and the clear length of tubing that ran from it to the nasal cannula taped to his nose.

A tall, well-muscled man, obviously a bodyguard, walked behind him as they moved at a turtle's pace. They finally arrived at the old man's destination. "Go away," Russo barked. The bodyguard went to sit on a bench in front of a fancy mausoleum, about thirty feet away.

Ashriel stood nearby and remained cloaked. It took all his willpower not to cause this human monster grievous injury. But he took comfort in knowing that soon Hell would do a far better job of it than he ever could.

Octavio approached Emma's grave. He stood and glared down at the freshly turned earth for a long time, then spat on the grave. "Well, here we are, you little bitch. At long last. You gave me a good run for my money."

Ashriel sensed Thorne coming back. The demon materialized at Russo's side.

The old man flinched, his eyes wary. "What are you doing here? I still have sixty days now!"

The demon smiled. "Relax, Monsieur Russo. I'm well aware of that stipulation in our contract. I'm not here to collect your soul. Besides, it doesn't work that way, n'est-ce pas? Brilliant, monsieur, to have the girl killed before the cancer could take you, since only her death could invoke that stipulation, and our contract did not specify the cause of her death. You would have been mine by nightfall tomorrow, but now? Sixty long days to put your affairs in order. Such intellect, such je ne sais quoi. A maneuver worthy of yours truly."

A twinge of suspicion made Ashriel take a step closer and listen more intently. The demon's usually condescending and arrogant French accent was respectful and soothing. Clearly, he was up to something.

"Thank you," Russo said, but he still sounded wary. As well, he should. "So, why are you here?"

Ashriel wanted to know the answer to that very question. Why was the demon there? The deal was done, and the countdown had begun. He had no reason to be.

Thorne reached into his coat, produced two silver flasks, and handed one to Russo. "My favorite. Rémy Martin Louis VIII Cognac. Aged for more than one hundred years. Call me sentimental. I wanted to mark the occasion. The deal I made with you—that kind of out-of-the-box thinking? I believe that deal marked the true beginning of my road to success. What you taught me about leverage and negotiation has served me well.

My lord Hades recently named me Hell's regional manager in charge of the entire Eastern Seaboard of the US, plus Canada."

"Congratulations."

"The same to you, Monsieur Russo. For seven long years, you made that girl suffer. Well played, sir. Well played."

Russo nodded and clinked his flask against Thorne's. They both enjoyed a sip of the expensive and rare brandy.

Ashriel wanted to shove the flasks down their throats!

Thorne surreptitiously observed Russo, his pale blue eyes flashing demonic black for a split second. "Octavio, after your...um, regretfully compulsory initiation program downstairs—it is Hell, after all—come and see me. I have room at the top of my organization for a man as sadistic and intelligent as you. You'd be surprised at how rare that combination of traits is."

"I will."

"Excellent. Consider this a signing bonus." Thorne muttered a few words in a language Ashriel didn't recognize. "You can lose that cane and the oxygen now."

Octavio ripped the oxygen tubing off his head, took a deep, easy breath, and stood up, ramrod straight. With a muttered expletive, he hurled the cane as far as he could throw it.

"Amusez-vous bien! Enjoy your sixty days, mon ami."

Man and demon went their separate ways.

But the angel remained, keeping vigil over the dead.

Several hours later, in the war room at the citadel, Ben sat at the large rectangular strategy table, bathed in the glow from a wall of monitors where weather and news stations and world maps with current terrorist or known and suspected Illuminati operations ran around the clock. He took slight comfort in the extra light on this dark night, when so much was at stake and nothing was certain. He aimed a remote at one monitor and changed the channel from CNN to Nick at Nite.

He shoved his hand into his jeans pocket, came up with a roll of antacids, and popped several in his mouth. His stomach burned like he'd swallowed battery acid, which he figured was from the stress or the coffee alternated with beer he'd been downing since they got home from the funeral. Probably both. He'd made sandwiches earlier for Chase and himself, but neither ate much.

Chase stepped into the room, carrying a pot of coffee and an untouched box of donuts. "After midnight. Any time now." He put the pot and the donuts on the table and dropped into a seat across from Ben. With a combination of a groan and a growl, he scrubbed his hands over his face, frustration and anxiety evident in his every movement.

Ben frowned as his chest tightened. "You okay?"

"Hell, no, I'm not okay! *Thorne?* It had to be Thorne? I swear, that guy's like herpes. Just when you think you're rid of him, he's back. Of all the fucking soultrader demons in Hell, why did it have to be him?"

"Kincaid luck?"

"If he ever finds out about this, if he tells Hades—"

"We'll just have to make sure he never finds out. And if he does, we'll deal with it. Like always."

Chase blew out a long sigh. "Yeah. Yeah, damn right. Nothing we can do about it right now, anyway." He sat back, put his feet up on the table, crossed his arms, and closed his eyes.

Ben eyed his cousin. To a casual observer, it might look as if he were relaxed, but he knew Chase too well. His cousin was wound up tighter than a coil spring. Maybe he should keep his mouth shut, but he was worried. "Ash warned us about the risks going in. He's still on Michael's shit list after disobeying him to save your butt, and with him unwilling to risk accessing his torc's power, it's a crapshoot. A dangerous crapshoot. There's no guarantee here. If this thing goes sideways or flat out fails completely, you gonna be okay?"

Chase didn't move a muscle; he didn't even open his eyes. "You listen to me, Benji. We ain't having this conversation. It's gonna work, and I don't wanna hear another damn word about it."

Ben gritted his teeth, but he held his tongue. When Chase got like this, there was no reasoning with him. Only time would tell.

It wasn't long before Ashriel appeared in the room with Emma's corpse in his arms. "Where?"

Chase jumped up and led the way down the main hall to a guest bedroom. "Any trouble?"

"Not from Thorne, but I had to kill three ghouls that attempted to get to her body. Even dead, she's a beacon for the unnatural." He laid her gently on the bed. "I don't know how long this will take. I may be back in a few hours. Or never."

Ben glanced at Chase, who stared down at Emma as if mesmerized, and turned his gaze back to Ashriel. His heart pounded, his thoughts racing, and his emotions torn. He wanted to help her; he really did, but he feared for his friend and for his cousin. "You sure about this, Ash?"

"No. But I have to try."

Chase clasped Ash on the shoulder and gave it a firm shake. "Thanks for doing this, man. I owe you."

"You don't owe me anything. I'm doing this for her, not you."

Chase nodded. "Even so."

Ben hated the whole thing, but it wasn't his call. In truth, he might have made the same decision if it were. But *God Almighty*, it was a lot to risk on such an uncertain margin of success. "Just don't melt, Icarus."

"Luckily, my wings aren't made of wax." Ashriel disappeared.

Chase fell back onto the chair and quirked a brow. "What the hell is Icarus?"

Chapter Six

As he traveled faster than the speed of light, Ashriel battled an emotion that was completely foreign to him.

Fear.

Heart-pounding, gut-twisting fear.

What he planned to do was inordinately dangerous. Potentially suicidal. Hypothetically, it was possible, but as far as he knew, no other angel had ever attempted what he was about to do. But what choice did he have? He needed enormous power to accomplish his goal, and without the power of his torc, this was his only option.

There was no way he could draw upon his torc for such an immense amount of energy without raising an alarm in Heaven. He wasn't breaking angelic law. But risking himself to save a human without orders to do so bordered on insubordination. Something Chase said came to mind—*Sometimes it's better to ask forgiveness than permission.*

Ashriel hadn't agreed with that at the time. But in this case, he did. Michael might have given his permission had he not already been furious with him, but the archangel was mercurial and often wrathful. His actions were noble and warranted, and he wouldn't take the chance of being denied. He had to proceed. He was committed to this course of action, way past the point of no return. If Michael ever found out? Well, he would cross that galaxy if he came to it. He had bigger worries at present.

His journey complete, he phased out of the space-time continuum and into normal space. He shielded his eyes from the blinding light as the sun burst into view, so close to the star that all he could see was undulating, molten fire. The sudden, incredible blast of heat curled the ends of his feathers, and gravity hit him like an iron fist to his chest. His breath came in weak gasps. He doubled over in pain, his wings pinned against his body, and he was pulled forward headfirst.

In a heartbeat, he was rocketing toward the gaseous giant, caught like a fly in the incredibly strong web of the star's gravitational pull. He panicked at the horror of his miscalculation—the sun was 333,000 times heavier than Earth! For over an hour, he fought with all his strength to spread his wings and regain control, but his power depleted at an exponential rate. Exhausted, part of him let go and accepted his fate—accepted his failure—but what he carried within himself cried out in fear.

That tiny voice meant everything.

His strength of will resurged. He focused and refused to succumb to the heaviness, the vertigo, and the spots dancing in front of his eyes. But although he fought with all his might, his energy faltered. Another hour passed, and he was pulled closer and closer to disaster. Drained, with nothing more to give, exhausted and broken-hearted, he accepted failure. His last thought before he lost consciousness was a plea for forgiveness.

Senator Richard Zyro gazed at the expansive nighttime view of Los Angeles offered by the wall of windows that formed the eastern side of his penthouse home. Cheerful lights twinkled in buildings great and small and in seemingly artistic patterns along the highways and bridges that crisscrossed and clover-leafed among the sprawling city. Stars glittered in a velvet sky unusually devoid of smog thanks to a torrential storm earlier, and palm trees, beautifully illuminated by landscape lighting, swayed lazily in the warm California breeze.

He had little appreciation for the stunning view.

His world was cold and dark, and he liked it that way. But it amused him to make his home in the City of Angels.

He enjoyed the irony.

His focus shifted to his own reflection. His dark brown hair bore only a slight dusting of gray at the temples, and his clean-shaven skin was smooth except for the tiny crow's feet at the sides of his hazel eyes. He'd exchanged his usual designer suit for jeans and a tight T-shirt that showed his tall, muscular build to perfection.

In fantastic physical shape for a man nearing forty-five, he hadn't seen the inside of a gym since his teens. He laughed at the hordes of people who wasted their time and money sweating in gyms, when all it took for him to remain youthful and fit was a simple magical spell.

Most people were so incredibly stupid. Mindless, cowardly sheep led about by the nose, easily controlled by the censored media, organized religion, widely accepted social mores, and corrupt corporations like big food and big pharma. And politicians.

Of course, it was all to his advantage. And theirs. Sheep needed a powerful sheepherder to keep them in line.

His hands clenched and unclenched at his sides as he waited. He hated waiting, but patience was required of a man in his position. The tattoo on his left forearm of an *ouroboros*—a snake coiled in the shape of an infinity symbol and eating its own tail—proclaimed his high-ranking familial status within the Illuminati.

A phone rang. Not his personal iPhone; the ringtone was different. The untraceable burner phone. He retrieved the cellphone that sat on a shelf above the bar, checked the caller ID, and blew out a harsh sigh. *What now?* He checked to make sure the app that would disguise his voice was activated and then answered. "*What?*"

A man's harassed voice said, "The girl is being a fucking pain in the ass!"

He ground his teeth and resisted the urge to throw the phone across the room. That was what he got for using civilians. But he wanted to keep it simple, and once the matter was closed, it would be far easier to make a couple of nobodies disappear than members of the military. "If you can't handle the assignment, I'll find someone who can."

"She won't eat, and now she won't drink. She spits on me every fucking time I go near her!"

How annoying. Damn brat. But he wanted her alive and well. Collateral loses its value when imperfect; she'd be worth far less dead or damaged. Unfortunately, his first gambit failed. How the Kincaids got past that vampire ambush was a mystery.

But he would use the kid again.

Waste not, want not.

He simply had to decide how. "Tell her if she won't cooperate, she'll lose shower privileges, and we'll chain her to the wall, put her on intravenous fluids, and shove pureed food down her throat with a feeding tube. Get her pizza and Coke. I never met a teenager who could resist pizza. And I reiterate, do not harm a hair on her head if you want to get paid." He hung up and glared out the window.

His doorbell chimed, but he didn't turn around. The reflection of his front door was mirrored in the window glass. Besides, he expected the visitor, and she would let herself in. The dark witch needed no key.

Santana entered, and the door closed on its own behind her. She locked it with a careless flick of her wrist as she stepped down from the foyer to the sunken living room. The movements of her lithe body were sensual and sinuous, stiletto heels clicking on the marble floor as she crossed the expansive, ultra-modern room to stand beside him.

Taking in the view, she tucked a stray lock of blonde hair behind her ear, the large blood rubies dangling from her earlobes sparkling in the glass. Her fragrance swirled around him—something musky and earthy, with undertones of bergamot and vanilla. But beneath the banal scent, he detected the harsh, acrid stench of brimstone.

The Hell-born perfume intoxicated him.

Lust slithered into his groin, making him rock hard in seconds. While it thrilled him, it annoyed him as well. Why was it that neither kinky nor sadomasochistic porn nor the most experienced whore could arouse him lately? Yet this woman's mere presence always made him want to fuck her brains out.

A spell? Had she bewitched him? After a second of disquiet, he laughed inwardly. Of course not. She wouldn't dare. Still...he would further consider that possibility later. "What's wrong? It must be important for you to come here so quickly."

She caught his eye in the reflective glass. "It began with a vision in my scrying mirror. A young brunette woman. She's connected somehow, strongly, with Chase Kincaid and the angel Ashriel. It's unclear how. The vision was strange. Murky, and just a flash. She was there, and then she wasn't. It's very odd, unlike anything I've ever encountered. Perhaps she died, or the knights warded her as they've done themselves."

"Templar spells only work on those with Templar blood."

"Yes."

"Interesting. But let the damn shoe drop, Santana. What has this woman to do with me?"

"Visions in the scrying mirror are mere glances at a possible timeline, subject to flux and the whim of fate. Nothing is written in stone except epitaphs. The vision was confusing, but assuming she still lives, one thing was clear. She could be a great threat to you."

He stiffened imperceptibly. "Oh? How great?"

"Unless the future changes, unless the path she walks is altered—she is the instrument of your death. I dealt the tarot cards thirteen times using thirteen different decks, and each time the same cards came forward, led by the death card. There is no mistake."

He shrugged, giving no sign of the fear that turned his bowels to jelly. He'd never show weakness to this powerful witch. Having her as an ally was like owning a pet tiger. One never knew if it would pounce with no warning and rip you to shreds. "Then I'll have to alter her path, now, won't I?"

"How? That fortress is warded against magic and beyond even my power. It's protected against demons and all manner of evil and unnatural creatures, and now psychic energy as well. Our failure at Polaris Citadel only served to increase the security of all citadels."

"Excellent. We know what won't work. The process of elimination is a valuable first step in determining what will." He strolled to the bar and drew the stopper from a crystal decanter of brandy. "A drink, my dear?"

Santana dropped onto the black leather sofa, tossing her hair over her shoulder in an impatient gesture. "How can you be so calm?"

"Panic is for the weak-minded. Panic leads to mistakes." His hazel eyes locked with her dark brown eyes in the bar mirror for a long moment. "I don't make mistakes." If she caught the cloaked warning in his words, she gave no sign. But then, she wouldn't.

He carried their drinks to the sofa, handed Santana hers, and put his glass on the lamp table. He left the room for a moment and returned carrying a pair of white cotton gloves and a thick ancient book, which he carefully laid on the glass coffee table. The aged leather cover was hand-etched with cryptic symbols, the largest of which was the Sigil of Satan, deeply etched into the center of the cover. "There's a solution to every problem. It cost a small fortune, but well worth the price. It pays to prepare."

Santana gasped and stared at the book. "This belonged to an extremely powerful warlock. I can feel his energy still locked in the pages."

Zyro nodded. "Indeed. According to the seller, this codex is one of a set of three written by the warlock Egemon Gornlaith. Included in this book are hundreds of spells for various purposes, including those that will call extinct creatures from beyond. Yes, the citadel is warded and protected against all known creatures, but perhaps not against creatures long extinct."

"Clever, very clever. You would need a witch of considerable power and skill to cast such a spell."

Annoyance made his eyes narrow and his tone derisive. "Are you not up to the task?"

She gave a huff of indignation and moved to the edge of the sofa, as if to leave. "Of course I am. But you assume too much, Zyro. I'm not one of your kiss-ass lackeys, to be ordered around at your whim and will."

A mistake, after all. He had to tread lightly with her. He needed her powers to achieve his goals. But he had to make it clear who was in charge.

"Of course not." He smiled and trailed a manicured fingertip down her cheek. "My apologies. You can, of course, assist me or not, as you wish." His hand moved to encircle her slim neck in a gentle grip. "But, my dear, you would do well to remember exactly who and what I am."

Her gaze dropped to the tattoo on his arm, a tattoo only those in the highest echelon of Illuminati leadership were permitted to wear. But she lifted her chin and looked him boldly in the eye. "And you would do well to remember the same about me."

With a chuckle, he released her. "Touché, my dear. What do you require as payment to help me with this insignificant problem?"

"Insignificant problem? It's an enormous problem, and so it will require enormous recompense. One million dollars."

He didn't even blink at the hefty sum. "Agreed. Assuming the bitch still lives. This is why we deal so well together. We both know our own worth." He slipped on the gloves and reverently thumbed through delicate parchment pages gone yellow with age, hundreds of pages of handwritten Latin words and cryptic symbols, and hand-drawn images of monsters and other unnatural creatures, some of which still existed: vampires, werewolves, wraiths, goblins, hellhounds, and ghouls. But others were now considered mere legends or had gone extinct over the centuries.

"Those Kincaid boys have been a pebble in my shoe for long enough. I'd hoped to be rid of them already. But perhaps it was for the best now that I know about the woman. Perhaps I can kill three annoying birds with one well-aimed stone. We need a very special creature, one that can slip past the citadel's warding, a creature so lethal that it can kill quickly and silently." His hand stilled on a page. He smiled as a wave of excitement sent his heart pounding. "This one. This one is perfect! Mere legend, or did the creature live?"

Santana, a woman who wore evil like a designer label, a woman who had seen—and caused—all manner of unspeakable horror, stared at the creature and shuddered. "I believe it lived, although who knows? Ancient lore is filled with stories about its ferocity, so I would lay odds that it was real."

She read the opposite page before speaking again. "I must cast the spell in a polar magic circle to contain and focus my energy. When I call the beast to this dimension, it will manifest within the circle, but this book says nothing about how to contain it! *Are you insane?* It could kill us!"

"Simply a matter of control, my dear. All power lies in control, and with those who know how to wield it." He walked to his desk and picked up the phone, hit a button on the speed dial, and placed the call on speaker.

A woman answered, her voice croaky and barely above a whisper, clearly roused from sleep. "Good evening, Senator. How may I help you?"

"Tricia, place a call to General Colton at the Army Corps of Engineers. It's late; call his home number. Better yet, his private cell."

"Yes, sir."

Moments later, General Colton's gruff voice came over the line. "Zyro, it's been a long time, my friend."

"Indeed. We must do lunch next time you're in town. There were some interesting news headlines this morning, wouldn't you agree?" Zyro couldn't have cared less about the news. The seemingly innocuous statement was the current Illuminati greeting code to ensure identity and establish that it was safe to talk. As safe as it could be, anyway, in the technologically advanced times that made absolute electronic communications privacy impossible.

"Yes, it's depressing, isn't it? The world is in sad shape."

Zyro smiled. Colton supplied the correct countercode. "I'm doing my best to change that, but the wheels of politics grind slowly."

"True. What can I do for you?"

"I need to borrow your engineers for a matter of utmost discretion. A project of vital importance to national security."

"Of course. Engineering has many specialties. What do you need?"

"A cage. A very strong, very special cage."

Ashriel woke up in the quiet stillness of the space-time continuum. He spread his wings and flexed his limbs. He was physically sound, and his power was restored to normal. Stunned and disoriented, he searched his memory, but he didn't know who or what had saved him. Although he was giddy with relief, it was also perplexing and alarming. He remembered a similar occurrence—waking up in the Maine woods with no knowledge of how he came to be there. But that anomaly ended well.

Thrilled and relieved to be given a second chance, he had no time now to solve the puzzle. He needed to complete his mission. He flew out of the continuum and burst into normal space. Again, he shielded his eyes from the blinding light as the sun burst into view, so close that all he could see was undulating molten fire. Again, the sudden, incredible blast of heat curled the ends of his feathers, and again, gravity hit him like an iron fist to his chest.

But this time, he corrected his mistake, increasing his speed, changing the divergence of his wings into an adverse yaw, and altering his angle of trajectory by thirty degrees to compensate for the enormous gravitational pull of the gaseous giant.

The tips of his wings were singed, but otherwise he was impervious to the heat. The gamma radiation? That was the X-factor. While he was there to harvest that incredible source of energy, it would be like standing at the mouth of an active volcano spitting lava. There was no way to predict if or when a dangerous solar flare would occur, or worse, a mass coronal ejection, where high-speed particles raced off the sun, an event of such magnitude—such an enormous, explosive burst of magnetic energy—that it could spell his doom.

While that thought gave him pause, he was even more concerned about the precious cargo he carried.

He came to a full stop and spread his wings toward the gigantic burning sphere. Buffeted by the solar wind—the continuous flow of charged particles released from the upper atmosphere of the sun and into space—he struggled to maintain his position. His wings acted as a solar array, with the feathers absorbing sunlight and gamma radiation. He jolted as intense warmth spread through his wings and into his body, making his blood sizzle and his bones tingle, but after the initial shock to his system, it wasn't an unpleasant sensation.

His heart pounded, and he experienced a thrilling moment of elation as his power surged beyond anything he'd ever known. Did the archangels feel like this? Within minutes, his feathers sparkled and then glowed with power, but when his vision blurred, he decided enough was enough. Triumphant, he folded his wings, phased out of normal space and back into the space-time continuum, and headed back to Earth.

"Over seven hours!" Benji scrubbed his hands over his face. "We thought you were a goner, for sure."

"As did I," Ashriel said. "I have much to tell you, but it can wait. We must proceed." Ashriel shrugged out of his leather coat and began rolling up his shirtsleeves as he turned to Chase. "As I told you, before I can transfer power—"

"Yeah, yeah, you told us three times, Ash. You gotta step down the voltage by passing it through my body first, and basically use me as a transformer." He flexed his biceps and deepened his voice. "*I am Optimus Prime.*"

Benji hurled his water bottle across the room. "For God's sake! Can't you ever be serious? Do you realize how dangerous this is?"

Trying to control the fear that made his heart pound, Chase slid into the chair next to the bed. "Chill, dude. I know the friggin' risks, so save the surgeon general's warning. Believe me, I been through worse. Do it, Ash."

"You're wearing rubber-soled shoes as I instructed?"

"Yep. Bought 'em from an electrician's supply store, and the rubber mats for under the chairs, too. Hey, I'm sure I'd taste freakin' awesome, but I don't wanna be a piece of Chase jerky."

"As long as you don't ground yourself, the transfer won't be pleasant, but you probably won't sustain any injuries I can't heal."

Benji frowned and blew out a harsh breath. "*Probably?* Let's be real. You've never done this before, so you're only guessing."

"That is correct. The energy I'm using is not precisely electricity, but it seems prudent to take these precautions."

"Chase, I don't like this!" Benji raked his fingers through his hair. "Anything could go wrong. Besides, you're still recovering from being a vampire's milkshake. Why don't I do it?"

"No! No. I hear you, and I appreciate the offer, but *I'm* doing this, end of discussion." He caught Ashriel's eye. "Just don't screw the pooch. Exploding ain't on my bucket list."

Ash finished exposing his arm, and Chase shrugged out of his T-shirt, took a few deep breaths, and braced himself. It was gonna hurt like a bitch, but he wanted to do it for her. He *needed* to do it for her, and he didn't even try to explain it to his cousin.

Benji wouldn't understand.

How could his cousin understand when he didn't really understand either?

But Emma wasn't the only reason. He'd be damned if he'd run away from pain again. Maybe this would take him one step closer to looking in his mirror and seeing an honorable knight again, instead of a gutless coward.

Ashriel moved a chair directly across from him, adjusted the rubber mat under the chair legs, and sat down. He handed him a soft plastic seizure stick. "Bite on this."

He grinned. "What, no bullet? Real men bite on bullets."

"Chase, shut your damn pie hole!"

To his astonishment, this order came from Ashriel. He grinned at Benji and dramatically placed his hand over his heart. "I'm so proud."

Ash slapped his hand on his bare chest. And he wasn't gentle about it. *Ouch!* Jeez, did he break a damn rib?

"Seriously, shut up! I need to concentrate. This is far more dangerous for her than for you."

That sobered him up. "Sorry. Just trying to lighten the mood."

"Put your hand on her forehead. Don't release the connection, no matter what, until I say you may."

"But what if my arm jerks or I have a seizure or something? Maybe we should strap my hand to her head."

"Not a bad idea," Benji said. "I'll get a belt."

Once they'd secured Chase's hand to Emma's forehead with the belt, Ashriel began the procedure. He placed his hand on Chase's chest. "Ready?"

Fuck, no. But he took a deep breath and nodded. Gripping the chair arm with his free hand, he jerked and helplessly groaned as energy flowed through his body. He was swimming in an ocean of electric eels. *Angry* electric eels. The skin under and surrounding Ashriel's hand reddened and sizzled, like bacon in a skillet, and Chase flashed back to the day he'd received his Templar sigil brand. But that had only taken a few seconds.

God, would it *never* end? He alternated between strangled moans and gasps for air as tiny blisters formed and grew larger as Ashriel continued to transfer energy. Larger and larger, until the fat blisters popped, and fluid and blood seeped out and ran down his chest in rivulets.

Emma convulsed as the power flowed from Chase's hand into her body. As Ashriel released more and more power, his eyes glowed like blue neon, and the veins in his neck and face bulged. Chase lost control and screamed in pain, and the angel's face contorted as he struggled to control the strong current that flowed from his body into Chase's.

Finally, after what seemed like hours, the agony stopped. Ash ended the transfer and removed his hand, and Chase gulped air, hoping it was done. He didn't think he could take any more. He reflexively jerked away when Ashriel moved to touch him again.

"I just want to heal you."

He nodded, unable to speak. What he'd just experienced was right up there with some of the best torture Hell had to offer.

Ash did his healing thing and then turned his attention to Emma. Thankfully, Benji kept a steadying hand on his shoulder as he slumped in his chair, because he might have tumbled off and onto the floor otherwise. His head rested in his hands as he tried to catch his breath.

Close to puking, he was woozy and weak from the trauma. His entire body tingled, and his eyelids and muscles twitched. Although Ashriel had healed the burns and broken flesh, he felt like someone had ripped his guts out, roasted them over an open fire, and then shoved them back inside him while they were still on fire.

And he should know.

Elated, Ashriel gazed down at Emma's body. He was victorious! Her skin was a healthy pink, and her chest rose and fell with easy, steady breathing. He stood beside her, closed his eyes, and spread his arms wide. A sparkling cloud of white light flowed from his body, swirled gracefully in the air, and then gently settled down into hers. But afterward, Ashriel pressed his hand to his chest, as if in pain.

And it was pain as he mourned the loss of her soul as she departed from him.

The empty place she left behind was cold.

And lonely.

He didn't realize until that moment how lonely he had been before her. Their time together hadn't been long enough. He wished the procedure had failed, so he could have kept her with him forever. But the selfish thought shamed him. Tears pricked his eyes as he leaned down and caressed her soft cheek. *Be happy, my sweet Emma.*

"It work?" Chase asked, his voice raspy and weak. "She good?"

Ashriel composed himself. Rolling down his sleeve, he turned to the cousins. "Yes. She'll sleep now."

Without a word, Ben patted Chase's shoulder and slipped out of the room.

"Ash, you did it. You should be proud of yourself, man."

"Not exactly proud, Chase. Happy. I still believe it is angels' purpose to protect humanity, and so often I've failed. But to save this innocent woman..."

Chase grinned at him. "Yeah, buddy. It's a big, fat win for the home team."

Ben called from down the hallway, "Ash, can you come here for a minute?"

"Stay with her, please. She could awaken at any time." Chase nodded, and Ashriel headed down the hallway to where Ben leaned out from around a corner and beckoned to him.

"Look at this."

Ashriel rounded the corner and stopped short, a shock of alarm sending a sudden feeling of cold through his body as his feet became inexorably locked to the floor. "Ben? *What are you doing?*"

Chapter Seven

Ash's shocked expression when he recognized the scattering of Celtic runestones glowing green at his feet sent a splinter of guilt into Ben's heart, but he couldn't let it go. Too damn much was at stake.

"You would use the Runes of Calyx against *me?*"

"Just the immobilization spell." Ben crossed his arms. "The truth, Ash. Now. *All of it.* Or I summon Michael, and the shit hits the fan, whether you like it or not." He was bluffing. He'd never do that to Ash, but he had a decent poker face, and he wore it now.

"What are you talking about? Every word I've told you is the truth."

Annoyance pricked, and Ben's eyes narrowed. He knew subterfuge when he heard it. "Maybe so. But it's not the whole truth, is it?"

Ashriel couldn't meet his eyes and looked away.

Ben's chest tightened. *Damn.* He was right. "Look, I've let it go until now because that girl saved our lives, so I wanted to save Emma as much as you did. But she's safe now. I saw the way you looked at her and Chase back in the hospital. Before she wakes up, I want to know what's going on between her and my cousin. It's not like Chase to be so head-over-heels over a girl he's never slept with, much less never even met before! I don't think he was this upset when Holly dumped him. And after Santana's hold on him? I'm not gonna just stand by and let another woman put him in danger."

"It's not like that."

"Then just how the hell is it?"

Ashriel momentarily closed his eyes and heaved an annoyed sigh. "You've left me no choice now, but I urge you to think about this carefully before you tell Chase. I strongly suspect it would upset him, and I believe it is best that he doesn't know."

Alarm bells clanged in Ben's head. "Know *what?*"

"You're aware that a human soul, although encased in a flesh and blood body, is pure energy. Just like an angelic coruscentia. Like all matter, like all energy, the soul vibrates on a molecular level. Every soul vibrates at a unique frequency. Think of it like human fingerprints."

Ben raised a brow and held up his hand, palm toward Ash.

"Yes, I know, but for people *with* fingerprints, no two are alike. But there are rare exceptions to the rule when it comes to souls, meaning two souls that vibrate at the exact same frequency. Like Chase and Emma."

"What does that even mean?"

"Emma and Chase are soulmates."

"*Soulmates?* That's really a thing?"

"Yes. Not necessarily the human notion of soulmates being perfect love-mates, but literally two halves of one soul, divided in two by God at the time of its creation."

"Why?"

"I don't know. It's a divine mystery. It's extremely rare. In all my time on Earth, I've never seen it before. Emma and Chase have a spiritual connection, but God gifted human beings with free will. What they choose to do about it is up to them."

Chase and Emma were soulmates. Ben's head spun, and his knees turned to jelly. He fell back against the wall and slid down to sit on the floor. This was unbelievable! Never in a million years would he have imagined such a thing were possible. "That's what Chase said in the hospital—that they have a connection. I thought he was losing it, or it was the meds, but now, to know it's real? Wow! She could be meant for him?"

Ashriel turned away. "I told you; I don't know."

Ben sat cross-legged and leaned his head back against the wall. Should he tell Chase or not? His first impulse, to tell him, was born of training—Chase was his Laird, and all decisions affecting the citadel lay with him. But this was different. This was personal, on the deepest level.

Chase deserved a chance to be happy, and what better chance than with his soulmate? Emma was alone in the world, and that was the key. With no outside ties, it was far less likely that there would be complications. After just a few months, Holly had resented living in the citadel, separated from her friends and family. She'd left too much behind, and the constant danger of Chase's life as a Templar Knight had been too much for her.

But Emma was used to danger and being alone. She could cope with the isolation of life at the citadel. For her, it was a drastic improvement! But after what Holly had done, Chase was already skittish when it came to anything resembling a relationship. And he was sure to get his back up if he thought that an outside force was pulling the strings—even if it was God himself. He would hate the idea of a woman being destined for him;

he would hate that he had no choice. He could very well sabotage his one chance to have everything he'd ever wanted.

Ben wasn't going to let him.

And if Chase settled down and produced an heir for Orion Citadel...

Hope exploded in his heart. It was a win-win situation! But he had to handle it right. "I get it, Ash, why you don't want Chase to know. You're right; he wouldn't like this. Does Emma know?"

"No."

Ben rolled to his feet and retrieved a small wooden box from where it sat on the floor. He opened the acacia-wood chest that housed the ancient runes. The polished square stones levitated and floated back into the chest of their own accord. "All right, we'll keep this between us. For now."

Twenty minutes later, Chase sat with Benji by Emma's bedside as she slept. It was ridiculous, but he couldn't help the sweaty palms or the butterflies doing jumping jacks in his gut, like a teenager on his first date. Ash had read her mind in the hospital, so the angel knew pretty much everything about her. But he'd told him and Benji only what they needed to know to complete the mission, and that wasn't much—only that her name was Emma Borello, she was twenty-five years old, and she was alone in the world.

And she'd been hexed with a terrible curse that made her a human lure for monsters.

Ashriel refused to violate her privacy any more than that. He insisted Emma would tell them what she wanted them to know when she wanted them to know it. Chase appreciated and respected Ashriel's decision.

A moment later, she stretched and opened her eyes, and his heart skipped a beat and started pounding. Their eyes met, and her face lit up.

"Hi," she said.

She smiled at him, and Chase had to take a gulp of air. This was the first time he'd seen her eyes clearly, and they floored him. The color of honey, with little gold flecks, like someone sprinkled glitter in them. The butterflies in his gut multiplied. "Hi, Emma. I'm Chase. Chase Kincaid. And this is my cousin, Ben. Also Kincaid."

But the butterflies disappeared when her eyes widened, and with a soft cry of distress, her smile vanished. Her breath coming shallow and fast, she clawed and kicked at the bedcovers, struggling to free her legs. She launched herself out of bed, but he caught her before her feet hit the floor.

"No, let me go," she pleaded, clutching at his shirt. "I need to leave here. Please, you don't understand. You're in danger with me here!"

"Easy there, sweetheart," he said. "No danger here, I swear. We know all about your curse, and we're gonna help you get rid of it. C'mon back and relax, okay? Everything's fine." He guided her back onto the bed and pulled up the covers. "You're catnip for all things that go bump in the night, but this place is better than Fort Knox, protected against every evil thing you've been running from and from any human threat, too. Safest place on the planet, I swear. You got nothing to worry about."

Emma leaned back against the pillows and gazed into the familiar gray eyes that had graced her dreams since early childhood. She knew that handsome face, and she wasn't afraid. But she was confused. Where was she? And how did she get here? She wore a long-sleeve, navy-blue blouse. She ran her fingertips over the smooth, delicate material. It felt like real silk. But it wasn't hers; she hadn't owned anything so nice in a long time.

The unfamiliar room reminded her of a guest bedroom in a European castle turned Airbnb she'd seen in a travel blog. She sat in an elegant four-poster bed, covered with a lovely light-blue comforter and snow-white sheets with a floral embroidered edge. There were no personal belongings visible in the spacious chamber, but on the pastel-yellow walls hung several beautiful paintings of snow-capped mountains against an azure sky, surrounded by thick forest.

A large bay window with matching light-blue curtains let in brilliant sunlight that reflected on the polished hardwood floor. Wasn't a motel or hotel; the cherry-wood furniture looked like genuine antiques. "Where am I?"

"My house," Chase said. "Well, kinda. Not really a house." He looked at his cousin, the enormous red-haired guy who sat next to him, and shrugged. "How do we explain?"

The big guy—Ben, that was his name—pulled a cellphone from his pocket. "Guess a picture is worth a thousand words. Took these last time I went hunting. Really cool rainbow." He brought up a photo on his phone and handed it to her.

She stared at the picture. Lightheaded, she braced a hand on the mattress, and a knot formed in her stomach. What were they trying to pull? It had to be a screenshot from a video game. A castle integrated into the side of a mountain rose into the bluest of skies, and a spectacular rainbow arched over the tallest spire. The only things missing were a drawbridge, a moat, and a dragon flying in the distance.

She handed him back the phone. "Right. And I'm the princess in the tower. Again, where am I really, and what's going on?"

Chase laughed and scrubbed his hands over his face. "Listen, I know it looks freakin' unbelievable. But God's truth. Benji and me? We're Templar Knights, and you're at Orion Citadel in the Rocky Mountains of Colorado."

She nodded and smiled. "So, I suppose the airport offers sightseeing flights so passengers can take pictures. You got a gift shop in the lobby?"

"No," Ben said. "A cloaking spell hides the whole place."

"Oh, man." With a frustrated groan, Chase raked his fingers through his glossy black hair. "It really sounds sketchy." He shrugged. "Yeah, I wouldn't believe us, either." And then he smiled at her.

Despite whatever con game they were trying to run, she melted like a popsicle on a hot summer day. *Good lord*, what a smile! He should do toothpaste commercials. He should get an agent, go to Hollywood, and—

Oh, no.

A flood of disappointment brought the sting of tears.

She was dreaming. It was just another damn dream.

She slowly shook her head. "Damn. Had me going for a minute there. For a dream—even for me—this one's a real doozie."

"You're not dreaming," Ben said. He exchanged a look of concern with his cousin. "We're real." He waved his hand around the room. "This is all real."

She wanted to believe him, but how could she?

Chase touched her arm. "Emma, you acted like you recognized me. Have we already met?"

"Not in real life. Only in dreams. Like now." With a wistful smile, she trailed a finger along his bearded jawline. "All my life, I've dreamed about you. Except for—" Her gaze flicked to the doorway as someone new entered the room. She dropped her hand and, with a strangled gasp, scooted further back against the headboard.

Not in fear.

In awe.

"No worries," Chase said, patting her arm. "This is Ashriel. He's a friend, our guardian, actually."

She gazed up at Ashriel, enthralled. "*An angel*. You're so beautiful."

The angel smiled, and his incredible blue eyes widened. He seemed surprised, and from the soft blush that crept over his face, he seemed a little embarrassed. An angel could get embarrassed?

"Yes," Ashriel said. "I mean, yes, I'm an angel, not yes, that I'm beautiful. I appreciate the compliment, but physical beauty is a subjective concept, and as the proverb says, it is in the eye of the beholder and cannot be judged objectively, so it would really depend on one's personal pref—"

"Ash," Chase whispered loudly.

"Yes?"

"Babbling, dude."

"Oh."

Emma gasped as her memory sparked. "Wait. I remember now. The alley." She shuddered. "Oh, God. Vampires. And someone shot me, I think. Yeah, more than once. Oh, I get it now." Well, that explained the angel. Her gaze wandered again around the beautiful room. Not exactly what she might have expected, but it was still very nice. "This is Heaven?"

Chuckling, Ashriel lifted her hand. "No, Emma. This isn't Heaven. You're very much alive."

Her eyes widened at his touch. She looked at the hand that held hers and then up at the angel's face. Her breath caught. Something teased at the back of her mind—a memory of light and warmth and joy that she couldn't quite grab hold of. She narrowed her focus and tried to catch it, but Ben spoke and distracted her, and it was gone.

"Wait," Ben said. "How did you know Ash is an angel?"

She tore her gaze away from Ashriel and looked at Ben. Was he blind? "Seriously? Halo. Wings. Glowing. *Duh*."

"Emma is one of the special people who can see beyond my humanoid body to my spiritual being."

Eyes wide, Chase fell back into his chair. "Holy crap."

"Wait." She glanced from Chase to Ben. "You mean, you guys don't see it?"

They both shook their heads.

She pressed her hands to her cheeks, trying to wrap her spinning head around it all. "Okay, so I see an angel, but you tell me I'm not dead, and it's not a dream?" She stiffened as a wave of fear constricted her muscles. "*Oh, no!* A unicorn snagged me." She covered her face with her hands. "It's unicorn venom. Somehow, one of those bastards pricked me with its horn. I'm lying under a tree somewhere, living my perfect dream world in my head while a damn unicorn drains the life out of me for a snack."

Ashriel put his hand on her shoulder. "Emma, that is not happening to you."

"Absolutely not," Chase said. "I promise."

She threw her hands up, and her brittle voice revealed a bubble of hysteria that was close to bursting. "Oh, come on! It's the only logical explanation. I remember being shot multiple times, yet I'm fine? And I'm safe for the first time in years, sitting here in this impregnable, fairy-tale fortress with the man of my dreams—literally, the man of my dreams—and his cousin, who looks like an actor from that show *Vikings*. And then they tell me they're freaking knights in shining armor? Oh, and the icing on the cake? An angel who's so incredibly beautiful that I want to cry. Does any of that sound even remotely like reality to you? I mean, the odds of this being real are microscopic. Miniscule. Infinitesimal."

Chase leaned toward Ben and whispered, "That's really small, right?"

Despite the situation, she wanted to laugh. How cute was he?

"Yeah, Chase. For God's sake, read a book. You know, she's got a point. How do we prove to her that this is real?"

Chase tried to think of a way but came up empty. "Damned if I know." Why hadn't they thought about this before? Of course, she'd be wigged out. He'd been so focused on saving her life that he hadn't given a damn thought to her mental state. The poor girl just woke up in a freakin' episode of the Twilight Zone.

With a defeated sigh, she sat back and gave a dismissive wave of her hand. "Know what, guys? It's okay. Doesn't matter." She wrapped her arms around herself and stared at the wall.

After a moment, her eyes brimmed, and a tear trailed down her pretty face, sending a shard of anguish into his heart. "I'm tired of running. Tired of being alone. I'm so *damn tired* of being alone. Can't do it anymore. This is better, way better, even though it's not real."

Still staring at the wall—seeming to forget all about them—she rocked back and forth. The tears stopped, but her eyes clouded over and she got a faraway look. "Soon I'll be dead. Dead as a doornail, dead as a dodo, pushing up daisies. Shuffling off this mortal coil. But it'll finally be over." She gave a ragged sigh. "I'm glad; I really am."

She stopped rocking, and she looked a bit disgruntled. "But I have to say, I'm a little disappointed in myself. Not very imaginative. Damsel in distress, rescued by knights in shining armor, carried off to the safety of their castle? Total cliché. Clearly, way too much Disney when I was a kid. But the angel's an interesting wild card, though. Maybe Emmalina made him up. She was always more creative than me." She gave a little laugh and started rocking again. "Dead, dead, dead."

A chill skittered down Chase's spine. Ben grabbed his arm, and they exchanged a horrified look. Even Ash stared at her, looking panicked, his eyes wide.

"An angel, a beautiful, beautiful angel. Waiting here to take me to Heaven. Maybe Mama's there." Her eyes brimmed again, and a tiny whimper escaped. "Maybe not." But then she sighed, her face lost all expression, and her tone went eerily flat, almost robotic. "Huh. Maybe he represents a good wizard, like Gandalf or Dumbledore, or maybe a fairy godmother, or an advanced being like Q from Star Trek."

Chase's scalp crawled. *Shit*, she was losing it! "Oh, *hell*, no," he muttered. He wasn't gonna let her slip away down the rabbit hole! Lightning fast, he pulled his boot knife, grabbed her hand, and slashed her palm. She yelped and stopped rocking.

"Chase!" Ashriel stepped forward, his hands fisted and his face twisted in rage.

He kept a tight grip on her bleeding hand and wouldn't let her pull away. "Listen to me, Emma. Feel that pain. *Feel it!* That feel like something that would happen in your perfect dream world? It ain't a damn unicorn. You ain't gonna die. This is real, dammit, real! You gotta believe me!"

Tears streamed from her eyes, and her chin quivered, breaking his heart. The last thing he ever wanted to do was cause her more pain. But those tear-filled eyes were clear and focused again.

"Okay," she said, nodding. "Okay, real. It's real. I believe you."

He motioned to Ash. "Hurry, fix her up."

Ash glared at him and gently held her bleeding hand in his. He emitted the blue beam of healing light from his palm over the gaping wound, but he continued to glare at him as the gash closed and disappeared in seconds.

Chase blew out a harsh sigh. "Don't gimme the stink eye, Ash. What the hell was I supposed to do? She was fixin' to punch her ticket on the train to Oz."

"He's not wrong," Benji said.

Eyes wide, Emma examined her now-perfect hand and then gazed up at Ashriel with an expression of wonder. "Thank you, Ashriel."

"My pleasure. Are you all right now?"

"I think so."

"Good. Rest assured that you're safe here. I must go, but I'll return soon." And he vanished, making her mouth gape and her eyes go even wider.

Chase patted her arm and gave her a wink. "You'll get used to that. He beams in and outta here like it's the transporter room on the Enterprise."

Dammit, Ash! Why didn't he use the door and leave from the hallway? Wasn't she freaked out enough? He leaned over and reached for her hand again, but this time he pressed a gentle kiss to her palm where the deep, bloody gash had been. "So damn sorry I hurt you, sweetheart." He shrugged helplessly. "Didn't know what else to do. Can you forgive me?"

"Of course, I do." She raised a hand to cradle the side of his face, and that amazing feeling cascaded over him like a gentle summer rain. "You were right to do it." She leaned back against the headboard and took a deep, shuddering breath. "Wow, that was really scary. I was swimming in the deep end there for a minute, huh?"

"Happens to the best of us. It'll be okay, I promise. It's a hell of a lot for anyone to deal with." She'd given him a slight smile at the transporter joke, but what could he do to make her laugh and chase away the shadow of anxiety from her pretty eyes? "Hey, I really do got a tower if you wanna play princess." He grinned and lifted a lock of her long hair. "Rapunzel, Rapunzel, let down your hair."

She giggled, and it was music to his ears.

"My hair's not *that* long."

"No. But it's just as beautiful." He tilted his head and tapped his chin, giving her a teasing assessment. "Well, you could wind it up on the sides of your head and do the cinnamon roll thing, like Princess Leia."

She wrinkled her nose and gave a little headshake, but amusement sparkled in her eyes. "Not my style."

"Yeah, you're right. And this place couldn't pass for the bridge of a Star Cruiser or the Millennium Falcon, so that would totally ruin the vibe. Although I know someone who'd make a great Wookie." He winked and bobbed his head toward Benji. Another giggle. *Yes!* He was on a roll. Hmmm...surely, she'd seen *The Princess Bride*. "Oh, I know. How about Buttercup?"

"And I suppose you're Westley?"

"Of course." He jerked a thumb at his cousin and grinned. "And he's Fezzik."

As she laughed, Benji rolled his eyes, gave a long-suffering sigh, and got to his feet. His cousin stood behind him, gave his shoulders a couple of quick, hard squeezes, and gave his hair a rough but affectionate tousle. "Emma, I apologize for my idiot cousin playing movie trivia while you're probably starving. Do you need or want anything? Anything at all, just name it."

"I'd kill for a cheeseburger." She sniffed and wrinkled her nose. "And what's that funky chemical smell? It's making me a little nauseated." She sniffed her forearm and cringed. "Oh, yuck, it's me? A shower would be nice."

Emma stared at her naked body in the bathroom mirror. Shaking like a leaf, she ran her hands over her skin. Her mind reeled with shock and disbelief, even as her heart soared with elation. Nothing but soft, flawless skin.

Her scars were gone?

This had to be a dream; it had to!

She rubbed her eyes and looked again. A normal woman looked back at her instead of the ugly thing she had become over the years.

The thick, gnarled scar tissue that disfigured her neck from when she was held captive and fed upon by vampires. Gone.

A werewolf's hideous claw mark that slashed across her chest, starting at her left shoulder, across her breast, and continued down her belly and flank. Gone.

The enormous, ragged chunk missing from her right thigh and the long, deep gouges on both her legs—grotesque souvenirs from her tangle with a wendigo that tried to drag her into the Utah woods. Gone.

She gathered her hair to the side and looked at her back in the mirror. No trace of a bullet wound.

Even the scars on her forearms from the surgery to repair her broken wrists were gone. She kneeled on the tile floor and clasped her hands in prayer. "Dear God, please don't let this be a dream. Please, please, *please*, let it be real."

Feeling better for the hot shower and clean clothes, Emma walked through the magnificent Gothic architecture of Orion Citadel—the fortress Chase had told her served both as the Kincaid ancestral home and their command center. She carefully followed the verbal directions he gave her before leaving her alone to bathe. The place was enormous. It seemed to her like miles of hallways, which—despite the glorious architecture—were all granite block walls and floors and identical solid oak doors.

Although she paused at several windows to admire the astounding views of mountains and forest, there was not a painting or a picture. Not a single plant, not even a fake one. Not a decoration of any kind. The place needed some color. Some life. Good thing all the rooms had numbers, or how the heck would someone find where they were going?

She arrived at her destination and stepped into the immense Great Hall.

And froze.

Chapter Eight

Emma stood in the center of the Great Hall with her mouth ajar, staring goggle-eyed like a sun-burned, camera-toting, fanny-pack-wearing tourist. They had their very own Hogwarts! She wouldn't have been surprised to see a snowy owl swoop past her with mail clamped in its talons or students in long black robes run by, carrying books and magic wands.

She nearly gave herself whiplash, trying to look everywhere at once.

At one end of the large rectangular room was a stone Gothic archway, the distinctive pointed arch featuring a center keystone inlaid with a Templar cross. Beyond the arch gleamed a stunning stained glass window interpretation of Raphael's painting of the archangel Michael vanquishing Satan.

Marble columns marched across each side of the room and rose to a soaring, coffered ceiling crisscrossed with massive oak beams. Built-in arched bookshelves with glass doors burgeoned with books, scrolls, and displayed artifacts, many of which looked like they belonged in an antiquities museum.

The biggest fireplace she'd ever seen held court at one end of the room. She crossed the room to get a closer look. A fire blazed inside the hearth, but there was no firewood or even fake logs. Some kind of gas fire? On closer inspection, she couldn't see the source of the flames, nor a gas line or valve. How odd!

Above the fireplace hung a three-foot-long broadsword, and assuming the jewels set in the handle were real, it was worth a fortune! Above the sword—so high she had to step back and crane her neck—hung an ornate coat of arms bearing the name *Kincaid* along the bottom and the motto *Justice, Honor, and Family, These I will Defend,* emblazoned on a ribbon scroll across the top.

Like sentinels on watch, two gleaming suits of armor draped with the Templars' signature white mantle adorned with the red Templar cross flanked the fireplace.

Stunning wrought-iron light fixtures hung from the ceiling, with matching sconces on the walls and columns. Set into deep embrasures along one side of the enormous room, sunlight streamed through three sets of floor-to-ceiling leaded-glass windows and reflected across what seemed like an acre of gleaming hardwood.

Her wide eyes were agog at the assorted ancient weaponry on display, at the sigils and warding symbols within the frieze that ran along the ceiling, and at those inlaid into the wall above each arched bookshelf.

At each entry point, there were a series of sigils integrated right into the floor. A magical security system? But the things that had her nearly drooling in nerdy lust were the countless volumes of ancient and obviously priceless books and scrolls housed there. Her fingers itched to crack a few of those gems open.

A staircase tucked away in a round alcove caught her attention. Where did those stairs go? She stood on the bottom step of the circular staircase and looked up through the hole in the middle of the spiral. The stairs rose at least five stories above her. Sunlight shone in abundance at the top. Just windows? Or did it lead to some kind of exterior space, like a balcony or terrace?

She was afraid of the night—and the danger that prowled the dark—so she hadn't viewed the night sky in years. Perhaps she would have the opportunity to enjoy the night sky from such a safe vantage point. She'd loved visiting the Vanderbilt Planetarium and Observatory on Long Island as a child, fascinated by the mythology behind the constellations.

Boot steps caught her attention. She turned to find Ben walking toward her, smiling and holding a laptop computer and a small bottle of orange juice.

"Feel free to check it out, but it's a big climb. I'd wait a few days."

"What's up there?" she asked.

"Chase wasn't kidding. That staircase is inside a turret, pretty much a castle tower. It opens to a wide terrace that narrows off into a walkway that encircles the fifth floor. The views are amazing. You can see for miles, even the river."

She clapped her hands together. "Oh, I'd love to see that! It must look amazing with all the trees turning color. Maybe tomorrow?"

"Sure. Just say the word."

She pointed to the fireplace. "What's the deal? No wood, no gas source."

"Come. I'll show you."

She followed him to the fireplace and watched as he took an old coin off the mantel and held it toward the blaze. "Ignis extinctus fueris." The blaze immediately died.

Her mouth fell open with a small gasp. "Magic?"

Ben nodded. "A family heirloom, old Templar magic."

"May I?" Fascinated, she held out her hand, and he handed her the coin.

She examined both sides of the weighty gold disk. If there had ever been an inscription, it was gone, worn away by time and many fingers. Giggling, she held it toward the hearth. "Fire, come back!" She flinched when the blaze returned with a *whoosh*. "Wow, that was cool—"

Ben stared at her like she'd sprouted three heads.

"What? Did I do something wrong?"

"Uh, no. No, it's fine." He smiled, held out his hand for the coin, and returned it to the mantel. "You must be hungry."

"Understatement."

"I brought a snack for you."

Her gaze fell upon the framed photos on the mantel. She wanted to ask about them, but a wave of dizziness that accompanied an embarrassingly loud stomach growl made her choose instead to follow Ben to one of the long tables. He set his laptop down, pulled a granola bar from his pocket, and slid it and the bottle of orange juice across the table to her. "Here you go. Should hold you over until Chase gets back with the food."

She sat across from him, tore open the wrapper, and bit off a chunk. She moaned. "Chocolate chip, my favorite. Manna from Heaven. Feel like I haven't eaten for a week."

"Feeling better now?"

"Yeah, much. Nothing like a long, hot shower. A word of advice, though? Ever have any more guests here? Give them a map."

"Yeah, I guess it would take a while to learn your way around. I'll put up lots of Post-it Notes with arrows for you. You know, this way to the kitchen, that way to the Great Hall."

She laughed. "That's very considerate, but I got it now. I'm good at remembering directions. How did you guys even get this place? And what are Templar Knights? Obviously, not exactly what I've read."

"To answer your first question, Chase and I were born here, as were our fathers and grandfather, all our Kincaid ancestors, from the day the angels built this citadel. As for your second question about the Templars, well, probably very little of what you've heard or read is true. Misinformation campaigns aren't a recent invention. It is true that the original Templars were warrior monks and were considered the special military forces of their day.

"But most info floating around out there about the Templars is well-crafted propaganda, meant to keep our true purpose a secret. I believe the current story has it that all the remaining Templars were killed off long ago after they pissed off the French king, and that the Freemasons are descended from the Templars. Not true.

"Well, King Philip the Fourth had some French Templars murdered over a supposed money deal gone wrong, but the truth is, the king was dabbling in witchcraft and sorcery. He had to be stopped to maintain the balance of power..."

He raked his fingers through that thick, red mane. "I'm sorry, I didn't mean to launch into a history lesson."

"Oh, no. Please, don't stop. I love history. It was my favorite subject in high school."

"Okay. Anyway, long story short, modern-day Templar Knights work in service to the archangel Michael against Satan and his human minions, the Illuminati. Michael is our commander. Being a Templar Knight, well, it's not a choice. You can't just enlist like the army or Marines. It's a bloodline. Chase and me, our fathers and grandfather, and so on, all the Kincaids back to Scotland. There are other citadels like this one, thirty-three in all, spread across the globe. Each is assigned to a Templar family, passed on from father to eldest son. Chase's dad was my dad's older brother, so Chase became laird when his father died."

"Laird? Scottish word for lord, isn't it?"

"Yeah. Not in the sense of nobility anymore in our case, but in the sense of being in charge. Commander, head honcho. This citadel is his to command and to protect, unless he dies without an heir, and then the responsibility would fall to me, or to my oldest son, if I'm gone."

"So, why castles? I mean, call it what you want, a citadel or whatever, but it's a freaking castle."

He laughed. "I guess it is. For protection. Defense. Stored within the citadels are countless items of historical and practical value—including God-given holy relics like the Ark of the Covenant and the Holy Grail, although no one but Michael knows exactly where they are. Originally, they stored these items at the Temple Mount in Jerusalem, where the Templars had their headquarters. Hence the name Templars, because their duty was to guard the temple and its treasures. You're familiar with the Crusades, right?"

"Yeah, sure."

"Well, in 1187, Saladin's Muslim army attacked Jerusalem with a force of over thirty thousand. Total massacre. In the end, only a handful of Templars who were on guard within the temple itself were left alive. While Saladin was smashing down the city walls, they escaped from beneath the Temple Mount, taking the treasure and relics with them through a labyrinth of caves.

"Touched by God and directed by the archangel Michael, those men split up, each taking a portion of the treasure and relics with them. Those thirty-three men became the founding fathers of today's Templar family bloodlines."

"You said Chase's official title is laird. So, are all Templars Scottish?"

"No, sorry for the confusion. Here in the States, they are. But the other family patriarchs use their own titles, depending on their nationality of origin. Of the thirty-three original Templars, only four were Scotsmen. Actually, the Knights Templar order was originally started by a Frenchman named Hugues de Payens, but eventually orders were found across Europe.

"Since the British Isles are relatively small, only one citadel is needed to cover that area, and that one was assigned to a British baron. When the new world was discovered, Michael sent Henry Sinclair here first, and then the other three Scot families in the group followed later, when their citadels were completed. Including Artair Kincaid, our ancestor."

"That's incredible." She covered her mouth as she yawned. "So sorry! Your story isn't boring at all. I'm just tired."

"No wonder. You've been through the wringer. I'll tell you more later."

"Oh, please don't stop. It's fascinating. I've heard about the Illuminati, too, but all I've read are what seem to be a bunch of conspiracy theories about world domination."

"Unfortunately, much of it's true. Illuminati members hold high-ranking positions in nearly every country's government, including ours. Especially ours. They're stealthily working to bring about a world government. Their propaganda sounds like it would ultimately benefit mankind, but the truth is, the leader of that so-called government would be the Devil himself in disguise. Lucifer. Our primary mission is to prevent that from happening."

A chill ran down her spine, and she shuddered. How terrifying was that? "Wait. Illuminati...Lucifer? The Illuminati claim to possess enlightenment, and Satan's angelic name means light-bringer. That's damn scary. It really fits."

"Yep. Sometimes the best place to hide is in plain sight."

"But if they already have bad guys in our government..."

She must have looked as scared as she felt, because he leaned across the table and patted her hand. "No worries. We have people in top positions, too, all over the world."

"Good! Tell me who, so I can vote for them."

He chuckled. "Sorry. Need to know basis only, for security. Not just talking about you. Chase and I don't even know them all."

That made sense. It made her feel a lot better. "Why doesn't God just, I don't know, wipe them off the earth, like Sodom and Gomorrah?"

"Good question. But I gave up questioning the why of it long ago. Waste of time. I asked Michael once, back when I was in training. He told me in no uncertain terms not to question God's will."

"Where does Ashriel fit into all of this?"

"Ash is a seraph, a lesser angel than an archangel, but he still packs a punch. He's our family guardian and has been for countless generations. He reports to Michael, too." Ben smiled. "Most of the time. Ash is a bit of a rebel. More on that later. Right now, you need to eat."

Ben slipped on a pair of reading glasses and turned his attention to his laptop.

As Emma ate her snack, she took in the unusual man sitting before her. One word in particular came to mind: *big*. No doubt, he spent serious time in a gym. Shoulders like a linebacker, bulging biceps, a neck like a California redwood, and just as tall. Thick, wavy red hair skimmed his shoulders. He had a rugged, clean-shaven masculine face armed with killer dimples when he smiled. A strong square jaw. Long-lashed, moss-green eyes shone with intelligence behind the round, wire-rimmed glasses.

He looked like a cross between a young college professor and a Viking warrior-king of olde. About thirty, give or take. She liked him right away and was completely at ease in his company. Did that have anything to do with the fact that his coloring was much like her mother's?

To better protect herself, she'd read every book she could find on how to read body language, so it was second nature for her to observe anyone in her vicinity for signs of danger, but there was nothing amiss with Ben. He seemed warm, steady, and genuinely nice. "Ben, you want to tell me why I reeked like biology class? Formaldehyde, right? Or something like it?

And what happened to all my scars? Not that I'm complaining, mind you, because it's totally and amazingly awesome that they're gone, but it's kind of freaking me out."

"Uh...I don't...scars?"

The distant sound of a door opening and then closing drew her attention. Footsteps echoed, and then Chase emerged through the arch carrying bags of takeout food. "C'mon, kids, let's get our grub on."

Her heart flip-flopped as he strode across the room toward her. *Dear Lord*, the man was ridiculously handsome! He moved confidently, each step of his cowboy boots laying claim to the place where they landed. His strides were long, his pace unhurried, his gaze steady, and his shoulders relaxed. This was a man in charge of his domain, a man accustomed to calling the shots.

He aimed that lethal smile at her as he crossed the last few feet to the table. Setting the bags on the table in front of her, he bowed gallantly, charming her into a blush that warmed her cheeks. "As per Milady's request, we have cheeseburgers, fries, and chocolate shakes—a meal truly fit for a princess."

"Thank you, kind sir." She opened a bag, sniffed deeply, and sighed with pleasure. "God bless us, every one. I forgot to ask, but did you happen to get any of those little pies? I do love me some pie."

"Of course." Chase reached into the bag and pulled out a small cardboard box. "Hope you like apple." He handed it to her and then grinned at Ben as he shrugged out of his black leather jacket and tossed it on a chair. "Girl after my own heart."

"Chase thinks sugar is one of the four food groups." Ben rifled through the bags and took a burger and a salad. He glanced pointedly at his cousin. "Emma has questions."

"I'm sure you do, sweetheart." Chase dropped into a chair and grabbed a burger. "I'm gonna answer every single one, but how about we strap on the old feedbag first and then we talk? I'm starving."

"Sounds like a plan," Emma mumbled, her mouth already full of delicious, salty fries. But where was the angel? "Isn't Ashriel going to eat?"

Ben shrugged. "Angels don't have to eat. He can eat for pleasure. He just doesn't do it very often."

"Is he here?" she asked.

"Yeah, where is fly-boy, anyway?" asked Chase.

"You got me." Ben eased back into his chair with a chocolate shake. "Popped back in earlier for five minutes, then said he had to go check on something and that he'd be back."

While they ate, Emma watched Chase from under her lashes. She'd have thought she'd be immune to his looks by now, having seen him in her dreams for most of her life. But the live, up-close-and-personal Chase was, well, damn intimidating.

Between bites, he chatted with Ben about specs for a box truck, and his voice sent shivers down her spine. Deep as the ocean and resonant, like the seductive growl of a luxury supercar at idle. She detected the undercurrent of a southern accent—no, more like a charming drawl that reminded her of Texas Pete. The memory of a dream from long ago made her smile: Chase was seated on a cow pony, trailing after a herd of steers. Texas maybe? That would explain it. He must have spent quite a bit of time there.

He'd been fine-featured, almost pretty, as a boy, but no longer. A little too rough around the edges; too much wear and tear. But the hardening of his countenance by maturity and life experience only added to his masculine attraction. Thick, black lashes framed stunning light-gray eyes ringed with black, the irises shimmering with silver striations.

His midnight-black hair glistened blue under the lights and was on the short side and carelessly fashionable, and a neatly trimmed mustache and beard accentuated the hard line of his jaw. Full, eminently kissable-looking lips made her heartbeat quicken and her cheeks burn as she imagined them pressed to hers.

His narrow, once-straight nose now sported a slight crook to the left. Accident or fistfight? Most likely a fistfight. He'd been nothing but nice to her, but at first glance, he came off as a tough guy, the kind of man who'd shoot first and ask questions never, who'd be quick with his fists or with a smooth pickup line, depending on his quarry.

Although he didn't have the extreme bodybuilder physique of his larger cousin, muscles rippled under the long sleeves of his black shirt and across his broad shoulders and chest when he moved. He reminded her of a black panther—dark, powerful, and dangerous.

She imagined, assuming he was single, that on any given night he had his choice of leggy, big-breasted blondes or sultry brunettes with blood-red lipstick and stiletto heels.

By comparison, she was as remarkable as a field mouse.

With a half-eaten cheeseburger in her hand, she sighed, stared down at her thigh, and picked at a ragged little rip in her jeans. Her backpack had been waiting for her in her temporary bedroom. After her shower, she'd changed out of the soft, warm robe Chase had loaned her—which was miles too big and caused her to lift the hem like the train of a wedding gown—and put on her usual attire.

Although her clothes were clean and comfortable, she was suddenly acutely aware of the worn, faded jeans and the old T-shirt she wore—her complete lack of adornment. Her hair hadn't seen a professional stylist in years. She wore no makeup or jewelry. Plain Jane in every way. She hadn't given any thought to her appearance since cooking school. When was the last time she wore lipstick and heels? The prom. She'd been fifteen, a princess in pastel-pink satin, walking into the gym on quarterback Matt Corwin's arm and walking back out with a crown on her head, music echoing in her heart, and her feet tired from dancing.

Well, those days were long gone. A lifetime ago.

Her gaze moved back to Chase when his cellphone pinged. As he read the text message, his mouth set in a hard line, and those silver eyes sparked with obvious anger. He set the phone on the table without responding. She flinched when he slammed his fist down next to it and jabbed a finger at Ben.

"You deal with MacDonald. I see that sonofabitch again, and I'll stab him in his ugly face. Don't know where the hell he got his intel, but it's time for him to hang it up and head back to the ranch. And tell him to stay there. His services are no longer needed."

Emma's heart stuttered at Chase's sudden outburst and harsh voice. Beyond the obvious charm, a savage glint lurked in his eyes. There was steel in him, and it had a deadly serrated edge. Whoever that man was, he would be wise to stay far away. It gave her a momentary pause, but so far, there had been nothing but caring and softness in Chase's eyes when he cast them her way.

It sounded like he fired the guy, but surely that kind of angry outburst was born of deep emotion. A personal issue, not just business. A betrayal by a friend or trusted colleague?

She suspected all that tough-guy swagger camouflaged a carefully constructed wall of defense. She wouldn't blame him. God knew; she'd built her own emotional walls, brick by brick, thick, high, and wide. She'd learned over the years that those walls weren't built only to keep things out, but to keep things in. To shelter the little parts of herself that, by some miracle, remained intact after the pain, the loss, and the loneliness destroyed the rest.

Perhaps he did the same.

She didn't know much about the Kincaid cousins. Were they husbands or fathers? So far, other than the photos on the mantel that didn't appear to be recent, she'd seen no sign of a female presence in the citadel. There was none of the clutter a family brings to a home and none of the comfortable touches a woman would surely have added to the place. No toys or other children's paraphernalia; nothing to show that either had a wife or children. Neither man wore a wedding ring, but many men didn't wear rings, so that wasn't telling. Of course, the place was enormous, so maybe she just hadn't seen the family wing yet.

Or maybe they were as alone in the world as she was.

The lights flickered, and the room spun.

She dropped her cheeseburger and leaned forward with her face in her hands as the world went topsy-turvy.

"Emma?" Chase's voice. A chair leg squeaked and scraped across the hardwood, and someone put an arm around her shoulders.

"You okay?" Ben asked.

"Dizzy. Lights...flickering. Didn't you notice?"

"No," Chase said. "You, Benji?"

"No. Maybe we should call for Ash."

The world settled, and the ringing in her ears faded away. She lifted her head and blinked a few times as her vision cleared. "Oh. It's all right now."

"You sure?" Chase asked, his arm still around her shoulders.

"Yeah, I'm fine." She smiled up at him. "Guess I just need to eat more. Probably low blood sugar."

Chase patted her shoulder, then sat and slid another burger across the table to her. "Probably. Well, eat up, sweetheart. Got plenty."

Chapter Nine

EMMA FELT MUCH BETTER with a full stomach, and her anxiety was eased by the amazing story Chase and Ben had just told her. Fast food wrappers littered the table by the time she tossed back the last bite of her apple pie. "Okay, guys, let's see if I got this straight. Ashriel—an honest-to-God angel—read my mind in the hospital and found out about my curse. He gathered up my soul when I died, and after Russo knocked over the last domino of his devil deal by spitting on my grave, Ashriel stole my dead body and came here, brought me back to life, and then reinstalled my soul."

Chase nodded. "Yeah, in a nutshell."

"And the procedure—I guess it could be called a resurrection—was what erased all my scars?"

"Must be," Chase said. "Pretty cool, huh? I noticed a few surgical scars on your wrist in the hospital, but we didn't know you had such bad ones until you told us."

Cool? He had no idea what it meant to her. But how could he? Her eyes stung with tears. It was a miracle. Not just because she'd been so ugly, but because, without the visible reminders every day of her life, she could finally lock those terrible memories behind the wall. "So, when Russo dies and goes to Hell, my curse will be over?"

Ben and Chase exchanged an uneasy glance. "We're pretty sure," Ben said.

"But you're not certain?" She couldn't keep the disappointment out of her voice.

Chase took her hand and gave it a squeeze. "No, we're not sure. But if it don't end when that bastard takes the express elevator down to the heated basement, we'll look for another way. It's a curse, which means it's just a spell, and every spell can be broken. Just gotta find the right counter-spell. And this place? Chock-a-block full of books and files on spells and magic.

And if we can't find a counter-spell here, I know a couple of witches we can go to for help."

They were buddies with witches? She could imagine what Indy would have to say about that, and it wouldn't be pretty. "What about Michael? He's an archangel. If he's so powerful, can't he remove my curse?"

"Sorry," Ben said. "Spells don't work like that. And even if Michael could, he probably wouldn't. Except for the halo and wings, he's nothing like Ash. One human who has nothing to do with the Illuminati wouldn't mean anything to him. His entire purpose is to wage war against Lucifer and his minions. An important job, to be sure, but he can be a real jerk."

An archangel that was a jerk? A sudden surge of anxiety made her heart pound. "Hey, you got anything stronger than a chocolate milkshake? I could use a drink."

"Got beer or Jack Daniel's," Chase said.

"Perfect. Jack, please. Make it a double, neat." Emma stood and gathered up the trash from their meal.

Chase rose to go make her drink. "Emma, you don't have to do that."

"Hey, you fly and buy? I'm gonna clean up. Not like there's dishes to wash." She paused and looked back at the cousins. "And guys, thank you again for letting me stay here until this is over."

Ben smiled at her. "You're totally welcome. Not that we wouldn't have helped you anyway, but we'd have been goners if not for you. It's the least we can do."

"Damn straight," added Chase. "Anything, anytime. I mean it, sweetheart. You ask, you get. Need a kidney? No problemo. Pick which one you want. Want me to father your children? Just say the word." He punctuated the last statement with a saucy wink.

She laughed. Did these men have any idea how amazing they were? She went to each cousin and kissed his cheek. "Knighthood becomes you both." She scooped up the trash into her arms. "Where am I going with this?"

Ben pointed to the arch. "Kitchen's that way, second door on the left."

Chase watched her leave through the arch. While they ate, he hadn't been able to keep himself from checking her out. On the sly, of course. She'd been through hell, and he didn't want to come off like a horny douchebag. But, damn, the woman was smokin' hot. She smelled awesome, like flowers, and looked even better. Her long, silky hair streamed down her back like a waterfall of Captain Morgan rum, and her beautiful face was all flushed, the kind of pink a fair-skinned woman gets from a long, steamy shower.

Or from hot sex.

He wanted to see that pink on her face in both scenarios, preferably at the same time. He'd been so turned on that he'd barely tasted his food. When she'd innocently licked french fry salt off her fingers, all sorts of erotic images had flooded his mind, and he'd had to shift in his seat to make room for a raging hard-on.

She wore sexy ragged jeans with little holes that teased with glimpses of firm thigh, a faded Bobby Flay T-shirt that hugged every curve, and hot-pink socks. He wanted to scoop her up, carry her to his room, and not come out for a week. At least.

Slow your roll, Kincaid. All good things come to those who wait. He was just so freakin' thrilled that she was there, alive, well, and safe.

And with him.

No need to rush.

For once, time was on his side.

As he walked past Benji's chair on his way to the liquor cabinet, he leaned down and whispered in his cousin's ear, "She awesome, or what?" But as he crossed the room, his legs went shaky.

Shaky, because he'd meant what he said to her.

He picked up the liquor decanter and withdrew the stopper, but then he set the crystal bottle down, none too gently. Whiskey splashed and dripped down his chin. His breath caught as panic rose and slapped him in the face.

Slapped hard.

Adrenaline shot through his system, giving him palpitations and making his shoulder muscles rigid.

Father her children?

Had he really said that? Okay, it was time to take it down a hundred notches.

Yeah, he was drawn to her on a level he'd never experienced before in all his twenty-five years, even with Holly. Yeah, he was hot for her, and hell, there was nothing wrong with some good, healthy lust. But he was jumping off the high dive here, and he hadn't even stuck his toe in the freakin' water yet.

He was acting like a dumbass, a lovesick fool, and he wasn't gonna act the fool for anyone. Not again. He'd had the excuse of youth and inexperience with Holly. Reeling from Dad's death, he'd fallen head over heels with no restraint or thought of repercussions.

Too young, way too young.

That love had led to disaster.

He'd locked up what she'd left of his heart in a lead box, and that's where it was staying. Once he had Emma in his bed, he'd get this...thing, this obsession, whatever the hell it was, out of his system. Be lovers? Absolutely. She was amazing and hot, and he wanted her bad—had wanted her from the first time she touched him.

But a long-term relationship with her was out of the question. Holly proved that. He couldn't say it was Holly's fault because it wasn't, not really. It was his.

He'd thought she understood the danger.

No woman known to be associated with him would ever be safe in the real world. He'd accepted that his love life would be limited to meaningless hook-ups with willing women whose faces he'd never see in the light of day. And one day—way, way, *way* far in the future—when the time came that he absolutely had to get a wife to fulfill his obligations, he'd use his head and not his heart and choose from one of their own, a sealgair's daughter.

A loveless marriage? Maybe. But his noble-born ancestors had arranged marriages, and it had worked for them. At least she'd be someone who knew the score, someone he could be reasonably sure wouldn't get a glimpse behind the curtain and run away from the Emerald City.

Run away from him.

Besides, Emma was out of his league anyway. He should have seen it right away, as soon as she used freakin' words like *infinitesimal* and *impregnable*, as soon as she'd asked him, her eyes sparkling with excitement, if she could read the dusty old books and unroll the yellowed scrolls. In truth, Benji was far more her type and her intellectual equal than he was.

While Benji had loved school and studying and reading books, Chase had done the bare minimum to get the hell out of the classroom. He was a Templar Knight, a future laird, and his destiny was settled before he was even born. What the hell did he need with algebra and chemistry and all that crap?

He'd learned the important stuff from Michael, Dad, Pete, and Wyatt, like paranormal battle techniques, weapons and armaments, defensive and offensive strategy, espionage, and wilderness survival.

And thanks to Pete, he could ride a horse, rope a steer, and wrangle a stray heifer with the best of 'em. Horsemanship wasn't in the modern-day Templar Knights' job description, but he'd often thought he had a genetic affinity for horses carried down from the days when knights clad in chain mail and suits of armor rode destriers into battle.

Emma was beautiful and wicked smart, and once her curse was over, she could leave all this supernatural crap behind and go out into the normal world. She could be anything she wanted, have any life she wanted, have any man she wanted.

A little voice in his head whispered, *That curse is the least of her worries. The girl sees angels. She's Chosen. Just like you, and Ben, and Kenny. She ain't getting out, ever.*

He ignored the little voice. No, after the fucking hell she'd been through, she deserved a normal life! A pretty house in the burbs with a porch swing, a couple of kids playing in the backyard, a minivan, and a golden retriever napping at her feet. And she deserved a man who shouldn't have *Danger, keep back!* tattooed on his forehead. A nice, safe dentist, accountant, or teacher would fit the bill.

It was exactly where she belonged.

But not yet.

For now, she would be his. And after her curse was over, they helped her to get on her feet and helped her to move on—when she was happily tucked away in the safety of that pretty house in suburbia, she'd think of him now and then and smile.

Or maybe she wouldn't think of him at all.

He ignored the shaft of pain that tore through him at that thought. He poured Emma's drink and one for himself and carried them back to the table.

Emma felt Ashriel returning. She sensed even before he appeared that he was back, but she didn't question it or wonder how or why. She jumped up from the table and turned in time to see him appear out of thin air on the other side of the room.

"Hello," Ashriel said.

Ben looked up. "Hey, Ash. Everything okay?"

Ashriel didn't answer; his gaze riveted on Emma as she walked slowly toward him.

She stopped a few feet away and gazed up at him. Was she dreaming, after all? He was as amazing as she remembered. He appeared to be in his early thirties. Tall. Not as tall as Chase—and nowhere near as tall as Ben—but then, at only five-foot-three, just about every man seemed tall to her. He wore a long black leather coat that reminded her of a cowboy duster, a blue T-shirt, jeans, and black leather boots. Around his neck hung a hammered silver torc inset with a large, glowing blue sapphire that matched his eyes perfectly. Light sparkled on the unusual crystal hilt of the short sword that hung in a leather scabbard at his side.

His curly blond hair had the hue and sheen of freshwater pearls. A handsome, angular face with chiseled features. High cheekbones. A straight nose with flaring nostrils. Lush, full lips with a striking cupid's bow. A triangular jaw shadowed by a night's stubble. Even the fine lines around his eyes and across his forehead appealed to her because those slight flaws gave his face warmth, charm, and character and kept him from being too perfect.

But his eyes?

His eyes took her breath away. Deep, clear pools of luminous sapphire blue seemed to look right into her soul. They were simply magical.

He smiled at her, and her world tilted.

"Are you all right, Emma?" he asked.

Tears blurred her vision. Her heart swelled with gratitude and admiration. The emotion that blossomed in her chest was almost painful. "Ashriel, what you've done for me? The first time I saw you, I thought I was dreaming. A part of me still does. If I am, I pray to God I never wake up. You saved me. There's no other way to say it. You gave me a whole new life, literally. And my scars..."

She choked back a sob, the effort brutal. The first tear spilled over and trailed down her cheek. "My scars are gone. All gone. I was so ugly. Hideous. And the memories—so many terrible memories. But now? Now, even if my curse never ends, you've given me everything. A simple thank you doesn't cut it, doesn't even come close. But it's all I've got." Tears streaming down her face, she ran to him. Stretching up on her toes, she kissed his cheek and threw her arms around his neck. "Thank you, Ashriel. Thank you, *thank you*, times a hundred billion."

He stood stock-still for a few seconds, then put his arms around her and awkwardly patted her back. "You're welcome. Um, times a hundred billion."

With a watery laugh, she stepped out of his arms and glanced back at the cousins. "Are all angels this adorable?"

"No!" Their simultaneous answer was immediate and loud.

A rush of air sent her hair flying. She looked back, and Ashriel was gone.

Ben chuckled. "I think you embarrassed him."

Her heart sank. "Oh, no. I didn't mean to make him leave."

"No worries." Chase lifted her drink, beckoning her back to the table. "He'll be back. And for the record, some angels are dark angels in league with Lucifer. You might be able to tell the difference, but we can't count on that." He handed her the drink after she sat down. "You ever see an angel that ain't Ash? You run the other way, and you tell one of us as soon as you can. Better yet, pray for Ash while you run. Got it?"

Eyes wide, she nodded. "I figured angels protected people or just sat around on clouds and played harps."

Chase huffed a jaded laugh. "Yeah, not so much. Most are okay, I guess, doing their own thing. But some of 'em would sooner smite you than look at you, and if we weren't under Michael's protection, it probably wouldn't be pretty. And they're a suspicious bunch for the most part. For a while, Ash was Earthbound, 'cause he lost his feathers, and he was kinda shunned and looked down on by other angels. Wait, strike that. *Lost* ain't the right word. Stolen. That's the right word. A bitch of a witch stole his feathers, and I'm not trying to be funny."

"But I don't understand. Ashriel has beautiful wings."

"That weirdness just happened. Coincidentally, the same day you saved our butts."

Her heart skittered as another wave of dizziness passed over her. Indy's voice whispered in her head. *There's no such thing as a coincidence. Not that I've ever seen, anyway.*

"Look, Emma, I got a few questions I wanna ask, but you don't have to answer if you don't want to. And we can stop any time you want. Okay?"

She nodded, although her stomach rolled and her fingers went numb. She didn't want to unlock and relive the terrible memories, but after all they'd done to help her, they deserved her honesty.

"First, how in the hell did you just happen to have consecrated blood for your arrows with you when you ran into us? That stuff don't keep."

That was an easy question. She grinned and shrugged. "Catholic hospital blood bank." Her chin rose a fraction. "I didn't steal it. I left payment. And it keeps because I use preservatives. Not only for junk food anymore. You can order them online; prep the arrows way ahead of time."

Ben slapped his forehead. "Brilliant! Why didn't we ever think of that?"

"I'll show you how to do it. Next question?"

"When you first woke up, you said that you dreamed about me all your life, except for…and then Ash walked in, and you never finished. What were you gonna say?"

"Oh, yeah. Four years ago, there were three months, starting in April, that the dreams about you stopped. Just suddenly stopped. I don't know why. I was thinking it was over, but then I dreamed about you again the night of July twenty-eighth. It was a Tuesday."

Ben and Chase's eyes locked.

Emma stiffened, and the hair rose on the back of her neck. What the heck was that about? "Okay, Stevie Wonder could see the freak-out on your faces. What's going on?"

Chase shrugged at Ben. "No point in keeping it a secret." He turned to her. "Four years ago, I died and did a three-month stint in Hell before Ash rescued my ass. On July twenty-eighth, and yeah, I think it was a Tuesday."

Her head reeling, Emma stared at him. What the heck was going on? None of it made any sense! He had died? And why in the world would he go to Hell? And how could she have known? *In her dreams?* She reached for her drink and threw back a big gulp of whiskey. She immediately regretted it. The burn in her throat and sinuses nearly sent her to her knees. She coughed and struggled for breath.

Chase patted her a few times between the shoulder blades. "You okay? Went down the wrong pipe?"

She shook her head, her eyes watering. "First one," she wheezed.

The cousins exchanged puzzled looks. "First drink of whiskey?" Ben asked.

She shook her head, coughing again.

"Wait. First drink ever?" Chase asked. At her nod, he shook his head in amazement. "And you pick Jack Daniel's, *straight?*"

"Didn't know," she rasped. "Indy drank it like water."

"Who's Indy?" Ben asked.

Chase gave his cousin an exasperated look. "Jeez, let her catch her breath, will ya? I'll get her some water." He ran toward the kitchen and quickly came back with a bottle of water he put into her eager hands. He also placed a small box on the table. "I figure you probably want this back."

Ben got up. "Gonna get a beer. Want one, Chase?"

"Sky still blue?"

Emma chugged half the bottle of water before she opened the little box. Mama's locket! With a cry of joy, she pressed it to her heart. She leaped up and gave Chase a quick hug. "Thank you so much! This is all I have of my mother. I was afraid it was gone forever; I thought I lost it in the alley when it wasn't with the rest of my things."

"Wish I could say I found it for you, but truth be told, a nurse said you were wearing it when you got to the hospital. She thought if there was a picture inside, it could help us find out who you were. I couldn't figure out how to open it, but then Ash found out who you were, and I didn't want to force it open and break it. It's really pretty. That's a Celtic knot design, right?"

"Yes. My mother's people are of Scottish heritage. But it doesn't open. I don't know if its broken or glued shut. I've never seen the picture, and I never want to. But the locket was hers, and my grandmother's before that. That's all that matters to me."

Chase swallowed convulsively, and it shocked her to see his eyes brim with tears.

"I get it," he said in a husky voice. "Lost my mom, too. Lost everyone, except Benji."

Her heart went out to him, and she covered his hand with hers. She wasn't the only one who had suffered. "My father—the man I thought was my father—burned all the pictures of my mother, erased all the digital photos, and gave all her things away when I was still a baby. I only have this locket because Mama stipulated it in her will. She left it with her lawyer before…well, the lawyer kept it for me until my seventeenth birthday."

"What a shit thing for a dad to do. Even if he wasn't your biological father, he still raised you. How could he do that?"

She shrugged. "I've asked myself that question a thousand times."

Chase took the beer Ben handed him and took a long draw before he asked, "But why don't you want to see the picture in your locket? Maybe it's you."

"I know it's not me." She didn't want to talk about that picture. She clasped the locket around her neck. "Next question?"

"Like I said, you don't have to talk about it if you don't want to, okay?"

Chase waited for her nod before continuing. "Why does that old man Russo hate you so much that he was willing to sell his soul just to curse you? What could you possibly have done, and why the crypt-keeper torture? Why didn't he just have you killed?"

"Long story. It was a few months after my fifteenth birthday. I'd just won a karate tournament…"

After she finished her story, Chase jumped up and strode to the fireplace.

He stood with his back to them, his hands fisted, staring at the flames. His harsh, rapid breathing was audible from all the way across the room. He stayed there for a moment before he whirled and came back, his handsome face twisted with rage and the promise of murder in his eyes. "You were barely fifteen years old, and that old bastard blames you for accidentally killing his son in *self-defense?* He trashed your life for doing nothing but defending yourself? If he wasn't already going to Hell, I'd send him there myself!"

Ben frowned at his cousin. "Chase, get a grip. Seriously, you're gonna give yourself a stroke. He'll get what's coming to him and more. Hades will make sure of that." Ben turned back to her. "What happened then? Vincent murdered your father. I assume there was a trial?"

"Yes, of course. I testified, and Vincent was convicted." She watched as Chase strode to the liquor cabinet. His face beet red, he poured himself another drink and returned to his chair. She could practically feel the anger coming off him in waves. Although she didn't enjoy seeing him so upset, it touched her deeply that he was so enraged on her behalf. "I was accepted into Witness Protection, and eventually, I started my new life. Or so I thought."

Chapter Ten

Seven Years Ago - Napa Valley, California

EMMA BIT HER LIP as she watched Nick plate his entrée. His Alaskan salmon was as aesthetically pleasing as her own creation. But something was different about his dish. What was the green herb in the aioli swirled artfully across the plate? She wiped damp palms down the front of her chef whites. Nick would not best her again! Hmmm…basil? Tarragon? Maybe mint? No, mint was unlikely to be paired with salmon—

She grunted as Rachel elbowed her in the ribs. "Em, you're up."

Chef Webb stood at their station, staring expectantly at her, a pronounced note of annoyance on his face. "*Miss Prescott?*" he asked, apparently not for the first time. "Are you going to present your dish, or shall I move on?"

Her face heated to what she imagined was cherry red as the cheerful cacophony of clanking pots, clattering plates, and the dozens of soft voices that filled the enormous teaching kitchen returned to her conscious mind. *When* would she get used to the name Prescott?

It had been almost two years since she entered the Witness Security Program and chose a new last name, over a year since she began her training at the Culinary Institute of America's Greystone Campus. "My apologies, Chef. I've prepared King Salmon fillet poached in local white wine with a lemon-mustard hollandaise containing shallots, goat butter, lemon zest, thyme, ground white pepper, and garlic, served on a bed of sautéed broccoli rabe with cranberry and walnut chutney."

The annoyance faded from Chef's face as he tasted her food. "Very nicely done, Miss Prescott. I enjoyed the savory, creamy fish combined with the sweet and tangy elements of the chutney. All is forgiven."

As Chef moved on to Rachel's dish, Emma sighed inwardly. *Thank goodness.* She glanced up and found Nick smiling at her and silently clapping his hands. Before she could respond, he winked and turned to his stationmate, who was speaking to him.

Her face heated again. Her nemesis was handsome, smart, and talented. Dark blond hair and blue eyes, a charming smile, and the easy confidence born of belonging to a family of wealthy restaurateurs. Nothing in his life was uncertain.

He'd asked her out several times over the semester. To which she'd always answered, no. Why couldn't he have bad acne, stinky breath, or something? Did he have to be so damn perfect? Well, not perfect. He didn't have raven-black hair or silver eyes.

Ugh! Enough with the dream man, Emma! Vincent Russo was behind bars, and she'd been given a new identity and a new life. It was time for her to let go of the past and get on with her life. A life based in reality, not fantasy. If Nick asked her out again, she would say yes.

When class was over, she and Rachel gathered their belongings and exited the teaching kitchens. As they walked among a throng of students moving down the main hall toward the atrium stairs, Rachel grinned. "Friday, girl. You know what that means."

"Truffles!" they said in unison.

"Let's get there before the raspberry ones are gone," Emma said.

They hurried down the stairs, but Emma paused as they reached the grand piano in an alcove on the second floor that overlooked the three-story glass atrium stairway. She ran her hand over the polished wood, a wistful longing tugging at her heart. In her memory, she could see the notes, hear the music, and feel her fingers dancing across the keys.

But her fingers no longer had the dexterity or span of reach required to play anything of complexity. Three surgeries and years of physical therapy couldn't restore what Antonio Russo had stolen from her. The damage to her nerves was too severe. As it was, she spent an extra hour every morning before class practicing her knife skills to make up for the physical limitation.

Rachel put her arm around Emma's shoulders and gave her a gentle squeeze. "Come on, Em. Chocolate is the path to inner peace."

They made their way down the stairs to the ground floor and headed down the distinctive two-foot-thick granite block hallways of Graystone's main building, originally a winery. They turned a corner and came to the Ghirardelli Chocolate Discovery Center, where students learned to work with chocolate and create amazing confections and desserts. Even before they walked through the double-glass doors into the chill air of the chocolate preparation area to join the already-burgeoning line of students waiting for a treat, a sweet, heady aroma wafted through the air.

Once inside, Emma inhaled deeply, allowing the incredible smell to overwhelm her as her eyes feasted on the array of tantalizing morsels laid out on chilled marble tables. As they waited in line for their turn, her mouth watered in anticipation. It thrilled her to see a three-tiered display of ornately decorated truffles, including her favorite raspberry truffles. She selected several when her turn came.

Rachel, a plate of treats in hand, glanced at her watch. Her brown eyes warmed, and her pretty face broke into a big smile. "Clayton said to meet him at the Illy after class."

"What time are you guys heading out?"

"After I pack, we're gonna catch a bite to eat and then hit the road. Six and a half hours to LA. Should get to my parents' house by ten. I hope. Depends on traffic. Dress fitting in the morning at eleven, so I need my beauty sleep."

As they stepped around the corner, Emma paused just outside the doors of the Illy Café and reached for Rachel's hand. She held it up to the light for a few seconds, admiring the contrast of the sparkling diamond engagement ring against Rachel's brown skin. "You're a lucky woman, Rach. Clayton is a total catch."

Patting the neat cornrows of black hair at the back of her head, Rachel nodded. "Don't I know it, girl!" Her eyes widened as she grabbed Emma's arm. "Forgot to tell you, I found the perfect bridesmaid's dress! You'll look drop-dead gorgeous. I'll show you when we go back to the dorm."

They walked into the Illy Café just as a handsome black man stepped out of a pair of double stainless-steel swing doors that led from the bakery to the café. He carried a small but elaborate two-tiered cake with shimmering, blush-pink fondant icing, white and pink roses, and strings of edible white pearls. When he spotted Emma and Rachel, he broke into a smile. "Happy Birthday, little lady." He leaned over the bakery display case and presented the cake with a dramatic flourish. "Ta dah!"

Emma gasped. "Clayton, you didn't have to do this! It's so beautiful!"

He gave her a wink. "Nothing on God's green earth is too good for the best friend of my queen." He carried the cake around the bakery's glass display cases and led the way to a café table sporting a *reserved* sign, where plates and cutlery were already waiting, along with a large envelope that obviously held a birthday card. "Besides, you only turn eighteen once, don't you know?"

"That's true," said Rachel. "It's twenty-nine you get to do over. And over, and over, and over. According to my mama, at least."

Emma laughed as Clayton gave Rachel a quick kiss. "Sexy woman, even when you're eighty and old and gray, you'll still be twenty-nine in my eyes."

Rachel propped her hands on her hips and cocked a brow in feigned annoyance. "Well, baker-man, that's sweet, but I'm only twenty-one now, so let's not rush it, okay?"

"Sorry, I'm late," Nick said as he came up to their table. "Hope you saved some for me."

Clayton pointed to the fourth chair. "Didn't miss a thing."

Before he sat, Nick reached for Emma's hand, raised it to his lips, and placed a gentle kiss on her knuckles. "Happy birthday, Chef Prescott."

Her face heated at the sensation of his soft lips on her skin. She gazed up at him and smiled. "Thank you, Nick."

She spent a lovely hour with her friends, enjoyed the delicious cake, shed a happy tear at the sweet sentiment of the birthday card, and gave thanks in her heart for the new life with which she'd been blessed. A world-class culinary education, good friends, and good health. So, she couldn't play piano anymore, but she could still practice karate as long as she wore protective wrist braces.

And Nick asked her out again, for dinner and a movie the following night, and this time she said yes.

The future was bright, indeed.

If only she could forget a pair of silver eyes that were etched into her heart.

Later that evening, someone knocked on the door to the dorm room she and Rachel shared. She muted the TV. Had Rachel forgotten something? But she and Clayton had left Graystone over an hour ago, so probably not. She opened the door to find Elizabeth from down the hall, holding a bouquet of flowers and a large pink envelope. Melting—assuming the gifts were from Nick—it surprised her when Elizabeth waggled her eyebrows and said, "A uniformed chauffeur left these for you. Nice."

Nick came from a wealthy family, but having a chauffeur deliver his gifts? That was...weird. And a bit off-putting. He didn't seem like the kind of guy who would try to impress a girl by flaunting his status. Had she been wrong about him?

She put the bouquet on her desk, sat on her bed, and opened the card. Her brows rose as she discovered that it wasn't a birthday card at all. It was a folded sheet of thin cardboard that held a handwritten letter. She glanced at the bold but elegant signature.

And her blood ran cold.

It was from Octavio Russo.

Vincent and Antonio's father.

Her scalp crawled, and the room spun for a few seconds as the horror sank in. *How?* How had he found her after all the Marshals' Service had done to protect and hide her? They'd moved her six times, finally winding up on the other side of the country. She had a new identity, a new name, a new birth certificate, and a new social security number. It was impossible!

The letter was still clutched in her shaking hand, and she ran to make sure the door was locked, as well as the sliding glass doors that led to the courtyard. She closed the blinds, trying to catch her heaving breath. She grabbed her phone from the desk to call the emergency number given to her by the US Marshals' Service, but when she dropped the letter onto the desk so she could use her cellphone, the first sentence, written in bold and all caps, sank into her shocked brain.

> *Miss Borello, DO NOT SEEK HELP, or your roommate and her fiancé will never make it to Los Angeles. Such a lovely couple. That would be a shame, wouldn't it? Come out to the limo parked near the vineyard. Tell no one. Carry nothing. No harm will come to you; I only wish to speak to you. I assure you that you will return to your dorm room as healthy as you are at this moment. Please do not keep me waiting.*

> *Octavio Russo*

Precious minutes ticked by as her panicked mind tried to process what was happening. *God, oh, God, what should she do?* Her gaze landed on a framed photo of Rachel and Clayton that sat on Rachel's desk. Their engagement portrait. Emma's heart sank, and a wave of nausea made her swallow convulsively. She had no choice but to do exactly what Russo wanted.

On shaky legs, she left her dorm room and walked out to the parking lot that overlooked acres of green vineyards. The warmth of the late-afternoon sunshine and cheerful birdsong faded from her conscious mind. Her brain seemed to shut down and switch to autopilot.

In a state of numbness, she slowly approached the black stretch limousine. A uniformed chauffeur stood waiting and, with a slight bow, politely opened the door. A hysterical bubble of laughter caught in her throat. What a strange and genteel way to welcome her to death!

She knew she would die.

Her memory, as always, was crystal clear. After the judge sentenced his remaining son and the guards escorted Vincent from the courtroom in chains and handcuffs to be incarcerated in a New York maximum-security prison, Octavio Russo had shouted his vow to make her pay, even if it took every penny he had.

He had many pennies. He was a billionaire, in fact. Apparently, he had made good on his vow and had directed enough of that wealth in the right direction to buy the information he wanted.

To find her. To make her pay.

She ducked her head, stepped into the darkness of the luxurious car, and sank onto a cushioned leather seat. And trembled.

On the adjacent bench seat, an enormous man in a dark suit—obviously a bodyguard—held a pistol aimed at her chest. Seated across from her, Octavio smiled, poured a glass of champagne, and held it out to her. "Would you care for a drink, my dear? It is your birthday, is it not?"

Laughter threatened again as she noticed a brightly wrapped gift on the seat beside him. "I'm only eighteen," she blurted, confused by his calm demeanor. She'd expected anger and violence, not decorum, gifts, and polite conversation. Maybe the gift was a bomb. She reached for the glass. What difference did it make when she was about to die? But as she raised the crystal flute to her lips, she hesitated. *Poisoned?*

Russo chuckled, the fatty jowls of his face jiggling, seeming to read her mind. "The drink is not poisoned or otherwise medicated, I assure you." He refilled his own glass from the same bottle and drank.

Still, she didn't drink. If she had any chance of getting out of this—doubtful—she needed to stay alert. Besides, her stomach was already churning, and she refused to spend the last few moments of her life vomiting alcohol. "How did you find me? I assume you bribed someone for the info. I'd like to know who it was before you kill me."

He shook his head. "I'm not going to harm you." He tilted his head toward the guard. "And neither will he unless you attack me. To answer your question, no one significant enough to hold that information accepted my bribes, which was a disappointment and a revelation. I've always believed money was the answer to all questions, the solution to all problems, and the power in this world. I was shocked to discover that it isn't.

"Oh, it helps; don't get me wrong. My blood-sucking attorneys will get Vincent out of jail. Eventually. But do you know what the *real* power in this world is, Miss Borello? The power that can get one anything they desire, as long as one is prepared to pay the price?" He peered expectantly at her.

"The power of love?" she quipped, startling herself.

He chuckled again, but his expression grew serious.

Deadly serious.

"The real power in this world is magic. More precisely, black magic. Witchcraft, sorcery, Satanism. There are many names for the same thing—harnessing the power of darkness to do one's bidding. Which is exactly what I have done."

Her jaw gaped. She didn't know what she'd expected, but certainly not this. A chill that had nothing to do with the temperature gave her goosebumps. He actually believed what he was saying. "You've lost your mind," she whispered.

"Perhaps I have." He shrugged and drank the rest of his champagne in one gulp. "We shall see. But, down to the matter at hand. You have taken both my sons from me, and that shall not go unavenged. I considered simply having you killed or tortured first and then killed, but even that would be too quick. I want you to suffer, Miss Borello. As I have suffered every day since you murdered Antonio, and as I shall suffer every day that they keep Vincent behind bars like an animal."

"But I didn't murder Anto—"

"Shut up!" he shouted, spittle flying from his mouth, finally showing his true self.

He leaned toward her, his hate and what she feared was madness burning in his brown eyes, so close that she could smell the alcohol on his hot breath. Her heart stuttered, and she pressed back as far as the cushioned seat would allow as his voice dropped to a whisper.

"No amount of money could buy what I wanted, and so I searched and searched and searched for a way, until I thought I would go mad with desperation." He seemed to gather his dignity and moved back into his seat. "I purchased an old book, a book of witchcraft, of occult spells. And in that book, I found my salvation. I found a spell that would summon a demon from Hell who would grant me anything I wanted. Anything at all. For a price."

"A price? You said money wouldn't help."

"I didn't pay with money. I paid with my soul. The bargain I struck with the demon exchanged my soul for a five-year minimum of guaranteed suffering for you."

Although she didn't believe the nonsense he was spouting about demons and spells, she asked, "What kind of suffering?"

"Beginning at the stroke of midnight tonight, you will be cursed, my dear. All things foul, unnatural, and otherworldly will be drawn to you like moths to a flame. Oh, there are all manner of creatures we humans, for the most part, believe are myths or superstitions, but in fact, they exist. Werewolves, vampires, wendigos—oh, the list is long and quite interesting. You will be hunted day and night, and no matter where you run, *something* will be coming for you. But not demons, so you need not concern yourself with them."

He winked and smiled, obviously quite pleased with himself. "Demons are too powerful and not surprisingly unethical and would likely kill you no matter what, so I negotiated them out of the equation. And the best part? For five long years, no matter what horrible things they do to you, no matter if you're torn limb from limb or drained of every drop of blood—even if you try to die by suicide—you will not die. You'll heal slowly and painfully every time."

How could he believe this stuff? Although his delusion could work in her favor. It appeared as if he would really let her go. Maybe she could get out of this yet.

He refilled his glass, emptying the bottle, and continued. "So, to recap, you will suffer for five full years; there is no doubt about that. Then, it's up to you. The standard contractual agreement for a so-called soul deal is limited to thirteen years, but I negotiated more interesting terms in that you are the one who determines the length of the contract.

"If you manage to stay alive for twenty years? I highly doubt it, but if you do, I will also live twenty years." He reached for the gift on the seat and handed it to her. "Happy Birthday, Miss Borello. You'll need these." The smile that lit his face didn't reach his cold, hard eyes. When she didn't take the box, he thrust it at her, the mask of cordiality slipping again. "Open it!" He took a calming breath and smiled. "Please, it's rude not to accept a gift."

Fingers trembling, still afraid it might explode, Emma tentatively unwrapped the gift. It was a shoebox. Inside was a pair of designer-brand running shoes in her size.

"Run, Miss Borello," he said with delight. "Run fast and run far." He laughed and knocked on the window to signal the chauffeur to open the door. As Emma got out, he said, "Remember, my people will track your friends from here on out, so no calls for help. Their lives are in your hands."

She did the only thing she could do.

She ran.

Chapter Eleven

Chase unclenched his aching fists and fought the urge to pound on something. Benji was right. If he didn't get control of himself, he was gonna give himself a damn stroke. Looking at Emma's sad, tired face, he wanted to gather her into his arms and make it all better. Like he could?

Now he got why Ash had been so pissed after he read her mind at the hospital, so bent and determined to help this innocent young woman who had been so unjustly punished. "So, I assume Vincent Russo is in jail for the rest of his miserable freakin' life?"

She stared down at her hands once again and shook her head. "He should be." Her voice trembled. "But his high-priced Park Avenue attorneys appealed the case and whittled it down to aggravated manslaughter. Something about a technical error in some report. He's eligible for parole after ten years' total time served, and that includes the time he was in prison all during the trial."

Benji's head jerked up. "Wait, ten years? That's done, right? Is he eligible for parole now?"

She nodded. "They post official information online. Last time I checked, he was on the list for parole consideration. In New York, a convict can apply for parole every two years after they've served the minimum. And with billions of dollars to grease the exit door?"

"That bastard could actually get out?" Chase asked.

She shivered. "Yes."

Chase caught Benji's eye and saw his own thoughts reflected there. He gave a slight nod, which was returned, a silent agreement made. No way was Vincent Russo ever gonna leave that prison still breathing.

She held her hands up in a gesture of bafflement. "I just don't understand why he hired a hitman to finish me off. Maybe he got bored with the game and just wanted to see me dead already after seven years? Although that would end his own life too and send his soul to Hell. Why would he do that? I just don't get it."

"Ash told us why." Chase took her small hand in his. "The old bastard is dying of cancer. Gotta love karma. Guess he forgot to add protection against disease to his deal, but he put in a little bonus for himself if you died before him. Your death bought him sixty extra days to kiss his own ass goodbye."

Emma pressed a hand against her chest. "My life for two lousy months?" She gave a bitter laugh. "Don't know why I'm surprised. After everything he's done to me? Anyway, after he clued me in, he just drove away in his chauffeur-driven limo. Never touched me. I thought he was totally off the wall. I mean, who wouldn't? Monsters were real? And they were gonna hunt me? *Sure*. Russo was the only monster I could see, but I had to protect Rachel and Clayton, so I did what he said. I ran as far and as fast as I could. But I should've believed him. I wish I had believed him."

She took a few more sips, her hands trembling so badly that the scotch nearly splashed over the edge of her glass. "Wasn't long before I was locked in a cage in a vampire den. I put up a good fight, and they wanted my skills on their side, so they tried to turn me into one of them, but it didn't work. The curse stopped it. Wouldn't be suffering if I was a vamp, right? Then they tried to kill me, but of course, at that point, I couldn't die.

"So, they kept me. Fed me stolen scraps and restaurant leftovers from dumpsters. Like an unloved pet. No, more like a backup food supply. The alpha fed on me when hunting was bad." She stopped talking and stared down at the table.

Chase waited for her to go on, but she didn't.

Benji looked at him and shrugged. Mouthed, *Ask her*.

Chase wanted to know, too, and there were more questions that needed asking, but she looked really upset. They needed to know everything so they could form an effective plan to help her, but he didn't want to be the one to upset her even more. He glared back at his cousin and mouthed, *Bite me. You ask her*.

Benji threw him an irritated look, but he did it. "How long were you there? How did you get away?"

Emma looked up, took a deep breath, and blew it out slowly. "Over a year. An amazing man rescued me. He busted in like Indiana Jones, throwing flash-bangs left and right, and all hell broke loose. I had no idea what was going on, but I was sick and weak, so I pressed myself as far back into my cage as I could. By the time I could see again, all the vampires were dead, and then Indy found me." She met Chase's gaze. "He's a sealgair."

A sealgair? Well, this was new and interesting information, but not surprising. Not like just any guy off the street, even a seasoned cop, coulda handled that scuffle and lived to tell about it. He exchanged a quick glance with Benji, but neither commented on this revelation.

She continued. "He said his name was George, but I don't think it was. Didn't matter, anyway." A soft smile curved her mouth. "I called him Indy. He took me to a cabin out in the middle of the woods, and he and three friends took care of me. I barely remember the first week. I was in really bad shape. Pneumonia. If not for the curse, I'm sure I would have died. So weak I couldn't even walk.

"Indy brought a doctor, and as soon as I was strong enough, he taught me how to survive, how to protect myself, hide my scent. He knew how to fight the things that hunted me, and he taught me well. He kicked my butt until I got it right, until I learned everything he could teach me. I'd have been dead long ago if not for him. I owe him. I promised that someday I'd repay him for all he did for me. And I will."

The hair stood at attention on the back of Chase's neck. At the mention of the name George, Benji's eyes had widened too. Chase didn't know of any sealgair named George, and it looked like Benji didn't either. But maybe there was, and he'd just forgotten. He'd check on that later. "If you were so sick, why didn't he take you to a hospital instead of a cabin?"

She seemed surprised by that question. "He knew I'd endanger people around me. He knew...about my curse." Her forehead furrowed, and she gave a little shake of her head. "I never questioned that. How did he know?" But she waved a dismissive hand. "I must have told him and just don't remember. Like I said, I barely remember the first week."

Benji set his empty beer bottle down. "Why do you think Indy lied about his name?"

"I don't know, just a feeling. And he had this silver medallion he wore. Looked like a badge, with a lamb holding a waving flag. The initials engraved on it were H.R. There was no G. Hey, I don't blame him for lying. If I didn't know his real name, I couldn't spill it, right? Indy's very smart."

Chase's heart pounded, his thoughts racing. What were the odds that another man had a silver Agnus Dei medallion with the initials H.R. on it?

Damn low, pretty much zilch.

But Dad did, and the H.R. stood for Harold Kincaid, their grandfather. But George Kincaid was no sealgair; he was a Templar Knight. Chase jumped up and practically ran from the Great Hall. "Be right back," he called over his shoulder. He retrieved the medallion from his dresser drawer and raced back to the table. He handed it to her. "This it?"

Her face lit up. "Yes. Where did you—"

"How long were you and Indy together?" Benji asked.

She cradled the medallion to her chest like a treasure. "Sixty-four days."

What? Chase stiffened as a red flag popped up and whacked him in the face. That wasn't long enough to learn jackshit. She'd said Indy taught her everything he knew. But it had taken him and Benji nearly that long just to pass Werewolves 101. And she was sick to begin with? He could tell his cousin was thinking the same thing because he looked across the table in time to see Benji get that bullshit-detector smirk and lean over the table toward her.

"Just two months?" Benji asked. "How could you possibly learn all that in such a short time?"

"Get a book. Any book. Something I wouldn't have read."

Benji shot her a questioning look, but he crossed the Great Hall and grabbed a thick old book from a shelf. He returned to the table and held it out to her, but she held up a hand to stop him. "Pick a page," she said.

Benji opened the book in the middle and handed it to her. She barely glanced at the page, gave it back to him, closed her eyes, and recited. "Who knows now that ancient tongue of the Viridian moon? And who speaks still with that goddess of silver-green light? Who sings the paean to invoke her blessed favor? The long-forgotten magic of the land of druids—"

"You have an eidetic memory?" Benji asked, his eyes wide.

She nodded.

Chase frowned. An eye *what* memory? "Plain old English, please?"

"She has a photographic memory."

Emma rolled her eyes. "Yeah, and then some."

Well, that explained it. Chase leaned back in his chair. "Wait. You mean you can just look at something real quick, and your brain does what? Takes a picture? Like a human camera? Cool."

"At times, it's a blessing, but mostly, it's just another curse."

A curse? Hell, he'd love to have a superpower like that. *Memory Man—the newest Avenger.* "How can a gift like that be a curse?"

She leaned forward and looked him in the eye. "Chase, think about every terrible thing that's ever happened to you. Every mistake. Every loss. Every nightmare. Every horrible thing you shove to the back of your mind, where it fades with time, and you can pretty much forget about it. And when you remember, it's not so bad because it happened a long time ago, and the images and feelings have dimmed with time. You've gotten over it.

"Now imagine that when you remember those things, it's like they just happened. Every tiny detail. Sounds, smells. Visuals. Physical pain, emotional pain, all crystal clear in your mind. I don't forget, Chase. Not anything. Ever. I've learned to block the memories, but they never fade. If they're triggered, they come back full force."

Well, shit. Not knowing what to say, he reached over and patted her arm. He couldn't imagine what kind of loony bin he'd be locked away in if he couldn't shove back his memories of Hell and a thousand other nightmares. And God knew; she'd been through her own version of Hell, too. It really did sound like another fucking curse.

She gasped, and her face lit up with a brilliant smile. "Wait! If you have Indy's medallion, you must know him. Is he close? Can he come here? Can I see him?"

Benji ducked his head and grimaced. He looked at Chase and gave a half-shrug.

Chase's gut twisted. *Dammit.* He didn't want to tell her, but he had no choice. "Sweetheart, your Indy didn't lie. His name was George. George Kincaid. He was my dad and Ben's uncle, but he wasn't a sealgair. He was a Templar Knight, the laird of this citadel."

Her smile vanished as his words sank in. "Wait...was?"

"I'm so sorry to have to tell you this, but he died almost five years ago."

"How?" When neither answered, she asked again, but she screamed it this time. "*How did he die, goddammit?*"

His bad ear ringing from the shrill assault, Chase leaned back, shocked by her extreme reaction. He'd expected tears, but not the snarling wildcat sitting across from him. "A demon working with the Illuminati killed him."

Her eyes narrowed and blazed with anger. "The demon Eligos?"

"No," Benji said. "Just some random demon during battle. Wait, you know about Eligos?"

She didn't answer. Instead, she schooled her features. A lesson he'd learned from Dad, too. Without another word, her pale face now a careful blank, although unshed tears shimmered golden in her eyes, she carefully handed the medallion back to him and left the table.

Left the Great Hall.

Left him with his jaw hanging and his head spinning.

What the actual fuck? He couldn't take it all in. The possibilities, the consequences. "My dad and Emma?" A shocking and unwanted thought blasted into his brain. "You don't think..."

"It's possible. Two consenting adults. Creepy, given the age difference, but possible. And they were so close that he told her about the demon that killed your mom and the twins? He didn't talk about that. *Ever.*"

Chase's stomach spasmed, and for a moment, he was afraid he was going to puke. Nope, nope, *nope!* He had to block it. He couldn't allow *that* picture to form in his mind.

"That's not all," Benji said. "Brace yourself."

He groaned and pressed his fists against his temples. "What now?"

"The fire coin worked for her, and she didn't even say the right incantation."

He'd expected the other shoe to drop—it always did—but not that fast. "*What?* She commanded Templar magic?"

"Yes. Proof she carries Templar blood. Can't say I'm surprised." He cupped a hand to his ear. "Hear that clicking sound?"

Chase listened but heard only the ringing in his left ear. "Don't hear nothin'."

"Dominoes toppling. She's Chosen, I know it. Too much here to be anything else."

"Okay, slow your roll, Benji. Gonna break your neck, jumping to conclusions. Yeah, this is some weird ass shit, but I'm sure there's lots of people out there who carry Templar blood and don't know it. Modern knights ain't monks. The source could go generations back."

Benji considered for a moment. "Yeah, maybe you're right. Or not. Still, it could be one of her parents. Could be her biological father."

"Oh, shit, that's right. Borello ain't her real dad." His gaze went to where she'd disappeared into the hallway. If he was freaking out, he couldn't imagine how she felt. "Think we should go see if she's okay?"

"She didn't seem to want company. Should probably give her a while first."

After what seemed to him to be a while later, Chase checked the time on his phone. He still sat with Benji at the table, nursing a beer and discussing what their next move should be, but he couldn't concentrate because he was worried about her. "Okay, that's it. It's been over an hour. I'm gonna go check on her."

Before he could get up, Emma stormed through the arch and into the Great Hall, wearing her boots and jacket and carrying her backpack. She headed for the main stairs.

"I take it the exit is this way?" she asked curtly.

"Uh-oh." Chase got up to go after her, but Benji, seated on the side of the table nearest to the arch, jumped up and, with his long strides, got to her before Chase even made it around the long table.

"Emma, wait," Benji said. "You shouldn't leave." He caught up to her as she got to the stairs and reached for her arm. "And you can't get out—" In the blink of an eye, he was flat on his back on the floor with her straddling him, her knee jammed against his liver, and a knife at his throat.

Chase froze, gaping. *Holy crap!* Had he really just seen that?

"I can. And I will," she said, the soft but forceful words growled more than spoken.

Chase didn't grab the gun out of his thigh holster and blow her head off, as he would have done with just about anyone else who threatened his cousin's life. He was pretty sure she wouldn't purposely hurt Benji. She'd intended on leaving the safety of the citadel. She was distraught, and clearly, she wasn't thinking straight.

But what to do?

It was almost funny, seeing that pocket-sized woman holding his six-foot-six, two hundred-and-eighty-pound cousin at bay.

He knew size wasn't always a factor—obviously—especially with Emma's martial arts expertise. But this was one for the books. Benji had told him how she'd gone all Bruce Lee on the vampires while he'd been unconscious and getting his blood sucked, and since he didn't want his nose broken again, he'd try diplomacy before he tangled with this little warrior. First time for everything, he guessed. He made sure his voice was calm and soothing. "Hey, what's going on? Problem here, guys?"

Benji cleared his throat. "Uh, yeah, Chase. Didn't you hear her? She wants to leave."

Of course, he'd heard her, but he wanted to know her reasoning. "Leave? Why, sweetheart?"

Emma turned her fierce gaze to him, her face a mask of fury. Her tight voice trembled. "Because if it takes me the rest of my miserable, God-forsaken life...if it's the last thing I ever do...if I have to sell *my* soul to the Devil, I'm gonna hunt down the demon that killed my Indy, and it will suffer greatly."

"Can't." Benji squirmed, his voice strained. No wonder since she had her knee jammed into his gut. "Told you, just some random demon during battle. Don't even know its name."

"I don't care! How could you do that? How could you let his death go unavenged? I know you can't kill it, but...*something*. You should have done something to make it pay!"

Chase sized her up. She was on the edge, her face flushed, and her pupils dilated. She had fire in her eyes—the worst kind of fire—the kind that exploded and made sane people do insane things.

He had to talk her down.

And fast.

He didn't want to hurt her, but there was a trickle of blood going down Benji's neck where the knife pressed against his skin, and if her sharp little knee went any deeper into his gut, his insides were gonna see daylight. "You're wrong, sweetheart." He took two slow steps toward her. "We can kill it."

She glared at him, suspicion written all over her face. "I heard you couldn't kill a demon."

"Indy didn't mention the Aegis of Solomon when he taught you about demons?"

"Demons aren't part of my curse. What's that?"

"It's a dagger, kind of, that belonged to King Solomon. Made from a dragon's tooth and meteorite iron. There's a spell—we assume it's a spell but might be a prayer—engraved on the tooth, supposedly put there by Moses's own hand. Takes out demons and most kinds of monster."

Her eyes narrowed. "A dragon's tooth? You mean a dinosaur's, right?"

He shrugged. "Don't know, don't care. It works. I used it to kill Eligos." He swallowed hard as guilt squeezed his heart. "You're right, sweetheart. We shoulda tried harder to find that demon. I swear, as soon as things settle down with you, we'll get right to work to find that murdering bastard, and when we find it, if you want, I'll let you be the one to take it out."

She stared at him with frantic, suspicious eyes. "Swear it, Chase. Swear it to God!"

Nodding, he walked slowly toward her, holding his hands in plain sight. "And there's something else you should know. Indy died to save Benji's life, threw himself in front of a bullet meant for him. He died a hero, just like he lived. So, when you ask me to swear it to God, well, I'll do even better than that. I swear on the soul of George Kincaid. Now, why don't you give me that knife, okay, sweetheart? Don't wanna make Indy's sacrifice for nothing, do you?"

She stared at him for another long, tense moment, her chin trembling. Eyes glittering with tears, she took a shuddering breath, handed him the knife, and rolled away from Benji and onto her knees. Her slim shoulders shook as the towering wall of rage crumbled and fell, leaving only grief in the ruins. Terrible screams tore from her throat as tears coursed down her face.

Chase knew that kind of soul-deep grief; he knew it too fucking well. He dropped to his knees, pulled her into his arms, and held her as she sobbed. His own vision blurred with tears as he looked up and met Benji's stricken eyes.

Holding his head to keep it from exploding, Chase paced the width of the dungeon. His booted feet crunched on loose particles shed by decaying brick as he walked and prayed. "Ash, it's Chase. I need you here, man. In the dungeon. Now. Please!"

In a rush of air that sent dust motes flying, Ashriel appeared. He glanced around him. "What's wrong? Why are we down here? Is Emma all right?"

"She's fine. Well, not fine, but okay. Just shut up a minute and listen to me. Look, I know you said you wouldn't violate Emma's privacy, that it's up to her what she tells us, but I gotta know this, or I'm gonna freakin' lose it. She spent time with my dad, and she's totally blown away that he's dead. I gotta ask. Were they...did they..." He covered his face with his hands. "God help me. I can't even say it!"

"Are you asking if they were involved sexually?"

Chase took a breath before answering, not sure if he really wanted to know the answer. "Yeah. That."

"No. She loved Indy—George—very much, but to her, he was like a father. Much more so than Borello ever was."

Oh, thank God! His relief was so great that he had to bend forward and brace his hands on his knees as the room spun.

"Chase, Emma is..." Ashriel hesitated.

"She's what?"

"She's *innocent*."

"Yeah, I know, that's why we did all..." He jerked his head up as he got the angel's meaning. He straightened and huffed a laugh of disbelief. "Aww, come on, Ash. A virgin? No friggin' way. She's my age."

"So? Look at her life. She was hardly more than a child when the Russos destroyed her world. She's been on the run all these years. What opportunity did she have for a relationship? After her curse, who could she ever trust enough to risk the vulnerability of intimacy? I'm glad you brought this up. You cannot,"—Ashriel made air quotes with his fingers—"*hit that*, Chase."

He feigned innocence, although he'd been thinking along those lines earlier. "You think? I wouldn't..."

Ashriel raised a brow and gave him a deadpan stare.

"Okay, fair enough." A zing of guilt shamed him. But it's not like he woulda forced her to do anything she didn't want to do! But maybe he was jumping the gun with her. As hot as she was, as much as he wanted her, she'd been through the wringer times ten. He didn't wanna do anything to make things worse for her. And she was a virgin, to boot?

Damn. That invoked number five on his don't-do list. She wasn't one of the experienced women he played with. They knew the score, and he always made it real clear he wasn't relationship material. Maybe it would be best to take a hands-off policy with her. "Yeah, I got a track record. But not her. She's special."

Ashriel nodded vigorously. "Yes. She is special—very special. And vulnerable. Don't hurt her. She's not to be trifled with. I mean it."

"Already said I wouldn't! Anyway, who died and made you fucking boss over two consenting adults? What are you, her guardian angel?"

Ashriel's eyes narrowed. "Yes. Yes, I am. You and I have been friends all your life. I bounced you on my knee when you were a baby. I stood by your side when you buried your lost loved ones. We've traveled many a difficult road together, fought the enemy shoulder to shoulder. I've saved your life, and you've saved mine. But heed my warning, Laird Kincaid. If you hurt Emma, you'll answer to me."

Chase breathed deeply and forced his tight muscles to relax. He'd seen the results of Ashriel's iron fists more than once and had no desire to be pounded to a bloody pulp. "So, that's how it is?"

"That's how it is."

"Guardian angel, huh?" His gut burned with anger he fought hard to repress. "Just wondering—seeing as how you're currently on Michael's shit list—but would that title be official or self-appointed?"

Ashriel moved a step closer. "Does it matter?"

He forced himself to stand his ground, and he stared at the angel, intimidated for the first time in a long time by his old friend. He sure as hell didn't like the feeling. "Guess it don't. Well, no worries, so don't get your feathers ruffled. Last thing I wanna do is hurt her, so we're both on the same page. You asked if she's okay, and I don't think she is. Had a couple dizzy spells and told us the lights were flickering, but they weren't. And now, finding out about my dad's death? She's wrecked. I think you should check on her."

Chapter Twelve

EMMA YAWNED AND CAREFULLY placed her hairbrush on the antique cherry-wood dresser in her beautiful, albeit temporary, bedroom. It was a herculean effort just to raise her arm to brush her hair. She should braid it, but screw the damn tangles. She'd deal with it in the morning. Just too tired. Sleep-for-a-week tired—more tired than she could remember being in her entire life—and that was saying something.

She cringed as she studied her reflection in the beveled-glass mirror. *Good lord*, she looked awful! Hair a mess, complexion sallow, and dark circles under eyes that were dull and bloodshot.

Ashriel warned her it might happen as a result of the trauma her body sustained on a molecular level during its reanimation, a trauma he couldn't completely heal. She needed to rest. Sleep, sleep, and more sleep, he'd advised. Although her mind reeled from the events of the day and she still had a million questions, the way she felt, she wasn't about to argue.

She pulled back the comforter, crawled onto the bed, and fell face down on the pillow. Only the need for oxygen convinced her to make the effort to turn her head. But more than an hour later, much to her dismay, she was still awake. Her hope that sheer exhaustion would allow her to fall asleep easily was dashed because her mind was in overdrive. With a groan, she rolled onto her back and then lay staring at the coffered ceiling as chaotic thoughts bounced around in her head like tumbleweeds on a windy day.

After seeing to her every need, the Kincaids had excused themselves and gone to bed, and Ashriel had wished her a good night, told her he'd see her in the morning, and disappeared.

Literally. Right in front of her eyes. That really was going to take some getting used to.

She'd apologized profusely to Ben, and he'd accepted warmly and told her not to give it another thought, but guilt and regret weighed heavily on her heart. How had she done that? Attacked someone who had shown her only kindness? Her face heated at the memory. She'd make it up to him somehow.

Chase had been especially nice. A walkie-talkie sat on her nightstand, and he had the other in his room. He'd told her if she needed anything, anything at all, to just press the button, and he'd come running. Easier than using a cellphone. Like she was going to interrupt his much-needed sleep like that?

It was tempting, though.

When she hadn't found her Glock in her backpack, assuming she'd lost it in the alley, she'd almost pressed that button so she could ask him if she could borrow a gun. She always slept with her gun under her pillow and her machete within reach. But he'd taken such pains to assure her she was safe in the citadel under his and Ben's protection that she'd been afraid of insulting him.

Still, after so many years of sleeping with her weapons close at hand, without them, she felt vulnerable. Exposed. And although she was accustomed to sleeping in a different place every night, this was different. She was used to an endless stream of cheap motel rooms, but motel rooms have a door to the outside for escape. While her bedroom had a window, it was at least a hundred feet up, far too high off the ground to even consider using for escape, and her door opened into a hallway. The only exit to the outside that she knew of was on the other end of the building and down several flights of stairs.

Instead of insulated, she felt trapped.

Claustrophobic instead of protected.

For a harrowing second that sent her heart pounding, she thought she saw the ceiling move closer to her. Despite Chase's assurance that he and Ben were just down the hall if she needed them and that the citadel was safe, there was no such thing.

Safety was an illusion.

She took a deep breath to calm her racing heart and deliberately switched her train of thought. It was difficult to wrap her head around the fact that she had died and that an angel—a literal angel from Heaven—had saved her, not only from death but maybe from her curse as well.

Her temporary death, just long enough for Octavio Russo to have the satisfaction of spitting on her grave, started the countdown clock ticking. In sixty days, he would die and go to Hell, and she would be free.

Free!

No more running, no more hiding, no more dousing herself with strong deodorant, choking on stinky incense, and keeping mothballs in her pockets and cramming them into her car and motel room heater and air conditioner vents. And people. She could be with people again. Get a job, an apartment, and make friends. Have a life!

She could contact her old friends. According to Facebook, Rachel and Clayton had two kids and lived in San Francisco. And Heather was married, had a daughter, and now lived in Brooklyn.

Well, maybe.

There was no guarantee. None of them were sure if her curse would end, but at least she had a shot. Only time would tell—sixty days' worth of time—and she wasn't sure if she wanted those sixty days to fly by or to crawl. At least during the waiting, she would have hope. And if, wonder of wonders, her curse ended? What then?

Or worse, what if it didn't end? What then?

She had no answer to either question.

And then there was Ashriel. How was it she could see the actual angel—not just his humanoid body with the handsome face and pretty blue eyes, but the angel within? Why? How? And when? Was this an ability she always had? Had she just never encountered an angel before? Or was it a new thing? Did that mean she could see other angels as well?

She always knew she was a freak, but this took freaky to a whole new level.

Earlier, when Ben asked her to describe what the angel in Ashriel looked like, she had been at a loss. Aside from wings and a halo, there literally weren't words to describe what she saw and felt—because her perception of Ashriel was not only visual, but it was also a physical sensation. She could literally feel him near her, and the closest comparison she could come up with was warm bubbles in the air, and that didn't even begin to cover it.

And his appearance? How could she describe the incredibly beautiful being of light and energy that she saw? So, she had asked Ben, *How would you describe colors to a person born blind?* He'd thought about it for a minute and understood. You couldn't, because they would have no frame of reference, and neither did he.

Ashriel. Her unfamiliar room had become darker and seemed more isolated after the angel left and took with him that soft blue glow and the comfort of his presence. With a sudden realization, she knew she was wrong. There was such a thing as real safety. When Ashriel was there, she was safe. She didn't even know if he was still in the building. Did he live there with Ben and Chase and sleep in his own room? Or did he go back to Heaven at night?

Questions, so many questions she wanted to ask him.

With a sigh, she gave up on sleep for the moment. She hauled herself up into a sitting position, fluffed her pillow, and stuck it behind her back. Her heart pounded from the effort, and each arm felt like it weighed a hundred pounds. A spell of dizziness crashed over her, spawning nausea that rose like a tidal wave, so intense it took her breath away. She should get up and go to the bathroom in case she got sick, but every tiny move made it worse.

A cold sweat beaded on her forehead, and she trembled from an onslaught of chills. Maybe eating greasy fast food as her first post-resurrection meal hadn't been such a smart idea. A sour taste filled her mouth. Oh, no! She forced herself to shimmy, inch by inch, to the edge of the mattress. She didn't want to vomit all over the gorgeous bed. Then she slowly dragged the blanket up and concentrated on taking deep, even breaths, and after what seemed like hours, the nausea subsided. She scooted back down to try to sleep.

It was a good thing the lamp was already on, because she didn't think she had the energy to reach across the nightstand and turn the switch.

She never slept in the dark.

Monstrous things waited in the dark.

Chase's face appeared in her mind's eye. She still couldn't believe Indy's son was the one she'd dreamed about all her life! While at face value it seemed like kismet, like it was meant to be—and, oh, didn't she want to believe it was—it still worried her.

She didn't believe in destiny or fate, not anymore.

But she believed in manipulation.

Something strange was going on. It would be so easy just to go with it. So easy, after all the years of being alone, to let someone else take care of her and be strong for her. So easy to assume it was all okay and accept that finally good things were going to happen in her life.

She wanted to, but she couldn't.

Suspicion was ingrained in her, drilled into her by both experience and Indy's instruction.

A pang of guilt struck. Was she being disloyal? Chase was Indy's son! She knew his face from her dreams, and in person, he was even more handsome. But that shouldn't matter, because how a person looked had nothing to do with their character. She was no longer a dew-eyed girl, head over heels in love with a fantasy man who lived in her dreams. She'd given up on that fairy tale long ago. In reality? She knew next to nothing about him.

But Ben told her Chase had suffered an extremely painful procedure to help Ashriel resurrect her body. How could she be suspicious after hearing that? And yet, she was.

On the other hand, she innately trusted Ashriel, and he trusted the cousins.

She yawned and rubbed her temples. Her thoughts were all muddled. She couldn't think straight. Way too tired to think straight.

Both Chase and Ben had been incredibly nice to her. Look at all they had done for her, and now their home was her temporary sanctuary. Nevertheless, Indy's voice lectured in her head. *Listen to your gut, little girl. You have good instincts. Things aren't always what they seem. If something doesn't sit right with you, protect yourself first, and then find out the truth. Always search for the truth. It could mean your life.*

Tears stung her eyes as the memory of learning of Indy's death popped into her head for a moment before she pushed it back.

Ashriel, I wish you were here with me.

That thought took her by surprise, because she was used to being alone and because, even though he saved her life, they had met only hours ago. It was strange, and she couldn't explain it, but she missed him.

She missed his kind, gentle presence and soothing voice that somehow seemed familiar, and his soft, bubbly blue glow that was so comforting and relaxing, like sitting in warm sunshine on a chilly day. She could use some of that warmth right now.

The memory of Indy's death surged forward again, refusing to be denied. She closed her eyes and concentrated, tried to close the door to that memory, tried to keep the pain at bay, but it was too new and too raw. She was too tired, and the door wasn't strong enough yet.

Indy was dead.

Gone forever.

She would never see him again. Never make good on her vow to repay his kindness.

She'd been nothing but a burden, after all.

The grief and guilt welled up and spilled over. She covered her face with her hands and sobbed.

As soothing warmth surrounded her, she jumped at a soft touch on her shoulder. Ashriel stood next to the bed, gazing at her with such tenderness, warmth, and compassion, that she didn't hesitate at all before moving into the comforting embrace of his open arms.

It felt like coming home.

Ashriel carried Emma to the chair and sat with her cradled in his arms as she cried. She tucked her face against his neck and grabbed hold of his coat with both hands, but he didn't mind at all that his neck and shirt grew wet with her tears.

He longed to take her pain away.

Although he could easily erase the memory with the touch of his hand on her head, what would be the point? She would find out again, sooner rather than later, that George Kincaid was dead. She needed to grieve to heal, as much as she could heal with her extraordinary memory. The grief would remain crystal clear in her mind, would never fade, and would hurt just as much every time she remembered it. But in time, she would build a door in her mind and trap the memory behind it.

Trapped, unless something or someone acted as a key to open the door and release the memory. And the devastating pain would hit her, like the trauma, the loss, and the pain had only just happened. The mental doors were her coping mechanism—the way her unusual brain worked to protect her from the psychic pain of constantly reliving the excruciating memories of her past.

He would do everything within his power to make sure the old memories stayed locked away and the only fresh memories she made were good ones.

Emma cried herself to sleep right there in his arms. Her trust humbled him. It was difficult for her to trust, so he appreciated what a rare and precious gift it was.

When he'd taken her soul into his body, he hadn't known it would create a connection, a bond, between them. She'd been so pure, so bright, so beautiful, that he hadn't kept her separated from him. He couldn't have known or even imagined the intimacy he and Emma would share.

Their spiritual joining was the most joyful and deeply personal experience of his lifetime.

It had only been a few hours since he bid her a good night and left her room, but he'd missed her terribly. Only now, when he touched her, did the aching loneliness within him cease.

Earlier in the Great Hall, moved beyond words at her expression of gratitude, he could only stand there and fight the tears that stung his eyes. He couldn't let them fall—wouldn't let them fall—and let the Kincaids see what he assumed they would consider weakness.

He'd wanted to tell her that even with her scars, she'd been beautiful, but he couldn't get the words out. He'd tried to steel himself against the unfamiliar emotions that had buffeted him, but her touch, her scent, the warmth of her soft body pressed against him—it had been too much. The sweetness of her had seeped in and left him dazed. It had taken a few seconds for him to regain control and to remember that he was supposed to hug her back.

And when he did? His body's reaction had shocked him.

He'd panicked and fled, going to sit on the roof of the citadel to compose himself and think, returning only when Chase summoned him.

When she'd gone to bed, he hadn't gone far. He'd returned to his favorite perch on the roof, keeping watch and looking up at the stars, waiting for morning to come so he could be with her again. But she'd wished for him—simply for the comfort of his presence—and his heart had leaped with joy.

She squirmed now in his arms, settling into a more comfortable position in her sleep. He stroked the silky hair that fell over her shoulder in a gleaming tangle of burnished copper. Her physical body was almost as lovely as her sweet soul. As he gazed down at her tear-streaked face, an intense surge of protectiveness, tenderness, and desire welled up in him—a fierce, staggering feeling unlike anything he'd ever known.

He was in love with her.

The wonder of it, the enormity of it! His heart pounded, and his breath seemed to catch in his lungs. That he was capable of such depth of feeling? His mind reeled.

As centuries passed, he understood that his time among humans changed him, but he hadn't realized how profoundly or how significantly until that moment.

Sweet, brave, strong Emma. She had endured so much, and yet her soul remained untarnished. He loved her, and in that moment, he knew with absolute certainty his purpose.

His true mission.

The words he'd said to Chase in anger were prophetic. He would be Emma's guardian, and he would do anything to make her happy and to keep her safe. *Anything*.

He would fight for her.

Kill for her.

Die for her.

With the knowing came peace. Contentment. She was in his arms and safe, although he had much work left to do to ensure her safety. But that was a concern for another day. For now, he would simply enjoy the gift.

Her body cooled as she relaxed, so he unfolded a wing and gently covered her with it. He still held her that way almost three hours later, when she woke up. He knew the moment she did, and yet she remained perfectly still and said nothing. What was she thinking? "Are you all right, Emma?"

"I have to get up, but I don't want to. This is nice, and I'm so tired...and I'm afraid if I move, I'll wake up."

"You're not dreaming. Why must you get up?"

She whispered the words, pressing her face against his shoulder. "I have to pee."

Ashriel smiled. He carried her to the bathroom. "Call for me in your mind when you're done." He set her down, made sure she was steady on her feet, and vanished.

When he took her back to the chair, he hesitated before sitting down. "Do you want to sleep in your bed now or sit with me again?"

She clutched at his coat. "With you."

Her answer pleased him because he enjoyed holding her. He understood why she wanted to be held. Except for a few fatherly hugs from George Kincaid, no one had held her in a long time, not since the last of a seemingly endless procession of uniformed nannies quit and left the cold, loveless house of her childhood.

Quit and left her alone with a man who valued money above all else and resented the child he knew was not his own, the gifted little girl he treated like just another possession to show off to his wealthy friends. And then came Russo and her curse, and she let no one get close enough to touch her.

"But wait. Don't you need to get some sleep, too?"

"I don't sleep." He settled them back into the chair, just as they had been, and covered her again with a wing. She settled in on his lap, gazing up at him, looking cozy as a kitten. "Comfortable?" he asked.

"Uh-huh. Angels don't sleep?"

"We don't require sleep."

"Do you mind if I ask you a few questions?"

"Not at all."

"Do you live here or in Heaven?"

"I haven't been to Heaven in centuries. My work is on Earth. I have my own room on the next floor above this one."

"What's it like, being an angel? How old are you?"

"Oh, many millennia old. Being an angel is very different from being a human, and it depends on what kind of angel you are. I am seraphim, which is a class under the archangels, which are the most powerful angels and the fewest."

She touched a fingertip to his torc. "This is beautiful. Is that a sapphire?"

"Similar. It's a crystal from another dimension, like the colorless crystal God used to craft my sword."

"Do angels die?"

"Not from what you would call natural causes. We're created to live until the end of time. I don't know of anything that could kill an archangel, except God, of course. Modern technology holds many new dangers as well. I suspect a nuclear weapon would kill angels, possibly even archangels. Hopefully, that possibility will never be tested.

"But we lesser angels can be killed by an angel sword and by the enchanted swords held by each Templar family. And potentially by Hades's scepter since it's made of the same crystal as angels' swords. And hypothetically by a spell, but I'm certain such a spell does not yet exist, or I would surely be dead." He laughed softly. "And Michael often threatens to throw me into the sun or into a black hole."

She was silent for a moment. "In the Book of Enoch from the Dead Sea Scrolls, the angel Uriel says, 'This dark place is the prison house of the fallen angels, and they are detained here forever.' Some people believe he's talking about a black hole."

The extent of her knowledge stunned him—although it shouldn't, since he knew she'd spent countless hours listening to audiobooks while she drove and reading eBooks at night. "That is true."

Her brow furrowed. "Michael wouldn't really do that to you, would he?"

The concern in her voice warmed him. "It is unlikely."

"Hades is really the King of Hell? It's not just a myth?"

"He really is. After the War of the Titans, that was the punishment he accepted from God in lieu of death."

"Wow. And he has a scepter." She gave a small laugh. "An artist's silly drawing in a book I read on mythology depicted it like the Devil's pitchfork from a Halloween costume."

"That artist was not entirely incorrect. However, it is a bident, having two prongs, not three."

She gaped. "Does he have horns and a tail, too?"

He laughed. "No. Hades is not Lucifer, nor does Lucifer have horns or a tail. Remember, Lucifer is an archangel, one of the most beautiful angels in Heaven before he fell from grace. While history and mythology carry threads of truth, much is convoluted with pagan beliefs. Cloven hooves, horns, a pointy beard, and a tail—these things are more Satyr or faun, or Pan, or even goat. Although Hades has a pointed goatee, which I suspect is a purposeful effort to create that exact effect."

She was silent again for a few moments. "Ash, how did you know?"

He smiled at her use of the shortened version of his name. "Know what?"

"That I needed you."

"Angels can hear those who pray to them."

"But I didn't pray."

"It doesn't have to be a formal prayer. It could just be a thought or a longing directed at me. Or a wish. Any time you need me, I'll come to you."

"Like a guardian angel?"

"Exactly. I'm your guardian angel."

"You're my..." She gave an exasperated sigh. "Come on now, are you *sure* this isn't a dream? I hope it's not, but sometimes it's hard for me to tell because my dreams are so vivid, and I remember them clearly."

He wished he could make her believe him, but only time could do that. "It's all real. I promise."

"I did wish that you were here with me. Felt really sick, but it passed. And...I missed you. I'm sorry. Is that weird?"

"No." He rested his cheek on top of her head, enjoying the silky texture and lovely scent of her hair. "I missed you, too. Wait. You were ill?"

"Uh-huh. Really dizzy and nauseated."

"May I heal you, just in case? If your stomach is inflamed, the nausea might return."

"Yes, please."

He placed his hand over her abdomen and emitted his healing power. "Any difference?"

She gave a hum of pleasure. "The muscles relaxed, like I had a nice, long, hot bath. Thank you."

"You're welcome." Did Emma realize she was gently stroking his wing? No one, angel or human, had ever touched his wings. It was a pleasurable sensation, and he didn't want her to stop.

"Is it because you're an angel that I feel like this? Like I've known you for a long time, instead of just a few hours?"

"That might be part of it. But just for hours...isn't exactly true."

"What do you mean?"

"When your body died, I carried your soul inside this body with me. We were together until I brought you back to life."

"My soul?" She moved a hand to his chest. "Everything that makes me who I am was in here with you all that time?"

"Yes."

"I think that's what I remembered when you held my hand after I first woke up here. Light, not light I could see, but light I was part of somehow, and warmth, and...you. I could feel...no, not exactly feel, but I could sense you, and..." She sighed. "Gone again. Too tired to think." She tucked her head back under his chin, yawned, and her eyes drifted closed. "Are we friends now?"

"I'd like that very much."

"Me, too. Haven't had a real friend in a long time."

"I know." His heart broke for her. So many years she'd spent alone and afraid, staying away from others as much as possible, speaking to people only when necessary, for fear she would put them in danger.

All that time! If only he'd known.

Well, he knew now, and she would never be alone again.

She slept.

She remembered her soul linked with his coruscentia while they shared his body? How was it possible? But then, he hadn't known she was one of the special humans who could see his angelic form, either. There were many things he still didn't know about her, even after their joining, even after he'd read her mind in the hospital, when he'd found psychic doors through which he could not see.

A wave of anxiety flooded his heart. Why was she gifted in these ways? For what purpose? And what would it mean for her future? What other secrets did she possess—secrets even he couldn't reach in the labyrinth of her extraordinary mind?

Chapter Thirteen

Yawning and tying his robe, Chase stepped out of his room and stopped. Music drifted through the hallway. And what was that awesome smell? He sniffed deeply. *Holy crap.* Bacon. Coffee. Blueberry. Cinnamon. And something else he couldn't place, but whatever it was, he sure as hell wanted it.

His cousin rounded a corner and walked toward him.

"Smell that, Benji? That is the best smell of any smell ever smelled in the freakin' world history of smells."

Benji hurried past him and kept going. He called over his shoulder, "Yeah, and if you're really lucky, just might be some crumbs left for you." And the jerk took off running.

Chase raced after him, slippers slapping against the polished granite floor. "Won't be able to chew if I knock all your damn teeth out!"

They locked shoulders at the kitchen door, grunting, shoving, and blocking, each trying to be the first into the room. Chase ducked down and made it through first. "Ha! Brains beats brawn every damn time."

"Dream on. I let you win."

Emma giggled and looked over her shoulder from where she stood, plating blueberry pancakes at the stove. She'd brought the vintage record player from the Great Hall into the kitchen and had cheerful swing music playing. "Good morning, children." She pointed the spatula at them and said sternly, "Behave or no dessert tonight."

Chase's heart did something funny inside his chest when he saw her standing at the stove. It seemed to expand and fill with something so rare for him that it took him a few seconds to recognize what it was.

Happiness.

"Morning, Emma." She looked so damn beautiful; it was everything he could do not to take her in his arms and kiss her the way he really wanted to. But his hands-off policy was still in full effect. Instead, he sidled up to her and planted a gentle, chaste kiss on her cheek that made her smile and blush. "Okay, we'll be good." He pointed over his shoulder at Benji. "But he started it." He winked at her and snagged a slice of crisp bacon off a platter on the island on his way to the coffee.

Benji poured a steaming cup of brew. "Morning, Emma. Glad to see you up and about, but you're supposed to be taking it easy. You're recovering from…well, death. You shouldn't have done all this." He grunted and winced when Chase elbowed him in the ribs and gave him a look that clearly said, *Shut up, stupid!*

"Don't worry," Emma said. "I have Ashriel's official permission to get back to normal activities, as long as I feel up to it. Good thing, too, because I'm absolutely bursting with energy this morning. And we need to talk while you guys eat." She spooned fluffy scrambled eggs onto two plates. "This was so much fun! Been so long since I had a full kitchen to use."

She waved a hand around the room. "This big old kitchen is beautiful. I love the hand-painted flowers on the white cabinets and the pretty green tile countertops. And this vintage O'Keefe and Merritt range is a dream! They don't make them like this anymore. Cost a small fortune if you wanted to buy one from an antiques dealer." She opened the oven door and pulled out a muffin tin, holding it up for them to see. "I made coconut-almond muffins, too, just in case either of you don't like blueberries."

Benji grinned at her. "My mom would be happy to hear you say that about the cabinets. She was the one who painted the flowers on them. And our grandpa built them for our grandma."

"Well, they're lovely. She was quite the artist, and he was a real craftsman. You don't see dovetailed drawers every day."

Chase waited while she dumped the muffins into a basket, and then he nabbed one, juggling it from hand to hand for a moment until it had cooled enough to handle. He held it up to his nose, drew a deep breath, and exhaled a sigh of pleasure. That was the smell he couldn't place—coconut. He sat at the table, and his eyebrows quirked. "Wait, we had coconut and almonds?"

She laughed as she carried a loaded plate for each of them to the table. "No, and you didn't have flour, baking powder, almond extract, or vanilla either. I'm actually kinda shocked you had eggs. Ashriel took me to the grocery store. Teleportation is amazing. One second we were standing here in the kitchen, and it seemed the next second we were in town."

Chase was glad she could teleport with no issues. He hadn't had any problems with it either—until his stay in Hell. Now it knocked him on his ass. Lucky him. "Aren't you gonna eat, sweetheart?"

"Already did." She slipped into the chair across from him. "Woke up starving."

Chase took a big bite of the sticky, sweet, fluffy muffin. His eyes crossing with pleasure, he slapped a hand down on the table. "Oh, sweet Mother of God! Marry me, woman!"

She laughed and winked at Benji. "Guess it's true. The way to a man's heart is through his stomach."

Benji gave him a dumbfounded and somewhat horrified glare. "Yeah, I'm sure it's every woman's dream to have a marriage proposal mumbled through a mouthful of food."

Chase ignored the reprimand and shoved the rest of the muffin past his teeth. Grinning, his cheeks bulging like a chipmunk's in autumn, he chewed with his mouth open. Benji was still so damn easy—and hella fun—to bait. For a moment, he felt like a little kid again, when his most pressing concern had been inventing new ways to annoy the crap out of his older cousins. He shot Emma a wink.

The smile she tried to hide behind her hand and the amusement sparkling in her pretty eyes told him she knew exactly what he was doing.

Benji's face twisted in disgust, but then he shook his head, sighed, and turned his attention back to Emma. "So, what's on your mind?"

"We have fifty-nine days until my curse is broken. Or not. And until then, I'm gonna pull my weight around here. And don't give me the speech about how *you saved our asses, and we owe you* because you guys saved mine, too. In my book, we're even. So, here's the deal. I'll do the cooking and help with the other chores, and I want to help in any way I can with your work. You guys help people. You make a real difference in the world. Only way I've ever helped anyone is to stay away from them, so it will really make me happy to do it."

"Heck, yeah!" Benji put down his juice. "I'd love some help. Doing a computerized inventory, bringing this place into the twenty-first century. I can teach you how to handle research, too, in case we get marching orders and need info stat. That would be a huge help. Anything we can do to improve efficiency makes Michael happy. Well, as close to happy as he ever gets."

"Sounds good, but you do realize that anything I read is gonna get stuck in my head forever. Spells, lore, maps, the Templars' secret handshake." She tapped her head. "You okay with me carrying all that around in here?"

"Just don't tell anyone," Benji said.

"Who would I tell? You're the only people I know. And if I ever do know anyone else, I swear not to breathe a word."

"Good with that, Chase?" his cousin asked.

"Okay, by me. She can have access to anything in the Great Hall." He sought Benji's eye to make sure he understood that the Laird's Library and the Templar Repository weren't included. While he trusted Emma, he alone was responsible for the top-level secrets and treasures hidden within his walls. A need-to-know basis for access was embedded in all Templar systems. There was plenty of work for her to do within the Great Hall.

"Great, then we're agreed." She stood, swiping a slice of bacon off Chase's plate with a wink. But she wobbled and leaned on the table, the bacon falling to the floor.

Uh-oh. Afraid she might fall, Chase jumped up and put his arm around her. "Hey, you okay?"

"Yeah. Yeah, sure. Just a little dizzy. Got up too quickly, I guess." She smiled up at him and patted his arm. "I'm okay now. I'm gonna go take a shower." As she left, she paused in the doorway and looked back at them over her shoulder. "By the way, guys, I'm a fantastic cook, but I don't do dishes." She shot them a sassy wink and left.

In unison, they looked at the kitchen sink, piled high with bowls, pots, and pans.

Chase shrugged. "Totally worth it."

"Sounds like she's going to be cooking a lot."

"If we're lucky."

"Guess our days of paper plates and plastic forks are over for a while. I'm thinking it's high time we get that new dishwasher."

Chase dropped his fork with a clatter. "Dude, you're a genius!"

"Just hate washing dishes."

Footsteps echoed through the Great Hall as Ben led Emma up the circular tower stairs to the battlement terrace so she could check out the spectacular views for the first time.

He'd prepared a little surprise for her. She'd mentioned an interest in astronomy and the constellations, so he'd dug out his old telescope and set it up for her on the terrace. It was daytime, but looking at the moon during the day was pretty cool, and she could return after dark to look at the stars. They emerged into a crisp afternoon filled with golden sunlight. "Here you go, Princess Emma. Your very own tower."

He sighed with pleasure as he gazed out over the stunning view of snow-capped mountains, green pines, and deciduous trees in their full yellow and orange autumn splendor. In the distance, a sparkling blue river wound its way across the land. He'd never get his fill of the pristine beauty.

She stood next to him but said nothing. He glanced down, but the odd expression on her face wasn't what he'd expected. Her eyes looked glassy and seemed unfocused, and then she swayed on her feet...

Oh, shit! He caught her just in time as she passed out. He carried her down the stairs, intending on settling her into her bed and summoning Ash, but she woke up before he hit the last step and would have none of it.

Ten minutes later, he set a steaming cup of tea on the table in front of her. As he lowered himself onto a chair, he noted her still-pale cheeks and that she reached for her tea with trembling hands. He cursed himself ten times over. Why had he made her climb all those stairs so soon? *Idiot!* He should have known better.

He'd already been worried about her. In the few days they'd been working together in the Great Hall, she'd developed dark circles under her eyes, and although she cooked wonderful meals for them, she didn't seem to eat much. Was she losing weight? When he'd carried her down the tower stairs, her slight weight had been like nothing in his arms. "I wish you'd listen to me and go have a nap." He patted her forearm, noting that she had goosebumps. "Are you cold?"

"Yeah, it's kinda chilly in here."

He retrieved her jacket from a row of coat hooks on the back of the kitchen door, glancing at the thermometer built into the wall clock. Chilly? It was seventy-five degrees. He draped the jacket over her shoulders.

"Thanks." She gave him a grateful smile, raised her cup to her lips, and took a few sips. "How about we continue our work tomorrow?"

"Of course, whatever you want. Are you sure you don't want to take a nap? And I'd feel better if we got Ash to take a look at you."

"No, please don't bother him. I'm okay now, I promise. How about we watch TV? I think Hulu just uploaded a bunch of old sitcoms. Let's have a *Perfect Strangers* marathon."

"You're on." He liked that silly old show, but old reruns yet again? What was up with that? "May I ask you a question?"

"Sure."

"I've noticed that the only TV shows and movies you watch are old or straight-up comedies—which is totally fine—but I'm curious. Why nothing currently running or at least recent? There are a lot of pretty decent new shows."

"I do that?" She seemed at a loss for a moment and stared down at her cup. Then she shrugged and gave him a sad little smile that broke his heart. "I guess because I already know the ending."

When would he learn to keep his damn mouth shut? He lifted her hand and placed a kiss on her knuckles. "Come on, Balki's waiting."

But as they stood to leave the kitchen, she moaned. "Oh, no." She rushed to the sink, reaching it just in time as she vomited up the tea.

Just tea had made her sick? He hurried to her side, rescued her hair, and put his arm around her shoulders to steady her. When she was finished, he picked her up again and carried her from the kitchen. "Damn, I'm sorry, Emma. I knew you were overdoing it, and I just made it worse. Traipsing up and down the stairs to the tower is a far cry from sitting and reading. You're going to bed, like it or not, and I'm getting Ash to check on you."

She didn't argue this time, which worried him even more.

Ashriel gently placed Emma on her bed and tucked the covers around her. He moved his chair close to her side. She'd awoken from a bad dream in the middle of the night with a nosebleed and a puddle of blood on her pillow and had called for him in a disoriented panic. He'd healed her, but he was growing concerned.

When he'd been called to check on her a few days earlier, he'd assumed that Ben was right and that her relapse was because of overexertion. But now he wasn't at all sure of that. Her body still hadn't fully recovered from her resurrection; in fact, it seemed to have deteriorated. She had little appetite and was losing weight, and her delicate skin was far too pale and marred by several unexplained bruises.

He would have liked to continue to hold her, but after several hours, he feared her body would become stiff from being in one position for so long. She slept comfortably and deeply, and she didn't wake up when he moved her. It was a natural, healing sleep, exactly what she needed, but he'd have to wake her soon, just long enough so she could drink and eat.

There was a soft knock on the door. With a flick of his wrist, Ashriel opened the door from across the room.

Chase walked in, a steaming mug in his hand, his eyes widening as he spotted him. His gaze darted to Emma, sleeping in bed, and he whispered, "Why are you in here? Is she all right?"

"She had difficulty last night." He told Chase what had happened.

Chase tiptoed to the other side of the bed, smiling softly as he gazed down at Emma. She lay on her side with her hands tucked under her face, her hair spread out over the pillow.

"I'm afraid her body is reacting worse than I feared to her reanimation. She'll need to sleep for some time yet. But I'd like her to eat. Will you bring her milk and food? She likes scrambled eggs and buttered toast. Lots of butter. She needs the calories."

"I'm on it. Want this? I brought it for her, but I guess she shouldn't fill up on a cup of flavored water. Just tea, but it's hot and black."

With a nod of thanks, Ashriel took the mug.

"Should we be worried? I mean, is it dangerous?"

"Any unknown is potentially dangerous. As I've told you, the procedure damaged her body on a molecular level that I can't fully heal. I resurrected her body, which was embalmed with chemicals and dead for almost a week, using the power of gamma radiation, which I could barely control. As far as I know, that's never been done.

"I took her soul inside me and then put her back into her body, and as far as I know, that's never been done, either. And on top of that, Emma's body is under the influence of her curse, a powerful spell. We simply don't know the ramifications or the complications that may arise. But don't worry, I won't leave her side until she's completely recovered."

Not leave her side? Chase frowned as jealousy uncoiled and bit him in the ass. "Don't you think that's overreacting? The girl's sick and sleeping, not dying. This is Colorado, dude. We've all had a bloody nose from time to time. The air is even dryer than normal this time of year. Except for a couple of dizzy spells, she seemed just fine yesterday. But, hey, if you think she needs watching, we can help, too. Take turns; give you a break."

"You and Ben are welcome to join me, but I will not leave her side. Emma is my responsibility. I did this to her. And I'm her guardian. It's my duty to protect her and care for her. I can constantly monitor her condition. She needs me."

It wasn't easy, but Chase let go of his jealousy. If she really was in danger, Ash was right. He and Benji couldn't do what Ash, with all his angelic powers, could. "If it's that bad, maybe we should take her to the hospital."

Ashriel's face mirrored his disdain. "If I can't heal her, what do you think human doctors could do? And she doesn't exist anymore, remember? To the world—and to the Russos and Thorne—she's dead. If she were identified, all we have done would be for naught."

"Yeah. That's true. Can she hear us?"

"She's in a deep sleep. You can speak freely, but quietly."

"What in the hell is going on with her? She dreams about me, and she sees angels? And you got your wings back at the same time we find her? All coincidence? My ass, it is. Something weird is going on here."

"Perhaps. But her ability to see my true angelic form might result from me taking her soul into my body. Her soul touched my coruscentia. This is unheard of. She may or may not see other angels. And my new wings may have nothing to do with her. Coincidences happen occasionally. The only thing I know for sure is that I have to protect her."

"Protect her from what?" When Ashriel's intense blue gaze turned toward him, the angel's terse answer sent a chill up Chase's spine.

"Everything."

Ben glanced up from where he sat cross-legged on the floor when Chase returned to Emma's room a short time later with her breakfast on a tray. "Morning."

"Morning, Benji."

"Where's mine?"

Chase snorted. "Bite me. You know how to crack a damn egg."

"Well, someone woke up on the cranky side of the bed."

"Sue me."

Ashriel gently shook Emma's shoulder to wake her up to eat. "Emma. Emma, wake up. Time for breakfast."

Anxiety made Ben's heart pound when she didn't wake up.

She didn't even move.

Chase arched his brows at Ashriel. "Did you give her some of your angelic Ambien?"

"All I gave her was comfort and a feeling of security." He shook her again, a little harder this time. "Emma. Emma, wake up."

Still nothing.

Ben sought his cousin's eye and exchanged a look of concern. The same terrible feeling of dread he'd felt in the hospital, watching her die, hit him again. He imagined Chase felt even worse, and the haunted look in his cousin's eyes confirmed it.

Ashriel frowned. "She must drink, or she'll become dehydrated. I'm going to give her a small amount of stimulant." He touched his palm to Emma's forehead.

She whimpered and opened her bleary eyes. "Ash?"

"I'm here. Can you sit up? You need to eat and drink."

"Not hungry," she mumbled. Her eyes drifted closed.

Ash motioned to Chase. "I'm going to pick her up and hold her. Will you try to get her to drink and feed her?"

Ben stood and waited nearby in case he was needed. "Ash, I'm no doctor, but don't you think she should be—"

"Already been through that," Chase said.

Ashriel looked up at him, and Ben saw something he couldn't ever remember seeing in the angel's eyes.

Fear.

Although Emma was safe from her curse in the citadel, she wasn't out of danger yet. Far from it.

Ashriel moved the chair away from the bed, picked Emma up, and sat with her on his lap with her head propped against his shoulder. He kept her as straight as he could manage, but she was like a limp rag doll in his arms. It took a while, and it was like feeding a baby, but they got her to drink all the milk and eat some of the food.

"All right, Chase. That's enough for now." Ashriel laid Emma back in bed and covered her with the blanket. Her weak voice, barely a whisper, stopped him.

"Ash? Don't leave me."

He sank to his knees next to the bed and stroked her hair. "I won't leave you, little one. I promise."

She moaned. "Don't feel good."

"I know. I'll take care of you."

Chase leaned over the bed and patted her shoulder. "Me and Benji are here, too. You're not alone, Emma. Not anymore."

Over the next twenty-four hours, Ben and Chase took turns sitting with Ashriel as she lingered in a semi-comatose state, roused only by the angel's small doses of stimulant when it was time for her to drink or eat.

They became more worried as every hour passed.

She wasn't getting enough fluid or nutrition, and Ashriel, with his angelic powers, could sense that her electrolyte levels were becoming dangerously unbalanced.

It was late afternoon the next day when Chase stepped into Emma's room carrying two beers. He handed one to Ashriel before sitting in a chair he'd brought in from his room. "Tried Benji again. The beamer's gone, but I don't know where the hell he took off to. Still ain't answering his phone." He took a swallow of his beer, the flavor going bitter in his mouth as he gazed at Emma's pale face and motionless body.

There was a bit of dried blood on her upper lip from another nosebleed. His heart ached, the memory of her lying in a hospital bed, dying—and hearing her last, soft breath—still fresh in his mind, cycling over and over like a video on a loop. "Think maybe it's the curse that's keeping you from healing her?"

"Perhaps. Some things I can heal, and some things I can't. Some seem to heal, but the tissues break down again. There's no pattern I can discern. It could all be from the molecular damage, or it could be her curse, or it could be a combination of both. Or it could be something else we're not aware of. Chase, I'm extremely concerned. I don't know what else to do. We may have to risk taking her to a hospital, although I can't imagine what they could do. Or call on Michael."

Chase's gut twisted. If Ash was willing to take a chance like that—to risk pissing off Michael, or to take her away from the safety of the citadel to seek help from human doctors and possibly put others in danger—it was bad.

Really bad.

"Hold the phone." Ben bustled into the room, carrying a shiny metal pole mounted on a rolling base and a couple of large white bags. "You don't have to do that. Not yet, anyway."

"Dammit, Benji! Where in the hell have you been? Don't we have enough to worry about? You can't just go AWOL like that! Why didn't you answer your freakin' cell?"

"Sorry, man. Battery died. Been so distracted with Emma, I didn't notice." He put the bags down and set the pole next to the head of Emma's bed, as he explained. "I hit a medical supply company in Denver and got what we needed to set her up with IV fluid. This should take care of her hydration and electrolyte problems. Got antibiotics, too, just in case."

Relief made Chase weak in the knees. What would he ever do without Benji's brainpower? He jumped up and gave his cousin a bear hug. "I'll say it again. You're a freakin' *genius*."

"Just made sense."

"Leave payment?" asked Chase.

Benji shot him a glare. "What am I, a thief? I left more than enough."

Chase sighed and dropped back into his chair. "Sorry, Benji. Of course, you did. Not thinking straight."

Ashriel stared at the apparatus. "Do either of you know how to hook her up to it?"

"No worries," Benji said. "I got this." He hung a fluid bag from the IV pole from where he'd stood it next to the bed. "Dozens of instructional videos online on how to do it. Looked pretty easy." And it was. A few minutes later, he taped the butterfly needle to her hand, set the IV drip rate according to the height and weight chart he'd saved on his phone, and stood back. "Okay, that should do it."

An hour later, Ashriel was happy to report that her electrolyte levels were improving.

But the next morning, as Chase sat slumped in a chair in Emma's room, his head tucked against his chest as he dozed, he was startled from his sleep by Ashriel's panicked voice.

"Chase! Hold her down so I can heal her. Hurry!"

Emma's body arched like a bow, her arms flailing. Ashriel moved aside as Chase flung himself down on top of her and grabbed her wrists—the only way to keep her from hurting herself or throwing herself off the bed.

Ashriel placed his healing hands on her head. She stopped flailing and fell motionless.

Chase carefully got off her, his heart slamming in his chest. "What the hell happened?"

"Seizure. A blood clot went to her brain." Starting at the top of her head, Ashriel moved hands that emitted a healing light slowly over her body to her feet. "I have to find where the clot came from and make sure it heals completely." As he moved back up, he stopped at her belly. "Her spleen. A spontaneous rupture. I've never seen anything like this. The molecular damage seems to ebb and flow. I heal one thing, and something else fails. Her body tissues are very fragile."

He concentrated his healing power on that spot. "I think that got it. I'll check again in a minute. Check her IV and make sure she didn't pull out the needle." Keeping one hand on Emma's shoulder, Ash sank into the chair and leaned forward with his head in his free hand.

Chase glanced up as he checked Emma's IV. Ash's hand shook so badly that his head was wobbling. "Dude, I don't get it. Why are you so freaked out? I mean, God forbid she dies, of course. But if she does, can't you take her soul inside you and fix up her body up again?"

"It's not that simple anymore. Her physical body is in jeopardy, and I can't even heal it completely, much less resurrect it again. I dare not remove my hand from her body because she's declining at a rapid rate, and it's all I can do to keep her alive. It may be the resurrection procedure that damaged her in the first place. And Chase... My power is dangerously low, and even if I could leave Emma for such a period of time, I wouldn't survive an attempt to reach the sun again.

"The resurrection consumed even more power than I expected—all the extra power I harvested from the sun and most of my own power as well. I'm having a hard time keeping up with healing her as her body breaks down. And without her physical body in which to return her soul, I have no right to take her soul inside me and prevent her from going to Heaven. It would be sacrilege! Should I commit such a heinous crime, Michael would surely put me to death. And rightly so.

"I'm not sure I would survive even the brief journey to the veil right now. If Emma were to die and her soul moved into the veil, I couldn't go there and bring her back."

Ashriel took a shuddering breath. "If she dies there's a good chance we'll lose her forever."

Chapter Fourteen

Known only as Vector 7, the Black Ops military warehouse and no-fly zone in the Sonoran Desert of California—a facility that existed on no publicly known roster or map—appeared to be under siege, surrounded by dozens of army tanks and Multipurpose Combat Jeeps with their combined firepower aimed at a nondescript, sand-tan building.

It was a precautionary measure just in case what they brought back into the world proved too much to handle.

Inside the warehouse, under the watchful eyes of Senator Zyro, Army General Colton, and the two army engineers who designed the cage, the dark witch Santana prepared to call forth the beast.

She stood within a large circle of flickering black wax candles and began chanting in Latin, swaying back and forth, holding a large green chalice of polished malachite engraved with demonic symbols. Over and over, she chanted the words until the candle flames suddenly blazed high before they settled down to normal. Turning toward the east, she drew a small, bejeweled dagger from the pocket of the long black dress she wore and sliced her palm, letting her blood drip onto the chalice.

At the first drop of blood, a small, hideous mouth formed at the bottom of the cup—a mouth that hungrily devoured the blood. Santana fed the demon spirit all it wanted until the mouth sated itself and closed.

Her hand dripping blood, she lifted the chalice toward the east. "I call upon the warrior demon guardian of the East Gate and the element of air to watch over and protect me within this sacred circle." The candles flared and died down to normal.

She turned toward the south. "I call upon the warrior demon guardian of the South Gate and the element of fire to watch over and protect me within the sacred circle." The candles flared up again and died down.

She turned toward the west. "I call upon the warrior demon guardian of the West Gate and the element of water to watch over and protect me within the sacred circle." Again, the candles flared and died down.

She turned again. "I call upon the demon warrior guardian of the North Gate and the element of earth to watch over and protect me within this sacred circle." The candles flared yet again.

The dark witch pointed to the ground beneath her feet. She let her blood drip onto the concrete floor. "I call upon the power of Satan and all Hell's darkness to aid me in my quest!" The candles flared up, impossibly high, nearly to the thirty-foot ceiling, and went out.

Santana nodded to Zyro. He motioned to a guard standing nearby. The guard opened a wide roll-up door, and a group of young soldiers pushed a cage that sat on a rolling sled into the circle. The cage was a soundproof, perfect cube, twelve feet square. Framed with steel-reinforced iron bars, encased in six-inch-thick, bullet-proof polycarbonate plastic, one side was fitted with a door that held a single tiny, latched hole, just large enough to insert and maneuver the muzzle of a rifle. When the cage was in position, General Colton called the soldiers to attention. "You've seen nothing here today. Any word of this gets out, even the tiniest whisper, and I will have each and every one of you executed, and your bodies will never be found. Do I make myself clear?"

As a group, they replied, "Yes, sir!" Colton dismissed the soldiers, and they hurried to exit the building. Santana waited until the area was clear and the warehouse doors were closed and locked before she reentered the circle. She walked into the cage, cut her palm again, and let more of her blood drip onto the bottom of the cage. Murmuring a few words in Latin, she retrieved a plastic baggie from her dress pocket. With a smile, she opened the baggie and tossed its contents—a small swatch of blue and white checked fabric—into a corner of the cage before returning to Zyro's side.

"What's that?" asked Zyro.

Her smile was smug. "A little souvenir from Chase Kincaid. Unfortunately for him, he left a pair of his jockey shorts at my place during our time together. And he'd worn them, too. Such bad manners to leave dirty laundry at someone's home. But I thought they might come in handy someday, so I kept them nice and dirty in a plastic bag. His scent and DNA are on that cloth, so our new pet should have no problem tracking his way through the forest to the citadel."

Zyro smiled, nodded, and made a mental note to keep extremely good track of all his clothing. "Did you cast the other spell?"

"Yes, last night. Neither Chase nor Ben Kincaid's prayers to their angel guardian will penetrate the telepathic barrier. They could pray to him from the next room, and he wouldn't hear them."

"Very good. What about the archangel? Michael could be dangerous for us."

"I can't be sure. He may sense the disturbance in the ether. Do you accept the risk?"

"I do."

Santana returned to stand within the circle of candles. She wrapped her injured hand as the two engineers closed and sealed the cage door. There was no latch or handle; a remote control would open the door at the proper time. The men moved out of the circle. Santana raised her arms, chanting softly in Latin. Louder and louder, over and over, she chanted, "*Potestate Satanae praecipio tibi proferet manticore! Potestate Satanae praecipio tibi proferet manticore!*"

The rows of electric lights that hung from the warehouse ceiling flickered and blew out one by one, tiny explosions that had Zyro and Colton flinching and sharing concerned glances. Suddenly, all the electric lights went out, and then there was an explosion of green light within the cage.

Pitch dark.

When the emergency lights turned on a few seconds later, within the cage stood the horrible beast, snarling and posturing, its poisonous tail raised—poised and ready for battle.

A manticore.

Zyro couldn't help the wave of fear that passed through him or the pounding of his heart, even as he gloried in his triumph. The creature was everything he'd hoped for and more. It was huge, the size of an adult male Bengal tiger, about nine-and-a-half feet long, about four feet high at the shoulder. Its head and face were eerily like a man's, with a long, dark gray beard and humanistic blue eyes, but it had curved red and black striped horns that gave it a decidedly satanic appearance.

Its body was that of a lion with enormous paws armed with lethal-looking, razor-sharp claws. Its short fur was scarlet red, and its shaggy, full lion's mane was dark gray, thick and curly. The monster's mouth was much wider than a man's and had multiple rows of sharp teeth, like a shark's mouth. But the creepiest thing of all was the black scorpion-like tail that curved over its body, long and thick, with shiny armor-like scales and multiple spikes on the end.

General Colton took a step forward to get a better look. His movement sent the beast into attack mode. It curled its tail like a scorpion and flung it forward, shooting spikes like arrows from the tip that bounced off the clear walls and fell to the bottom of the cage. The small group watched in fascination—and horror—as new spikes immediately formed and grew to full size in less than a minute.

"Holy crap," Santana said in a weak voice.

"Well said, my dear. But there's nothing holy about this magnificent creature." Zyro motioned to the engineers. "Trank him and get the collar on." When neither of the men moved, their wide eyes glued to the manticore, Zyro clapped his hands together loudly. "Move it!" One engineer retrieved a rifle from a nearby table and loaded a tranquilizer dart, while the second engineer handed out military-grade noise-canceling headphones to all.

Zyro gazed at the fearsome creature. The lore warned that the manticore's trumpet-like song was used by the creature to lull its prey into a trance-like state, making the prey easy to strike with a venomous spike that would paralyze the victim. Then the manticore would drag its living prey back to its den, sometimes traveling for miles, so it could eat the still-fresh meat in peace.

The engineer with the rifle used a stepladder to reach the gun port. Although six inches of solid acrylic stood between him and the manticore, the man's hands shook visibly as the creature fired round after round of spikes at him that fell harmlessly to the floor of the cage. He took a deep breath to steady himself and fired, the tranquilizer dart hitting the manticore's flank and enraging the beast. It reared up on its hind legs, roaring like a lion and baring razor-sharp rows of teeth, clawing at the sides of the cage with sharp talons that were, luckily for all, impotent against the bullet-proof glass.

"How long till he drops?" Zyro asked.

The engineer shrugged. "I'm no vet, but I used big cat trank, and according to the instructions, it should only take about ten minutes. If that doesn't work, I have elephant trank."

Zyro glared at the man. "Elephant trank? I didn't go through all this trouble just to kill it."

Twenty minutes later, they were still waiting. The manticore seemed unaffected by the tranquilizer. "Hit him again," ordered Zyro. "Cat trank. He does me no good if he's dead."

The second dose did the trick. The manticore slowly swayed, his eyes rolling and his tail relaxing into a resting position on his back. Finally, he sank to the floor and passed out. They could see the rise and fall of his body as he breathed. "Poke him," Zyro ordered. "We can't afford a mistake here." The engineer used a length of rebar to poke none-to-gently at the manticore's body, but the creature didn't so much as twitch. "Okay, open the door and get that collar on, and make sure the camera's working. And hurry. We don't know how long he'll be out."

Ben closed his eyes and let his fingers dance over the guitar strings, willing the familiar music to fill his soul and soothe him, but even the beloved chords of his favorite songs only jangled his nerves. He set the acoustic guitar back on its stand and paced the length of his spacious bedroom. The walls were closing in. Anxiety was like a rattlesnake coiled in his chest, ready to strike. He *had* to get out of the citadel for a while! Although he'd just awoken from a few hours of fitful sleep, he was mentally and emotionally exhausted—totally strung out. They all were.

It was afternoon by the clock, but the days had lost any semblance of normalcy as Emma's life hung by a thread. He and Chase took turns sleeping, and Chase wouldn't even leave her room, preferring instead to sack out in a sleeping bag on the floor.

And the worst part was that there was nothing more they could do for her.

They'd decided not to risk taking her to a hospital. Her curse could draw any monster within miles, and they would place innocent people at risk. What could they do for her there, anyway? No doctor would know how to treat the molecular damage breaking down her body. Ash was doing all he could just to keep her alive, the angel always maintaining constant contact with her body, diverting all his torc's energy to his power of healing.

Ben left his room and hurried to the kitchen. He heated the leftover coffee and poured two mugs, then headed to Emma's room.

Chase glanced up with bloodshot eyes from Emma's bedside as Ben walked in. He handed his grateful cousin and Ashriel each a mug. "Any change?"

Chase shook his head.

"Need me for anything? If not, I'm going for a run, guys, before I lose it."

Chase ran a hand through his hair. It stayed mussed in tufts and clumps, and his beard and mustache were unkept. When had the poor guy last taken a shower?

"Go ahead. But do me a fave, and before you go, bring me something to eat. Don't care what. Long as it ain't green."

"Sure, I'll make you a sandwich. I'm gonna make something decent for dinner when I get back. We won't do her any good if we drop from malnutrition."

Chase gazed at Emma's pale face, his bloodshot eyes brimming, his features wreathed in sadness. He shrugged helplessly. "Not doing her much good now."

His heart aching for Emma and for his cousin, Ben gave Chase's shoulder a squeeze and hurried back to the kitchen to make him a tuna sandwich. He peered into the freezer and took out a lasagna to make for dinner. He wished he had fresh salad, but he'd make do with frozen broccoli. Chase was eating green with dinner, whether he liked it or not.

Noting the freezer's meager contents, he sighed. The only meat left was a split deer carcass hanging in the frozen food locker. Meat was essential. He didn't want to make the long drive to the grocery store, not while things with Emma were at such a crisis point, but he had to make sure they stayed healthy and strong, and protein was vital. He'd bagged the buck in August but hadn't had a chance to butcher it properly before they were called out on assignment. He unloaded one side of the venison from the meat locker and left it on the cart in the kitchen to defrost. He'd take care of it later.

He took Chase the sandwich, an apple, and a glass of milk. "Okay, I'm heading out. Won't be more than an hour. I'll have my phone."

He changed into his running clothes and shoulder holster, pocketed his phone and knife, transferred his gun from his thigh holster, and ran down the stairs to the front entry. After putting on a warm hoodie, he muttered the magical incantation that unlocked the heavy iron door and moved outside into the sunshine with a sigh of relief. He made sure the door closed securely behind him and headed down the pebbled path that led to the driveway at a brisk pace. Reveling in the fresh air, he sucked in several deep breaths. *God*, he needed this!

The air was chilly, but the sun was warm on his back, and the cloudless sky above the mountains looked impossibly blue. He considered listening to music as he ran but decided to enjoy the sounds of nature instead—the breeze stirring Ponderosa pine needles and rustling the last of the autumn leaves, which clung stubbornly to the trees; a skyborne vee of migrating Canadian geese honking to one another; the lonely cry of a circling hawk.

He jogged along the switchback road leading down the mountain. At the base of the mountain, where an old logging road led to the highway, he automatically braced himself for the strong tingling sensation that centered on his upper chest as his Templar sigil brand allowed him to pass through the magical domed barrier that protected the citadel. He turned around, jogging in place for a moment.

It never ceased to amaze him.

The magical barrier, a dome that encapsulated the mountain and extended to encompass the adjacent woodlands, completely camouflaged the citadel and any trace of the road going up the mountain. Anyone passing by would see only a steep, rocky, brush-cluttered slope.

The muted whirr of a helicopter reached his ears. The forestry service, making their usual rounds, hopefully. No sign of smoke on the skyline. As he ran along the side of the seldom-traveled logging road, the rhythmic movement brought his lax muscles to life, and his pumping heart made his blood sing and surge through his veins. He emptied his mind and concentrated on the physical sensations. Felt so damn good!

But as he ran, his unruly thoughts circled back to Emma. And he did something he hadn't done in a long time, not since he was twelve—not since the nightmarish day he laid his parents and brother to rest.

He prayed.

Please, God. Please don't take her away from us. I have to believe that our paths crossed for a reason. I have to believe there's a plan somewhere in all of this pain and chaos. Why would you give Chase a soulmate only to rip her away from him? Haven't they both suffered enough? Please have mercy just this once. Please!

He harnessed the sadness and anger and exploded into a sprint, pushing himself to his limit until he was breathless, until his heart battered his ribs and his calves and thighs burned like fire. Exercise was important. He needed to stay strong mentally and physically. Chase was floundering, and if Emma died? He had to be there for his cousin to help him pick up the pieces.

Again, the sound of a helicopter. It seemed closer this time. He stopped running and jogged in place, searching the sky in every direction. Soundwaves would bounce between the mountains, so without a visual, it was impossible to figure out which direction the sound came from. No sign that anything was amiss. But was that a trace of smoke in the air? He stopped jogging and sniffed.

Nothing. Just his imagination.

But even the imagined smell of smoke took him back in time...

He remembered that day nearly five years earlier as if it were yesterday—shouts and screams, gunfire and the clash of swords, his heart thundering and his parched throat tight and stinging, as much from fear as from the swirling motes of hot air that carried stinging embers and gray woodsmoke that clogged his lungs and blurred his vision.

The all-hands-on-deck emergency summons had come only two weeks before he would graduate with dual degrees in computer programming and cyber security, but Michael's order had brooked no refusal. While a week earlier, Ben had been sipping chai lattes on the quad and discussing string theory, now bullets whizzed past his head and flaming arrows rained down around him.

Would he live to hold his diplomas in his hand?

Knights from three citadels fought side by side, defending Polaris Citadel, which had fallen prey to psychic espionage by a remote viewer—a new tactic by the enemy—who had gained the incantation to disarm the fortress's magical security dome. The Illuminati surrounded them on three sides, and a wall of flame would soon block the only way to safety. Michael, watching from above, gave the order to fall back and regroup within the citadel's gates.

With a thundering crash, a dead oak tree exploded into a towering column of flame as its dry body fed the ravenous fire. Blistering flames consumed grass and trees, eating up every inch of the land surrounding the citadel. "Chase! Ben! Follow me!" Uncle George fired round after round at the enemy force as his son and nephew, aces at virtual battle practice but still inexperienced in actual combat, made their way through the chaotic melee to his side. "Keep down!" He ushered the boys in front of him, and they steadily made their way toward the citadel's gate.

From the corner of his eye, Ben saw movement—a demon sniper in a burning tree, the Hell-spawned creature oblivious to the intense heat and flames. Ben's sharp eye and mathematician's brain estimated the trajectory of the demon's aim. It was centered on *his* chest! Frozen in fear, he braced for impact as the bullet burst from the gun. He was knocked to the ground, but it wasn't the bullet that hit him. It was Uncle George who threw himself in front of Ben and took the bullet meant for his nephew.

Although Ben and Chase prayed frantically for Ashriel, the angel didn't respond. Chase sobbed as he kneeled by his father, who lay in a pool of his own blood. Uncle George held up a shaky hand to draw another knight's attention, a hulking mountain of a man who stood nearby. "Alec! Get Chase to safety now!"

The knight tried to pull Chase away from his father's side, but Chase was having none of it. So, the enormous knight simply tossed him over his shoulder and strode away toward the citadel as Chase yelled and kicked and pummeled his back.

Uncle George grabbed Ben's shirt in a bloody fist and pulled him close. "It's my time. Swear it, Ben. Swear to me, you'll watch out for him. He's Laird now. He needs you. Make sure he's prepared for the responsibility. Make sure he has an heir to carry on." Uncle George took a shuddering, wheezy breath. Bloody foam trickled from the sides of his mouth and coated his lips. "And take care of Aunt Sarah and the twins for me. Swear it, Ben, so I can rest in peace."

Ben's heart broke even more. Severe blood loss was clouding Uncle George's mind, confusing him. Aunt Sarah and the twins had been dead for years. As tears ran down his face for the man who raised him into adulthood, Ben pulled his knife and sliced his palm. He pressed his hand to the bloody hole in his beloved uncle's chest, over the bullet that would have ended his own life. "A Templar blood oath, Uncle. I swear it."

Ben shook off the terrible memories and continued his run. When his phone pinged to signal that a half hour had passed, he reluctantly turned around and headed back home.

An unmarked black-ops army helicopter hovered over a small clearing in the forest, the prop wash from the large chopper's tandem blades whipping the trees and sending leaves and pinecones flying. The pilot carefully maneuvered the craft to set down its heavy cargo: the manticore's tarped cage that hung suspended by cables from the Boeing CH-47D Chinook.

"Careful!" Senator Zyro yelled. "Precious cargo."

"Yes, sir!" The experienced pilot set the cage on the ground with barely a bump. He pressed the button on the hand controller that released the cable and ascended high above the trees, the cage's tarp, connected to the cable, pulled up with it.

Zyro leaned over and clapped the pilot on the shoulder. "Good job. What's your rank, son?"

The pilot pushed the sleeve of his flight jacket up to show the tattoo on his inner arm, a triangle that contained the Illuminati's all-seeing eye. Zyro nodded. "Expect a promotion."

"Thank you, Senator."

Zyro pulled a remote control from his coat pocket. "Time for my pet to take a walk." He peered down at the cage as he pressed the button to open the cage's door. When the manticore burst out and ran into the trees—and toward Orion Citadel—Zyro laughed with glee. He loved it when a plan came off without a hitch.

Ben ambled up the pebble path to the citadel's front entry. With a sigh, he paused and turned around, drinking in the stunning mountain and valley views that always bolstered his mood. The sun was setting, bathing him in golden rays. A flock of blackbirds broke from the trees and flew overhead, circling several times before taking off toward the east.

If only the peaceful interlude didn't have to end. But duty called, pulling him back to reality and his worry about Emma. He felt guilty now for leaving her, although there was nothing he could do for her, and if her condition worsened, Chase would have called him. He turned and spoke the incantation to open the door.

When the lock clicked, he pushed the heavy door open and moved to step inside, but a beautiful sound distracted him, like a cross between a trumpet and a flute, a lilting, lyrical, clarion sound like nothing he'd ever heard before. The sound was intoxicating, filling him with warmth and a sudden calm. All worry, all thought of duty melted away, leaving only peace and wonder.

He turned and, with mild curiosity—but absolutely no fear—watched an animal approach. It was an unusual creature, and it looked somewhat familiar, but he couldn't place it.

The creature thrust its tail forward, shooting a spike deep into Ben's shoulder. There was no pain, only a dull thud, and a pleasant, cool, liquid sensation flowed through his body. The world tilted as he sank bonelessly to the stone floor of the citadel's entry, his body straddling the doorway. He stared up at the heavy iron chandelier that hung suspended from the ceiling in the entry hall, making a mental note to dust the cobwebs.

The beautiful sound ended, and so did Ben's stupor. Horror flooded his body with adrenaline, but he couldn't move, couldn't speak, and couldn't even turn his eyes. He was paralyzed! He blinked automatically, and he was breathing, but he couldn't control either. His mind clearing, he remembered where he'd seen this creature before, in the pages of a book of extinct monsters. A manticore!

The enormous creature moved to stand over him, pausing for a few seconds to sniff and lick his cheek. Was it *tasting him?* Ben stared up at an enormous mouth filled with dual rows of yellow, razor-sharp teeth. Malodorous saliva dripped from its mouth and down its gray beard as it growled low in its throat—a harsh, grinding sound like rusty, unlubricated ball bearings slamming around in a metal housing. Stark fear made Ben's throat fill with acid. Would it eat him alive?

His gaze landed on the the thick collar around the beast's neck—a collar with a small video camara attached to it. What the hell? *The Illuminati!* The beast's breath reeked like rotting meat; a glob of thick saliva plopped onto his cheek and oozed down his neck. Fighting panic and nausea, he prayed frantically in his mind for Ashriel. If he heaved, he'd likely drown in his own vomit. *Ash! Help! A manticore! Help me! I'm paralyzed!*

The manticore raised its head and sniffed. Another low growl rumbled in its throat. The creature seemed to forget all about him as its creepy, human-like blue eyes narrowed. He stepped over Ben and walked through the front door.

Ben's heart slammed against his ribs, and he screamed in his mind, but he could do nothing as danger entered the citadel.

Chapter Fifteen

MINDLESSLY STARING AT THE TV in Emma's room, Chase jerked upright in his chair as an alarm on his cellphone went off. It was the ringtone he had linked to the citadel's security system. He grabbed his phone off Emma's dresser. The front door was ajar. They'd set the system to sound an alert if the door was open for more than one full minute. "What the hell? It's not like Benji to forget to close the door. But I guess we're all running on empty."

Ashriel nodded. "Better close it."

Chase yawned as he pocketed his phone. "Yeah. Need to stretch my legs and hit the head anyway." He leaned over and smoothed his hand over Emma's hair. "Be right back, sweetheart. Any improvement, Ash?"

"No." Ash flexed his neck and switched from his right hand to his left, always keeping one hand in contact with Emma's shoulder. "She drifts in and out of consciousness. But she hasn't worsened in the last few hours, either."

"Well, that's something, I guess." He took in the angel's haggard appearance. "Dude, you okay?"

"Like you said, I'm running on empty. I'm routing every bit of my power that regenerates to my healing power."

"I'll bring coffee." He paused at the door. "Lock this behind me. I'm sure it's nothing, but let's follow intruder protocol. Better safe than sorry." He left Emma's room, stopped at the powder room, and trudged down the stairs to the entry level. Intending to shut the front door, he passed into the foyer and froze.

What the fuck?

Benji lay sprawled and motionless on the entry floor, with the front door wide open!

Thankful for his training that required a knight to always be armed—with a few notably naked exceptions—Chase drew the Beretta 92FS from his ever-present thigh holster, held it in front of him in a two-handed grip, and raced in a serpentine pattern across the foyer, scanning the area for intruders as he ran. Seeing nothing, he fell to his knees beside Benji, relieved to see no sign of blood. "What happened?"

Benji didn't answer, staring up at him with wild eyes. But except that he wasn't moving or talking, his cousin looked fine. Then he saw the small object protruding from his shoulder. It looked like some kind of polished stick. The wound wasn't bleeding, and his chest rose and fell with regular breathing, so Chase didn't remove the object yet. It could do more harm than good if the object had damaged any blood vessels.

He put his ear to his cousin's chest; his heartbeat was strong and regular. "Benji, what the..." Something foul-smelling insulted his nose. He scanned the area. Across the wide entry hall, right in front of the double steps that led up to the armory, was a huge pile of fresh poop. A second later, something metallic hit stone—a noise that sounded like it came from the kitchen. A stainless-steel bowl rolling on the floor?

Something alive—and big, from the size of that pile of crap—was inside the citadel. His training kicked in. *First, secure your safety and the safety of anyone alive.* He hurried outside and scanned the area, seeing nothing out of place. "Okay, I don't know what this thing is, but I think you'll be safer outside for now. No worries, I'll keep an eye on you." He grabbed Benji's feet and dragged him the rest of the way out of the door. Not an easy feat. "Dude, you weigh a freakin' ton." He snapped a photo of the object protruding from Benji's shoulder, leaned down, and patted his cousin on the cheek. "Hang tight. I'll come back for you as soon as I take care of this bitch."

He accessed the security system and locked the camera feed from the entryway on his phone's screen. Perfect. Ben lay in plain sight of the camera. He palmed his gun and quickly scanned the exterior area again. Finding no obvious danger, he went back inside and closed and locked the front door. Gun at the ready, he rushed back up the stairs to Emma's room and gave a quick succession of three and then two knocks.

When the door opened, he flung himself inside and relocked it.

"What's wrong?" Ashriel asked.

"Something's in here, in the kitchen, sounds like, and it got Benji in the shoulder with some kind of spike or thorn. I think he'll be all right. I hope. He's paralyzed but conscious and breathing. Left him outside for now." He put his gun on the dresser and showed Ash the picture he'd taken of the spike. "What can do this? Whatever the hell it is, it's a big sonofabitch. It left a pile of crap you wouldn't believe."

"Only thing I know of that size that shoots a stinger that paralyzes its victim is a manticore. But they died off thousands of years ago."

"Maybe this one missed the memo." Chase accessed the database of creatures Ben had downloaded onto both their phones. "Damn! Not in here. Talk to me, Ash. Kill it, how?"

"I...I don't know. I've never encountered one."

"Well, *fuck!*" Chase grabbed the pistol and headed for the door. "I'll have to check the archives. Or maybe Benji has some info on his computer about this thing."

"Don't." Emma's raspy voice, barely a whisper, had him whirling and hurrying toward the bed.

Ashriel supported her head and held a cup while she took a sip of water. Just that slight movement had her panting. After a moment, she spoke again.

Chase had to drop to his knees and lean in close to hear her weak voice. His heart stuttered when she opened her eyes. Blood streaked the whites and pooled in the corners; a single blood tear trailed down her temple. He'd had that happen after getting his nose fractured and knew it was from broken blood vessels, but she hadn't endured any trauma to her face. *God, what was happening to her?*

"Only way to kill...manticore...beheading...silver blade," she rasped. "But you don't know...what you're...up against. Its song...relaxation so deep...you'd be defenseless...must be how...got Ben. Will wear off...twenty-four hours... Ben okay. But careful. Spikes shoot...twenty feet...regenerate immediately."

"Sweetheart, you're amazing." He leaned down to kiss her forehead. When she didn't respond, for a panicked second, he feared the worst. Her eyes were closed again, but the shallow and rapid rise and fall of her chest told him she was breathing.

Chase moved to the door, pulled his earbuds from his pocket, and selected hard rock music on his phone. But there was a second or two of silence between each song. *Dammit!* That wouldn't work; he had to block out the manticore noise completely. He had a ten-hour box fan noise recording he sometimes used to help himself sleep better when away from home and selected that instead, turning the volume to max.

"Okay, I got this. Listen to me, Ash, and this is an order. Your only priority is Emma, you hear me? This thing's as old as a freakin' dinosaur, so I don't know if her curse is gonna draw it. But if he comes after her, this door should hold him off for a while, and I'll close every door I can between her and it." He took a second to appreciate the centuries-old craftsmanship of the five-inch-thick, solid-oak door. "I don't care what happens. If that thing gets through me and you think it's gonna get through this door, you take her and wing the hell outta here, and don't worry about us. You got me?"

"I hear you. And I wish I could comply, Laird. But I don't have enough power to fly or to teleport."

"*Crap!*" Chase raked his fingers through his hair. "So, I assume you can't smite, either."

"You assume correctly."

"Okay, Plan B. I'll recon. Maybe I can shut some doors and contain it for a while. If we can, we'll take Emma down to the dungeon. I doubt this thing can chew through iron doors. I hope. Don't know what we'll do from there, but one thing at a time. Got your cell?"

"Yes."

"I'll keep you posted. If you don't hear from me again within an hour, assume I'm dead and go with Plan C." Chase couldn't believe he was saying this, but desperate times. "Summon Michael. Yeah, he'll probably throw you into a black hole when he finds out about Emma, but maybe he'll save her and Benji first."

"Agreed. Good luck, Chase."

"Thanks. I'll need it." Chase firmly pushed the earbuds into his ears, the blaring static noise sure to block any sound. He drew his gun, and even though regular bullets wouldn't kill the manticore, they might slow it down. He paused and looked back at Emma, his heart aching.

Would this be the last time he ever saw her?

He hurried to her side and kissed her gently on the cheek. At the door, he took one last look over his shoulder, and then he slipped out of the room.

The white noise that would protect him from the manticore's song was a double-edged sword; it spooked him not to rely on his hearing. His heart pounded as he snuck downstairs and down the hallway toward the armory, closing every door he passed through.

He made it to his destination, side-stepped around the dung heap, and peered into the armory. Good, empty. Hurrying inside, he eased the thick oak door shut behind him. He reloaded his gun with a magazine of silver bullets—just in case they proved more effective than regular ones—put two more mags in his pocket, and he grabbed a wicked-looking silver scimitar that hung on the wall along with other swords and cutlasses. Its edge was razor sharp, and it had a good heft, just what he needed to behead a large animal. But how to get within striking distance and not get nailed with a stinger? He had to buy himself time to figure it out. But first, he had to determine his quarry's location.

Before he slipped out of the armory, he took several deep, calming breaths, then sneaked down the hallway that led to the kitchen. He paused just outside the door and mentally prepared himself, praying to his Templar ancestors for guidance as his heart pounded, knowing his lethal opponent may lie just beyond that doorway. But a grin slowly spread as his Templar blood sizzled and rushed through his veins, and he welcomed the white-hot, focused rage that accompanied the throes of battle—a rage that gave him strength, focus, and clarity of mind.

He was a warrior.

He was born for this.

He raised the Beretta and peeked into the kitchen. The manticore *was* there.

The creature's size, demonic-looking horns, and foul stench sent a chill down Chase's spine. At the same time, he bit back a chuckle at the ridiculous picture it made—the manticore lay on the floor, gnawing on a frozen deer carcass like a happy dog with a bone. *Perfect.* Fido had a chew toy to keep him busy for a while. But the manticore's shark-like jaws were making quick work of the frozen venison, and the wicked-looking spikes on the monster's insectoid tail sobered him.

Should he burn a mag into the creature's brain as it lay there? It was tempting, but he wasn't sure if silver bullets would do the trick. Might just piss it off, and then what?

No, it was too risky. Might not get a second chance; he had to wait for the sure kill. The clock was ticking. The manticore was already halfway through the frozen deer, consuming bone and all. Chase shut the solid oak kitchen door as quietly as possible, then he turned and ran like hell, throwing glances behind him to see if the creature was in pursuit.

He skidded to a stop in the Great Hall as a voice in his head shouted. Dad's voice—a memory from his boyhood. *Slow down, son! You can't find the right path unless you know your destination. Think before you act!*

He took a few deep breaths. Okay, what was his destination? What did he want to accomplish? *Duh.* He wanted to kill the fucking manticore. He had the weapon to do it. His problem was getting close enough to do the deed and not get himself killed.

He evaluated the collection of ancient shields that hung on the walls, dismissing them as too small or too unwieldy. He was heading back to the armory to grab one of their modern, transparent acrylic shields when his gaze fell upon the twin suits of armor that flanked the fireplace.

The suits were imbued with an ancient Templar spell that made them impervious to mundane weapons like knives and bullets. But would they withstand the manticore's biologic and possibly magical spikes?

No clue, but he had no better option. He couldn't cover his entire body with a handheld shield. It took over twenty minutes to put on one of the heavy suits. How the hell did their ancestors walk around in these getups? Of course, they had squires to help them. He dripped with sweat by the time he figured out how to put it on and had maneuvered himself into the heavy metal rig. He just hoped he could walk without tipping over.

He checked his phone to make sure Ben was okay before he put on the helmet and pulled on the heavy metal gauntlets. *Shit*, just in the nick of time. Through the eye slots of the helmet, he spotted the manticore standing in the archway, bristling and snarling, its tail curled over its back. *Holy crap!* Hadn't taken long for it to get through the solid-oak kitchen door.

In a lightning-fast move, the manticore flicked its scorpion-like tail forward. Several heavy thuds against his chest knocked Chase back. He struggled for a few seconds to keep himself upright, but he stayed on his feet, and he wasn't injured. The spikes had hit the armor and fallen harmlessly to the floor.

Crouched like a tiger, the creature stalked him.

Chase glanced into the antique floor mirror that leaned against the wall opposite him and assessed the damage. The suit may have stopped the spikes, but there were deep dents where each one hit. Repeated hits in the same spot would likely result in penetration.

He raised the scimitar and hoped he'd get a chance to use it.

But the manticore stopped.

Almost comically, it cocked its head from side to side, like a confused dog, as it stared at him. It shuddered and shook its head, and then looked toward the arch, sniffing the air. It raked the floor with razor-sharp claws and bared its hideous teeth, saliva dripping onto the scarred hardwood, looking back and forth between Chase and the archway. Finally, the manticore turned and walked toward the arch that led to the main staircase, seeming to forget all about him.

Chase braced for an attack. Was this a fakeout or a hunting tactic? Would it turn around and rush him? But seconds ticked past and turned into minutes. The manticore really had left the Great Hall altogether.

What the hell?

Understanding hit like a fist to his gut—*Emma's curse!*

Ashriel tensed at a strange noise. A scraping sound reverberated through the stone walls and floor, causing a small vibration under his feet. Concentrating, he tried to place the sound. He jumped as his cellphone pinged with a text from Chase.

> Curse is drawing the bitch! Clawed thru kitchen door in like 10 min. Got 4 doors between it and you. Working on it.

Ash pocketed his phone and gazed down at Emma. He'd never been so helpless—or useless—in all his life. He could barely feel the slight movement of her chest as she took each shallow breath. Pale and thin, she was barely alive, sustained only by the tiny amount of power he transferred into her body through his hand.

He drew his sword. The crystalline blade wasn't made of pure silver, but God himself crafted it. It might kill the beast. But if he had to fight, he would surely be forced to lift his hand from Emma's chest. She would die within seconds.

He was tempted to call for Michael.

But he had his orders from the Laird of Orion Citadel, and he was duty-bound to obey. He understood Chase's reasoning and agreed with him. Calling upon the archangel would be what Chase called a hail Mary pass, a last-ditch attempt with little chance of success.

Ashriel wouldn't do that and risk the archangel's wrath until he was certain the manticore would breach the last door.

He had to give Chase a chance to save them.

Chase found that trying to lure the beast away from its intent to reach Emma proved to be a waste of time. Using himself as bait, even slicing his hand to entice the beast with the scent of his blood, was of no use. All it earned him was a bloody palm and another set of dents in the suit of armor.

The manticore was obsessed with getting to Emma and viewed him only as a minor annoyance as it clawed at the door.

Chase lumbered as fast as he could in the suit of armor back to the Great Hall. Maybe he could find a spell to immobilize the creature. If only his cousin wasn't laid out, he could use the Runes of Calyx against the sonofabitch. Well, no use in wishing. The runes obeyed only Benji.

Precious minutes ticked past as he scrolled through the spells Benji and Emma had cataloged on the computer. *Shit*, there were hundreds of them! As acid churned in his belly, one spell caught his eye. His heart pounded with triumph as he read the description. The spell could transfer any bewitchment, hex, talisman, charm—or curse—from one person to another, lasting until the next sunrise.

But with few exceptions, magic demanded a price be paid, and this one was no exception. The spell made one beholden to the goddess Hecate, the ancient Grecian goddess of magic and witchcraft. Her price? One year of the conjurer's life would be spent in servitude, payable at the goddess's convenience.

What? For a harrowing few seconds, the world tilted, and he got tunnel vision as he stared down at the page. An entire *year* of his life, bowing and scraping to a freakin' old-time goddess? And there was no mention of when he would serve that year. Would it be at the end of his lifetime, or would something immediately whisk him away to wherever Hecate presently set up housekeeping?

He needed time to kill the manticore!

He checked his phone. Benji looked fine, but he'd spent half an hour searching the database. The manticore would soon tear at the last door if it wasn't already.

Well, fate had handed him a gun, and he'd be a fool to toss it away. He prayed it was loaded and wouldn't misfire and blow up in his face. He gave a humorless laugh as he lifted the visor and wiped the sweat from his brow. "Necessity is the mutha of decision. I like that. Gonna put that on a T-shirt. Maybe I'll get real lucky and live to wear it."

And maybe the penance of such a sacrifice would be exactly what he needed to look at himself in the mirror and see a noble knight once again.

Maybe then the nightmares would stop.

He dragged the second suit of armor until it faced the fireplace, rubbed blood from his still-bleeding hand onto it, then gathered the equipment and ingredients the spell required. He followed the instructions step by step: lit a peat moss fire in a marble bowl and added dried sage, three tears of a griffin, a hummingbird feather, and a few drops of his blood, then recited the incantation. The fire blazed up and died out, emptying the bowl and sending an iridescent purple cloud toward the ceiling.

Moving as quickly as the suit of armor allowed, he positioned himself to wait just inside the arch, concealed behind the wall.

If the spell worked—and that was a big *if*, because they didn't always work, he'd learned over the years—the manticore would now be attracted to him, not Emma.

It would smell the blood lure on the decoy suit of armor and give Chase the opportunity to make his move.

That was the plan, anyway.

Chase waited, hoping for the best.

Minutes ticked past. Sweat trickled down his body and made him itch in several extremely uncomfortable places. *Come on, Fido. Here, boy, here, boy...*

Nothing.

He didn't feel any different, either. Maybe the spell was a dud? What the fuck would he do now? But then there was movement on the floor—an enormous shadow moving closer to the archway.

Chase backed up and held his breath. Without his sense of hearing, it was pure torture waiting for the beast to show itself. He held the sword high, ready to bring it down on the manticore's neck when it passed through the arch.

The manticore's head poked through the archway, sniffing. It moved toward the decoy.

Chase swung the scimitar with all his considerable might. As the beast's severed head rolled across the room and came to rest near the fireplace, he pulled the helmet off and shouted a cry of triumph. Now that the danger was past, he struggled to get himself out of the suit of armor. Breath heaving, soaked in sweat, he set the last piece of armor on the floor and sank into a chair to call Ash. "Got him. Coast is clear."

He hung up and laughed. "And to think, I used to wish these freakin' suits of armor were in the scrap heap when Mom used to make us polish 'em." He looked heavenward, kissed two fingers, and flicked them skyward. "Thanks, Mom. Owe you big time."

He pushed himself up to go get his cousin, but something caught his eye. A collar lay on the floor near the beast's head—a collar fitted with a camera. *"Son of a bitch!"* He snatched up the bloody collar and growled deep in his throat as a medallion like a dog's rabies vaccination tag glinted in the light. He wiped away the blood and experienced a moment of rage so profound that his vision blurred, his pulse pounded in his ears, and heat rushed through his body like a flash fire. His lips pulled back, baring his teeth in a feral snarl.

The tag was etched with an ouroboros and the letter Z.

Zyro!

Chase aimed the camera at his face. His voice reverberated with fury. "Zyro, you fucking bastard, you just signed your own death warrant." Chase grabbed a silver bullet from his pocket and held it in front of the camera lens. "This bullet's got your name on it." He turned the camera toward the dead manticore and then back to his face. "Epic. Fucking. Fail. Nice try, *Zero*, but you'll have to do better than that. You think you're all safe and protected in that fancy office up on Capitol Hill? Be warned, you dick. It won't be today, and it probably won't be tomorrow, but I'm coming for you. Real soon. And when I do, I'm gonna kill you. *With this bullet*. I'm gonna sleep with it under my pillow and dream about sinking it into your brain. My face is gonna be the last thing you see before the fires of Hell."

Chase dropped the camera on the floor and stomped on it with his boot heel until there was nothing left but fragments.

Emma woke up to find Ashriel standing next to her bed, gazing down at her and holding her hand. Chase stood at the foot of the bed, staring at her like she was some kind of fascinating zoo exhibit.

Both looked terrible.

"Emma? How do you feel?" Ashriel asked.

"Thirsty. *Hungry*." She sat up and scooted back against the pillows. "What's going on?" Her voice was a rasp. Why was her throat so dry? She grasped the bottle of water Ashriel gave her and downed almost the whole thing in one go. Something pinched her hand. Her eyes widened when she saw the IV needle taped to her skin. *What the heck?* Her gaze swung back to Ashriel. "What'd I miss?" She was astonished to see his eyes brim with tears, and he vanished. "Ash?" She looked at Chase. "Why'd he leave? Chase, what's going on?"

Shaking his head, he ground the heels of his hands against his eyes. Was he crying, too? What in the world had happened?

He lowered his hands. "You don't remember?" His eyes were bloodshot, and he had dark circles. His usually shiny black hair was dull and rumpled, and dark stubble shadowed his cheeks and neck around an uncharacteristically scruffy mustache and beard.

"No. What's wrong?" Oh, no! Her heart stuttered. "Is Ben all right?"

"Yeah, he's recovering in his room. We had an intruder. A manticore got in, and it—"

"I remember now!" Relief that Ben was okay slammed right back into panic. "Is it still here?"

"No worries, sweetheart. I killed it. With your help. We didn't know how to take it down, but you did. Probably saved us all."

She blew out a sigh and pressed a hand to her chest, where her heart still pounded. Thank God they were all okay. "Yeah, I'm a whiz at Trivial Pursuit. Especially the supernatural creatures category."

"I'll bet."

"But if everything's okay now, why did Ash fly off like that?"

"Probably just needed some fresh air. He hasn't left your side, not even for a second, this whole time."

"Whole time? What do you mean?"

Chase sat next to her on the edge of the bed. "You almost died, sweetheart. It was touch-and-go for a while. You scared the crap out of us."

Stunned, she rubbed her hands over her face. "Oh, God. How long?"

"Just about nine days."

Nine days? It took her a few seconds to absorb. It seemed like she'd fallen asleep only a few hours ago. And Ash had stayed with her all that time? A rush of emotion had her blinking back tears. She gestured to the IV needle, pinching her hand. "This thing hurts."

Chase carefully removed the needle and put a bandage over the puncture wound. "Better?"

"Yes. Thank you." She reached for his hand and drew him close enough that she could lay her hand along the side of his face. She searched his bloodshot eyes. The poor guy looked ready to drop where he stood. "Are you all right?"

He covered her hand with his own, closed his eyes, and leaned into her palm. His weary sigh made her heart ache. "I am now."

She understood. He'd nearly lost Ben—his cousin, his only remaining family. He had to be greatly relieved, even more than she was. "Why don't you go get some sleep?"

"Can't yet. Gotta keep an eye on Benji for a while."

"Can I help? I could sit with him so you can sleep."

"Maybe after you eat something."

"Okay. Would you mind leaving for just a little while? I want to change my clothes."

Chase nodded and headed for the door, but hesitated. "Know what? Lemme see you get up and walk around first. Gotta make sure you're steady on those pins."

She walked around the room twice, with him shadowing her every step. She could tell from the looseness of her clothes that she'd lost significant weight. "I feel skinny—and hungry—but perfectly fine otherwise. Like I woke up on a regular morning."

"Good. Just take it easy and stay in bed until you've eaten. Don't rush it, okay?"

"I won't. Promise."

He saw her safely back in bed. "I'll go get you some chow. What would you like?"

"Just something light. Toast and scrambled eggs, a cup of tea?"

"You got it."

He left and closed the door behind him. She sent out a silent prayer. *Ashriel, I'm alone now. Please come back.* With a flutter of wings, he appeared, but he stood on the other side of the room. He tried to hide it, but she could tell he'd been crying.

An angel crying?

Over her?

She slid out of bed and padded across the room to him. Her arms went around his waist, and she rested her cheek against the warm, solid wall of his chest.

Taking a ragged breath, he wrapped her in his arms and pressed a kiss to the top of her head. "We were losing you. And there was nothing I could do to stop it."

"Then why am I okay now?"

"I honestly don't know. Something...changed, and suddenly, my power worked and healed you completely."

She lifted her head and gazed up at Ashriel's face. She was deeply moved that he cared so much, and she saw the anxiety still in his eyes. She needed to take it away. "Well, it's over. I'm fine now, Ash; truly, I am." She reached up and patted his cheek, sighing in her heart over the pleasure of touching him. "I'm sorry I worried you. But you're not gonna get rid of me so easily. I'm afraid you're stuck with me. Because that's what friends do, Ash. They stick."

He lowered his brow to hers and took a deep, shuddering breath. "Yes, they do."

Chapter Sixteen

RICHARD ZYRO LEISURELY SIPPED imported organic coffee as he lounged on the sofa in his private office on Capitol Hill. No one would have guessed that he could barely contain the rage boiling within him as he waited for his guest to arrive. The intercom buzzed. "Yes?"

"Senator, you have a visitor. He says he has an appointment, but you asked me to keep this afternoon clear, and I don't have him on your calendar. A Mr. Alteo."

"Yes, he's expected. I forgot to tell you. Please show him in. Go ahead and take your lunch break. In fact, take the rest of the afternoon off. It's Friday. Get started on your weekend early. You deserve it."

"Yes, Senator. Thank you. Oh, your father called while you were in your last meeting. He confirmed for Saturday morning and said tee time is ten sharp, followed by lunch at the clubhouse. Shall I call President Zyro back to confirm before I leave?"

"No need. I'll call my father this evening and confirm myself."

The secretary opened the door and stepped aside, allowing a short, bald, muscular man to enter. "Senator, here is Mr. Alteo."

"Thank you, Tricia. See you Monday."

"Have a good weekend, sir."

Neither man spoke. The man—the demon—had the prominent nose bridge, deeply tan skin, and protrusive lips of an Egyptian man. Richard's gaze lingered for several seconds on the tattoo of a three-inch scarab beetle decorating the demon's thick neck. After Tricia left, Richard rose and left his office, crossed the reception room to the door that led to the hallway, and made sure the door was locked. This conversation required the utmost privacy. He returned to his office, closed the door, and gestured to his guest to have a seat. "Would you care for a drink, Alteo-ra?"

The man bowed deeply. "No, thank you, Exalted One. I do not partake in alcohol. Nor do I sit."

Richard regained his seat on the sofa. He opened his mouth to speak, but his words caught in his throat. The scarab beetle tattoo was no longer on Alteo-ra's neck; it was on his cheek. He tapped his own cheek. "Explain."

Alteo-ra respectfully inclined his head. He held out a hand, palm up, pushed his shirtsleeve up to his elbow, and uttered several words Richard assumed were ancient Egyptian. The tattoo crawled off the demon's face, scuttled down his neck, and emerged on his bare forearm, coming to a stop in his palm. Several more unintelligible words, and the tattoo transmuted into a three-dimensional, living beetle that hissed and clacked its powerful mandible in a clearly threatening posture.

"A pet?" Zyro asked.

"Not precisely. Katado has many talents. As was our tradition, the priest placed him within my funerary mummy wrappings to help me navigate the spells within the Book of the Dead."

Richard held back a shudder. Creepy fucking thing. "Fascinating, but put it away. We have important matters to discuss."

The demon uttered several words. The living beetle became a tattoo again and returned to Alteo-ra's neck.

"I've heard interesting things about you. They say you're cunning. Ruthless. Tireless. And most of all, intelligent. Your tracking skills are legendary, as are your torture techniques. I can only hope these things are true."

"I shall endeavor to exceed your expectations."

"That would be wise. I want three humans eliminated. Two knights and a young woman. They're presently beyond my reach, locked up in a Templar citadel. I tried stealth and brute force and nearly succeeded, but the knight Chase Kincaid—"

Richard had to stop and take a sip of his brandy as his temper flared. He gave a small cough, pretending to soothe his throat with the drink. It wouldn't be appropriate—or wise—to show the weakness of emotion to a demon underling. "The knight Chase Kincaid is clever and strong. A worthy opponent. As is his cousin. And I understand you have a previous relationship with that particular Templar family."

"Indeed, I do. I killed Laird George Kincaid in the battle for Polaris Citadel."

"Excellent. I expect you to eliminate his son and nephew as well. And the woman they harbor. I don't care how you do it as long as it gets done. Beware of their guardian angel, Ashriel. We've enacted a spell that blocks the knights' prayers to him, and he lost his feathers, poor thing, so he can't fly, so that should make your task easier.

"But he is still powerful and dangerous. Use whatever means you deem necessary. Cost is no object. Bring me proof of their deaths—preferably their heads—and your future is assured. Bring me the bonus of the angel's head and the powerful torc he wears, and your future will be bright, indeed." He locked eyes with the demon. "However, fail me, and you'll regret it. Do we understand each other?"

Alteo-ra bowed deeply. "We do, your excellence. I shall not fail you."

"Good. The sooner, the better, but don't rush. I want it done right. I'll prepare a dossier with all the information I have. You'll be notified when it's ready."

"This may take time, your excellence. Knights are hidden from us and well protected."

"I am aware." Santana's warning about the woman was repeated in his memory. *She is the instrument of your death.* "You must not let the woman slip away. Don't be deceived by her gender. She's a worthy foe."

"Understood."

"Leave me."

The demon minion bowed yet again and backed out of the room, showing the proper deference for its master.

Smiling now, Richard poured another brandy and put his feet up.

Under a cloudy night sky, Ashriel rolled his wings into a banked position and circled above the rectangular cluster of low-slung, two-story brick buildings that made up the prison compound of Patroon Creek Correctional Facility in upstate New York. Selecting the largest building, which comprised a main hub with wing offshoots that formed a half-star, he made himself invisible and landed in the inmates' common room of the maximum-security prison. It was four in the morning, and the room was empty, although he could hear the clanking of pots and the murmur of voices from the nearby kitchen as the staff prepared breakfast.

His gaze took in the sterile, ugly, monotonous surroundings. Shiny gray walls and an equally shiny gray concrete floor. Bolted to the floor were rows of stainless-steel tables that seated four with attached, backless stools painted a dull blue. A flight above, thick blue bars cordoned off catwalks that encircled the area, the narrow walkways lined with cells. Heavy steel doors with tiny windows safely contained the convicts, two men per cell.

Ashriel had no idea where to begin his search. He opened himself up psychically, but the onslaught of brainwaves from the inmates was overpowering. So much rage! Even some of the dreams were nothing but violent, bloody, horrifying images. But just as he prepared to break the excruciating connection, a quiet voice caught his attention.

A voice lifted to God in praise.

Ashriel blocked out the chaos and zeroed in on that voice. He followed it to its source, down a long, bleak corridor to a cell where one man lay asleep on the top bunk, and a man who appeared to be in his early sixties kneeled on the concrete floor, his bald head bowed and his hands folded in prayer. A Bible lay on the man's bunk.

Still invisible, Ashriel phased through the cell bars, touched the sleeping man to ensure he remained asleep, and stood beside the praying man. He placed his palm above the man's head and read the man's thoughts, then opened a psychic connection so he could speak mind-to-mind and induce a state of calm. "Be not afraid, but do not speak aloud. I am Ashriel, and I am an angel of the Lord. You are a good man—an innocent man—and your prayer has been heard. Do you believe, Marcus?"

His tired, brown eyes glistening with tears, the man nodded.

"Then have faith. You will be delivered from this miscarriage of justice. I will help, but you must be patient. If I could, I would simply remove you from this terrible place, but I cannot. They would hunt you down. Miracles are not accepted in these times, so I must find the actual killer and bring him to human justice in order to clear your name. But I have another mission, and I must complete that task before I help you. In the meantime, you must say nothing of this visitation to anyone, not even your wife. Do you agree?"

Marcus nodded as tears coursed down his stubble-covered cheeks. *Thank you!*

"It is my honor and my sacred duty to help a righteous man in need. I must go now, but I will not forget you. Be at peace."

Ashriel left the good man and continued his search for the evil man he sought. There were fifteen hundred men incarcerated at the facility, and he had no time to walk up and down each cell block searching for one man. He needed to get home before Emma woke up.

There had to be an easier way to find his quarry.

He moved through the building, finally locating the guards' control room. Two men were on duty, sipping coffee, listening to talk radio, thumbing through magazines, and glancing only occasionally at the large bank of monitors fed by cameras placed throughout the prison.

On the wall behind the guards, a large clipboard held a thick computer printout that listed the inmates alphabetically by name and their cell assignments. Ashriel, still invisible, silently took the clipboard off its hook and quickly found the name he sought.

Vincent Russo.

His cell assignment was in the Special Housing Unit. Ashriel read further, learning that he was scheduled to be released on parole in two days' time. But the SHU was used to house inmates under disciplinary action. The notation said Russo was in solitary confinement because of repeated fighting with one fellow inmate in particular, Jarvis Obermeyer, who was also being kept in solitary. Fighting? Then why was Vincent being released on parole? Wasn't good behavior a major factor in such a decision?

He studied a map on the wall that showed the entire prison complex, found the SHU, and teleported himself there.

He found Russo sitting on the bunk in his one-man cell. It was odd that Russo was awake and alert when he should have been sleeping. Ashriel stared at the man who helped make Emma's life a nightmare—the man who had brutally murdered her stepfather and set her on a path to misery.

The man whose release from prison had been approved by the parole board even though he'd done nothing to earn it, bribed for their votes by Octavio Russo, no doubt.

His lip curling in distaste, Ashriel peeked into Vincent's mind and shuddered. This man had much blood on his hands and knew no remorse. Hate exploded within him. Never in his life had Ashriel wanted so much to cause someone pain!

The unexpected sound of careful footsteps drew Ashriel's attention. As they came closer, Russo moved to the door. Ashriel teleported to the corridor in time to see a prison guard pass a cellphone through the narrow slot in the cell door into Russo's waiting hand. "Ten minutes," the guard whispered.

Russo took the phone back to his bunk, sat down, and dialed.

Ashriel returned to the cell, his angelic hearing enabling him to hear both sides of the conversation.

"This better be important," Russo whispered. "I'm taking a serious fucking risk here."

"The Borello girl is alive," a man said.

"*What*? That's impossible. We had the pictures and her prints. They buried her body!"

"Yeah, we did, and they buried something. But unless she's got an identical twin, she ain't dead. The auto-search bots Kirby deployed way back for us to keep track of her just sounded the alarm. Guess he didn't bother deactivating the program when we all thought she was a stiff. I tell ya, I'm sittin' here looking at a series of still pics taken by a traffic cam of her walking into a grocery store in Colorado and then coming out again."

"I can't believe it!"

"Believe it. I called him first, and Kirby swears by those bots. He got us linked to just about every public camera system in the country. Said he uses the same facial recognition software the military uses. There's no mistake. It's her, all right."

"You tell my old man?"

"No, I wouldn't go over your head like that."

"Good, don't. He's likely to freak out, and I don't need that dying old fool fucking up my release. That psycho Obermeyer almost wasted me this time. If the guards hadn't pulled him offa me, I'd be countin' worms on the wrong side of the grass. I gotta get out of this fucking hole! No, we'll take care of this as soon as I'm out. I don't know how that little bitch pulled it off, but we'll find her. Gotta go." Russo ended the call, slipped the phone back to the guard, and paced the tiny cell.

Ashriel's hands fisted. *No, no, no!* All they had done, and now Emma was still in danger? And it was his fault for simply taking her out to the store? He hadn't considered the threat of modern technology, only that he could easily protect her from any preternatural creatures that her curse might attract. But a computer program watching for her face on nearly every surveillance camera in the country? And it would only get worse as biometric technology advanced. She'd never be able to leave the citadel. All her choices, taken away once again.

Enraged to the point of smiting, he took two steps forward before he hesitated. Taking the life of a human without authorization was against angelic law. If found guilty, he could be imprisoned or even put to death. But wasn't the string of murders and other terrible crimes that blackened this man's soul and the horrible tortures inflicted against Emma just cause for such a punishment? Most assuredly so!

The correct course of action would be to present his case to Michael and ask for the commander's approval. But he dared not. Michael didn't know anything about Emma or her death and subsequent resurrection at Ashriel's hands. Michael had been livid when Ashriel disobeyed his orders and rescued Chase—*the Kincaid Laird*—from Hell.

How much worse would he react regarding one human woman who was, to Michael, a nobody? What if Michael became so angry that he cast him into angelic prison, or worse? Russo would be free, and Emma would never be safe. And what about Chase and Ben? They needed him!

If only the guards hadn't intervened and the prisoner Obermeyer had murdered Vincent. That would have solved everything. Ashriel smiled grimly as a thought came to him. Perhaps there was another way to rid the world of Vincent Russo, a way that would not cast suspicion on him.

Yes, it was the perfect plan.

But first, he had to freeze the surveillance cameras in the corridor.

"Your turn or mine?" Ben hoped he'd lost count, and it was Chase's. He loathed washing dishes.

"Yours." Chase smiled cockily and shoveled a forkload of hash browns into his mouth.

"Ugh." Ben eyed the pile of dirty dishes in the sink again. Looked even bigger this time. "We're getting that new dishwasher soon, right?"

"Yeah, we'll go after breakfast. Just gotta see what parts I need first."

A little while later, Chase kneeled on the floor, disconnecting their old, broken dishwasher.

Ben sipped his second coffee and, as was his morning habit, logged into his laptop and checked his favorite news feeds. With a *beep*, a pop-up notification filled the center of the screen. "Something triggered one of my auto-alert search programs."

Chase waited and spread his hands. "Am I supposed to guess?"

"Hang on. *Son of a bitch*. Vincent Russo, serving time for the death of accountant Mario Borello, was found murdered at Patroon Creek Correctional Facility early this morning, severely beaten, and his throat slashed. Russo was scheduled to be released on parole. According to prison spokesperson Gail Jones, the body was discovered in the unlocked solitary confinement cell of another inmate, and Russo's cell was also found unlocked, although according to prison staff, the usual stringent lock-down protocols had been followed to the letter.

"New York State homicide investigators are working with the New York Department of Corrections Internal Investigative Division. So far, the murder has been deemed to have been committed by fellow inmate and convicted serial killer Jarvis Obermeyer, as the murder weapon, a homemade weapon known as a shiv, was found in the cell with Obermeyers' prints on it. Investigators are also looking into malfeasance and bribery among prison staff, although no charges have yet been filed."

Chase barked a laugh and gave a fist pump of satisfaction. "Karma's a bitch, ain't it? Well, one less thing on my to-do list. Going behind the wall to end that sonofabitch would've been a major pain in the ass. We gotta send that dude Obermeyer a fruit basket."

"Think we should tell Emma?"

"Yeah, but not yet. She looks great this morning, but the girl just got vertical. Let her get her sea legs back first."

"Good call. We do anything to set her back, and Ash is likely to smite first and ask questions later."

Ashriel appeared in the kitchen. "Hello."

Chase shot Ben a look. "Speak of the devil."

Ashriel frowned. "Excuse me?"

"No, Ash, it's just a figure of speech," Ben said. "He means we were just talking about you."

Ashriel gave him an exasperated look. "Yes, of course. But by comparing me with Lucifer, I take it that whatever you were saying wasn't complimentary."

Chase rolled his eyes as he pulled a length of plumbing pipe from under the sink. "Dude, chill. I was just goofing around. We were just saying how great it is that you got your pilot's license back, that's all."

Ben gestured to the coffeepot. "It's old and crappy. I was just gonna put on fresh, so get while the getting's good."

Ashriel poured a cup and sat down at the table with Ben as Emma rushed into the room. Her hair, still damp from her shower, hung in a curtain of lustrous mahogany. Her face was pink and fresh, and the floral scents of soap and shampoo floated around her in a fragrant cloud that had Ben—and Chase, from the besotted expression on his face—reeling.

As soon as she saw Ashriel, her face lit up with a huge smile. "Thought I felt you here." She kissed his cheek and linked her hand with his while they spoke. "Good morning, Ashriel."

"Good morning, Emma. You're not overdoing it, are you?"

"No, I'm fine. Made a simple breakfast and took a shower. That's all, I promise."

Chase watched her go to the stove and pull a plate of food from the oven. "Excuse me... *you felt him here?*"

"Uh-huh. Don't ask me to explain, because I can't. It's an angel thing."

Chase frowned. "Okay." He tossed aside the screwdriver he'd been using and got to his feet. "Gonna hit the shower. Be ready to go in thirty, Benji." He yanked the tape measure off his belt, dropped it onto the counter, and stalked from the room.

Ben stared at the screwdriver, half hidden under the fridge. It wasn't like Chase to treat his tools carelessly. But he understood his cousin's change of mood. What Emma had described seemed oddly intimate.

Ashriel looked up in surprise as Emma slid the plate of food in front of him.

"I saved this for you."

"Thank you, Emma. But I don't need to eat."

"I know. Ben told me. But he also said you can eat, so here you go. Eat it or don't eat it; I'm fine with it. Made plenty." She glanced at his coffee cup and grimaced. "Oh, that coffee looks muddy. Let me get you some fresh."

He smiled as she reached for his cup, but he intercepted her hand. "I like it this way."

"*Really*?" Emma considered that for a moment. "You trust me, Ash?"

"Of course."

She carried his plate back to the stove, sprinkled a liberal amount of black pepper and hot sauce on the scrambled eggs, spread a thin layer of grape jelly on the toast, and then placed it back in front of him. "Okay, we're gonna do a little experiment. I'd like for you to take a bite of each food on your plate and rate it on a scale of one to ten. Ten being delicious, one being disgusting. And don't worry that you might hurt my feelings, because you won't. Will you do that for me?"

"All right."

While Ashriel did as she asked, Emma found a pen and a pad of paper in a drawer and started writing.

"I'm finished, Emma," Ashriel said.

"What'd you come up with?"

"Are you sure?"

"I told you. No worries. Go ahead."

"The coffee is a ten. The eggs are nine. The toast, one. The orange juice, two. The bacon, six."

"Pretty much what I figured. Ben, I've got a list of things I need from the store. If you guys have time, can you pick them up?"

Ben was scrolling through the in-stock dishwashers on the home center's website and answered without looking up. "Sure. Grocery store right next to the Home Depot."

Emma gave a small gasp. "Is that *blood?* Are you hurt?"

Although Ben's attention had been mostly on his laptop, trying to decide which dishwasher would best suit their needs, he'd also been listening to Emma and Ash's conversation. Utterly dull and domestic and normal. And so, for him, it was unusual and entertaining. But at the mention of blood, his head came up. He followed Emma's gaze to the spattering of blood spots on Ashriel's clothes.

"Oh," Ash said. "Um...no. I'm fine. Just a shaving nick this morning. I didn't notice the spots."

"Oh, no," Emma said, looking up. She reached high above Ash's shoulder and touched...nothing. "There's a few spots on your wing, too." She closed her eyes for a few seconds. "Dried blood stains...here it is. I'll need hydrogen peroxide and an iron. Of course, I won't be able to use that method on your feathers, but it'll work on your clothes." She looked at Ben. "Do you have those things here?"

"Emma, don't worry about it," Ash said. "You don't have to clean my clothes or my wings."

"I know I don't have to. But I want to."

Ben, suspicion flaring in his mind, stared at Ashriel as he answered Emma. "We have an iron, but I think you're out of luck on the peroxide."

"Can you please get a bottle while you're out?"

Ben tore his speculative gaze away from Ashriel and managed a small smile for her. "Yeah, sure. Make a list of whatever you want. And by the way, if you want to order anything online, you can have it delivered, and we'll pick it up. I'll email you the list of our post-office boxes."

"Great. I do want to order some things."

"Hey, Em, you know what? Now that I think about it, there just might be some peroxide in the linen closet in the hallway outside my room." Ben didn't think that at all, but he wanted a moment alone with Ashriel.

"Thanks." She hurried off.

As soon as he was sure she was out of earshot, he turned back to Ashriel. He was trying to wrap his head around what he thought he just saw. "Two things, Ash. First, did I just see Emma actually touch your wing?" At Ashriel's nod, his mouth fell open in amazement. "But, how? Don't your wings exist in a different spatial dimension or something?" Before Ashriel could answer, Ben drew a sharp breath. "Is that part of her being able to see you, the real you?"

"I assume so. The few humans I've met previously who could see my angelic form never had occasion to touch me."

"Wow! Amazing." Ben just sat there, trying to absorb it. And trying to make sense of the feeling of unease that came along with it.

"You said there were two things?"

"The blood spots? I'm thinking you paid a little visit to the Patroon Creek Correctional Facility last night."

An hour later, Ben, Chase, and Ashriel cruised down the highway in Chimera, which was a red Dodge Challenger at the moment.

"You know," Ben said, glancing out the back window, "we're going to be hauling a dishwasher back, so we may as well switch over to the truck while no one else is around. Coast is clear."

"Good idea." Chase turned the gearshift head to the right and then to the left. The cap popped open, revealing a large, glowing moonstone embedded in the head. He placed his thumb on the stone. "Dodge Ram, four by four, crew cab, black." The Challenger soundlessly morphed into the desired truck.

In the back seat, Ashriel frowned. "You two, go ahead. I'll catch up." He vanished.

A muscle twitched in Chase's cheek. "You know, sometimes I think I liked it better when he was plucked."

"Actually, I'm glad he flew the coop." Ben reached over and turned off the stereo. "I need to give you the head's up about something, and I didn't want to tell you when Ash or Emma might overhear."

"Oh, goody. That's not disturbing at all."

Chapter Seventeen

Emma cowered on her bed, scrunched up against the headboard with her arms wrapped around her drawn-up legs, trembling, her palms sweaty, and her gun clenched in her hand. Her machete lay on the bed beside her.

That weird creaking noise again!

Her heart pounded so hard that she could hear her heartbeat in her ears.

A soft *whoosh*. The ventilation system? Or something...*breathing?* An intruder? Another monster that somehow breached the security dome?

When Ashriel appeared in the room, she almost burst into tears of relief, but guilt quickly followed. "Oh, no! I'm so sorry. I didn't pray or wish, I swear!"

"You didn't have to." With a tender smile, he held out his arms.

She practically flew into them.

He sat on the chair again, with her on his lap. She moaned and buried her face against his neck. "When did I turn into such a complete wuss? I've been fine here, but a couple of creaks and groans in this old place, and I'm scared to death. It's ridiculous. It's embarrassing, is what it is."

He laughed softly. "You're one of the bravest people I've ever known."

"*Brave?* I've spent years of my life running and hiding."

"Yes, brave. Like when you testified against your father's killer, although they'd threatened your life. Like when you saved Ben and Chase from the vampires. Like when you deliberately lured that wendigo away from those campers in Utah. You suffered horrifically, but that family is alive today because of your bravery." When she looked up at him in shock, he gently tapped her head. "I read your mind in the hospital, remember?"

She bit her lip, her cheeks heating. "Oh, yeah."

"But you're used to being outside driving all day and tiny motel rooms at night. It's only natural that you'd be nervous, trapped here alone in this big, still unfamiliar place for the first time. I'm the one who should apologize. It's too soon. I should have stayed here with you."

"It's not your fault, Ash. I know there's gonna be times I have to be here alone, and the sooner I get used to that, the better." But her actions belied her words. She stayed where she was, her face pressed against the stubbled skin of his neck, taking comfort and pleasure in the steady pulse that beat just below the surface, his warm breath as it fanned over her cheek, and the powerful, protective arms that held her.

Arms to hold her.

How often she'd dreamed of that. First, as a child, yearning for her mother's arms, wishing for a father's loving hugs. And now, as a woman, longing for a man's passionate embrace. Ashriel was an angel, and of course neither father nor lover, but being wrapped in his arms touched her heart and comforted her in a way she could never have imagined.

She wished she could stay in his arms forever.

Her new friend—her very own guardian angel. He was a miracle. Her miracle. But it was like catching lightning in a bottle. She had no illusions that she'd keep him for long. She'd done the math, and each scenario for the truth played out to the same conclusion.

If this was—as she still often suspected—just a dream, she would eventually wake up.

If, even after Chase's painful reality check, it was a unicorn-induced dream world, when the beast consumed her life force, she'd die.

And if it were real, Chase promised one way or another that her curse would end, and Ashriel would no doubt move on to some other unfortunate human who needed a guardian angel. Then, after a while, the Kincaids would—very nicely, of course—ask her to leave the citadel. And she'd be alone again.

Alone.

She pushed back the pain, pushed back the fear. The truth didn't matter because she was going to enjoy every moment. Grab on to what she had with both hands and hold on for as long as she could until it was taken from her.

Everything she ever loved was taken from her.

But in the meantime, she vowed not to be a burden to her angel and would instead seek ways to make him happy. And maybe when they parted, Ashriel would think of her now and then. Maybe even visit her from time to time.

Or maybe he wouldn't...

The pain that thought caused her was almost more than she could bear.

She raised her head and pushed her hair off her brow so she could look at him. "Thank you for staying with me the last few nights and watching over me. I slept like a rock, knowing you were here. I don't usually sleep well. Too many years listening for every little sound, I guess."

"It was my pleasure. I was still concerned for your health, but I can watch over you every night if you like."

Her heart took a happy little leap, but caution had a line appearing between her brows. "But don't you have important angel things to do?"

He gave her hair a gentle tug, the corners of his eyes crinkling as he gave her a slightly exasperated smile. "You are my important angel thing to do."

She pressed a trembling hand to her throat, as if to stop the immediate *yes* that wanted to burst out. She didn't want to be a burden, but to sleep in absolute safety every night? What could be more wonderful? "Are you sure it's not a bother?"

"I'm completely sure. I'd prefer it. That way, I won't have to worry about you. But if it makes you uncomfortable, or if you change your mind for any reason, just tell me, and I'll stop."

"Okay, then. I'd like that." It was on the tip of her tongue to ask him why.

Why her?

Why—after all this time—did she rate a guardian angel? Was it because she'd saved the Kincaids' lives? Of course, that must be it. She'd saved his friends.

"Emma, let's continue to keep this just between us, all right? I once offered to watch over Chase as he slept, but for some reason, it seemed to disturb him."

He appeared perplexed by that, but she could imagine big, strong He-man Chase reacting to such an offer. A giggle bubbled up inside, but she bit her lip, thinking that laughter would be out of place. "Okay."

She didn't want to leave the bliss of his arms, but she shouldn't press her luck. Besides, she needed the items on her list for dinner and to begin her experiments. "You can leave now. I'll be okay." She touched his cheek and gave him a little smile. "But maybe you better turn down the volume on the angel intercom, because if you come flying back here every time I feel nervous, or if I just miss you and want you here with me, you're gonna sprain your wings."

Ashriel's heart swelled with emotion. She had no idea how her words affected him. That he meant so much to her? He'd never been so important to anyone. Of course, he had his good friends, the Kincaids. And over the centuries, he'd had the Kincaid's ancestors and angel friends and held positions of angelic authority, both as a Templar Guardian and as commander of his own battalion of angels during the long-ago Xenohari War, but that was different.

No one ever looked at him the way she did.

Like he was a hero.

Certainly, no one had ever needed him the way she did. And he had never *needed* anyone, not really.

Until now.

Until her.

Whenever he closed his eyes, all he could see was her. That sweet smile, those dazzling gold eyes, the reflection of himself drowning in them. Now that she was well, he hungered for her. Desire, once only a rare and passing acquaintance, was suddenly a constant companion. His mind reeled with it, his body ached with it, pulsed with it.

He'd allowed his imagination to run wild last night as he sat in the chair, watching over her as she slept. He'd imagined taking off his clothes and slipping into bed with her. Imagined pulling her close to him, kissing her soft lips, and holding her in his arms, every inch of her skin against his. Imagined mating with her, giving and receiving pleasure, and keeping her snuggled against him, warm and protected under his wings, as she slept.

He didn't, of course.

And he wouldn't, no matter his feelings for her .

She was innocent and traumatized, and she trusted him. He would sooner die than betray that trust. Friendship, he ordered himself. Nothing more. Be her friend and her protector. A hand to steady her, arms to comfort her, until the danger of her curse was past. Until she said the words he dreaded hearing.

Until she didn't need him anymore and sent him away.

It was inevitable. Yes, she needed him now, but one day she'd come to resent his overwhelming need to protect her.

Unless Chase took her from him even sooner.

She giggled softly. "Maybe you should only come if I send out a formal prayer. You know, *dear Ashriel, please hear my prayer*. That way, you know I mean to call you to me."

"We can try that. But I can't promise that I won't come if I sense you need me."

She smiled and patted his cheek. "I'm good with that."

After Ash returned to the truck, Chase hit the brakes, cut the wheel, and veered off to the side of the road, coming to a skidding stop on the gravelly shoulder. He slammed it into park and threw open the driver's door. "Outside, Ash. We gotta talk."

Both Ash and Benji joined him on the shoulder of the road. "What's wrong?" Ash asked.

He must have looked as pissed off as he felt, because Benji put a restraining hand on his arm. "Keep your cool."

But he growled and jerked away. *Cool?* He was as far from cool as the fucking surface of the sun!

Holding his palms up, his cousin stepped back. "Your funeral."

He glared at Ashriel. "Just where in the fucking hell do you get off? You just went off alone and did the deed and didn't even talk to us first? *I* wanted to be the one to end that motherfucker! I wanted to do it for her!"

"Perhaps I didn't make myself clear on this matter." Ashriel's voice was low, as usual, but his eyes grew frosty. The fact that he was speaking softly didn't lessen the power or intimidation behind his words. "Your ego is of no concern to me. However, I have no intention of telling Emma that it was I who facilitated Vincent Russo's death."

Chase tensed as Ash advanced on him, taking a reflexive step back and nearly stumbling on the uneven ground that sloped steeply down behind him. He glanced behind him as a shower of pebbles slid down and splashed into the muddy water. He stood dangerously close to a drainage ditch filled with runoff. *Not good.* He flinched when he turned back and stared into angry blue eyes inches from his face. Friend or not, guardian or not, Ash was still an angel and could kill him with the ease of swatting a mosquito.

"Hear my words, Laird Kincaid. In all other things, I am duty-bound to obey your orders. But *I* am Emma's guardian. *Not you.* In this regard, I don't need or want your permission, and I won't apologize for doing what I deem to be in her best interests. I eliminated a great threat to her in the safest and most expedient way possible. As an angel, I moved through the prison undetected.

"Yes, I purposely put Vincent Russo in mortal danger by unlocking his cell and the cell of a serial killer already serving life in prison with no possibility of parole, a violent man known for aggressive behavior toward his fellow inmates and toward Russo in particular.

"Yes, I bore witness to his death so we could be sure, once and for all, that Emma would be safe. As I witnessed firsthand, unscrupulousness and bribery are rife in places like that, so no one, including Thorne, should it come to his attention, will question it."

In an explosion of air that had pebbles and sand flying up, Ash was gone. Chase yelled into the sky after him, "Well, screw you very fucking much!"

After they'd pulled back onto the road, Ben popped a few antacids into his mouth and then twisted in his seat to face his cousin. He hated it when Chase and Ash butted heads. It wasn't often, thankfully, but he'd never seen them so at odds. They'd nearly come to blows! "Chase, what's going on? An hour ago, you wanted to send the guy who did the deed a fruit basket, and now you're angry because it was Ash who made it happen and not you?"

"Just pisses me off that he went behind our backs to do it. Not our first rodeo with an Ash gone rogue, and it usually don't end well, now does it?"

"I don't know about that. If Ash didn't go rogue now and then, your charred ass would've spent a year in Hell."

Chase sighed. "Look, don't get me wrong, I'm freakin' thrilled he's protecting Emma. With her curse, she needs that kinda muscle. But if I didn't know any better..."

When Chase didn't continue, Ben pressed. "Didn't know any better about what?"

"Nothing. Forget it."

Ben bit his tongue. Clearly, it wasn't nothing, but he let it go for the moment. "Yeah, he should've talked to you first, but it sounds like he did the right thing. I'd have done the same in his place. What did he mean when he said he's Emma's guardian?"

"Exactly what it sounds like. Apparently, now he's her official guardian angel. Told me that when I asked him about my dad and Emma. Right before he warned me off her."

What? That didn't sit right. The guardian angel thing was a possibility, sure. But warning Chase away from her? That didn't make any sense. Ashriel was the one who told him Emma was Chase's soulmate. It was Ash's idea not to tell Chase, for fear he might reject her out of hand, and Ben agreed. Even though they sometimes argued, like today, Ash was Chase's friend and his guardian as well. Why would he warn him off? "What did he say about Emma? Tell me his exact words."

"Well, he told me she's a virgin and not to hit that, and that she wasn't to be...what was the word? Oh, yeah, *trifled with*. That I shouldn't hurt her, or I'd answer to him."

Emma was a virgin? Surprising, given her age, but he could see how it could be true. She'd been hunted, running, and hiding since she was a teenager. Every time he thought about her, so young, so alone for so many years, his heart ached.

Sure, his and Chase's lives hadn't been a walk in the park, either. But they'd had Uncle George until they were grown men, and they'd always had each other and the safety of the citadel as their home. Except for the short time Emma spent with Uncle George, she'd had no one and no place to call home.

How had she gone on alone like that, putting one foot in front of the other, day after day, year after year? And then risked her life by saving theirs? His gratitude and admiration for her knew no bounds. He stared at his cousin's profile. For a moment, he considered telling Chase the truth—that Emma was his soulmate—but he rejected the idea. Nothing had changed. He still believed the truth would send Chase running in the opposite direction.

But perhaps a bit of reverse psychology was in order.

"I know this is gonna piss you off, but you know what, Chase? I don't care. Ash is right."

Chase slammed on the brakes and brought the truck to a screeching halt in the middle of the road. Luckily, they were alone on that stretch of asphalt. "You, too, Benji? When the fuck did I turn into the world's biggest douchebag?"

"I'm not saying that, and neither is Ash. But it's clear you've got a thing for her, and you've said it yourself. Patience isn't your strong suit. A beautiful woman like that, staying in the citadel with us? Close quarters, man. It would tempt a saint. But she's been through the wringer. She needs time to adjust, to decompress, and to decide what she wants to do with her life. To see if her curse will end, for starters. The last thing she needs—"

"Is a jerk like me? Well, you're both right, I guess."

"Stop putting words in my mouth! That's not what I'm saying. I'm saying you should give her some time. I know you wouldn't purposely hurt her, but she'd be putty in your hands. She's been starved for companionship and affection. For love. And yeah, for sex, but if you think you can have a no-strings fling with her, smile, and walk away with no consequences, you're wrong. She'd fall in love with you, and you'd break her heart."

"In the hospital, you said that you and Emma are connected. It's clear she means something to you. Well, be her friend first. Get to know each other and spend time with her. Put sex on the back burner and lay the foundation for a genuine relationship, and when she's ready for more, you'll know. But if all you really want from her is sex, then back the hell off! And stay off! After all she's been through, she deserves better than that."

Chase's murderous glare gave Ben pause, but he didn't back down. It was too important. He wouldn't let his cousin hurt Emma and shoot himself in the foot. Chase could easily ruin what could be his one chance at happiness by dragging Emma onto an emotional roller coaster before she'd even had a chance to ride the carousel. "Yeah, Chase. This is me warning you off, too. If you hurt her, you won't answer only to Ash."

By the time Chase pulled Chimera into a parking space at the home improvement center, his anger had burned itself out, and he'd accepted the truth.

Benji and Ash were right.

He remembered the first night she was with them, when his very real feelings for her punched him in the gut and scared the crap out of him. He'd told himself he only wanted to get her into his bed. And then she'd gone sick, and for over a week he lived in fear of losing her, and then he'd felt overwhelming relief when she opened her eyes, and he knew she would be okay. And every morning, when he awoke to a sweet dream—a real home, with laughter and food and music, the way it had been when they were kids.

Because of her.

When he'd jokingly asked her to marry him, she'd laughed it off, of course, but he'd found in that one moment—deep in his heart—he'd truly wanted nothing more than to put a gold band on her finger and see her pretty, smiling face in his kitchen every morning for the rest of his life.

Not even with Holly had he ever considered, even for a second, taking that terrifying plunge and doing the marriage thing.

But that moment had passed quickly, and sanity returned.

Besides, Emma had a chance to get out. A chance to walk away from the dark side of the moon and cross that line into the light, and for her, it could be a one-way trip. Once the last Russo was dead and her curse ended, she could start over, and no one would be the wiser.

He cared about her very much, and because he did, he was gonna do her a favor and stay the hell away from her. The best way to do that was to get out of the citadel. Even if things were quiet with the Illuminati, there were plenty of evil, unnatural things that needed killing. Emma was safe, healthy, and had an attack angel by her side, locked and loaded.

Time for the Kincaids to get back to work.

Emma put the last glass on the top rack of the dishwasher, closed the door, and pressed the start button. She made a cup of tea and carried it to the table, opened her laptop, and, for the first time since she arrived at the citadel, caught up on the news.

She glanced up when Ben, Chase, and Ashriel entered the room. Chase gave her a smile as he plucked three beers from the fridge, handed one to Ben, and tossed one to Ashriel. The three of them stood around the island, quietly talking. She went back to reading, although she caught *bodies dropping, truck stop*, and *kitsune*, but she didn't really pay attention. A news story she'd just discovered had her riveted.

As she read the article out of New York, her heart pounded. It all made sense now! He'd been lying. He was so bad at it, she couldn't believe she'd missed it. Her brain must have still been fuzzy from her illness. His wings, his clothes, and his entire person were always immaculate. Pristine. But that morning—the first time he'd left her side in nine days—there'd been blood?

There was no other explanation.

Her gaze settled on Ashriel, who was listening intently to what Ben was saying. A lump formed in her throat, and she couldn't quite take a full breath. She rose and slowly walked to stand across from him at the island. Although she reeled with emotions, her face was purposefully blank. She'd learned from Indy that it was best to hide her emotions when ferreting out the truth, lest the answers to her questions be tweaked in reaction to her mood, whether to appease or to deceive. *An interrogator must be stone-faced, Emma. They don't call it the cold, hard truth for nothing.*

"Something wrong, sweetheart?" Chase asked.

She stared at Ashriel as she answered. "Just read a very interesting news story from New York. Vincent Russo is dead." She said it matter-of-factly, without inflection. Ben and Chase exchanged a worried glance, but Ashriel looked like he was facing down a firing squad.

Could he feel the emotions roiling within her?

Since the day he'd flown back to be with her when she'd panicked at being alone in the citadel for the first time, she'd been working on building a door in her mind, a door she could close to keep Ashriel from sensing her emotions and keep herself from bothering him all the time. She reached into her mind and firmly closed that door now. She wanted the truth, not to be placated. "Someone unlocked the cell doors. You did it."

He took a deep breath before answering. "Yes."

"And the faceless coward who shot me in the back for money. He's dead, too?"

"Yes."

She nodded. "Did he suffer?"

"Yes." His chin rose a notch, and his voice held a decided note of satisfaction.

She nodded again. "Good."

Ben gasped, and his eyes went round. "Ash? You killed a *human?*"

"Don't worry. I made it look like an accident."

"Em, how did you know Ash killed the hitman?" Ben asked.

"Yeah," Chase said, glaring at Ashriel. "Me and Benji weren't in that loop. Again. That's gettin' to be a real bad habit."

"I didn't know," she said. "But it's what I would have done."

"Well, *shit!*" Chase blew out a harsh sigh. "Okay, if somehow it hits the fan with Michael, *I* did it. Got me, Ash? We'll talk later and get our stories straight."

Emma touched Chase's arm and gave him a grateful smile before she turned to Ashriel. He watched as she walked to him. She gazed up at him for a moment and then threw herself into his arms. As they hugged, she knew only Ashriel would hear her unspoken words. *Thank you, my angel. Thank you.*

She smiled at his silent answer. *You're welcome, little one.*

Chapter Eighteen

A FEW DAYS LATER, Ben led Emma down the hall to an open door. With an exaggerated flourish and a smile, he stepped aside. "As my mother taught me, ladies first." Her giggle as she passed him warmed his heart. Since Vincent Russo's death, she seemed to float around the citadel on a cloud of happiness.

It was a joy to watch.

"A gym!"

He followed her into the room. "Yep. Just the basics." He studied her face as she moved through the room, as she touched the treadmill, the bench press, and the weight racks, as if to make sure they were real. It was just exercise equipment, but from her delighted expression, she might have been looking at the jewelry displays at Tiffany's.

Her excited eyes turned to him. "Would it be all right if I used it while I'm here?"

"Of course. I'd welcome the company, unless you'd rather work out alone. We can set up a schedule in that case."

Her smile was just a little sad. "I'd like to work out together. The charm of alone is greatly exaggerated."

Cringing, he cursed himself for being a horse's-ass. "I'm sorry. Give me a hand to pull my foot out of my mouth."

Laughing, she patted his arm. "No worries. Ever had martial arts training?"

"No. Uncle George taught Chase and me how to fight. Saw him knock out a werewolf once with one bare-fisted blow. Man, he had some power behind his right. Could've punched a hole in a brick wall."

She smiled, but tears glistened in her eyes. Realizing he'd brought up her Indy, his death still new and so painful to her, he cursed himself. *Dammit!* What in the hell was wrong with him? "And there goes the other big foot. God, I'm sorry. I'm usually not such an idiot, I swear."

"Don't worry about it. I can't expect you and Chase to pretend like he didn't exist. Truthfully? I don't want you to. Even though it hurts, I'd like to hear stories about him. Hearing you talk about him makes him feel closer somehow."

"I get that." How had Uncle George ever let her out of his sight? A surge of anger at his uncle caught him off guard. Why had he let Emma go off on her own? She'd been a teenager, for God's sake! He should have made sure she was protected and brought her home to the citadel. Of course, Michael probably wouldn't have allowed that.

But he could have taken her to stay with his good friend Jimmy Barton, at the very least. With the sealgair's home set up like a fortress against the paranormal, she would've been safe there, and Jimmy would've been glad to take care of her. His wife was a real sweetheart, and they'd have been wonderful surrogate parents, their kids having grown up and left the nest.

"Ben, if you like, I could give you karate lessons while I'm here. The basics and a few kick-ass moves that could help out in a clinch. I need to practice, too, or I'm gonna get rusty." She glanced around the room again. "I can run through my routine anywhere, but we would need more space for lessons."

"Yeah, that'd be great. I know the perfect room we could use. It was my second choice for my gym, but I decided on this one because it was already empty."

She followed him down the hall. He opened a door, stepped inside, and flipped on the lights. "What do you think about this room?"

She went inside and nodded. "This space will do nicely. Huge, well lit. Once we move the metal shelving units out, it will be perfect. We'll need to cover the floor with tumbling mats. We'll need targets, sparring gear." Face wreathed in a grin, she bounced on her toes, practically dancing with glee. "Don't worry, I have money."

"You don't have to do that. We'll cover it."

"No, I got it. Please, it's the least I can do to pay you back for everything you're doing for me. Don't worry, I've got some money stashed away. It's no problem."

"Okay. Your call."

"So, what's the next stop on the tour?"

"The shooting range and the garage."

Emma followed as Ben led the way along several hallways and down two flights of stairs. He opened a door and flipped on the lights, revealing a single-alley shooting range.

"Not much to see here," he said. "It is what it is."

Then he opened another door, and they emerged into the citadel's massive garage. With a gasp of surprise, she stopped short. She knew that car! She hurried over to the muscle car that gleamed like polished red jade under the bright lights and laid her hand almost reverently on the hood. "Just as beautiful in person."

Ben leaned against a wall and crossed his arms. "Chase already showed you a picture?"

"No, I've seen him driving it in my dreams."

"Oh. Chase's Pilleum gift. She's a Dodge Challenger SRT Hellcat. V-8 engine, with over seven hundred horses under that hood. He named her Chimera."

Chimera? That was an odd name for a car. It was funny how some guys referred to their cars in the feminine sense—like an inanimate machine could be masculine or feminine. *Chimera*. She searched her memory. The dictionary had several connotations, most notably a mythological creature made up of various parts of different beings. And in genetics, an organism composed of two or more genetically different tissues, or an artificially produced individual having tissues of different species. Weird, but Chase's car, so he could name it whatever he wanted. "Pilleum? What's that?"

"It's the Templar celebration following the year-long rite of passage that signifies the transition from child to adult. During our sixteenth year, we go through our most difficult training, and on our seventeenth birthday, we endure the brand of initiation and take our pledge—"

"I'm sorry, but did you say *brand?*"

Ben lifted his shirt. On his heavily muscled chest was indeed a prominent scar about the size of a man's handprint, right over his heart, in the shape of the Templar Cross. "Our badge of honor as knights sworn in fealty to the archangel Michael. But it also magically marks us—a powerful sigil to hide us from our enemies, placed there by Michael's own hand." He pulled down his shirt. "On that day, we choose our Pilleum gift, which can be just about anything, within reason."

Something about the car caught her eye. She moved around the Challenger, zeroing in closely on the car's hood. Under the intense overhead halogen lights, something was barely visible—a design veiled within the car's shiny red finish. Looking closer, she saw it was a Templar cross with the three stars of Orion's belt in muted silver. "What's that for? You can barely see it, so I gather it's not a decoration."

"Good eye. That's what makes this car truly special and worthy of being a Pilleum gift. It's a sigil that links to the magical sword hanging above the fireplace in the Great Hall. Using the power of the sword, the car can morph into different vehicles at Chase's command. We're up to nine models now."

"Wow! Like Transformers?"

"Not exactly. They go through a mechanical rearrangement of their parts, but this car morphs on a molecular level. The system combines magic with DNA biometrics only Chase can command. Smooth and soundless. Takes just a couple seconds and can be done on the fly, which comes in really handy if you're trying to lose a tail. The sigil also hides the car and its occupants from detection by demons, angels, or black magic."

"Unbelievable. Oh! Now, I get the name. Why nine models? Can you add new ones?"

"Yeah, we can. Well, I can. Majored in computer programming and cyber security. I convert the vehicle specifications into code and program it into the Challenger's upgraded ECU, add the proper spell work to link it with the sigil and the sword, and there we go. Much easier said than done, though. Ton of work."

"I can imagine. What did you choose for your gift?"

"A year of my own. Just for me. Three hundred and sixty-five days to be normal. No Templar responsibility, no angels, no demons, no Illuminati. I spent it on my senior year of college, living on campus, and being a normal student. Until then, all my classes were online. Didn't use it until I was twenty-four, because too much was going on, and Uncle George couldn't spare me for that long. But then things got quiet, and he said I could go. Too quiet, it turned out. The Illuminati were planning something big."

Emma was dying of curiosity, but Ben said nothing more about it as he walked by her side, and she could tell he didn't want to discuss the subject further. Along one side of the garage, a pair of sleek, black Ducati motorcycles were parked alongside a few rusty old motorcycles that looked like they'd been hauled from the dump. On the other side were several antique cars that looked like they'd been rescued from the scrap yard, along with the motorcycles.

Ben reeled off the names and stats as they walked: his own car, a pearl-gray, late-model BMW sedan parked next to Ashriel's midnight-blue Porsche. A tan tarp covered their grandfather's 1957 Chevrolet Bel Air. In a large section of the garage that held several tall, professional-looking toolboxes and shelves of various tools and equipment, a sad-looking '56 Ford Thunderbird with round porthole windows in its tattered white fiberglass roof was up on ramps.

"The Thunderbird is Chase's current project." He then pointed across the garage at a small white convertible that looked like it had just rolled out of the showroom. "And that's the one he just finished."

She let out a small cry of delight when she spotted the little white car. What a beauty!

"She's a '58 MGA 1600 Roadster. Ask Chase to show you the before pictures. You won't believe the rusty bucket of bolts she used to be."

Emma hurried across the garage and trailed her hand over the glossy paint. "Oh, she's simply gorgeous!" She? Oh, gosh! She was doing it, too. But this elegant car did indeed look like a lady.

"I guess she is," Ben said.

"Does she run?"

"Purrs like a kitten. He finished working on her about a month back. Think he plans to sell. Just started on the Thunderbird. Cars are Chase's thing. He fixes them, washes, waxes, polishes. Did all the work himself, even the bodywork and the paint."

"Think he'd mind if I sat inside?"

"I'm sure he wouldn't mind. Go ahead."

Ben watched as Emma slid into the driver's seat, adjusted the mirror, and put her hands on the wheel. He couldn't help but grin at her enthusiasm. He hadn't given the diminutive car much notice, except to admire Chase's excellent skills, since it was clearly a chick car despite its kick-ass engine. And even if he wanted to, he could never have squeezed into it. Chase barely wedged himself behind the wheel. She honked the horn. It blared a nostalgic *ah-ooh-ga* sound. She laughed and did it again, her radiant smile giving him an idea. He tucked it away for the moment.

Ashriel appeared at his side. "Hello."

"Hey, Ash."

"You weren't going to let her go out to drive, were you?"

"No, of course not. Just trying it on for size. But you know, eventually she's going to leave these walls. Curse or not, I'd still feel better if she took some extra protection with her." Ben hoped she'd never leave, but still, she couldn't stay trapped within the citadel twenty-four-seven forever.

"What do you have in mind?" Ashriel asked.

"Chase tell you about the fire coin?"

"No, what about it?"

"It worked for Emma."

Ash's eyes widened. "She carries Templar blood? I had no idea."

"Apparently. So our warding sigil would work for her. A tattoo, maybe?"

"That's an excellent idea."

"I'm gonna speak to Chase about it. Will you be here for a bit?"

"Don't worry. I'll escort her back upstairs."

"Sure looks cute in there, doesn't she?"

"Yes."

Emma spotted Ashriel and gave him a cheerful wave. He smiled and waved back.

Ben waved at Emma and left the garage, leaving her in the very capable hands of her guardian angel.

Chase slapped the lid of his laptop closed and rubbed his throbbing temples. Another damn headache? He glared at the bright sunshine pouring in through the Great Hall's leaded glass windows. Maybe he'd order some blinds or something. Taking a swig of beer, he eyed his cousin, who sat on the other side of the reading table working on his own computer. "Benji, I got zip. Zilch. Nada. Since Dutch and Steve took down that banshee in Albuquerque last week, can't find a damn thing going on out there. Never this quiet when we were in training. What the hell? Evil take a holiday? Illuminati convention in Hawaii or something?"

"Seems like. I came up dry, too. No obvious sign of Illuminati activity. Nothing paranormal either, no odd, grisly deaths, no sudden drought or crop losses, no mass cattle deaths, no whales beaching, no disease outbreaks, no unexplained severe weather. Tornado in Florida took out a trailer park, but it's Florida, so there you go."

"Why do twisters always aim right for the tin-can brigade? One of these days, I'm gonna investigate that."

"Yeah, you do that, Jim Cantore."

"Dude. Say that name with respect. Jimbo is a national treasure. Thunder snow? You gotta admit, that's awesome." Grinning, he opened his laptop and hit a single key. As a clap of thunder boomed, Weather Channel icon Jim Cantore screamed out of the laptop's speakers, "*Yes! Whoo, whoo, whoo! Yes, yes, yes, we got it, baby! Listen to that! Listen to that! Oh, baby!*"

Benji raised a sardonic eyebrow, although his gaze remained fixed on his computer screen. "Cantore meme. On your desktop. You watch the Weather Channel for fun, and you call me a geek?"

"Not geek. Nerd. Subtle difference."

"Wait a sec...think I found something. Oh, hell, yeah. A big something."

"What?"

"You told me to deal with Pete, and I am. He said Wyatt was the one who brought the intel about the vampire den in Oklahoma City. So, I've been going down the digital rabbit hole. I hacked Pete's bank account and found nothing unusual. Just his biweekly payments from the trust and a reasonable savings account. But I also hacked Wyatt's bank account and found this." Benji turned his screen so Chase could see. "Besides his regular sealgair pay, there's a deposit for a million dollars made a day prior to the accident."

An explosion of anger had Chase clenching his fists and wincing as the pounding in his head got worse. "From where?"

"Don't know yet, but unless he won the lottery, we both know it'll be from a numbered offshore account or a string of dummy corporations so convoluted it would take a forensic accountant to follow the trail."

"Zyro."

"Most likely."

Grappling to accept the painful but obvious truth, Chase guzzled down the rest of his beer and then smacked the bottle down on the table. "*Dammit!* Well, looks like Wyatt sold us out. You think you fucking know a guy. Glad Dad ain't here to see this. If he wasn't already dead, this would kill him for damn sure."

"Yeah. Hard to believe a man could change that much." Benji gestured toward his computer screen. "See it with my own eyes, but still. Wyatt?" He shook his head sadly. "I just can't wrap my head around it."

"I know, right? Oh, that reminds me." Chase reached into his jeans pocket and tossed the medallion from the manticore onto the table along with the silver bullet. "Forgot to show you. My new good luck charms. The tag was attached to the manticore's collar. You believe the ego on this son of a bitch? Had to make sure we—or whoever found our bodies, if anything was left after the manticore had his fill—knew it was *his* doing. Like those dumbass taggers who gotta sign their work at the scene of a crime and then get sent up the river because of it. Well, I'm gonna leave it on his corpse." He lifted the bullet and gazed at it. "When I sink this baby into his fucking skull."

Benji slammed his chair back so hard that it toppled. "*Don't move,*" he growled. "I'll be right back." He strode toward the arch without even setting the chair back on its feet.

Less than an hour later, Ashriel and Emma appeared in the Great Hall. "How'd it go, Em?" Ben asked.

She skewered him with a dark look. *How'd it go?* Was he kidding? It felt like she'd been branded like a damn steer! And she had PMS to boot—bloated like a dead fish, head throbbing, lower back aching—and she hadn't slept more than three hours last night. If her butt cheek didn't sting so badly, she'd be tempted to kick something—or someone—across the room. "Awesome. Just awesome, Ben. Spending hours being stabbed a zillion times with a motorized needle is definitely my idea of a good time. I'm putting another tattoo at the top of my freakin' Christmas list. And make it a big one!"

Ben leaned back in his chair, his eyes going wide.

Chase motioned for her to come closer. "Let's see."

"I got the damn tattoo, all right? No need for show and tell."

"C'mon, just show me."

She didn't move a muscle. Just glared at him. *Why* had she agreed to this? She could have drawn the apotropaic hexafoil symbol on her skin with a permanent marker. But permanent was a misnomer; it would still wash off after a few days of showers. And she liked the idea that when she eventually left the safety of the citadel, the tattoo would help keep her safe. Still, she hadn't known it would hurt so damn much!

Chase gave her a questioning look. "Sweetheart, we talked about this, and you agreed. And while you're here, your safety is my responsibility, and I need to know they did it right."

When she still didn't move, he jumped up and strode to where she stood. He steepled his fingers in front of his face and closed his eyes for a moment, as if praying for patience. "*Please* show me?"

Well, well, well. So, he was finally interested in her chest? She'd give him something to look at! She yanked the square neckline of her new raspberry-pink sweater *way* down, giving him an eyeful of blush-pink lace and cleavage.

His gaze dropped, his nostrils flared, and his jaw tightened. Anger at the lack of tattoo he expected to see on her upper chest where he'd suggested it be placed? Or maybe it wasn't anger. Could those sparks in his eyes possibly be desire?

She waited.

For him to do or say something.

Anything.

If she'd learned one thing about Chase Kincaid, it was that he was decisive. A born leader. And while at first he couldn't have been more attentive, lately he seemed to avoid her. If he was interested, why didn't he make his damn move already? But what if he'd seen her scars in the hospital and they repulsed him? She wouldn't blame him. Her scars and mangled flesh had been disgusting. But they were gone now.

But once he saw something so horrible, he couldn't unsee it. Could he ever look at her and see smooth, sexy skin after that?

Wait, that couldn't be it. He'd said that he and Ben didn't know about her scars until she told them.

Well, he was sure taking his time looking, and his breathing seemed to have sped up. Her heart tripped and started pounding. Maybe this would be the moment...

His gaze flicked up to meet hers. "They use invisible ink?"

Disappointment and hurt sent her already-blazing temper into the red zone. She blinked back tears that only made her angrier. She pulled her sweater up and turned away from him, walking carefully and stiffly—as quickly as one could with her left ass cheek on fire—toward one of the cushioned club chairs. "FYI, Laird Kincaid, unlike the inked-up, silicone-stuffed bar-bimbos you probably prefer, I'm not the tattoo type. I don't want that ugly thing on my chest."

A quick intake of breath came from behind her, and someone said, "Oh." It sounded like Ben, but she wasn't sure.

She glanced over her shoulder on the way to the chair. Both Chase and Ben had their eyes glued to her ass.

Well, that was something, at least.

Ashriel unfolded a plastic donut pillow and inflated it by holding the tip of his index finger to the air valve. He hurried to where she stood, waiting, and handed it to her. "I'm so sorry, I can't take away your pain."

Forcing a smile—even dear Ashriel's voice sounded like nails on a blackboard today—she patted his cheek and said through clenched teeth, "Yeah, I know, sweetie. You've told me ten times already."

"Why don't you just heal her?" Ben asked.

"Unfortunately, the healing procedure would destroy the fresh ink of the tattoo." Ash turned to Chase. "You don't have to worry, Laird. She's safe now from evil spirits, demonic control, and dark magic. The hexafoil sigil was correctly delineated by the tattoo artist, and I paid the woman handsomely and erased her memory of our visit."

Chase's eyes narrowed. "Wait. You saw? *You watched?*"

"Yes, of course. You said to watch her."

"Yeah, watch her, Ash. As in, make sure she stayed safe, not stare at her naked ass while they—"

"Chase." Ben gave his cousin an amused shrug. "You did say that."

"Yeah, Chase," Emma taunted, some little gremlin in her hormone-flooded brain urging her to provoke him. Anything was better than his indifference! "You did say that." With a sassy and sarcastic smile, she batted her eyelashes at him.

A nerve twitched in Chase's cheek as he stared at her.

Ben stood. "Uh, I gotta go do…anything that isn't here." He almost ran out of the Great Hall.

"Having fun, sweetheart?" Chase's pleasant tone of voice contrasted sharply with his stormy expression.

She smiled sweetly. "Uh-huh."

He stared at her for a long moment, a muscle working in his jaw. What was he thinking? Was he tired of her already and wished he hadn't granted her sanctuary in his home? Was he going to kick her out on her sore ass? But then his expression softened, and with a small sigh, he gave a rueful shake of his head. Was that pity in his eyes? Or was it regret and…*affection?*

Was she only imagining what she wanted to see?

Hope surged again as he took two steps toward her. But then he stopped, schooling his features.

Right back to indifference.

He pivoted on his heel and stalked out of the Great Hall without another word.

She barely held back a scream of frustration. *Fuck you, Chase Kincaid!* She slapped the donut pillow onto the chair and gingerly lowered herself, trying to get the throbbing, burning tattoo centered in the hole. The damn numbing cream hadn't lasted long at all.

She grumbled as she twisted, squirmed, and winced, adjusting the pillow and trying to find a comfortable spot in the confines of the club chair. "They need a sofa in this place, Ash. Maybe I'll order one, and you can bring it here. Why is my backside any of his business anyway? *Ouch, damn it!* Not like he's made a move in my direction. Well, I officially give up. The man's a moron, anyway. Seriously? Like you could care one way or another about my naked ass."

With a forceful flap of wings and a turbulent gust of air, Ashriel was gone, sending papers flying off the table and her hair billowing. She looked up in surprise and rolled her eyes. "Sheesh! And they say women are moody?"

Chapter Nineteen

Chase tossed an empty Coke can into the garbage pail that sat in a corner of Malachi's garage. He reached in the cooler that sat on a workbench for another, but his growling stomach changed his mind. With zero chance of being heard over the deep, guttural roar of the Harley's powerful engine as Mal played with the throttle, he waved a hand to get his attention. Mal cut the engine and looked at him expectantly.

"Gettin' hungry. What say we take a break and get some chow?"

"Sure." Malachi, his wild mass of brown hair barely contained under a black do-rag, rose from where he was crouched next to his motorcycle. "Hell, I'm always starving." He set the socket wrench he'd been using on top of a tall red toolbox and wiped his greasy hands on a rag. "Let's hit the diner for burgers, but gotta tell ya, this dinky human food ain't gonna cut it for me much longer. Gonna be heading out soon. Gotta feed. Head up north, Alaska way, for a spell. Salmon run on the Kenai."

"No fishing gear, I take it."

Mal laughed. "Hell, no. Gonna get my Grizzly on. There's this spot I know, a shallow pool next to a waterfall where the salmon pile up. All you can eat, just shove 'em in your mouth, like a Vegas buffet."

Chase cringed inwardly. He couldn't imagine chowing down on slimy, flopping, live fish. "What's it like, man?"

Mal narrowed his eyes and made a low, suspiciously bear-like growl in his throat. "Tasty. And satisfying."

"Not what I meant. What's it like, being you? Being able to change into anything at the drop of a hat. What's your fave?"

"Hand's down, my fave is the wolf." He leaned a hip against the side of his truck and gazed at the rising half-moon visible through the open garage door. "What's it like? Imagine padding through the forest on soundless paws, with eyes that see farther and so much more clearly than a human's, even in the dark. A nose that can scent prey a mile, almost two miles away, if the wind's blowin' just right. Just a trace, a whiff, at first. That first scent that raises your hackles, makes your heart race and your saliva flow. You track it, nose to the ground, and you can tell exactly where every hoof landed. And the scent gets stronger and stronger, and then you know you're on it."

A tickle of fear gave Chase goosebumps as Mal's brown human eyes morphed into the golden, almond eyes of a predator.

Of a wolf.

Those uncanny eyes remained fixed on the moon, and Chase had the feeling a part of Malachi had left the building.

"You break into a lope, and then you spot it—a deer or an elk, maybe a moose, if it's small or weak—and it scents or sees you and bounds away. That's when the prey's scent changes and gets even stronger, laced with the delicious flavor of fear. Then the thrill of the chase. Heart pounding, lungs and muscles straining, running and then leaping onto its back, sinking your fangs into hot, quivering flesh, and pulling it to the ground—that satisfying moment of triumph! And then you rip into its gut, and the sweet flavor of bloody liver—"

"Whoa, whoa, *whoa!*" Holding his hands up in front of him, Chase couldn't stop himself from backing up a few feet. "TMI, dude." Mal's eyes returned to normal, but Benji's warning rang in his head. *Nature will win out, sooner or later. You're walking a dangerous line with that guy.* "Look, I gotta ask something. Something serious. Back with me now? Can you hear me clear? 'Cause you kinda went a little wolfy there for a minute."

Malachi raised his brows. "You asked, I told."

"Didn't ask you to turn your eyes into a wolf's!"

Mal seemed genuinely surprised. "I did? Sorry, man, didn't mean to do that."

"Yeah, well, you did that." Chase took a deep breath and rubbed the back of his neck. It struck too damn close to home that Mal's description was a lot like his memory of being a demon. The awful hunger, the dark pleasure, the urge to kill. Except demons didn't kill to eat, to survive. Demons killed simply for the thrill of it. Worse, far worse.

A young woman's terrified face flashed in his mind.

Blowing out a sigh, he raked his fingers through his hair. He might flush a good friendship down the crapper—might make a new enemy, to be real—but he had to know, or he had no right to call himself a knight. "Tell me straight up. You ever take down two-legged prey?"

Mal pulled the do-rag from his hair, the thick mane of dark-brown spirals falling halfway down his back. "Can't vouch for others of my kind. But I don't feed on people. Never have, never will."

Chase searched Mal's eyes—brown human eyes that gazed unwaveringly back at him—and saw nothing that indicated a lie. "Okay. I believe you. But if I ever find out different? Friend or no friend, I'll put you in the ground."

"I'd expect nothin' less."

"Good. Cause I am what I am, and you am what you am. And that's like mixing fire and gasoline. But as long as we both know what's what, and no one lights a match, we're good."

Malachi clapped him on the back. "That's what I like about you, Chase. Zero bullshit. Let's go eat."

Ben grinned and followed Emma's gaze as she stood next to him and took in the citadel's new karate dojo. Blue tumbling mats covered the floor, sparring equipment hung neatly on a wall, and a heavy bag hung from the ceiling. An extra-large body opponent bag, the top of which modeled a man's torso, sat next to an upper cut bag and a matching kick bag, both rounded bases filled with sand for stability. In one corner were two chairs. He and Chase had surprised her with something not on her list: a wall covered in mirrors.

She gave him a quick hug. "It's perfect!"

She'd insisted on paying for everything herself, even when Chase almost had a fit over it. But she'd wanted to do it, she'd said, because it made her happy to know she would leave it all for them as a gift when she left.

Ben hoped that was a gift he'd never have to open.

She headed for the center of the room. "Let's get started."

He followed her and kicked his shoes off before he stepped on the mats.

She grinned up at him. "You ready for this? Today, I need to evaluate what you can do. You haven't eaten for at least two hours, like we talked about?"

"Nope. We're good to go. Are you, Em? It's only been a week since you got your tattoo."

"All good. Ash said the ink is fully set and healed the bit of remaining redness this morning." A shadow of anxiety passed over her face. "You understand that I'm gonna hurt you, right? I don't want to, but it's the only way to see what you can do, so I know where to start your training. You've got plenty of fighting experience, and we don't have the luxury of time to waste. Might even break some bones. You still okay with that?"

"I'm ready." He bounced a few times on the balls of his feet and threw a few punches in the air. "Bring it on."

"Okay. Let me call for Ash, and we'll get started."

Ben had to bite back a smile. She was adorable. She actually believed she was going to hurt him—without a weapon—and hurt him badly enough that Ash would have to heal him? Yeah, she'd gotten the better of him that one time, but she'd taken him by surprise. Well, he'd try not to make her feel too bad. Maybe he'd fake a sprain or a pulled muscle.

Ashriel appeared, and after receiving his usual greeting from Emma of a kiss on the cheek and a hug, he took a seat on one of the observation chairs.

She moved to stand in the center of the room and motioned for him to join her. "Before every lesson, we bow to each other. We also bow to each other after we complete the lesson. This is a sign of mutual respect, to show humility and lack of arrogance, regardless of our individual skill level."

Chase walked in but stood off to the side and waited until Emma finished speaking and they had bowed to each other. "Sorry, guys. Benji? A word, please."

He jogged over to join his cousin. "Yeah?"

Chase surprised him when he grabbed a handful of his shirt. "She's less than half your size. Don't hurt her,"—he gave him a shake for emphasis—"or I'll hurt you."

Was he serious? Ben frowned as he jerked away from Chase's grip. "Get real. I'd sooner stick my arm in a woodchipper than hurt her." He tilted his head toward Ashriel and snorted. "Besides, you'd have to get in line."

Chase looked over at Ashriel, who had his eyes glued on Emma as she sat on the floor stretching, so limber her nose could touch her knee.

Chase nodded and slapped him on the back. "Yeah, he'd peel your freakin' face off. We're good here. Carry on." Chase headed for the door, but he paused at the threshold, his eyes drawn back to Emma as she rose to her feet. Arms extended above her head, she bent from side to side. She wore a sexy purple outfit, skintight from neck to ankles, that revealed every curve. Her feet were bare, and her painted toenails matched her clothes.

The intense glint in Chase's eyes and his lopsided grin, paired with his overprotective posturing, left little doubt in Ben's mind that his cousin was falling for her. That assumption was confirmed when Emma's gaze met Chase's, and he gave her his patented *Yeah, baby, I'm checking you out* leer, slipped his hand under his shirt, and mimed a pounding heart.

She rolled her eyes and, with a sassy grin, flipped him off.

With a bark of laughter, Chase left the dojo, and a soft blush crept over Emma's cheeks.

If Ben knew how to do cartwheels, he'd have been rolling around the dojo like a wagon wheel.

He rejoined Emma in the center of the room. "Okay," she said, "I want to discuss the hair." She turned her back to him, looked over her shoulder, and pointed to the French braid that held her hair tight to her head and disappeared under her shirt. "In a fight, hair can be a vulnerability. My loose hair almost got me killed when Antonio Russo used it to pull me down." She turned back to face him. "Your hair is all kinds of awesome, but the same thing could happen to you."

He shrugged. "Always worn my hair on the long side. Never had a problem."

Before he could blink twice, she stepped forward, reached up, and grabbed a generous fistful of his hair, pivoted to the side, and pulled him backward while driving her foot into the back of his knee. He landed on his back—hard—his breath exiting his lungs in a forceful *swoosh*. She leaned over him and patted his cheek. "I'd think about a haircut."

He looked up at her and nodded as he struggled to regain his breath. And his dignity. Damn, his scalp hurt. Still wasn't going to cut his hair, though.

"Oh, I almost forgot to ask. You're wearing a cup, right?"

"Uh...no."

"Well, unless you want to hit the really high notes when you sing in the shower, you better put one on."

A cup? What in the hell had he gotten himself into? After he'd added that important piece of equipment to his person and returned to the dojo, she continued.

"I'm gonna keep my back to you. I want you to attack me from behind. Try to take me by surprise. Wrap your arms around me to restrain me, like you're gonna abduct me. Got it?"

"Got it."

She walked away and stood with her back to him, totally relaxed, as if she were standing on a street corner waiting for a cab or a bus.

Picked a piece of lint from her sleeve.

Scratched her chin.

Inspected her fingernails.

And sidestepped smartly when he rushed her. She grabbed his arm as the momentum took him past her, twisted it behind him, yanked it upward, and used pain to force him easily to the ground, face down on the mat. Keeping his arm twisted behind his back, she pressed her knee into his spine and forced his arm even higher toward his head with a sudden jerk.

Ben cried out as his shoulder slipped out of its socket with an audible *pop*.

"I just separated your humerus from the glenoid socket, also known as a dislocated shoulder. If you were an attacker, I'd have no problem finishing you or escaping, because you'd be completely lost in the pain."

She was right. It wasn't his first dislocated shoulder by any means, but it's not something someone could get used to. He writhed in agony.

She gestured to Ashriel. "Ash, please."

After Ashriel healed him, Ben sat on the mat for a few minutes, trying to come to terms with the unexpected death of his male ego.

Emma came to sit beside him. "I'm sorry. I warned you."

"Yeah, you did. I owe you an apology. I didn't believe you'd be able to hurt me."

"Ben, don't feel bad. My greatest weapon is the element of surprise, and let's be real. That's the *only* reason I could take you down. This is real life, not some ridiculous Hollywood movie where a hundred-pound girl-boss can consistently kick the asses of full-grown men." She held her toned but still slim arm next to his heavily muscled arm. "Seriously? Look at that gun. Once I show you my bag of tricks, I won't stand a chance."

"Still." He shook his head in amazement. "Damn, woman. Even without a machete, you're a badass." His heart sank as sadness clouded her features. "No, I meant it as a compliment."

She patted his hand. "I know you did, it's just...I never wanted to be *this*. When my curse ends, I never want to raise a hand in real violence or pick up a weapon again!"

That surprised him. "But didn't you say you started taking karate lessons as a little kid? Didn't you want to?"

She scrunched up her face. "No. I like it now, and it's good exercise, but I asked for lessons because my mother told me to take them. She said a day would come when my life would be on the line, and I needed to defend myself even without a weapon."

Her mother told her? That didn't make any sense. He shook his head in confusion. "But you told me she died when you were a baby."

"I was a baby when she told me. When I was old enough to understand what she'd said, the memory came back to me."

"Wow. How did she know you'd remember?"

Emma's voice changed now and became infused with sadness and pain. "My mother had this freak memory, too. But she also had premonitions. That's how she knew to warn me. And that I'd remember."

"That's amazing. I don't have any special abilities, but as a little boy, Chase had premonitions all the time. He'd know when our dads were coming home, or when the phone was gonna ring, or what was inside a wrapped gift or a grocery bag—little things like that. But he grew out of them by like four."

"Weird how these things go, isn't it? You wonder about the why and the purpose. Or if it's just some random thing that the universe throws at you."

"Yeah." He knew exactly what she meant. Despite his heritage and training, the supernatural realm was often incomprehensible.

Ashriel, who until now had sat patiently, stood up. Frowning, he walked to Emma and rested a hand on her shoulder. "Are you all right?"

She gave him a smile and squeezed his hand. "I'm okay, Ash."

He nodded and went back to the chair.

Ben considered what he'd just witnessed. And it worried him. "I've known him my whole life, but I've never seen him the way he is with you."

"Ash is very kind, and we're friends now. He's just doing his guardian angel thing."

Ben wasn't so sure. Ashriel's eyes had been soft and filled with concern. Just friends? Maybe so on her part. But was there more to it on Ash's part? Protecting her safety was one thing, but getting all worked up every time she got a little bit emotional was another.

She rubbed her hands on her thighs. "Before Russo and my curse, I had lots of plans. Didn't want to be rich or famous. Didn't want to be a doctor, or a lawyer, or an engineer, or a concert pianist like my father was pushing me to be. I loved the music, but the idea of a job that meant career-long travel didn't appeal to me, because I wanted a family. Was going to go to cooking school, be a chef in a nice place, maybe have a little restaurant of my own someday. Find my Prince Charming and marry him, have some kids, make a home together. You know, just...normal. But even without the curse, I'm a freak. I'll never be normal. I know that now. But it is what it is."

He gave her shoulder a gentle squeeze. "Hey, you never know what the future will bring."

"No. But that's a double-edged sword, isn't it?" She gained her feet in one fluid movement. "Okay, break over. Come on, sweetie, we're just getting started. And I trust now you won't hold back? You've got to come at me like I'm the enemy, like your life is in real danger. If you hurt me, Ash is right here to fix it."

"Yeah, I got that now." Ben hauled himself up.

By the time an hour passed, she hadn't gotten a scratch on her, but she'd dislocated one of his fingers, broken his nose, gouged one of his eyes with a lethal little finger, cracked several of his ribs, fractured his right arm, and shattered his left kneecap.

It had been a grueling—and painful—exercise, but she knew exactly what he was capable of, and how to begin his instruction. He really wanted to learn this new skill set. Yeah, he could throw a right-handed punch that could take down a T-Rex. But this took hand-to-hand combat to a whole new level, and if he lost his weapon or suffered an injury to his dominant right arm, like when the vampire stabbed him, it could make all the difference.

They sat on the mats, cooling down and drinking water. "Tomorrow, we'll start your training. We're gonna start with your stance, because none of the moves I want to teach you will work unless you get that right. Height and weight can either be an asset or a liability, and right now, yours can be a liability. But with your muscle mass, we can change that into an enormous asset."

She drew her legs up, rolled into a backward somersault, and rose gracefully to her feet. "Martial arts are, at their core, applied physics. A strike of any kind is basically force plus momentum, whether it be a light touch, a punch, or a kick. Momentum is kinetic energy, which in martial arts is best described as power. How hard you strike, combined with how fast you move, *is* your power. And learning the best way to apply that power to combat your enemy is the goal. I'm going to teach you the most vulnerable points of the human body, the crumple zones, and how to use your opponent's own body against him."

Physics? She was speaking his language. Maybe this would be fun, after all.

Rubbing wax-gummy hands on his jeans, Chase hurried to the kitchen to hit the fridge for a beer. Maybe two. He stopped and sniffed deeply as a delicious meaty smell wafted down the hall and country music was playing, which could only mean one thing.

Emma was making dinner.

He had a case of water in the garage, and for a moment he considered turning around and going back to the garage without the beer, but he'd spent the last few hours washing and waxing the cars, and he wanted a cold one. He cursed the sudden pounding of his heart and the damn butterflies in his stomach. It was getting harder and harder to make himself avoid her when all he wanted was to be near her.

He'd come real close to losing control that day when Ash had taken Emma for her sigil tattoo. When she'd pulled down her sweater and he'd looked, expecting to see the tattoo, he hadn't expected all that oh-so-sexy cleavage. And her scent, floral and sweet and so feminine. It had taken all his willpower not to kiss her, not to pull her against him and cup the soft breasts he imagined lying cradled in all that pretty pink lace.

She probably woulda knocked him on his ass.

He wouldn't have blamed her.

And then that day a couple of weeks ago in the dojo, when he'd forgotten himself and flirted with her, and she'd rolled those pretty eyes and given him the finger.

Man, oh, *man*. What a woman.

When she first came to the citadel, he loved to see her light up with a big smile every time he entered a room. But then he'd felt like gutter slime to see her smile disappear when she asked him to do something with her and he refused, and he'd hated to see the hurt flash in her eyes as he turned away from her.

But lately, she didn't smile like that anymore when he entered a room. And she didn't ask him to do anything with her. And the hurt was gone from her eyes.

And now she turned away first.

He told himself he should be glad. But it hurt.

It hurt like hell.

He had to remember that he was doing it for her sake. So she didn't become attached, and neither did he. So it would be easier when it was time for her to move on to her new curse-free life, a normal life away from all things supernatural.

Away from him.

It was for the best.

He had to be strong, for her sake, and just do what he always did: grab what he wanted out of the fridge and go on his way. But he froze in the kitchen doorway, the beer forgotten as the blood left his brain for a southern vacation.

She stood at the stove with her back to him, stirring a big steaming pot. She sang along to Maggie Rose's "Body on Fire" as she moved sensuously to the lazy, sexy music, her long ponytail swaying as she rolled her shapely denim-clad bottom twice to the left, and twice to the right. Left, left. Right, right. Left, left. Right, right.

Mesmerized, he went rock-hard in seconds. All his good intentions to stay away from her burned up in flames of desire. He just had to kiss those beautiful lips he kissed every night in his dreams, just had to hold that sexy ass in his hands. Already, he could feel her in his arms. He was about to make his move when Ashriel materialized in the kitchen.

Silently cursing a blue streak, Chase backed up out of view. As Taylor Swift's cute and sassy "Our Song" began, he watched as Ashriel put a grocery bag on the island countertop.

Emma turned, her whole face alight with a radiant smile. Singing along with Taylor, she danced over to Ashriel. Standing on her toes, she kissed his cheek, reached up, and playfully ruffled his hair. As he grinned shyly and smoothed his hair, she rummaged in the bag and came up with a spice jar. She did a spin and kissed his cheek again. Then she feigned turning away, quickly reached up, and ruffled his hair again, giggling as she made him laugh.

She danced back to the stove, opened the jar, sprinkled spice into the pot, and stirred it, once again singing and moving her body to the beat of the music.

Ash stood there.

Watching her.

Unfortunately, because Ash's back was to him, Chase couldn't see his expression, but from the angle of his head, it sure looked like he was staring at her ass. He would've given anything to see Ash's face, to know for sure if what he suspected was true.

To know for sure if Ash had the hots for her.

Jealousy and frustration burning, Chase went back to the garage, empty-handed.

Chapter Twenty

CHASE LAY SPRAWLED ACROSS his bed, eyes closed, AirPods on, Lynyrd Skynyrd screaming in his ears, trying to get Emma off his mind. After midnight again and again, all he could think about was her, just down the hall, soft and warm and asleep in her bed.

What was she wearing?

Maybe she slept naked.

He cursed himself as he lay there, tense and throbbing. *Yeah, moron, that was helpful.* Masochist, much? He was losing his freakin' mind. He needed a distraction, and soon. Could only hang out at Malachi's place so much. They'd fixed the Harley's throttle and installed new shocks and brakes on Mal's truck, so no excuse there.

Two weeks.

Two freakin' weeks, and he still hadn't found a reason to get out of the citadel. Well, nothing close enough, anyway. He'd investigated something he'd read online about weird shit going on out on the West Coast in different towns. Nine people dead. Young, healthy, not a mark on 'em, nothing showed up in the autopsies. At first, he figured they were soul deals, and the time had come to pay up, but it didn't jive. Too young—a few in their early to mid-twenties. Were ten-year-old kids making deals with demons these days? Not likely. No lottery winners, either, or any other sign of unusual good fortune.

Maybe the mysterious deaths were an omen. A sign of the beginning of the end, the first domino that would lead to doomsday.

What? Okay, he needed to get a freakin' grip.

Could just be some weird disease or poisoning they hadn't identified yet. Couldn't let his imagination get away from him; couldn't let himself get spooked. Surely, if some serious mega-shit were in the works, the ever-vigilant Michael would have sounded the alarm.

Besides, California and Oregon? Too far. Didn't wanna travel that far away just in case Emma needed them. Besides, if the deaths turned out to be paranormal, there were teams of sealgair in that area that could handle it. And if it turned out to be some kinda new Illuminati shit, unless Michael said otherwise, it would fall to Antares Citadel located somewhere in the Klamath Mountains of Oregon. Didn't wanna go stepping on another laird's toes.

The annoying little voice in his head piped up. *Dude, just go! Won't hurt nothing to poke around a little, check it out. She got Ash. She don't need you.*

Damn, how he hated that fucking little voice! He wished he could reach in his head, grab him by the throat, and choke the life out of him. Of course, the voice was right, and that's what made him so damn annoying. What could him and Benji do for her that Ash, a freakin' angel, couldn't?

Jealousy was a new acquaintance he wished he'd never met. He'd never known this sense of inadequacy before, not when it came to women. Always had just about any woman he'd ever wanted. Didn't take much. A little sweet talk, a drink or two, sometimes didn't even need the alcohol. Sometimes they'd just throw themselves at him. Yeah, he'd always had a way with the ladies.

But not this time.

You haven't even tried, you lame-ass coward.

Hell, no, of course he hadn't. He was staying away from her on purpose! And even if he weren't, if it came right down to it—if his suspicions were right and Ash had a thing for Emma—he didn't stand a chance, anyway. How could he, against an angel?

Friend or no friend, the fact was, Ash could pound him into ground chuck with his bare hands or burn him to a crisp with just a touch. Not that he believed he would, but how in the hell was he supposed to compete with that on any level?

A smart man picked his battles wisely. No point in starting a fight he had no chance of winning.

Same reason he didn't compete with Benji in the gym. No way could he ever come close to his strength and build. As Laird, he wasn't allowed to show weakness. *To anyone.* A lesson drummed into his head again and again by both Dad and Grandpa.

But was he agonizing over nothing?

Okay, so Ash spent a lot of time with Emma. Not surprising, since he was her guardian and her friend. But was he hot for her, too?

Was it even allowed? The Bible told stories of angels mating with human women and producing Nephilim offspring, a powerful hybrid species that wreaked havoc on Earth in ancient times. But God had fixed that problem by eliminating both the Nephilim and angels' ability to reproduce. But had he also removed their desire for sex?

Holy crap! What the fuck had his life come to that he was even thinking about this kinda shit?

He grabbed his extra pillow, sucked in a deep breath, pressed it over his face, and bellowed his frustration. Pain exploded in his head, and he groaned. He tossed the pillow aside and rubbed his temples. *Smart move, idiot.* Giving himself another damn headache.

But the worst part was the way Emma looked at Ash. Like he was a rock star. Like it was hero worship or something. She'd sure never looked at him like that, not even close, not even before he started avoiding her.

Seemed as if she and Ash spent just about every minute of the day together. Of course, that was partly his fault. Okay, mostly his fault. Okay, dammit, *all* his fault. He'd purposely done the exact opposite of what Benji had advised by avoiding her instead of spending time with her.

But he watched her when she didn't know he was looking. When she worked with Benji in the Great Hall on the inventory project, or while she was cooking and cutting up vegetables into those impossibly tiny pieces or shapes. And when she was giving Benji his daily karate lesson. That one was easy, because he could watch her, unseen from the hallway, in the mirrored wall of the dojo. He'd even made a few video recordings of their lessons on his phone, so he could watch her any time he wanted.

But still, he avoided her. Hard to do while stuck in the citadel, and since she insisted that all four of them have dinner together every night at the kitchen table. Of course, he hadn't put up a fight about that. The woman was an awesome cook. He and Benji never had it so good. And neither had Ash, he figured. Every night, she made a special dinner for him of that toxic waste she called angel food, usually a different version of the normal food she made for the rest of them.

No wonder Ash was over the freakin' moon about her.

The truth? Chase lived for that single hour at the end of the day. It was a mistake, no doubt. Every morning he told himself he would make some excuse to cry off, but by four in the afternoon he was pacing the garage and checking the time every ten minutes, like a jonesing addict waiting for his dealer to show. And by six, he'd be fresh from the shower and pulling out a chair at the kitchen table.

He couldn't help himself.

An entire hour or more when he could freely watch her, talk with her, laugh with her?

But that's where he drew the line.

Since that close call in the kitchen—when he lost control and woulda put the moves on her if Ash hadn't interrupted—he made sure he didn't linger when they passed in the hall, or he went to the kitchen for a drink or snack and found her there.

He tried to keep busy and stay away from her, tried to keep his mind occupied and off her. But how many times could he wash and wax the cars? Gonna wear the paint right off 'em! He'd ordered a few outrageously expensive parts for the vintage Thunderbird, but they hadn't come in yet. Even his favorite video games didn't hold his interest anymore.

He missed her asking him to do things with her. Even though he would refuse, it was nice to be asked. Instead, she hung out with Ash, or with Benji, and sometimes with both. But mostly with Ash.

Ash always had time for her.

Like last week, when he'd followed the sound of old-fashioned music coming from the dojo and found Emma and Ashriel dancing. Some old-timey dance with fancy moves where the guy held the girl close, and they spun in circles. From the looks of it, she was giving him lessons.

An angel dancing.

Well, alert the press, because he'd officially seen it all.

Of course, if dancing was what Emma wanted, that's what Emma would get. She was Ash's new mission, and when an angel was on a mission, he was a feathered stealth bomber locked on target. Yeah, okay, so Ash was her guardian angel. He accepted that. Even if it was self-appointed.

Still, it was a good thing. With her curse, she needed that kind of protection. But she was safe inside the citadel, so why did Ash have to be with her *all the damn time?*

What would Ash do when Emma's curse ended? At the very least, he and Emma had become good friends. Best friends, it seemed. Would he let her go have a normal life? Or would he insist—would he and Emma both insist—that he remain a part of her life? Yeah, an angel for a pal. That sounded normal. Only reason he was keeping away from Emma was because he wanted her to have a normal life!

Fuck! He was making himself dizzy, going around and around in his head with this crap.

Bottom line, if Ash balked at letting her go, at cutting his ties with her completely, he would just have to convince him it was the right thing to do, for Emma's sake.

Yeah, that would work.

Or it wouldn't.

He could order him to do it. But did his authority as laird extend to Ash's personal life?

Not a clue.

Ash might insist on leaving with her, and if he did, there wasn't a damn thing he could do about it. Although, technically, Ash would be abandoning his post as guardian of the Kincaid family. If he went to Michael, ratted Ash out...

No! What the hell was he thinking? No matter what, he wouldn't betray Ash like that. Not only was Ash his friend, but he also owed the angel his life several times over.

No, he would handle this himself.

Was Ash with Emma right now?

Alone in her room with her?

Unwanted images that made his fists clench flitted through his mind. Jealousy grabbed him by the throat again. Son of a bitch! Why was he doing this to himself? The little bastard in his head opened his big, fat mouth again.

Because you want her, dumbass! You wanna keep her for yourself. Play the hero, but you know you do. But you know what? He could be doing her right now, and you wouldn't know, stupid. Ash coulda zapped into her room. Could be in her bed. On top of her. Inside of her. Right now, right down the hall.

As rage sent his blood boiling, he considered sneaking down the hall and pressing an ear to her door. Checking it out. But what then? What would he do if they were going at it? Pound on the door or break in, and then what? Get his ass pile-driven into the ground or smote into cinders? Have Emma hate him for invading her privacy?

What right did he have to do anything, even if he could? They were consenting adults, and he had no claim to her.

He ignored the part of him that didn't believe that. The part of him that craved that amazing feeling he got whenever he touched her, the part that kept whispering in his brain that he and Emma were connected, were meant to be.

He choked on a bitter laugh. *Meant to be?* Like they were part of a stupid fairy tale? It was too ridiculous to pay attention to, and the little bastard in his head was way louder, anyway.

He really couldn't blame Ash if he wanted her, and in truth, he'd be surprised if he didn't. All else aside, what straight male with a pulse, wings or not, wouldn't want Emma? So why did it twist his guts just to think about it?

Hellooooo! How many times do I gotta say this? 'Cause you want her for yourself, that's why, you pussy. So go get her! Or are you too scared? Little boy scared to go up against the big bad angel?

Growling, he sat up. Enough was enough! If he couldn't strangle the loudmouthed little bastard in his head, he'd drown him. In alcohol. Friday night, and the bars would be rocking. He jumped out of bed, got dressed, and pointed Chimera towards town.

He couldn't have Emma, but he wanted sex. So damn it, he was gonna get laid.

An hour later, a red Challenger shone under a three-quarter moon and blinking orange neon in the parking lot of The Black Cat Saloon.

Chase remained in the driver's seat, his fingers gripping the steering wheel. Through the bar's large front window, he could see Alicia deftly mixing drinks and pouring drafts, smiling, laughing, and tossing her curly brown hair as she flirted with her customers. They'd hooked up not long ago. She'd be glad to see him again, no doubt.

He'd come tonight specifically to do just that, but the inferno of lust and frustration that drove him to leave the citadel had gone cold.

He blew out a sigh, let go of the wheel, and let his head drop back against the headrest. He closed his eyes and tried to summon the memory of a naked Alicia, but all he could see was Emma's sweet face.

As hot as the bartender was, he didn't want her anymore.

He wanted Emma.

Only Emma.

"I am so, *so* screwed." He hooked an arm behind his head and sulked. A loud knocking on the passengers' side window made him jump and reach for his pistol, but he grinned when he saw who it was. He unlocked the doors and waved him into the car. "What in the hell you doing here?"

Malachi gave him a fist bump as he slid into the passenger's seat. "Everybody's gotta be somewhere."

"Figured you'd be freezing your nuts off in Alaska by now."

"Shit came up at work. Soon, though, real soon. Question is, what are you doing out here on a Friday night, instead of in there, gettin' your party on. Alicia was just asking me about you."

"Things are...complicated these days."

Mal sighed and rubbed a hand over his face as he peered through the windshield at the moon. "Yeah, they are."

Chase felt a twinge of unease. What did he mean by that? "Wanna tell me about it?"

Mal gave him a grin. "Well, I could tell you, but then I'd have to kill you."

Chase chuckled and rolled his eyes. "Fuck off, bitch. As if. At any rate, now that your rides are fixed, way overdue for that *Call of Duty* rematch. Gotta gimme a chance to kick your ass again."

"Dream on, hotshot. Rematch soon, but got a date meeting me here, so I only have a few minutes. What's up? What's the complication that's got you on the outside looking in?"

His face heating, Chase let his head drop back on the headrest again. "A woman."

"Oh. But not that woman, I take it?" Malachi tilted his head toward the bar.

"Different woman. But I can't have her." Emma's face flashed again in his mind—the way she'd looked last night at dinner, cheeks pink from the heat of the stove and her whiskey eyes sparkling with laughter at a story Benji was telling. He'd sneaked his phone out and taken a picture of her mid-laugh without her knowing. He pulled his phone out now, brought up the picture, and held it up for Mal to see.

Malachi gave a soft whistle of appreciation. "*Damn.*"

"I know, right?" He gazed at Emma's pretty face and acknowledged the ache in his chest, where his heart seemed to swell, and the knot in the pit of his stomach. "Jeez, Mal. Think I'm falling for her."

Saying the words out loud gave him the courage to accept the truth, as much as it scared him. And it scared him plenty. He'd gone and done it again, hadn't he? The one fucking thing he'd told himself he'd *never* do!

He lifted his head and looked Malachi in the eyes. For some reason, he felt okay to talk to Mal, to spill his guts without feeling like an emo wuss. "Hell, I *am* in love with her. TKO, face-planted into the mat, little birds circling my head, and the referee calling out ten. And you know how great that went last time." He rubbed his hands over his face. "Love ain't a good look for me."

Malachi nodded. "What are you gonna do about it?"

"Do? Nothing."

Malachi shimmered and morphed into Dr. Phil. "How's that working for you?" he asked, perfectly imitating the celebrity's catch phrase.

"Cut it out!" Chase glared at Malachi. "You might wanna consider a different gig than a night security guard, 'cause you watch too damn much TV. I don't even think that guy's on the air anymore. And some fake head-shrinker wouldn't know jack shit about my whacko life."

"He's a licensed psychologist. At least he was, and he's got a star on the Hollywood Walk of Fame."

Chase snorted. "Oh, well, in that case, make me an appointment."

Dr. Phil morphed back into Malachi. "Just trying to help."

Chase sighed. "I know. Sorry. But seriously, enough with the TV." He leaned his head back again and stared up at the moon. "Maybe I should just get a dog." A moment later, his eyes widened at the plaintive whine of a puppy. On the passenger's seat, a golden retriever puppy wagged its tail and held up a paw as it seemed to smile at him. Chase couldn't help but melt. "Aww, good boy." Grinning, he ruffled the puppy's head before yanking his hand back. "*Whoa!* Dammit, Mal! Now I gotta add a new rule to my don't-do list."

The puppy's whine turned into a human laugh as Malachi shimmered and morphed back into himself. "Sorry, just goofing around. Wait, you got a list? A literal list of don'ts?"

"Yeah."

Malachi twisted in the seat toward him. "Now this, I gotta hear. But just the highlights. Tammy should be here any minute."

Chase counted off on his fingers as he spoke. "One, don't show an enemy your back. Two, don't run outta ammo. Three, don't piss off an angel. Having a hard time with that one lately. Four, don't mess around with married women. Five, don't deflower virgins. My grandfather's words, not mine, but the image keeps me honest. Six, don't drink cheap tequila—learned that one the hard way—yada yada yada, and now, thanks to you, number twenty-four, *don't* pet other guys."

"Wouldn't have taken you for the homophobe type."

"I'm not. Hey, that's your jam? You do you. Makes no diff to me. But it ain't mine, hence the list."

"Not mine, either. But what's up with the no virgins thing? Not that I make a habit of it."

Chase shook his head. "No way. I don't wanna be that significant to any woman."

"Quite an ego you got there, stud."

"It's not that. First time's special, ain't it? Sure was for me. I can still see her face, remember her taking my hand and leading me upstairs to her room. Still remember...well, the details ain't important. What's important is I was fifteen, she was my first, and I caught a case of puppy love you wouldn't believe. But she was almost eighteen, and I sure as hell wasn't her first, so you can guess how that turned out. Ten years is a long time to remember details clear like that. And while I'd like to think I could pick every woman I ever been with out of a lineup, the details are all blurry. Just don't want any more complications in my life and don't wanna add any to theirs. Plenty of experienced women out there, just lookin' to play."

"So, this new woman you're pining away for. She ain't one of 'em?"

Chase huffed a laugh. "Not by a longshot."

Malachi tilted his head and gave him a questioning look. "Dude, I don't get it. You're the Kincaid Laird. You told me you got a duty to continue your family line. Somewhere along the way, you're gonna need a wife. Why not this woman, since you already love her? She ain't married, is she?"

Chase frowned. "Of course she ain't married. Rule number four? Listen, I don't need you to remind me about my duty. I'm only twenty-five, so there's no rush. When the time comes, I'll jump off that cliff. But it won't be soon, and it sure as hell won't be her. I wouldn't do that to her."

Mal shrugged. "You da boss." He leaned toward the windshield, his gaze drawn to the woman walking up to the bar. "There's my date. Late again, but totally worth it. Gotta bounce." He reached for the door handle. "Hate to leave ya high and dry, but priorities, man. But, hey, you're welcome to join us."

"Thanks, but no thanks. Third wheel, I ain't. And things could get awkward with Alicia. See ya around."

"Peace out." Another fist bump, and Malachi headed back into the bar.

Feeling off balance and anxious about his true feelings for Emma, Chase pulled out of the parking lot, hit up the drive-thru at the golden arches for a burger and fries, and headed home. It was almost three when he got there, and the citadel was silent. Yawning, he kicked off his boots at the door and smiled as he put on the cozy new slippers Emma had given him—that somehow always wound up by the door, waiting for him. But instead of going straight to his room, he went to the kitchen.

He stood at the table, took out his wallet, and put several ten-dollar bills in the swear jar. "That should cover it." He pushed down a corner of the clear packing tape covering his mother's handwriting that had lifted, and then glanced over his shoulder to make sure he was alone before he hugged the jar. "Sorry, Mom. Rough couple of days. I'll try to do better."

Chapter Twenty-One

Emma dropped onto a chair in the dojo and guzzled down half a bottle of water. She blotted the sweat from her heated face with a towel, smiling as she remembered discovering Chase's sweaty little secret earlier that afternoon. He never used Ben's well-equipped gym—that Ben knew of—and she'd wondered how Chase kept his fitness level and the powerful muscles that rippled under his clothes.

Her turn to do the wash, she'd been carrying a basket piled high with soiled towels to the laundry room when an odd noise caught her attention. She set the basket down at the laundry room door and continued down the long hall. The noise came from a staircase she hadn't seen since her tour, since she had had no reason to be on that side of the citadel. She stood at the bottom of the stairs, listening. It sounded like pounding footfalls coming down the stairs toward her.

The footsteps grew louder, and the light fixture at the top of the stairwell cast a clear shadow of someone coming down the stairs in a hurry. She backed up around the corner, bracing herself for a fight, her heart pounding. Had someone broken in? But the footfalls stopped. Then Chase's voice, hushed and breathy, counting.

She peeked around the corner. Chase was on the floor at the base of the stairs, doing one-handed pushups, twenty on one side, then twenty on the other. He'd obviously been at it for a while—sweat drenched his hair and sweats. He jumped to his feet and ran up the stairs again.

She'd tiptoed away, leaving him to his exercise. For whatever reason, he wanted to keep his workouts private. She wouldn't invade his solitude. She smiled at Ashriel as he came to sit beside her. "That was fun, Ash. You learn so fast! Dancing with you is so much nicer than dancing with all those clumsy teenage boys at those stupid society balls and country club dances I had to go to. I'm telling you, you're a natural."

"Thank you. But I have an excellent teacher."

"Thanks, but this teacher can't teach you anything else. Seriously, you've got it down. You've learned every dance I know. If this were a real dance school, you'd be ready for your recital."

He searched his memory. "Recital. A dance or musical performance. Did you have a recital?"

"With all those years of dance and piano lessons, I could have had lots of them. But I only had one."

"Why?"

She shrugged. "Recitals are held once a year so you can show off for your family. But I didn't participate after the first one. My father didn't show up. I knew he'd never go, so what was the point? And it was too boring to stand there on stage and wait while all the other kids' proud parents smiled and clapped and took video and pictures." She stood. "I'm gonna take a shower. See you later, sweetie."

After she left, Ashriel sat there for a while, fuming. She'd said boring, but what she really meant was painful and embarrassing. His heart ached as he recalled one of Emma's memories as a little girl, standing on stage in a cute kitten costume, her little chin trembling, blinking back tears because no one was there to clap for her.

He wished Mario Borello were still alive.

So he could kill him. Slowly, with his bare hands.

But he smiled as an idea came to him. Perhaps, in a small way, he could help make up for the missed recitals and the painful memory of her father's neglect.

But it would take some planning.

As Rascal Flatts played on Emma's laptop on the kitchen table, she poured a generous swig of dark ale into two frosty glasses and handed one to Ashriel. "Try this one."

She lifted her glass and took a sip. And cringed. *Yikes.*

Ash took a tentative sip. Then a bigger one. "Mmmm. Even better than the last one."

"I thought it might be your favorite. It's a strong, extremely bitter ale. Has the highest IBU of the locally available beers, although we can order even higher IBU beers online."

At his baffled look, she explained. "IBU is the acronym for International Bitterness Unit. It's a scale used to measure the amount of hops in any beer. The higher the concentration of hops, the higher the IBU, the more bitter the beer."

She smiled at Ben as he walked in and grabbed a bottle of water from the fridge. He joined them where they stood at the island. "Hey, guys. What's going on?"

"I'm working on a menu for Ashriel of foods he'll like for our football party." She smiled as her belly swirled with anticipation. Her knights had no idea they were going to watch the Colorado Buffaloes homecoming game on the new big-screen TV she was going to buy for them.

Ben's eyes widened. "Wow. Party food for angels? That's one for the books. Ash, before Emma came, I can't remember the last time I saw you eat anything."

"Food usually doesn't interest me. Although I've always liked beer. But Emma, how did you know I'd like the bitter ale even more?"

"Just like I know what to cook for you. Remember our experiments? You hated anything that was sweet or bland. The nasty, old, bitter, coffee was the clue. That's why when I cook for you, I only use strong, savory flavors. Salty, bitter, acidic, spicy, hot." She laughed. "Some people have a sweet tooth, but you have a bitter tooth."

She poured the rest of the ale into his glass. "To go with the beer, I made you special nachos. You wouldn't like nacho chips you can buy in the store, since they're made with corn, and corn is high in sugars. I made these out of a combination of low-carb grains. Quinoa, amaranth and millet, sea salt, lots of spice, *lots* of heat. That was a challenge. Couldn't get them crispy enough, but I played with the ratios and finally hit the jackpot."

A surge of pride had her grinning as she held up a spiral notebook. "Took thirty-two tries, but totally worth it. They're awesome, even if I do say so myself. I topped the chips with Pepper Jack cheese, melt-your-teeth hot sauce, extra-spicy Italian sausage, raw green tomatoes, jalapeños, ghost peppers, horseradish, avocado marinated in cayenne pepper-steeped vinegar, and bitter herbs." She glanced at the clock. "Should be done by now."

She slipped on her new hot-pink silicone oven mitts and pulled the platter of nachos from the oven. They looked perfect! An attractive, colorful palette of colors, cheese bubbling and lightly browned on the edges. She set it on the tile countertop, took off her mitts, and waited, holding her breath and twisting her hands together.

Would he like them? Or had she wasted all that time and effort?

Ashriel scooped up a few loaded chips and sniffed. He took a bite, his eyes closing in obvious pleasure. When he swallowed, he looked at her and grinned. "Best thing I've ever tasted. Ever." And he scooped up another portion.

His approval after all her hard work, combined with the *many* sips of beer she'd had along with him, sent a rush of joy through her so wild, so bright, she clapped her hands and burst into giddy laughter, unable to stop, gasping for air in between uncontrolled giggles. That kind of laughter is contagious, and Ben and Ashriel were soon laughing helplessly along with her.

Chase stepped into the Great Hall. Where was everybody? Hadn't seen Ash at all, and this time of day, Benji and Emma were usually working on their inventory project. Maybe taking a coffee break? He could use a little caffeine himself, so he headed for the kitchen. Laughter and music rolled down the long hallway, and the aroma of something spicy tickled his nose.

He paused at the kitchen threshold. Benji and Emma—*and Ash?*—were laughing like fools. If he didn't know better, he'd have thought they'd all smoked something a little sketchy and were trippin' out. "Hey, a party? And nobody invited me?" Since no one seemed capable of answering, he just shrugged. He stared at a laughing Ashriel for a moment.

This new Ash was practically unrecognizable. Gone was the serious, stoic, humorless angel he'd known all his life. Well, if anybody was finally gonna drag that giant stick out of Ash's ass, it would be Emma. A platter of nachos on the counter looked amazing. He picked up a gooey stack and stuck it in his mouth.

"Chase, don't!" Emma cried.

Holy fucking shit! His face burned as his sinuses filled with angry bees and his tongue burst into flames, his eyes flooding with spice-induced tears. He let the nachos tumble out of his mouth, stumbled to the sink, stuck his face under the faucet, and sucked up water like a dehydrated camel.

A heavy thud had him glancing behind him. Benji had collapsed to the floor, laughing even harder. *Jerk.* Chase stuck his face back under the water.

"Benjamin Kincaid, stop!" Emma sounded pissed. "That's not nice! Chase, I'm so sorry. Ash, can you help him?"

Still gulping water, someone touched his head, and the burning stopped. He wouldn't have asked for help, but he wasn't gonna bitch about getting it, either. "*Whew!* Thanks, Ash." Chase shut off the water and wiped his chin with his forearm. "Holy crap! I can throw down suicide wings with the best of 'em, but what the hell was that? Looked like nachos but tasted like friggin' napalm."

"That was angel food," Emma said. "It wasn't meant for you."

"Angel food nachos?"

"Yes."

Chase glanced around the kitchen at the explosion of bowls, knives, measuring spoons, bottles, and jars that cluttered the countertop, the stove, and the sink. There was even a little scale and glass beakers that reminded him of chemistry class. "Really? All that trouble just for nachos? Angels don't gotta eat, you know."

Silence dropped like a boulder.

Three sets of eyes glared at Chase. He frowned. "What?"

Ben gave his head a little shake and sent him a dark look. Ash looked away. And Emma? Chase figured if looks really could kill, he'd be gasping his last on the kitchen floor. What the hell did he do to piss everyone off?

She continued to glare at him, her angry gold eyes shooting sparks. "Ben, Ash, please give Chase and me a little privacy."

Ben pulled himself up from the floor and left the room, but Ash, standing behind Emma, hesitated and eased a hand onto her shoulder. Without looking back, she patted his hand. "Go ahead. It's all right." With a pointed glare aimed at Chase, Ash vanished.

Chase stiffened when Emma advanced on him.

Self-preservation had him taking a step back.

And then another.

"You selfish, inconsiderate son of a bitch!"

Uh-oh. He'd screwed the pooch. Big time. Wasn't sure how, but still. "Listen, sweetheart, I didn't mean—"

"Don't stand there and tell me what you didn't mean! I'm not stupid." Her breath came in shallow gulps, and her face was mottled with anger. She pointed to the table. "Sit! And stay there, or I swear I'll put you back there, bloody. This may be your place, and you've got every right to throw me out on my ass, but I've got some things to say to you, Chase Kincaid, and by God, you're gonna listen before you do!" She turned and stomped to the sink.

Chase—no fool—sat. And stayed.

His fairy had turned back into a warrior.

He'd heard all about how she'd broken Benji into bite-sized pieces, and if she wanted to, she could bend him, twist him, and fold him until he was staring at his own ass.

God, he wanted her.

It was scary how much he wanted her.

He pictured himself dragging her to the floor and taking her right there on the cool, smooth stone, her long hair fanned out around them. He'd kiss the fury right out of her until she was all soft and willing in his arms, until desire, instead of rage, burned in her eyes. Or maybe she'd keep an edge of that formidable temper and be wild. Play rough, leave scratches, marks on him, pain mixing with pleasure...

He shivered and struggled for control, every nerve ending in his body centered on the Louisville Slugger trying to rip its way through his jeans. He *had* to get away from her. Soon. Or, no matter the consequences, he wouldn't be able to keep his hands off her.

Good thing he'd finally found an excuse. Except for the odd deaths out west, things were eerily quiet out there. Too damn quiet, like the calm before the storm, and that, too, had him on edge.

He'd found a story online about how the alleged ghost of Billy the Kid was tearing it up at a hotel in Dodge City. Not something he would normally pursue. He'd had it pegged as a scam to lure in the tourists until he'd read that people were being hurt, and just yesterday, someone died in the hotel under mysterious circumstances. Now, it was interesting. Not close—a lot further than their usual stomping ground unless they teleported—but at this point, he just didn't care. He'd been looking for Benji to tell him about it when he'd walked into the kitchen.

And opened his big, fat, dumbass mouth.

Her breathing was harsh as she held her wrists under the cold water flow and then splashed her face. She grabbed a towel and dried off, then plucked two cold ones from the fridge, sat across from him at the table, and slid one across to him. He took out his pocketknife and used the end to pop the tops.

She took a long pull of her beer before she pinned him with an icy stare. "Chase, what's your favorite food? The thing you'd order as your last meal if this were your last night on Earth."

Oh, man. Was she that pissed? He gave her what he hoped was his most charming grin. "Am I dying tomorrow?" He angled his beer bottle toward her and winked. "In that case, sweetheart, I'll have you."

Her eyes narrowed, but he was relieved to see a glimmer of humor flash in them and her lips twitch. Thrilled to see a blush spread across her cheeks.

"Just answer the question, wiseass."

"Andrew's Diner, Chicago. Best burgers on the planet. Double cheeseburger on a pretzel bun, heavy on the onions, curly fries, deep-dish apple pie." He sighed. "Haven't been there in years, but that'd be my choice of gallows food."

"Why?"

"What d'ya mean, why? It's awesome."

"Let me tell you why. Taste, texture, appearance, and aroma. It's one reason I wanted to be a chef. Food is one of the great pleasures of life. I dare you to name a gathering, or a holiday, or a celebration that doesn't involve food. Social interaction revolves around food. Don't you get it, Chase? Good food does more than just fuel our bodies. Enjoying food brings us together and *makes us happy*." She leaned forward and stared at him, her brows arched.

It clicked. He grimaced, and his face heated. "Okay, I get it. I'll admit, not my finest hour. That was a dick thing for me to say. I didn't think."

"No, you didn't, and that's the problem. You take him for granted. Sometimes you act like he's a machine, like he's a Transformer or something. Just another weapon you keep in the trunk of your car and take out when you need the big gun. Yeah, he's an angel. But he's a person, too. I was inside him, so I know—"

"Whoa, whoa, *whoa*. Just wait a damn minute. You remember that?"

"Yeah, I do. A little more every day. It's not something I can explain to you, but we were together...connected somehow, while I was inside his body." When he frowned, she sighed. "I'm sorry if that bothers you, Chase, but it's an angel thing."

"An angel thing." A muscle worked in his jaw as his hands curled into fists under the table. "Yeah, got it."

"He feels just like we do. He hurts, and he worries, and he laughs, and he loves, and he feels sad, and he has regrets, just like we all do. He's good, kind, and loyal, and thinks only of doing the right thing, always. Even when you don't agree with it.

"You guys have told me so many stories already, right here at this table every night at dinner, and I know that's just the tip of the iceberg. None of us would be here if not for him. How many times has he saved you? Saved Ben? How many of your ancestors owed their lives to him over the centuries? Be nice to him, for God's sake. He deserves that. Chase, he's earned that."

She took a deep breath and blinked rapidly, clearly fighting back tears. "By some freak miracle I still don't understand, he's mine for a little while. I'm gonna make sure that when I'm gone, and he remembers me, he's not gonna wonder if I cared. Wonder if he mattered to me. Wonder if I appreciated what he did for me. He'll know because I'm gonna tell him *now*. Show him now."

She fingered the locket hanging around her neck. Tears brimmed and trickled down her face. "There are so many things I'd like to say to my mother. And to Indy. Especially to Indy. But I'll never get that chance. I had no choice with my mother because she died when I was a baby. But Indy? There were things I left unsaid. I thought he knew, thought that words weren't needed. But they were needed, Chase. If not for him, for me. I needed to say the words. Now, they're stuck inside me forever."

She downed the rest of her beer in a few long swallows, smacked the bottle down on the table, and wiped her tears with her sleeve. "Look, you know as well as I do that tomorrow isn't guaranteed for anybody in this world."

She walked around to his side of the table and shocked him speechless when she took his face gently in her hands. She looked into his eyes. "I care about you. You matter to me. And I appreciate everything you've done for me." She kissed his cheek and left the room.

Reeling from her touch and her words, he pressed a fist against his heart to ease the ache.

Chapter Twenty-Two

EMMA TRIED TO FOCUS on the blurry image of the daytime moon seen through the eyepiece of the telescope Ben had so kindly set up for her on the tower terrace. She leaned back and rubbed her tired eyes. This was a much-needed break after a long afternoon spent translating an ancient tablet. Sumerian cuneiform was so challenging! She was glad she'd already done the research on Dodge City ghost stories and Billy the Kid for Chase. It seemed like she'd been yawning more than reading for the past hour.

She stifled another yawn as she reached for the can of Red Bull she'd left on the flagstone terrace floor and then gulped the last of the energy drink, hoping it would kick in quickly. She'd slept fitfully last night, although she'd tried to hide it from Ashriel.

She peered again into the eyepiece of the telescope. The image was clear now. But she was too upset to enjoy the striking view of the terminator of the moon, the line between the light and dark sides. "What time do you leave?" She tried to sound casual, to keep the worry out of her voice, but wasn't sure she'd succeeded.

Don't be a burden!

She should have kept her mouth shut. Could she rewind the last minute and take the words back?

Ashriel sat nearby on a low section of the crenellated defensive wall that encircled the tower. "Leave? Where am I going?"

She leaned back away from the eyepiece and turned to look at him. "Chase found a mission."

"Yes. They leave for Dodge City first thing tomorrow morning. But what...oh." He scooted over and extended a hand to her. "Come sit beside me."

She grasped his hand and went to sit next to him on the three-foot-thick granite wall. He tucked her hair behind her ear. "You're worried?" At her hesitant nod, a pained expression crossed his face. "I'm sorry, but I can't sense what you're feeling since you shut me out."

She gasped in dismay. "You knew?"

"Of course, I knew. But you have every right to keep your feelings private."

"That's not why I did it, Ash. I just...I don't want to bother you all the time." She looked down at her hands gripped tightly together in her lap.

He slipped his hand under her chin and tilted her face up. "Emma, you are not a bother. You're...I've never been,"—he glanced up to the sky as if searching for the word—"*closer* to anyone, angel or human, in all my life. You're the best friend I've ever had."

She gave him a shy smile. "You're the best friend I've ever had, too." She almost said, *real friend*. But he wouldn't understand about Emmalina.

He kissed her forehead. "Now that we have that settled, I want to make something else clear to you. I'm not going with Ben and Chase. They don't need me to investigate a ghost, and I'm sure they'd be greatly insulted if I offered to go. But more importantly, as long as you're in danger, my place is with you. I won't leave you here alone. I promise."

A wave of relief flowed through her, and she kissed his cheek and slid her arms around his neck for a hug. The citadel was protected against every known evil, but what about the unknown? After all, the manticore had breached their defenses, hadn't it? Who was to say there wasn't another unknown evil or unnatural thing out there, drawn by the beacon of her curse, just waiting for the right time to strike?

Waiting for her to be alone.

But in truth, it wasn't only that.

Of course, she'd miss Ben and Chase while they were away, especially Ben, since Chase seemed to avoid her at all costs unless it was mealtime. But Ashriel? She would have missed him terribly if he'd gone. She wasn't ashamed to admit that she'd be lost without him. Not only because of his protection, but because simply being with him made her happier than she'd ever been in her life.

He was always nearby while she worked in the Great Hall with Ben during the day, and he kept her company in the kitchen while she cooked. In the evenings, they watched TV together sitting on her bed, played cards or board games in the Great Hall, many times with Ben joining in, or listened to music.

She missed their dancing lessons. She'd offered to teach him after they'd watched a few episodes of *Dancing with the Stars*, and he'd been so fascinated by the intricacies of the dances that he'd accepted her offer.

Who knew he'd learn so quickly?

Well, duh. She should have known. He was an angel, after all. She'd also been trying to teach him to play poker, something she'd gotten very good at by playing online late at night in motel rooms when she couldn't sleep. Although he'd grasped the rules of the game quickly, he couldn't bluff his way out of an open door.

Bluffing required lying and artifice, and Ash didn't have a dishonest bone in his body, even when it came to playing a game.

But they still had fun.

They always had fun together.

Her favorite part of the day was after she'd tucked herself into bed at night, when he would come sit in his chair to watch over her, and they would quietly talk until she grew sleepy.

It was like their own little world.

He told her stories of his long life and his adventures with the Kincaids. The stories amazed her. Sometimes they made her laugh, and many times they made her cry, but no matter what, she loved to listen to him. She loved his voice, so soft and deep, and more than a few times, not wanting him to stop, she'd fallen asleep to that soothing timbre.

Once, they'd talked straight through the night without even realizing until her alarm buzzed in the morning. That night would always be one of her favorite memories.

That reminded her. She reached into her jacket pocket and pulled out a cellphone. "You left your phone next to the clock on my dresser."

He sighed as he took it from her. "Thank you." He slipped it into the pocket of his leather coat. "I really must learn to keep better track of this thing. Chase said if I lost another one, he was going to glue the new one to my ass."

Giggling, she turned to look up at his face, but a colorful sparkle caught her eye. Projecting from the stone wall of the next story above them, a large window with gorgeous stained-glass windows reflected the sunlight. "Ash, what's that room?"

He followed her line of sight. "That's the laird's solar, which is meant to serve as his office and personal space. That entire floor is the laird's family quarters. But it's been closed off for years."

"Oh." Sadness flooded her heart. Poor Indy. "That's a shame. Maybe someday someone will use it again."

"Perhaps."

He gently stroked her hair as he continued to hold her. She loved being wrapped in his arms, basking in the warmth and comfort of his angelic glow, so intense and intoxicating when they touched. He would hold her for as long as she wanted, but she was pushing the time limits of a friendly hug, and she didn't want to make him uncomfortable.

Reluctantly, she eased out of his embrace and was about to tell him she was going to make his favorite dinner that night, but as she gazed up at him, her focus settled on his mouth. With a soft sigh, her train of thought jumped the tracks and plummeted headlong into a ravine.

He had beautiful lips.

Were they as soft as they looked?

She wanted to touch him and had to fight the powerful impulse to raise her hand and touch her fingertip to his lush upper lip, right there in the middle, to the indent of the cupid's bow.

Did angels kiss? How would it feel to have his lips pressed against hers? How would it feel to be pulled into his strong arms—not in comfort or friendship—but in passion? To be wrapped in them and pressed against his body as his mouth moved over hers...

She shivered and couldn't hold back the tiny whimper that escaped as a furious rush of desire swept over her. Her heavy-lidded eyes drifted up to his.

And her heart stumbled.

Although she was a virgin, and the last kiss on the lips she'd shared was with a teenage boy under the bleachers behind the football field in high school, she was no child. She instinctively recognized the arousal that revealed itself in his quickened breathing, the intensity of his expression, and the way his eyes locked with hers.

He slowly lowered his head, and for a few thrilling seconds, as tiny shocks of excitement skittered along every nerve ending, she waited for his kiss. Unconsciously, her lips parted, and her body swayed toward him, but then he was gone.

Poof.

Just like that.

Gone.

His rejection hit her like a slap. She could almost feel the burning welt of a handprint on her cheek. Disappointment, hurt, and humiliation had tears welling up in her eyes, had her sitting there frozen in shocked disbelief.

Well, what did she expect? Ashriel was an angel, for God's sake, beautiful and powerful and perfect, and she was just a woman, and not even a particularly attractive one. While she didn't think she'd make anyone lose his lunch now that her scars were gone, she was still a far cry from the paragons of perfection—tall, usually blonde, blue-eyed goddesses with legs that went on forever—who graced social media and the world of fashion and beauty.

She was too short, her hair a nothing color between red and brown, and she wouldn't even remember which end of a mascara wand to use anymore. Had she ruined their friendship? How would he ever be comfortable with her now?

Panic made her breathless. She had to fix it quickly.

She couldn't lose him; she couldn't!

Her mind in overdrive, she jumped up and ran down the spiral staircase. Already, she knew what to say.

Ashriel slowly banged his forehead against the garage wall and thought seriously about smiting himself. How could he have done that?

How could he have just left her sitting there like that? He'd panicked, that's how. Panicked and fled, like the sorry excuse for a guardian angel he was.

He hurt her feelings.

And it killed him to know it.

He hadn't known what else to do and still didn't. He'd come close—so very close—to kissing her. Even now, thinking of her lovely face turned up to his, her soft lips parted in welcome, he shuddered with desire. He couldn't kiss her because he was afraid that if he ever did, he wouldn't be able to stop. He didn't think he was strong enough, not when it came to her.

She thought she desired him.

But, of course, it was only gratitude.

Gratitude mixed with her feelings of friendship for him, magnified out of proportion by her need for love after being isolated for so long. She would willingly give herself to him, and he'd take her innocence. Betray her trust and destroy her faith in him. Perhaps ruin her chances at a normal life when her curse ended.

She liked him and trusted him. It was only natural that she would transfer those desires, those needs, onto him. Had he encouraged this and somehow revealed his true feelings for her? He didn't think so. He was so careful to keep his love for her—his desire for her—hidden under a veil of friendship.

She probably hated him now.

He couldn't lose her; he couldn't!

He had to think and come up with a plan.

How could he fix it? But he squeezed his eyes shut in despair as his head filled with her prayer. She was calling for him. Probably to ask him to leave. With a heavy heart, he went to her.

Chase tossed a party-size bag of Cheetos puffs into a grocery cart already loaded with road food for their trip.

Benji shot him a look of disapproval as he moved the bag of crunchy orange delight aside and set a twelve-pack of bottled water and a small bunch of bananas next to a jumbo package of chocolate chip cookies. "Don't you think this is overkill, Chase? Only about a seven-hour drive."

"Not just for the drive. Motel room stash. But did you look at the map? We get stuck in the middle of freakin' nowhere; I wanna be ready. Preparation is half the battle. Better to have pie we don't need than to need pie we don't have."

"No one needs pie."

"Speak for yourself."

"All that sugar and chemical-laden junk is gonna send you to an early grave."

Chase snorted and shot an incredulous look at his cousin. "Yeah, sure, I'll worry about that right after I check the balance in my 401k. You know my motto. Live fast, die young, and leave a good-lookin' corpse."

"Yeah, that was James Dean's motto."

"So, I stole it. Sue me." He pushed the cart forward as he scanned the aisle. "Where's the candy? I want licorice. The black kind, not that fake red crap."

"Yeah, there's always risk, but you could live a long life, father many children. Don't you want to be healthy enough to enjoy it?"

Chase stopped and stared at his cousin. His jaw tightened as realization dawned, and he shoved an index finger in Benji's face. "If this sudden concern for my health and optimism for my reproductive future has anything at all to do with Emma, you can damn well forget it! As soon as her curse is over, we're gonna help her get on her feet, and then she's gone. She's getting out of this crapstorm if I gotta carry her cute little ass all the way to Mayberry myself."

"Mayberry? There's no such place. It was a sixties TV show, a fantasy. And even if it were real, it sure wouldn't be the same today! And what would be waiting there for her?"

"A nice, normal life."

"No, it wouldn't. Emma isn't normal, Chase. Why don't you see that? Yeah, she wants a normal life, but she'll never *be* normal, and she'd be the first one to say it. Hell, she has said it! Cursed or not, she's one of us. She's in it up to her pretty little neck. You think by sending her away from us, away from the citadel, she'd be safer?"

"Damn straight."

"You're wrong. Maybe you just don't want to see it, but something's going on with her, and until we know what it is, she's better off with us, curse or not."

Fury and guilt made Chase want to lash out. "Oh, really? Were my mom and the twins safer with us? Was Kenny? Was Holly?"

Benji flinched after each name as if he'd been physically struck. He turned his face away and balled his fists.

Another pang of guilt made Chase's stomach twist. He was deliberately ripping open old wounds and rubbing salt in them, and he was a piece of shit for doing it, but he had to get him to understand! "I'm bad luck, Benji, ever since I went to Hell. Even before that. A bad penny, a jinx, a fucking one-man walking plague! And I'll be damned if I'm gonna add Emma to the list of people who've suffered or died because of me."

Ben threaded a shaky hand through his hair and turned to face him. "I know you believe that...and maybe you are. Hell, maybe I am, too. But this time, with Emma? What if something bad happens to her *because* you send her away? Look, you just have to take my word for it. This time, it's different. If you send her away, you'll regret it. And so will I." He pivoted and stalked off.

Chase stared after his cousin as a thorny seed of doubt took root. *Damn it, goddamn it!*

What if Benji was right?

Emma waited for Ashriel in the dojo, standing weak-kneed and trembling on the mats. She'd chosen the dojo because they'd have privacy. The guys went out for supplies for their trip, but even when they came back, Ben already had his karate lesson and worked out that morning with her, and she hadn't seen Chase in the dojo since that first day, so they wouldn't walk in on her humiliation.

As soon as Ashriel appeared, she held up her hands to stay his words. "Please, Ash. *Please.* Just sit and listen to me, and don't say anything." She waited until he reluctantly nodded and sat on one of the observation chairs.

He sat leaning forward, elbows braced against his thighs, hands gripped tightly together. His expression was blank.

She had no indication of what he was thinking.

Clasping her hands behind her back, she took a few seconds to organize her thoughts so she wouldn't sound like a complete moron. She drew in a long breath and squared her shoulders.

And stared at his boots while she spoke.

She hated her cowardice, but she couldn't look him in the eye, afraid to see pity. Or indifference.

She didn't know which would be worse.

She tried to sound formal. Matter of fact. Unemotional. "Ashriel, I want to apologize for offending you. I was way out of line, and I don't blame you at all for removing yourself from the situation. It's very clear to me now that there are lines that aren't to be crossed. Friendship is one thing, but you're an angel, and I'm just a woman, and never the twain shall meet.

"I don't know what came over me. Well, I do know, it's just that you're so very handsome and sweet, and,"—she took a shaky breath—"anyway, I only hope that you can find it in your heart to forgive me, and we can just put this whole thing behind us, and I sincerely hope I haven't ruined our friendship."

There, she'd said it. She took a deep breath and forced herself to look up to see his face.

He looked utterly horrified.

Her heart flooded with chilling fear. *Oh, God*. What had she done? She pressed her hands against her chest. "Please, Ash, please tell me I haven't ruined everything!" Panic made her voice crack on the last word.

He jumped to his feet, and to her surprise, he wrapped her in his arms and held her tight. "How could you think that? Think any of that?"

"Then what is it, Ash?" She leaned back and looked up at him. "I thought...I thought you were going to kiss me." She touched his cheek with a trembling hand and searched his eyes. "I want you to kiss me," she whispered shyly. "Why didn't you?"

He didn't answer her. But his continued silence said everything, didn't it? She'd been mistaken, after all. Again. Clearly, she had zero instincts when it came to men. He didn't want to kiss her, and because he was kind, he was trying to spare her feelings.

As a razor wire of pain whipped through her, she stepped out of his embrace. Turning away, she wrapped her arms around herself. Tears stung her eyes, and her lower jaw quivered uncontrollably, but she tried to sound blasé. "Hey, it's okay, Ash. I get it. You're just not attracted to me. It happens. No big deal."

Mortified, she squeezed her eyes shut, sending a tear sliding down her face. She'd failed. She sounded forlorn. Forlorn and pitiful. And pathetic. With a sob fighting to break free, she hurried for the door, wanting only to reach the privacy of her room before she burst into tears and humiliated herself even more.

With a rush of air, Ashriel stood directly in front of her, blocking her path. He reached out and gently cupped the side of her face, wiping her tear with his thumb. "Emma, that's not true at all. You're beautiful in every way, and I am *very* attracted to you. I did—I do—want to kiss you. And more. But I'm your guardian. It wouldn't be right. Your life is in upheaval, and you've been through so much in such a short time. I couldn't take advantage of that and still call myself a guardian angel. Once Russo is dead, things will be different. Do you understand?"

She did understand—although his admission that he wanted her sent a sizzling wave of desire through her that made her heart pound and her face heat. But he wasn't rejecting her. He was protecting her. Even from himself. And he was right; she saw that now. Everything in her life was topsy-turvy, and she had no idea what her future would bring. The sixty days were flying by. Perhaps it would be best to let things stay the way they were. For now.

Dear, sweet Ashriel. He was her guardian angel in every sense of the word.

Chase sat on the edge of his bed, picked up his ringing phone, and checked the caller ID.

He froze, his breath hitching and his face going numb.

666.

It was Hades!

A chill ran down his spine. Had Hades found out what they'd done? But there was no way he could have. Then what the hell did he want?

He set his alarm and put the phone down. It was late. They had an early morning, and he was in no mood to talk to that dick. Hades could leave a damn message. Chase shrugged out of his shirt, pulled down the blanket, and fluffed his pillow.

No follow-up text, no beep to signal that he'd received a voicemail. Well, it couldn't have been that important. Probably drunk dialing him, looking for a drinking buddy. Well, he could keep looking. Those days were long over, and they sure as hell weren't coming back. There was a knock on his door. "Yeah?"

Benji walked in, clad in pajamas, holding his phone. "Guess who just called me?"

"Hades?"

"You, too?"

"Yeah. You answer?"

"No. You?"

"Fuck, no."

"He didn't leave a message. Any idea what he wants?"

"Not a clue. Didn't leave a message for me, either. You don't think he knows, do you?"

"No. How could he?" Benji pocketed his phone and rubbed his eyes. "Okay, I can see him calling you if he's drunk. He still misses his Hell-buddy bromance with you. But why call me? He knows I'd just as soon stab him in the face as look at him."

"Maybe looking for me since I didn't answer. And jeez, don't call it a freakin' bromance. Drinking with that asshole got me off the rack and out of the pit, so don't judge."

"No judgment here. I'd have done the same thing."

No, you wouldn't. For a moment, Chase considered calling Hades back, but it would be like going unarmed into an enemy camp. Hades was a smarmy, evil douche, but he was smart, and he was a tricky sonofabitch.

Chase figured he couldn't say something wrong if he didn't say anything at all.

It was a long time before he fell asleep that night.

Chapter Twenty-Three

THE FIRST BLUSH OF dawn brightened the eastern sky by the time Chase shut the third box of shotgun shells he'd just replenished and made another quick visual sweep of the contents of Chimera's spacious trunk, checking again to ensure that his arsenal was well-stocked. The ghost wreaking havoc at the famed Dodge City Cornelius Rose Hotel sounded like a bitch and probably wouldn't go down easy. He grinned. How freakin' awesome would it be if it actually turned out to be the ghost of Billy the Kid?

Emma didn't think it was likely since Billy was buried in Fort Sumner, New Mexico, but Billy had slept several times at the Cornelius Rose, and the hotel boasted it had a wax figure of Billy in the saloon that supposedly wore the kid's own hat. Could be a haunted object, especially if any of the gunslinger's DNA remained.

Satisfied they were well armed, he shut the trunk. He looked to the other side of the garage, to where Emma stood with Ashriel and Benji, waiting to see them off. Benji stopped as Emma spoke to him. She took his face in her hands and kissed his cheek, and when he picked her up for a hug, Chase had to laugh. Looked like a little girl being hugged by a sasquatch.

Crossing his arms, he leaned back against the car. Benji walked toward him quickly and stiffly, his face almost as red as his hair, avoiding eye contact. Chase was surprised to see tears shimmering in his cousin's eyes. But, hell, that sweet woman could bring a death-row convict to his knees.

He looked toward Ash and Emma and raised a hand in goodbye, then slid behind the wheel, closed the door, and checked his mirrors. He hit the remote button to raise the garage door and turned the key in the ignition. Chimera's powerful engine roared to life, but he didn't put her in drive.

He shot a side-eyed glance at his cousin, who stared fixedly out of the passenger-side window.

Like they had for the past few days, Emma's words echoed in his mind, and Chase scrubbed his hands over his face and blew out a sigh. *There were things I left unsaid. I thought he knew, thought that words weren't needed. But they were needed, Chase. If not for him, for me. I needed to say the words. Now, they're stuck inside me forever.* He drummed his fingers on the wheel for a few seconds. "Son of a bitch," he muttered. He drew in a ragged breath and slammed both hands against the wheel. "*Sonofabitch!*" He squeezed his eyes shut and scowled.

But accepted the inevitable.

Benji grabbed his arm. "What the hell's wrong?"

"Nothing." Chase shut off the car and hit the remote to close the garage door. "Hang tight. Won't take long." He strode across the garage to Emma and Ashriel. "Sweetheart, I need to borrow your angel for a minute. Ash, can we talk? In private."

Ash nodded and followed as he led the way out of the garage.

Ben hurried over to Emma. "What's wrong? Where'd they go?"

She smiled up at him. "Not sure, but I think Chase went to answer his wake-up call."

Chase paced the Great Hall's hardwood as Ash waited. "Is something wrong, Laird?"

"Yeah. No. Damn it, gimme a second. I ain't good at this kinda thing." Chase continued to pace for a few seconds, then stopped and blew out a sigh. *Just suck it up and do it already.* Eyes closed, he pinched the bridge of his nose, prayed for guidance, turned, and looked his old friend in the eye. "I'm sorry, Ash. What I said the other day, that Emma shouldn't have bothered cooking for you? You know I didn't mean it like that, right?"

Ashriel inclined his head. "I understand."

"No, you don't. Emma says I take you for granted, and damn it, she's right. You're family, and I don't always treat you the way family should be treated. You're always there to lend a hand, to haul our asses out of the fire—mine, literally—and we've come to expect it. Like it's our due, but it's not.

"Yeah, you're guardian of the Templars of Orion Citadel, but as Michael would be the first to point out, the job is to keep us alive and help us win our battles. Period. You don't have to do what you do for us. What you've done for our family all these centuries? What you've done for me and Benji all these years? And now, what you've done for Emma? Way above and beyond. So, I'm saying thank you across the board—past, present, and future. And I hope you'll accept my apology."

"Apology accepted. It's forgotten."

Ashriel's voice was even huskier than usual. He held out his hand to shake Chase's, but Chase grabbed that hand, pulled him into a bear hug, and slapped him on the back.

"Thanks, Ash." He stepped away, suddenly embarrassed. He was just no good at this emotional stuff. "Okay, let's roll credits on this sappy Hallmark flick. We're burning daylight here, and I got work to do."

They returned to where Emma had waited. Chase nodded at them and headed for the Challenger, but he got about halfway across the garage and stopped. He needed to do one more thing. He turned around and crooked a finger at Emma. Clearly surprised, she hurried over to him.

"Chase, what—" Her eyes went round when he gently took her face in his hands.

He gazed down into her startled-fawn eyes, and like every time he touched her, he melted at the intense rush of pleasure that coursed through his body. He thought about telling her the truth, but he couldn't bring himself to say those three little words that could change everything.

He'd be a selfish sonofabitch to say them.

Because if he did, he'd never let her go.

But he knew what he could say. "I care about you. You matter to me. And I appreciate everything you've done for me." He kissed her—just a soft, sweet brush of lips—released her, and walked away.

He glanced in the rearview mirror as they pulled out of the garage. She stood where he'd left her, fingers pressed to her lips. Even if Benji hadn't crammed that friggin' doubt sandwich down his throat, it was getting hard to imagine himself letting her go—hard to picture himself sending her off to that pretty house in suburbia.

Hard to picture his life without her in it.

He loved her way too much for her own good.

And for his.

Absently sliding a metal tape measure in and out of its case, Emma bit her lip as she considered. "I think we could put a sofa here, and the TV stand could go against the wall. Unless we hang the TV on the wall. But that would mean putting holes in the brick, and I don't feel right doing that." She let go of the end and allowed the tape measure to retract back into its case with a metallic *kachink*. She looked to Ashriel for his opinion.

They stood in front of the fireplace, the area cleared now of the leather armchairs that had been there.

"I think that's an excellent arrangement. Of course, it will depend on the furniture you select. We may need to move the reading table."

"I don't think the guys would mind. Don't really need three tables. We could push the three of them together, or we could put this one in storage. For now, would you put it upstairs in that storeroom I showed you earlier? I'll remeasure."

Ashriel touched the table, and they both disappeared. He was back in a few seconds.

"I can't understand why they don't already have an actual living room set up. Didn't their mothers cozy up the place?"

"They did, but after Sarah's death, George put everything that reminded him of her away and out of sight. But I don't think it really helped."

Her heart ached. "Oh. Poor Indy." She drew a deep breath. "Well, it's time to move forward." Tapping a foot, she rested a hand on her hip. "I hate to pick furniture out from a picture online, though. Could look soft and comfy and yet feel like a park bench. I want them to enjoy it, not look at it."

"I agree. You should try it out first."

"Sweetie, how the heck am I supposed to do that?"

"I believe it's best to visit the store and try out the samples they have in the showroom."

As much as she'd love to go shopping, she'd grown accustomed—perhaps reliant—on the security of the citadel, made even stronger after the manticore attack. But she couldn't let herself become dependent. One day she would leave, and then what?

Ashriel seemed to read her thoughts. "There's no need to worry. You'll be safe with me."

"Okay. I can be ready in no time." She headed for her room but came back quickly. "I just remembered that after paying for the dojo, I won't have enough money for what I want. We'll need to go somewhere first. I need to dig up some cash."

The Kincaid cousins looked every bit like the FBI agents they really weren't, as Chase studied the Wild West mural painted high on the wall of the Ford County Sheriff's Office waiting room, and Ben checked out the framed pictures on the wall of *Gunsmoke* stars Burt Reynolds and Buck Taylor posing with the sheriff. Everything about Dodge City was rooted in the Old West motif, even the names of the streets.

Ben rolled his eyes. It was tacky, like a Hollywood wannabe. But he was sure Chase was in his glory. His cousin loved all this Old West stuff, ever since he'd started spending time at Pete's ranch. The more authentic, the better. He was sure there wasn't a cowboy movie ever made that Chase hadn't seen at least five times.

He could probably recite every word of dialogue from every Clint Eastwood and John Wayne movie, and he owned the complete collection of *Bonanza* episodes, even the black-and-white ones. The sound of a door opening made him turn around. A man in a sheriff's uniform strode toward them and handed them back their badges, which the deputy on reception duty had requested to verify their identities.

"Agents, here y'all go. Thanks for your cooperation. I'm Sheriff Dunwoody. What can I do for you?"

Chase shook the Stenson-wearing, middle-aged man's hand. "Sheriff. I'm Agent Morris, and this is my partner, Agent Stewart. We're investigating the death of Eli Isaacs. I understand his body is being kept at the local hospital morgue, and we need your official permission to view said body."

"Well, yes, that's true, agent. But I'm curious. Why is the FBI bothering with a case here in our little cow town? Eli was a local, well-known to me as a fine, upstanding citizen, and certainly wasn't involved in organized crime or the like."

"The details of this death," Ben said, "are very similar to another case we're working on in Nebraska, and that may mean that the assailant crossed state lines and committed this subsequent crime, which would make this a matter for the FBI."

"Yep, it would. Well, all righty then. Let me make a call and give the folks over at the hospital a head's up that you're on your way, and make sure somebody's available to assist you." The sheriff ambled toward his office but stopped and turned back toward them. "But just so you know, ain't much to see. I don't know what kind of assailant you're looking for, but Eli don't have a mark on him, except now from the autopsy, of course. Young, only thirty-five, and took good care of himself, too. Didn't smoke, did that jogging thing every morning."

Sheriff Dunwoody shook his head. "His poor wife is devastated. Just gave birth to their third child a few weeks ago. No financial worries, at least. Eli hit the lottery 'bout five years back. Guess he used up all his luck on that day. Thought for sure it was a freak heart attack or aneurysm, but the coroner says no. Nothing on the tox screens, so not drugs or the like, although the quantitative testing won't come in for another couple of weeks. Got the tests on a homicide rush, just in case. CYA, boys, am I right?

"But it's a waste of time and taxpayer dollars, you ask me. How can a substance that don't show up on a qualitative screen suddenly show up on a quantitative test? But thems the rules. Coroner's a poker buddy of mine, and I know for a fact that he couldn't find a damn thing wrong with Eli, not a damn thing. Driving him to distraction, too, cause it's the first time he's ever had to list the cause of death on a death certificate as unknown."

"Did Mr. Isaacs work at the hotel?" Ben asked.

"Nah, what with the lottery money, Eli didn't have to pull a nine-to-five. Had some investments and traveled a bit for those. He was staying there a few nights, is all. According to his wife, the new baby was leanin' a tad bit on Eli's nerves, so she sent him to spend a few days in the hotel for some peace and quiet. Young'uns that age don't seem to sleep much and cry a whole lot. Sweet, that wife of his. My wife never let me off the hook, that's for darn sure. Woulda come after me with the iron skillet if I'd tried to shirk my daddy duty. Missed a whole lotta sleep and changed a whole lotta diapers in my day, boys."

When the sheriff went back into his office, Ben turned to Chase. "A newborn in the house, and they already had two other kids? I don't care how sweet, I can't picture any woman sending her husband off for some R and R at a time like that. Could be wrong, but sounds to me like Eli was having an affair. And his wife just had a baby. Man, that's cold."

"Yup. Not exactly husband-of-the-year material."

"I feel bad for his widow."

Chase tugged at his shirt collar. "How do people wear suits and ties all day? I'd go nuts."

"Could be worse. Our ancestors had to wear chain mail and suits of armor."

"Yeah, been there, done that. Good point."

"On the other hand, a pissed-off, broken-hearted wife could mean we're dealing with a witch. Lottery winner? Hell hath no fury. She'd have plenty of money to pay for a death spell."

"Could be. Could be a lotta other things, too."

The sheriff stepped out of his office and headed toward them.

"Let's go have a look-see," Chase said.

Ashriel had assumed they were going to withdraw money from a bank, but when Emma said she needed to dig up some cash, she'd been speaking literally. He understood that now as they stood next to an enormous boulder that sat amid acres of scrub pines in the Central Pine Barrens region of Long Island.

"Ash, where is the exact location of the coordinates I gave you?"

He pointed to a spot on the ground a few feet away from where they stood. "There. Why did you bury your money? Were you afraid there would be monsters inside a bank?"

She shrugged and grinned. "Well, you never know. Bernie Madoff and Sam Bankman-Fried come to mind. But I didn't bury this money. My father did. He was a thief."

"This money was stolen?"

"Yeah, technically, but he stole it from Russo. Of course, I'm pretty sure Russo didn't come by it legally either, so every time I hit one of these stashes, I always give half to charity. If I turned it in to the cops, the government would get it, and they're the biggest thieves of all."

Ashriel's eyes narrowed. "The coordinates. Those are the numbers Russo wanted from your father."

She nodded. "Some of them. Apparently, he'd found out my father was embezzling. Although, is it really embezzling if you're stealing stolen money? Quite the ethical conundrum." She climbed up on the boulder and leaned back on her hands, turning her face upward. "The sun's warm today." She gave a little hum. "That feels good. I didn't know until after he was dead that Father was a thief. I found an envelope mixed in with the papers the attorney brought me—the contents of a safe deposit box. Just a list of seventeen sets of number pairs and a list of what turned out to be offshore bank account numbers. I memorized them, put the list in the sink, and burned it. Obviously, the number pairs were map coordinates, and I had no idea what they were for, but something told me I shouldn't leave that list just hanging around.

"Years later, when I was desperate for money, I thought maybe there was something valuable hidden there I could pawn. But when I located one, I was afraid to dig down. Thought maybe there was a dead body buried there or something. But I sucked it up and dug, and was I ever glad I did! Twenty-five thousand bucks wrapped up in layers of plastic bags. I've hit five of them over the years, and same thing every time—twenty-five grand. At least he was consistent." With a gasp of dismay, she sat up. "I forgot to bring a shovel."

"No need. How far beneath the surface is the money buried?"

"So far, it's been just a couple of feet each time."

"Shield your eyes." Ashriel zeroed in on the coordinates, held his hand over the spot, and emitted a beam of energy from his palm. Grass and dirt spewed as the beam cut through the ground. When he'd reached the desired depth, he pulled a dirty plastic package out of the hole.

Emma jumped down from the boulder, and together they opened the package. Ashriel neatly stacked the bundles of cash on the boulder as she counted each one and handed it to him. "Yep, twenty-five grand again." She put the money in the backpack she'd worn. "Okay, let's go shopping." She looked at him with beseeching eyes. "Ash, as long as we're already out, would it be okay if we make a quick stop somewhere first?"

A short time later, they stood before a grave marker in the oldest cemetery in Cleveland, Ohio. It was a small, nondescript flat slab that simply said, *Constance Borello.* Emma kneeled before her mother's grave and placed a bouquet of pink roses on the stone. With a sigh, she trailed her fingers over the granite, then sat back on her heels and shook her head. "Mama deserves more than this postage stamp marker. I tried to buy a nice one for her a few years ago, but this entire section is her family's plot, and the cemetery management wouldn't let me. I don't know why they care, since no one in the family but me is even still alive to protest if they don't like it. They told me a board of directors at some legal firm controls and directs a perpetual care trust fund, and I'd have to file a legal petition to make any changes. Of course, I couldn't do that because I don't exist."

She pointed to the graves right next to her mother's, which were marked by magnificent granite obelisks. "My mother's parents. They died in a car accident two years before I was born."

Ashriel kneeled beside her and slid a comforting arm around her shoulders.

She closed her eyes and leaned her head against him. "Let me tell you about one of my favorite memories. My mother was so beautiful, Ash. She had big green eyes and perfect skin, and her hair was a bright, true red, like Ben's, but long and straight, like mine. She smells like roses. She's holding me and singing to me while she rocks me to sleep. She has such a pretty voice. Soft and sweet. She's singing 'Starry, Starry Night'. To this day, it's my favorite song because she sang it to me. But it always makes me cry, because now I understand why she sang it." She gave a little laugh. "I see my own little baby hand, reaching up to play with her locket."

His heart ached for her. "She must have loved you very much."

"Yes." She turned her face away. "But I was a terrible burden."

Ashriel felt the wave of pain move through her; he felt it like it was his own—pain so deep and sharp it took his breath away. He put a finger under her chin and tipped her face up, so he could see her eyes. They glistened with tears. "Why do you say that?"

"She took her own life. I was only eight months old."

His mind reeling, he held her close and stroked her hair. He hadn't known. He didn't say anything; he just held her. What could he possibly say that could make her feel better? Now he understood. The walls in her mind—the walls so high and thick and locked so tightly that he couldn't see within—contained the memories she worked hardest and longest to lock away. But he had to ask her; he had to know. "Why do you think it had anything to do with you? How do you know?"

"She told me all about it one rainy day, just a few weeks before she died. She was holding me and crying. She did that a lot. Crying. She told me my father—my biological father—left her. No warning, no explanation. One day, he was just gone. He was the love of her life, and he broke her heart. When she discovered she was pregnant, she tried to get in touch with him, but he never responded. Didn't want her. Or me. My mother had this freaky memory, too. She tried to get over him, tried hard to lock the memories away—tried to forget. But she loved him too much, and there were too many memories of him."

She took a ragged breath. "I *know* it was my fault, Ash. How could she ever forget about him, with me as a constant reminder? She was pregnant with me when she met Mario Borello. She didn't love him, and he knew it. But he wanted her anyway because she was beautiful. Another rare and perfect item for his collection. She married him because she was alone and afraid, and he said he would raise me as his own."

She gave a bitter laugh. "He lied." After a moment, she shrugged. "I don't know. Maybe I'm too hard on him. Maybe he would have been different had she lived. Maybe he could have loved me."

"I'm so sorry for your loss. The picture in your locket. Is it your biological father?"

She nodded but offered nothing else. After a moment, she looked up at him. "Do you think she went to Heaven? Even though she killed herself? Most religions say if you take your own life, you go to Hell. I worry about that."

"Most people who die by suicide are in such pain, such mental anguish, that they aren't responsible for their actions. God is merciful, Emma. I believe your mother is in Heaven."

She took his hand, pressed a kiss to his knuckles, and held his hand to her cheek. "Would you mind giving me a moment alone with her?"

"Of course." Ashriel left her, but he didn't go far. He went only to the other side of her mother's family's section of the cemetery, which was partitioned by an ornate black-iron fence. He meandered through the rows. The grave markers' dates spanned centuries. Some were relatively recent, but a few weathered headstones dated back to the nineteenth century.

He noticed something that had the hairs on the back of his neck standing up. With a glance at Emma to make sure she wasn't looking his way, he took out his phone and drifted through the rows, snapping picture after picture. He stopped as he sensed a ghoul approaching. It was annoying, but not surprising, that there would be ghoul tunnels running under the cemetery since the disgusting creatures' preferred food was fresh corpses.

But ghouls were usually active at night, and it was midday. The beacon of Emma's curse must have attracted it.

He hurried back to her, surreptitiously taking a picture of her grandparents' markers as well before he spoke. "I'm sorry, but we must leave."

"Ghoul?"

"I'm afraid so."

"Ugh. I hate ghouls." Emma touched the marker again. "I'm sorry, Mama, but we have to go now."

Chase stood next to Benji in the morgue at Dodge City Community Hospital, looking down at Eli Isaac's corpse. What in the hell was going on? The sheriff was right. Other than the autopsy incisions, the guy didn't have a scratch on him, no puncture wounds that would show an injection, not even a bruise, not so much as a shaving nick. No trace of demonic sulfur, or EMF, or witchcraft. Nothing to show the cause of death.

The morgue attendant, a gawky kid of about eighteen equipped with equal measures of acne and attitude, shoved a thick file folder at him. "Here. I'm late for my lunch break. Do me a solid and refrigerate the leftovers when you're done."

Chase frowned as he grasped the file. "Dude, this was somebody's dad, somebody's husband. Have a little respect."

The boy gave a snide laugh. "Yeah, sure, like he cares anymore." He rolled his eyes, grabbed a pack of Marlboro off his desk, and headed for the door.

Smoking? There's a good life choice. "Hey, kid, those things will make your balls shrink."

There was that eye roll again. "Yeah, sure, gramps." And he left.

Chase fought the urge to go after the little jerk and pound on him. "Were we that obnoxious at that age?"

"No, we were too busy training and chasing things that go bump in the night."

Grinning, Chase wiggled his eyebrows. "Oh, yeah."

"Not what I meant."

"You got your memories; I got mine."

"Do you ever think about anything other than sex?"

"Not if I can help it."

Ben yanked the file folder from his grip and rifled through it. "They were thorough. Test after test after test. X-rays, an MRI, CAT scans, a battery of blood analyses, even genetic testing. Nothing. We got nothing. How does someone just drop dead for no reason?"

"Still thinking witch?"

"No. Even then, there'd be a reason. Sure, a spell can kill, but it causes physical harm, it leaves damage, evidence behind. Ever remember a witch kill that wasn't bloody? Or gross? Or both?"

"No. What then?" Chase blew out a frustrated breath and rubbed his temples as another headache set in. What the freakin' hell was going on here? But he took a sharp breath as he remembered something. "Hey, you know what? I think this might be the same crap that's going down out on the West Coast. We talked about it, remember? Young, healthy bodies dropping, and no one knows why."

A voice, both nasal and acerbic, came from behind them. "I can tell you why."

Ben and Chase whirled, Chase drawing the Aegis of Solomon from his jacket as he turned.

Hades smiled, elegant as usual in an all-black, custom-tailored Italian suit, but there was no mistaking the flames of anger dancing in his eyes. He stroked his dark, pointed goatee. "Hello, boys. Forget to pay our phone bill, did we?"

Chapter Twenty-Four

Emma grinned. "Now, this is living." She pulled the lever on the reclining module, where she sat next to Ashriel on the sectional sofa they'd purchased earlier. Sighing with pleasure, she eased back, kicked off her shoes, and wriggled her toes. The large sectional was even bigger than she'd intended, a long L-shape that dominated the space they'd cleared in the Great Hall. But she'd fallen in love with the wide, tufted-scrolled arms, the thickly cushioned upholstery, and the subtle buckskin-tan microsuede. And best of all? A built-in mini fridge.

Ashriel glanced around the Great Hall. "This space is full. Where do you want me to put the recliner?"

She bit back a smile. She'd purchased the oversized matching recliner as a surprise for Ashriel. He never complained, but the chair he sat on to watch over her at night was, in her opinion, about as comfortable as a cheap plastic lawn chair. "Oh, yeah, the recliner. Hmmm." Tapping her lip, she let her gaze roam around the room, pretending to consider where to put it. But her smile quickly broke free and grew into a laugh. "It goes in my room. It's for you." The stunned look on his face made her wonder if no one had ever given him a gift.

The thought made her heart ache.

His voice was thick and barely audible. "Thank you."

She patted his cheek. "You're welcome, sweetie." Her eyes grew misty. "But it's a very small thing to give to you when you've given me everything."

Blinking back tears, she coughed past the lump in her throat, afraid she was going to start blubbering like an idiot. She opened the built-in refrigerator that formed the corner section and took out the bottle of water for herself and the dark ale for Ashriel she'd put in earlier to test the unit. They were nice and cold. "Works like a charm." Before the guys got home, she'd stock the fridge with their favorite beer. The new seventy-inch flat-screen TV was the icing on the cake. She hoped her knights would love their new living room. She couldn't wait to surprise them with their gift when they returned home from Dodge City.

It was so good to have people in her life! People to be with, to do things for, and to take care of. To love. And she did love them—all three of her handsome knights. Living there with them was the first time since her mother died that she'd been part of a real family. Even if it was only temporary. She handed Ashriel his ale. "Where were we? Still my turn. What's your favorite TV show of all time?"

He considered it for a moment before answering. "I'd have to say *Star Trek*. Especially *Next Generation*, although the original series was very entertaining as well."

She'd expected him to say *Touched by an Angel* or *Little House on the Prairie*, or some other wholesome family show, but a sci-fi show? "Really? Why?"

"I started watching them with Ben. The stories were intriguing, and I found it quite interesting to see things that were mere science fiction back then become today's reality. Communicators were a preview of cellphones. They had voice-operated computers, touch-screen tablets, hand-held detectors, and video chat. The replicator was like 3-D printing, and the holodeck was virtual reality."

A shadow of sadness crossed his handsome features. "After Ben's parents and brother were killed, he sought the escapism of television, and *Star Trek* was his favorite at the time. He was only twelve years old, but even then, he kept his feelings deep inside. After their funeral, I never saw Ben cry, not once. He would sit and watch TV for hours and not say a single word.

"So I sat with him as much as I could. George arranged for him to have sessions with a grief counselor, and one thing she recommended was that Ben keep a journal or a diary, a place to get in touch with his feelings and get those feelings out onto the page instead of keeping them locked up inside. Ben scoffed at the idea and said diaries were for girls. But I suggested that instead he keep a video log, like the Star Trek captains did. *Captain's log, star date, whatever*. Ben liked that idea, and I think it helped him. I did the same thing, and I still do. And it helps."

"Really? You keep a captain's log?" How adorable was he?

"I call it my angel's log, but yes, I do. I've kept it up ever since then. Living as long as I do isn't...easy. It's difficult to grow attached to the people under my charge and then inevitably lose them. I keep a record of everything significant that happens to me, but especially things about the people I care about—things they've said or done, special things I want to remember as the decades and centuries pass. Even angels don't have the incredible memory that you have."

Emma's heart hurt for him. The concept of living forever sounded great—until you understood the cost. "May I use your phone for a second?" He gave her a quizzical glance but handed her his phone. She accessed the video recorder and aimed it at herself. She gave a brilliant smile. "Ashriel, I want you to remember that Emma Borello loves you *always*. You're special and amazing and my friend forever." She blew a kiss at the camera, ended the recording, and handed the phone back to Ashriel, whose blue eyes had gone glassy. "Okay, back to the game. Your turn now, Ash. Two questions about me. Anything you want to know."

He blinked rapidly, and his Adam's apple bobbed as he swallowed convulsively. It took him a moment before he could answer her, and his voice was thick. "Oh, um...favorite book?"

"That's an easy one. *Jonathan Livingston Seagull*. Ever read it?"

Following her example, Ashriel made his seat recline. He closed his eyes for a moment. "An interesting book. A unique perspective."

"Let me guess. The Akashic records again? Like the TV shows and movies you know but haven't watched? You never actually read the book yourself?" At his nod, she frowned. "So, Heaven just downloads all those books and TV shows and movies into your head, like downloading files onto a computer? Just zaps them all into your brain."

"Yes, in a manner of speaking. Does that matter?"

"Heck, yes, it matters! Just having the book in your memory banks isn't enough. It's like cheating yourself, Ash. You miss the experience of reading it, word by word, line by line, of taking the journey along with Jonathan, of considering what he's going through, and how it applies to your own life. A writer—a good writer—is an artist who paints pictures with words. What good is a painting if you shove it in the back of a closet and never look at it? Where's the pleasure in that? You should read it." Tilting her head, she gazed at him for a moment. "Now that I think about it, you remind me of Jonathan. Very much."

"I remind you of a scavenging sea bird?"

She laughed at his disgruntled expression. "No, silly. The story isn't really about a bird. It's a metaphor for humanity's struggle to reach a higher plane of existence, to find the courage to throw off the chains that bind them to Earth and attain the best version of themselves. To reach for Heaven, the divine. You did the same thing, but you flipped the script and did it exactly the opposite. You found the courage to cast off your

Heavenly chains and embrace humanity, and in doing that, you became a better version of yourself."

"Michael would disagree. He says I am the greatest bane of his existence."

Ben was right, it seemed. Michael really was a jerk. "Well, Michael's wrong. You're awesome. And just so you know, you're the greatest blessing of my existence."

He reached for her hand and raised it to his lips. "I'll read it."

"Good. You get one more question."

"What is your...favorite animal?"

"Good one. My favorite animal is the platypus."

His brows rose. "That's an unexpected choice. Why?"

"I feel very close to the platypus. We're both freaks."

"Don't say that. You are not a freak."

"Sure, I am. Webster's Dictionary defines a freak as 'one that is markedly unusual or abnormal.' I'm definitely a freak. Hey, not saying it's a bad thing, just like the platypus isn't a bad thing; it's just a weird thing. *The* weird thing. Defies the accepted laws of nature. A mammal that lays eggs, has a duck's bill, webbed feet, a beaver tail, and the males have venomous stingers on their hind legs? Gotta say, makes the rest of us freaks a little jealous."

"I believe God may have a sense of humor."

"I think he was just messing with us."

Ashriel laughed. "Have you noticed that at times our conversations are extremely odd?"

"Well, you're an angel, and I'm a cursed-human-female-mind-freak, so yeah, I think we can expect that our conversations are gonna lean toward the odd sometimes."

Laughing, he glided his hand over her hair. "You're my favorite person ever, you know that?"

She loved his husky laugh, although he always sounded just a little out of practice. Did he have any idea what it did to her to look into his beautiful angel eyes and know that for a little while he belonged to her? She leaned in and kissed his cheek. "Same goes, Ash. May I ask you a question now? This time, it's a serious one."

"Of course."

She wanted to ask him, but part of her was afraid to know the answer. But she had to ask, or it would always haunt her. "You have the power to heal. Why did you allow Indy, er, George, to die?"

A shadow fell over his face. "I'm so sorry I couldn't save him. The battle was intense that day. The laird of Polaris Citadel became sick and died without an adult heir, and in that moment of weakness, the Illuminati struck with an insidious plan. While human and demonic forces battled on the ground, we angels fought on our spiritual plane of existence. When George was shot, I was battling three dark angels and fighting for my life.

"If Michael hadn't thrown an energy bolt and taken out one of the enemy angels, I most likely would have died as well. By the time I made it back, George's soul had left the veil and was in Heaven. There was nothing I could do."

She imagined Indy in Heaven. She pictured him standing in a rushing creek, like the one that ran in back of the cabin where he'd taken her, looking just the way he'd looked that day, wearing those ugly hip waders, that ridiculous floppy green hat with all the fishing hooks and lures stuck all over it, with a fly-fishing pole in hand—and it made the pain ease. "But didn't Polaris Citadel have their own guardian angel? If that laird was sick, why didn't he just heal him?"

"I think you misunderstand angels' healing power. Let me explain. We simply expedite the body's natural processes on a cellular level to decrease inflammation and increase the speed of healing at an exponential rate. A wound or a burn or a broken bone that might take weeks or months to heal naturally can be coaxed to heal in seconds."

"Like my hand when Chase cut me?"

"Exactly. We can also extract foreign substances from the body, such as poison or drugs or alcohol, and time is a factor as well. The longer an injury goes without attention, the less effective the treatment."

"But you can't fix heart disease or diabetes or cancer or a bad cold—anything like that?"

"No."

She was silent for a moment, remembering what he'd said about Michael throwing an energy bolt. It sounded like something out of an Avengers movie. "If Michael is so strong, why doesn't he just blast all the bad guys?"

"There are rules, Emma, rules set forth by God. Angels are forbidden to injure humans, no matter how evil they may be, unless it is a direct order from our superior. We may battle our own kind and demons or monsters, but when an angel kills a human, it's investigated by Heaven's angelic leadership tribunal, and if that angel is convicted of wrongdoing, there are serious consequences, up to and including death."

"Does that happen often?"

"No. Not in thousands of years that I know of."

A sudden thought made her blood run cold. Ash had killed the hitman. *To protect her*. Now she understood why Ben and Chase had seemed so upset and why Chase had insisted on taking the blame if Michael ever found out. "You took a terrible risk for me," she whispered.

He smiled softly at her. "Some people are worth any risk. But don't worry. The chances of Michael finding out are negligible. And Chase has—what's the phrase?—got my back."

"Chase told me he died and went to Hell, but you rescued him. I've been wondering about that, too. How did he die? And why in the world would such a good man go to Hell? It doesn't make sense. Unless…"

He looked questioningly at her. "Unless what?"

"Unless he made a soul deal, just like Octavio Russo." A shiver ran down her spine. It was the only thing that made sense! "That's it, isn't it?"

He nodded. "It's not my story to tell. But I will say that he sacrificed himself to save an innocent."

More thoughts whirled in her head. Was she being annoying? Questions, questions, and more questions. Father—Mario—always said she asked too damn many questions. But this was Ash, and surely he didn't mind. "What will happen when time runs out for Russo? Does he just drop dead at the stroke of midnight?"

"It doesn't work like that. When a human has sold their soul, when the contracted time is up, Hades sends a hellhound to retrieve it."

"Retrieve? Sounds benign. What aren't you telling me? Don't hold back. I'm a big girl, and after what I've been through, not exactly squeamish."

"All right. The hellhound rips the person's soul from their body, consumes it, takes it back to Hell, and vomits it into the fiery pit. They leave the earthly physical remains intact, but the victim suffers terribly."

She shuddered. How awful! "Sorry, I asked. You know, even after what he did to me, I feel bad for him. No one deserves a fate like that."

"You have such a good heart. But don't waste your sympathy on Octavio Russo. He knew the price when he made the purchase, and if you ask me, he's an evil, black-hearted man who deserves that fate."

Her heart clutched. Chase had experienced the same thing. And all he did was try to help someone else? It wasn't fair! "Chase didn't deserve it," she whispered, tears clogging her throat and blurring her vision.

Ashriel frowned and patted her hand. "I hoped you wouldn't deduce that fact. I should have known you would. No, he didn't deserve that at all. You understand now why I couldn't stand by and leave him to suffer."

"Thank you for saving him." She wiped her eyes with the backs of her hands and struggled for control. She had to remember that he was fine now, and it was a long time ago. When the guys got back from Dodge City, she'd make Chase's favorite dinner and her special triple-chocolate cake, which he loved. "Why does God even allow evil to exist in the first place?"

"Well, I've never met God personally, but I asked Michael that same question many centuries ago."

"What was his answer?"

"He told me that the secret of the universe is balance, and that balance can only be achieved by polarity. Only in contrast to direct and equal opposition can anything exist. Some balances are esoteric and beyond my comprehension, but some are obvious: positive and negative, heavy and light, up and down, light and dark, hot and cold, masculine and feminine, joy and sorrow, pain and pleasure, and good and evil. Even Heaven and Hell exist in polarity with each other. Heaven is powered by the positive energy produced by happy and contented souls, but Hell gains its power from the negative energy produced by the pain and sorrow of damned souls.

"Think about it. Could there be light without darkness? No. The light *needs* the darkness to be the light. He said the same is true of what we perceive as good and evil. Good needs evil, and evil needs good, but we must maintain a balance between the two, or the world as we know it would cease to exist. That's why God created angels and the eligit deus, the special humans He calls His Chosen. We're charged with maintaining the balance."

Emma's head reeled. Absolutely mind-blowing. She blew out a long sigh. "Heavy. I think that's enough existentialism for today. Let's watch a movie—something funny and not even remotely serious. Know what? I'm in the mood for popcorn. You in?"

"Your popcorn? Always. Coco Loco?"

"You got it. You pick a movie, and I'll be back in like ten minutes." She headed for the kitchen but turned back to him. "May I ask you something personal? Last question, I swear."

"Yes."

"Why don't you relax and loosen up a little? Only time I've seen you take that sword off was during your dance lessons. It's just you and me. Do you need to wear that long leather coat indoors? Ditch a couple layers. Toss the sword, kick off your boots, put your feet up. Get comfy, sweetie."

Chapter Twenty-Five

CHASE HELD THE AEGIS of Solomon in a firm grip and pointed at the Overlord of Hell. He didn't know if the weapon could kill Hades, but the corner of his mouth lifted as he imagined plunging it into Hades's chest and watching the sonofabitch finally bite the dust. *Just gimme a reason, you dick.* "What are you doing here, Hades?"

"I might ask you the same question. Imagine my surprise at finding Beavis and Butt-Head here, at the very place I wanted them to meet me, and yet, no words to that effect were spoken because they couldn't be bothered to answer my calls!"

"Take a chill pill. I was busy, so you shoulda left a message, like a normal person. Oops, forgot. You ain't normal or a person."

"Busy? Too busy to answer a call from the Lord of Hell?"

"That's right. Too busy gettin' busy. I wasn't gonna climb down off the tall blonde I was doing just to answer a call from the likes of you, you ass—"

"Chase." Benji shot him a cautionary look before turning to Hades. "What do you know about what's going on here? And why did you want us to meet you here? Since when do you care about somebody dying?"

"I care when that person's soul—a soul that was contracted to me—is taken before its time. This client still had eight years remaining before his debt came due, but now he's dead, and his soul was not delivered to Hell. In fact, it's nowhere to be found. Gone without a trace."

Ben crossed his arms and glared warily at Hades. "Eli's soul is just gone? Not in Hell, not in Heaven, not still in the veil."

"Benjamin, were you dropped on your head as a child? Is that not what I just said? And this isn't the first one, either. It's happening around the globe. And it's affecting my bottom line. And so, *it must stop.* However, my agents could not crack the case, and that is why I called you."

Chase snorted. Hades fancied himself a savvy businessman. Elon Musk, move over. And he was calling his idiot demon minions agents now?

Puhleeze. He sheathed the Aegis but didn't snap the cover. Just in case. "And we should care about this. Why?"

Hades picked a piece of lint off his sleeve. "Because it isn't only souls earmarked for Hell that are going missing. Heaven is missing souls, as well."

Heaven was missing souls? Okay, it just got interesting. And concerning. But how would Hades know what was going on in Heaven? "And just how the fuck do you know that?"

"Because Heaven erroneously assumed that I was the thief and sent that overly aggressive, muscle-bound thug, Raphael, and his haloed henchmen to search every inch of Hell. Insulting that. To have an archangel poking into every nook and cranny of my kingdom was demoralizing." He shuddered. "The place felt so disgustingly clean afterward." He chuckled and straightened his jacket sleeves, his gold pitchfork cufflinks sparkling. "But who could blame them? I do enjoy a reputation for audacity and derring-do."

Chase smacked his forehead. "Look, if you're done brown-nosing your own ass, can we get back to brass tacks and hard facts?"

"So, if you don't have them, where could they be?" Benji asked. "I mean, how can souls just go missing? How is that even possible?"

"Good boy!" Hades's voice dripped with sarcasm. "Have you been doing those online brain exercises?"

Benji's lip curled, and his hands fisted. "Okay, you know what, Hades, you can—"

With a snap of his fingers, Hades paralyzed Benji's voice, and as he struggled to make a sound, Hades continued like nothing happened. "As we are all aware, the human soul is pure energy, each one like a tiny nuclear reactor—an extremely valuable, tiny nuclear reactor. Energy of that vast magnitude cannot simply disappear. Even if the power of the missing souls were exploded and thus transformed, there would be some evidence—a smoking gun, if you will. But somehow, something that cannot happen is happening. Sounds like a case for Scully and Mulder, does it not?"

Tugging at his tie, Chase sighed. So much for his plans for a fun little ghost hunt. "Yeah, it does, but first, fix Ben."

Hades snapped his fingers.

Chase looked at his cousin. "Good?"

Benji glared at Hades. "Yeah. Fine."

Chase crossed his arms. "Talk, Hades. Talk a lot. I wanna know everything you know about this before we agree to anything. No holding nothing back or we walk. The truth, the whole truth, and nothing but the friggin' truth."

"What's the matter, Chase? You don't trust me?"

Trust him? Rage made his ears buzz, his head pound, and his vision go blurry at the periphery, and his hand itched to grab the Aegis again. "*Trust you?* Where should I start? Oh, yeah, does the Crystal of Apep ring a bell?"

"Still holding on to that old grudge?"

"*Grudge?* You said it would cleanse my soul, but it turned me into a fucking demon!"

Hades laughed. "Yes, that was amusing. Come on, Chase. Admit it. As a demon, you had the time of your life. Besides, you're not a demon anymore, are you? So, shall we let bygones be bygones and move on to the pressing matter at hand?"

The time of his life? The image of that young woman's terrified face flashed again in Chase's memory. Grinding his teeth to the point of pain, he wished he could plunge the Aegis into Hades's neck and be done with it, but he'd probably be dead before he finished unsheathing it. "All the bodies the same? All young adults, no apparent cause of death."

"Correct."

"Even you can't tell how they died?" Benji asked.

"I know why they died, but not how. They died because their souls were ripped from their bodies. Not by hellhound, mind you, nor by spell, but in some manner of which I am unaware, suddenly and violently torn out. The cause of death was spiritual shock, which leaves no physical evidence. How this occurred? Well, that, gentlemen, is the billion-dollar question. And that is all I know." He held up his left hand in a three-finger salute. "Scout's honor."

Chase rolled his eyes. What an asshole! "Okay, fine. We'll look into it. For a price."

"A price?" asked Hades, looking wary. "Name it."

Chase was gonna do it regardless, for the poor souls being shanghaied who shoulda been relaxing up on a cloud somewhere, but he was still gonna play hardball. Hades was gonna pay. "No big deal. Just information on a certain Illuminati demon scum that killed my father. His name, rank, where I can find him, and anything else you got."

"Fair enough. Consider it done. When you complete the task."

"Not so fast." Chase slipped into his poker face and leaned back against the exam table. "I want a down payment. The bastard's name. Can't do much with just that, but I wanna know. It'll make me feel all warm and fuzzy."

Hades's nose wrinkled as annoyance flashed in his eyes. "Fine. Alteo-Ra."

"Deal. Email me a list of the vics and whatever deets you got about how, when, and where they died. And Hades? Don't call us; we'll call you. When we know something. If we know something."

"Fine. I hate to micromanage, anyway. Good luck, boys."

"Wait," Ben said. "Is this connected to the other people who were hurt at the Cornelius Rose Hotel?"

Hades raised a brow. "Only hurt? Benjamin, I deal in death, not boo-boos. But I doubt it." The Lord of Hell vanished in a cloud of sulfur.

"Chase, this is unbelievable. *Global?* Where do we even start?"

"No clue. But first things first. Eli here died at the Cornelius Rose, but I'm willing to bet whatever else is going on down there has nothing to do with Eli or the missing souls. Let's hit our motel, change clothes, and pack up."

"Why?"

Chase rubbed his hands together in glee. He'd gotten exactly what he wanted from Hades. Didn't even have to negotiate. He'd find that fucking demon, avenge Dad's death, and hopefully give Emma the revenge she wanted, too.

But first, he was gonna grab a little slice of life for himself. "Why, Benji? 'Cause we're checking into the Cornelius Rose Hotel, and I don't think ghost hunters wear suits."

While butter melted in the microwave, Emma started the popcorn and then broke up a bar of unsweetened baker's chocolate into a bowl, adding hot sauce, finely chopped jalapeños, and salt.

Soon, the sound of rapid popping and the delicious aroma of fresh popcorn filled the kitchen. She'd learned that popped kernels were called flakes while watching TV one rainy summer evening a few years back at the Red Maple Leaf Motel in Burlington, Vermont, during an episode of *Jeopardy*. It was a silly name. They looked more like blossoms.

"Better?"

She turned. Ashriel stood there with his arms spread wide. He'd taken her suggestion. He'd removed his coat, lost the sword, undid several buttons at the neck of his shirt, and pushed the sleeves up to his elbows. He looked down at his feet, clad only in socks, and wriggled his toes. "You're right; this is much more comfortable."

Emma's stomach dropped like she was plummeting on a roller coaster. He looked so delicious, it gave her goosebumps and turned her knees to jelly. And those crinkles he got at the sides of his eyes when he smiled always did her in. But she didn't let on. They'd had that discussion, and she didn't want to make him uncomfortable. "Yeah, that's much better. Want to grab a couple of drinks from the fridge? I'll be in soon." She turned back to her task, hoping he wouldn't see the fierce blush heating her face. Her eyes widened as a hand stroked down her hair. She turned to find him standing close—very close.

"I'm sorry, Emma. I couldn't help myself."

Her breath hitched as her heart skipped a beat and started pounding. "That's okay," she managed to force out.

He brushed his knuckles down her cheek and teased his thumb across her lower lip. "My sweet Emma," he whispered.

Slowly, he lowered his head.

And kissed her.

Her head spun as desire flamed up, sweet and hot, and she gave herself over to the heat and the need. She stood on her toes, wrapped her arms around his neck, and trembled as his mouth moved over hers, and his arms encircled her, and he pressed her close to his body—

"*Emma?* Are you all right?" Ashriel stood by the fridge, a bottle of beer in each hand. "Didn't you hear me?"

Yanked out of her fantasy, she couldn't answer for a few seconds. "What?"

"Do you want beer, hard cider, or cola?"

Even more heat rushed to her face, and she wished with all her heart that the floor would open up and swallow her. Where was a damn sinkhole when she needed one? "Oh, um...the hard cider, please." The beep of the microwave gave her something to do—a reason to turn away. "This won't take long, so you can start the movie without me."

He closed the fridge door. "You look flushed. Are you sure you're all right?"

She didn't look at him as she drizzled the chocolate mixture over his popcorn. "Yeah, just got a big whiff of hot sauce. Stuff takes my breath away." After he left the kitchen, she spread the chocolate-jalapeño popcorn she'd named Coco Loco out in a single layer on a baking sheet to cool and went to the sink to splash her burning face with cold water.

Crushing on an angel? She needed her head examined, even more than usual.

She needed a hard reality check. While he'd admitted that he was attracted to her, how could she think for one second she had a real chance with him? She'd just said it herself. She was a cursed-human-female-mind-freak. Even without her scars, she was a circus act. She was damn lucky that he even wanted to be her friend.

What about Chase and Ben? At least they were just men. Granted, totally hot, drop-dead gorgeous men, but even so, just men. Not that it mattered. While she adored Ben, she loved him like a brother. Zip on the chemistry scale.

And Chase? Chemistry, yes, for sure. Tons of it. He had only to pass her in the hall, and her heart pounded and her skin tingled. But that was a lost cause. The disappointment still stung. When she first came to the citadel, she thought things would be so different. She'd thought he was *The One*. She'd waited and waited for him to make a move, but except for two memorable instances, he'd made it abundantly clear that he wasn't interested in her on any level, except maybe as his personal chef.

While she recovered from her illness, he'd been sweet and attentive. But after she was well again, it was like someone flipped a switch. He lost all interest in her. She'd invited him to do things with her many times, but he'd avoided her like the plague. Still did, except for mealtime. Well, there was that one time in the dojo when he'd teased her with the cartoon-pounding-heart routine and the time he'd kissed her goodbye in the garage, but other than that, Chase made his feelings—or lack thereof—very clear.

He didn't even like her enough to want to be her friend.

That's why she'd been totally shocked when he kissed her in the garage. Talk about mixed messages! Chase, the man of her dreams, the one she'd imagined all those years as her Prince Charming, had finally kissed her. She always imagined that if he ever did, the world would stop spinning, the sky would explode with fireworks, and she'd fall blissfully into his arms, lost in passion.

She wasn't far off the mark. That kiss had burned all the way down to her toes, like a lightning bolt of desire. But Chase hadn't seemed particularly affected. Granted, he had far more experience with kissing than she did—now that was the understatement of the century—and it hadn't been a passionate kind of kiss. Not a bend-you-backward-and-ravage-your-mouth kind of kiss, the kind of kisses she's seen in the movies when the guy finally wins the girl.

Her face heated again with an embarrassed blush at the memory. She'd just stood there like a slack-jawed idiot, long after the garage door closed behind them, wondering if there was something seriously wrong with her. She was disturbed and confused by her reaction. How could she be strongly attracted to both Chase and Ashriel? Was that normal? Or was she some kind of repressed nymphomaniac?

Probably not a nympho. After all, there was Ben, who was objectively all manner of hot, and yet she felt no sexual attraction toward him.

It seemed most likely that her incredibly passionate response to Chase's kiss was a result of her subconscious expectations, built on the many years she'd fantasized about him being her Prince Charming, her dream man. But that fantasy was over. After Chase's lack of interest in her, she'd come to think lately that her dreams of him hadn't meant that he was her destiny.

Perhaps he was a guidepost to lead her to safety.

To lead her to Ashriel.

She was head over heels in lust with her guardian angel, with whom she hadn't even a snowball's chance in Hell. When did it happen? When had her love for Ashriel crossed that line from close friendship to desire?

Perhaps it had been inevitable, from a purely biological standpoint. After all, she was a young, healthy, unattached woman in the prime of her sexuality, and he was handsome and strong and sweet, and they were in constant proximity.

But so was Ben, and she spent considerable time with him, too, some of it in extreme physical contact.

The whole sexual dynamic was so confusing!

How would she react if Ashriel's lips ever touched hers—not just in a dream, not just in a fantasy, but for real? She was incredibly attracted to him. But would Ashriel's kiss affect her as much as Chase's had?

Ugh! She needed to put the whole subject aside for now. She had more important things to worry about. She'd gone without a man for this long. It wouldn't kill her to wait a while longer. The clock was ticking. She'd been marking off the days on her calendar with big red X's.

With an aggravated sigh, she splashed her face again and looked at her dripping face in the mirror that hung over the sink. "He's your guardian angel, and he's your friend, and that's amazing. Do yourself a favor, Emma, and don't screw it up."

She dried her face, put Ashriel's spicy-hot popcorn in one bowl, her salty buttered popcorn in another, and joined him in the living room.

Ash had picked a hilarious comedy, but her eyes didn't want to stay open, and if she yawned one more time, she was going to scream. Her restless night and early morning were catching up with her.

Cool air moved over her skin, and she shivered. Directly across from her was a vent set high in the wall. Surely the air conditioning wasn't on at this time of year! She wrapped her arms around herself and wished she'd thought of buying a throw blanket while they were out shopping. She didn't want to get up and go to her room for her robe. She pointed to the vent. "Can we turn that off?"

"Chilly?" Ash lifted a wing and held out his arm. "Come on. I'll keep you warm. I'm sorry, but the system was designed so that the vents could not be turned off. Without constant fresh air flow, the walls would soon be covered in mold. But it is getting chilly. No doubt, the heat will kick on in a moment."

In seconds, she was snuggled up against his side, comfy and cozy and blissful underneath the warmth of his wing, with his arm wrapped around her. She was out like a light.

The Challenger idled in a parking spot in front of the Dodge City Office Supply. Ben put his Big Gulp down next to his half-eaten burrito and examined the clip-on photo IDs Chase tossed into his lap as he slid behind the steering wheel.

Ben's eyebrows rose higher and higher as he read them. "Who Ya Gonna Call Paranormal Investigations? You're Egon Venkman, and I'm...*Harold Spengler?*" He cast baleful eyes toward his grinning cousin. "Seriously?"

"We're playing sealgair, and if you can't have a little fun with it, what's the point?"

"Oh, I don't know. Getting the job done, maybe? Without making fools of ourselves."

"Lighten up, already. I swear, Benji, you're worse than Michael sometimes. Always gotta be so serious. Michael could call us up at any minute and send us back to Africa, or Russia, or Buttcrack, Alabama. This'll be fun, like a blast from the past."

Chase stared up at fluffy white clouds floating in the blue sky and memories of Texas filled his mind. "I know you hated it there, but those summers we spent training with Pete and Wyatt in sealgair methodology were the best freakin' days of my life. Man, I loved it. It was simple and peaceful. Hard chores in the morning—feeding and watering the stock and then mucking stalls—then lessons, and then late afternoons riding along on horseback, following the herd, with nothin' but the creak of the saddle and the sun and the wind and the snorting of the steers. A man can really discover who he is out there. I found myself out there on the range. "

"Glad it was good for you. But you're right; I hated it. It was too damn hot and dusty; I didn't enjoy riding horseback—much less behind stinky, farting cows; I had to get library books delivered in the mail; the internet sucked; and no girls even close to my age within fifty miles. But you really got into that whole cowboy life." He laughed. "Remember how hard it was for Uncle George to get you to stop saying *y'all* after he brought us home?"

Chase chuckled. "Yep. Had to drop and give him fifty pushups every time he heard me say it."

"Still have a bit of Texas in the way you speak."

Chase shrugged. "You know what they say. You can take the boy out of Texas, but ya cain't take Texas outta the boy. Man, thinking back on all that...I just can't believe Pete or Wyatt set us up at that vampire den. I know what the evidence says, but my gut says somethin' else. We gotta find out what happened."

"We will. But people can change, Chase. A lot of years have gone by since then. We have to be objective and not let old childhood memories rule over our judgment."

"You're right. Told myself the same thing." He paused as a few more sweet memories flitted through his mind, and a grin spread. "Lost my virginity in Texas. Good times, man. Good times."

"Want some alone time to reminisce?"

"Maybe later." Chase's cellphone rang. He checked the caller ID and groaned. *Oh, great.* "What's wrong, Ash?"

"We need to talk. I discovered something odd about Emma's ancestry."

"Like what?"

"It will take a while to explain, and I need to show you pictures."

Chase sighed. "Look, is it life-threatening or dangerous to her or us in any way, or can it wait until we get back?"

"It's not dangerous to anyone that I am aware of."

"Good, then we'll talk about it when we get home. She okay?"

"Emma is fine."

"Good. Later." Chase ended the call. He turned to Ben. "Where were we? Oh, yeah. Back to why we're here. Look, we already know that dead guy Eli ain't linked to this, even if he died at the hotel. I'm telling you, all we got here is a ghost or maybe a poltergeist. I'm starting to have my doubts it's even Billy the Kid. Too bad. Owners are probably just milking that rumor to draw people in.

"I think if a real-life gunfighter with twenty-one bloody notches on his gun belt was haunting the joint, there'd be a lot more than broken plates and glasses and a few injuries. Relax, cuz. Have fun with it. Please? It's just for a few days. Don't we deserve some fun and a break from the fucking Illuminati nightmare that is our lives? Been a long time since we worked such an easy gig. Child's play. Piece a cake. Smooth sailing. Easy like Sunday morning."

"You done, Chase? 'Cause I got a few of my own. How about time suck. Avoiding the obvious. Skirting the issue. Beating around the bush. Hiding your head in the sand."

Chase put Chimera in reverse and backed out of the space. "I got no idea what you're talking about."

"Oh, so we're *not* gonna lower ourselves to Ghostbusters' level and work this case any newbie sealgair still wet behind the ears could handle just so you can stay out of the citadel and avoid Emma? It's so obvious that this trip is just a distraction—"

Country rock blared as Chase turned on the stereo. As they merged into traffic on the main road, Ben had to shout to be heard over the screaming guitar. He reached over and turned down the music. "Fine. You don't want to be at home? Then we should still outsource this Mickey Mouse case to the closest sealgairs and get started on the missing souls."

"Outsource? Listen to you, *outsource*. And you wonder why I call you a nerd." Chase turned the radio volume up again.

Chapter Twenty-Six

EYES SHINING LIKE A kid on Christmas morning, Chase couldn't help grinning as he and Ben stepped into the heirloom elegance of the Cornelius Rose Hotel's lobby. It was like stepping back in time, except the Cornelius Rose Hotel was better. It was everything he imagined the real Wild West to be, but with all the modern amenities.

The hotel was small by hotel standards, just a large Victorian house, but what it lacked in square footage it more than made up for in period opulence. He hummed along with the jaunty strains of the familiar ragtime favorite "The Entertainer" that drifted from a player piano in the attached saloon.

Ornate gold chandeliers made to look like old-fashioned gasoliers with frosted and etched white-ball glass shades hung from high ceilings dressed in copper-tin tiles. Thickly sculpted crimson and gold Aubusson rugs contrasted with dark hardwood floors.

Victorian-style furniture graced the lobby: curved triple oval-back settees and matching gentleman's chairs in mahogany wood upholstered in red velvet, and the coffee tables and side tables were matching mahogany with white marble tops.

An ornately carved staircase curved up to the cantilevered second floor, where oil paintings of western scenes in gold-filigreed frames hung on crimson silk-papered walls.

As they passed the louvered batwing doors that led to the saloon, two beautiful can-can dancers standing at the bar waved at them and winked. The girls wore colorful period-style dresses with low-cut bodices and high-cut skirts, their legs shown to advantage in fishnet stockings and high heels. He elbowed Benji. "Now we're talking, man. This place puts the *wild* in the Wild West."

Benji raised a brow. "Wild? Looks like Las Vegas's idea of the Wild West, not the real deal. I mean, look at this place. For an old house in the middle of nowhere, it's actually quite elegant."

"Website says it started off as a hotel and saloon, like it is now. But the little town around it turned into a ghost town when the gold rush petered out, and a fire took out most of the buildings. Then it was a working ranch for decades before the original owners sold out and the new owners restored it back to the way it was. Kept most of the acreage. Dude, they put on a big-ass rodeo and barbecue party twice a year. People come from miles around with campers and RV's. Maybe we'll come back for vacation."

Benji snorted. "Yeah, well, I was picturing sawdust on the floors and spittoons in the corners."

"That's the poor man's version. This here is the rich man's, the kinda place for men who struck it big in the gold rush, or cattle barons, or outlaws living it up on bank-robbery spoils."

"The two percenters. Some things never change, I guess." Benji came to a sudden halt. He looked around the place. "Wait. Notice anything weird?"

Chase gave the place a once-over. "Huh. Now that you mention it. Where is everybody? This time of day, this place should be crawling with guests. Come to think of it, I didn't even see anyone other than employees in the saloon."

"Exactly."

"Let's find out."

They continued to the front desk. The forty-something man behind the counter wore a period costume, dashing from head to toe in a black velvet coat with a red and white candy-striped vest, his trim dark hair parted in the center and neatly oiled down, and he sported an impressive handle-bar mustache. "Good afternoon, gents. How may I assist you?"

Chase nodded to the man. "Checking in. Name's Venkman. You Burrows, the manager?"

"Yes, sir."

"We spoke earlier." Chase grinned and flashed the fake ID that proclaimed him to be an employee of Who You Gonna Call Paranormal Investigations. "We're here to help."

Burrows blew out a sigh of obvious relief. "Thank God, you're here. The disturbances have gotten worse, and since that poor man died upstairs of no apparent cause, people are canceling their reservations, and new reservations have practically stopped. They think our ghost is murderous instead of just mischievous. Whereas mischievous brought the guests in droves, murderous has the exact opposite effect, I'm afraid."

"Yeah, well, when guests check in, they like to check out. Alive, that is. That why it's so quiet in here?"

As if on cue, a woman's scream echoed through the lobby. As they whirled toward the sound, one of the can-can dancers ran out of the saloon, screaming. Chase exchanged a quick look with Benji and then ran toward her.

Benji got to her first. "What's wrong?"

"Her hair's on fire!"

Chase ran into the saloon with Benji right behind him. The second dancer stood there, angry but apparently unhurt, looking down at the floor at what had once been a fancy blonde wig as the bartender dumped a pitcher of water on it to put out the flames.

The dancer ran a shaky hand through her short, spiky brown hair. "Damn thing cost me five hundred bucks!"

"What happened?" Chase asked.

"Nothing! Nothing happened. I was just standing at the bar chatting with Lacey, and suddenly my wig was on fire!"

"You weren't near a candle or a burning cigarette?"

"No. It was the ghost. I know it was. Well, I'm tired of this. I could've been hurt! *I quit!*" She gave the expensive pile of sodden ash on the floor a last look and stormed out.

Chase motioned to the bartender. "You see anything?"

"No. I was putting glasses away when Mia started screaming. Saw the flames, grabbed a pitcher of water, and ran out here. Mia got the wig off before she got burned, thank God." He crossed himself. "Man, I gotta find a new job. This place is getting dangerous. Not to mention, no guests means no tips. Not worth the gas to drive all the way out here last couple of weeks. Not gonna make my rent." With a sigh, he headed back behind the bar.

Benji shook his head. "A fire-starter? Fantastic."

"Leaning toward poltergeist."

"Looks that way. Hey, where's that wax figure of Billy the Kid you told me about? Let's rule him out before we move on."

Chase glanced around the saloon and spotted it. "There it is. Way back in the corner."

Benji pulled an EMF meter out of his jacket pocket as they headed for Billy. "Think that's really his hat?"

But Chase froze in his tracks, distracted by an enormous painting that hung over the bar of a woman reclining on a red velvet-covered bed piled with fancy pillows.

A bare-assed, naked woman with more curves than the Monaco Grand Prix.

Yowzah.

"Chase?"

"Yeah?" He tore his gaze away from the painting.

Benji stood fifteen feet away, scrubbing his hands over his face. "Work, remember? You're the one who insisted we do this job, so let's get it done, okay?"

"No appreciation for the finer things." With one last leer at the painting, Chase joined his cousin, where a life-size wax likeness of Billy the Kid glared menacingly from a corner of the bar.

"I was asking, do you think this is really his hat?"

Chase shrugged. "So they say. Looks like the one he's wearing in his pictures, but who knows? Dude was short, huh?"

"Article I read said five seven."

"No wonder he was cranky."

"Cranky? The man murdered at least twenty-one people. I'd say that's a bit more than cranky."

Chase made silly faces at Billy's unsmiling wax face as Ben ran the EMF meter all around the hat and the wax figure. Nothing. No trace of electromagnetic residue, which meant no ghost in the vicinity. *Bummer.*

"Sorry, Chase. Billy the Kid may have slept here, but Elvis has left the building."

"Yeah, thank you, Captain Obvious. Okay, first things first. Go out to the car and pack up what we need. I'll finish checking us in and see how many guests are here. I'm gonna see if I can get Burrows to empty the place for us. Fewer people we gotta trip over, the better."

Chase dropped his loaded duffle bag on the padded bench at the foot of his bed. "Burrows took no convincing at all. Only one other guest in the joint, and once he heard what happened, he wigged out, too." Chase chuckled. "Literally. Couldn't get outta here fast enough. Old dude was wearing a cheapo rug, totally noticeable. I mean, he looked like a freakin' Trump wannabe. Probably flammable as hell."

Benji, standing in the doorway, laughed. "Don't blame him for bolting. What's the plan?"

But Chase wasn't listening. He wandered through the place, taking it all in. He couldn't believe what an awesome room they'd been comped. Not room. It was a suite, *The Trapper's Den*, with a sitting room, a kitchenette, and two bedrooms. Looked like a rustic log cabin, with animal pelts hung on log walls and a stone fireplace in the sitting room, which was furnished with a red-and-black buffalo-plaid sofa and a big recliner. Mounted animal trophy heads hung on the walls. "This place is awesome. Two king-size beds, a big-ass flat screen in every room. Don't get much better than this."

Ben shrugged. "We're not here on vacation. I'd like it better if it had a sprinkler system instead of dead animals staring at us."

Chase wanted to laugh when Benji gave the stuffed moose head on the wall a side-eyed glance and stepped away from it.

"Giving me the creeps," Benji said. "Sorry, moose, but I'm not the one who shot you. I don't get why people think taxidermy is an art form. It's morbid. Feels like that moose's eyes are boring holes into me." He laid his hand on the log cabin siding that covered the walls. "Guess this place was grandfathered out of the fire-safety law that requires sprinklers in hotels. With a fire-starter spook around, all this wood is nothing but kindling, you ask me."

Chase shot an annoyed glance at his cousin as he headed to the kitchenette. "Seriously? Now you're quoting fire-safety laws? Do you gotta suck the fun out of *everything?*"

"Sorry, but I'd rather be at home eating Emma's cooking and working on the missing souls. What's the plan?"

Chase pulled an electronic key card out of his pocket and dropped it on the table before sinking into a chair. "First of all, you can untwist your panties, 'cause we're working on the missing souls, too. That's the key to the room where Eli died. Honeymoon suite."

Ben sighed. "So, I was right."

"Yeah. Well, kinda. Not an affair. Checked in alone, but every night he had company for a few hours. Same girl every night, and when the girl left the night he died—after only two hours—Eli was still alive and kicking. After she vamoosed, he ordered a surf-and-turf dinner from room service. Tipped the waiter a fifty. Girlfriend, or even just a recurring hookup, probably woulda stayed all night, he woulda bought her dinner at least. I'm thinking hooker."

"Sounds like."

"Let's sweep the love shack and see if we can find any clues the badges missed. After Eli did Miss Scarlet in the conservatory, maybe it was Colonel Mustard in the kitchen with a wrench."

"My money's on Professor Plum. In the bedroom. With a candlestick."

"That's just sick."

Standing on the immaculately groomed emerald-green fairway at Pebble Beach Country Club, Senator Richard Zyro watched as his father lined up his shot. Sunshine was warm on his back and sparkled like diamonds strewn across the white-capped Pacific, and the muted sound of waves crashing along the shore carried on the cool ocean breeze that caressed his skin.

He hated it.

Except for his father's well-trained personal caddie, who stood out of earshot when he wasn't performing his function and drove his own cart at a discreet distance, they were seemingly alone—as alone as a former President of the United States could ever be in public. But secret service agents stood watch at every entry point, crawled through every copse of trees, mingled within every public building, and patrolled the beach. They were given strict instructions to give the father and son some alone time. But should even so much as a seagull be unwise enough to fly toward them, it would probably get blasted out of the sky in short order.

He smiled at that thought.

His father swung, striking the ball with a solid crack of the club. Not a bad shot. About a hundred yards straight down the fairway, way farther than his own shot had gone. Richard couldn't have cared less. "Father, do you ever ponder the insignificance and utter waste of time that is the game of golf? Hitting a tiny ball as far as possible with a glorified stick, chasing it down, hitting it again, chasing it again, all in hopes of dispatching it into a little cup set in the grass."

"Golf is a game of strategy, accuracy, and excellence honed by experience. I should hope you've learned to value those attributions."

"Of course, I do."

Former President Zyro leveled a look at his son as he handed his club off to the caddie. "Retirement isn't all it's cracked up to be. Golf passes the time and gets me out of the house and away from your mother. More importantly, as far as you're concerned, the golf course is also where connections are made, alliances are formed, and careers are pushed forward."

"I have my own methods, thank you, and I've done very well in my career without having to spend hours broiling in the sun and practicing my chip shot."

"Have you?" his father asked as they walked to the golf cart. "You've yet to marry and produce children, as your mother nags me about incessantly.

And she's not wrong. The people expect their president to be a family man. You're also a senator and the son of a former president. So, what in the hell are you waiting for? When are you going to throw your hat into the ring for the Oval Office? The party leaders have been pressuring me for information."

Richard reined in his annoyance before answering as his father drove their cart to the next hole. "As to the first point, tell Mother that if *she* wants me married so badly, *she* can choose a wife for me. I'm sure she has a short list ready to go. But blueblood pedigree only goes so far. I want to approve the finalist. If I have to reproduce, she's got to be fuckable. As for the second point, soon. But not yet, so squash any rumors that I'll be running next year. I have things to put in order first."

"Hmmm. Let me guess. Does the name Kincaid fit in here somewhere?"

"It does. And you damn well know it."

"That misbegotten family is a millstone around my neck! If you'd managed to bring James into the fold, you'd be sitting in the White House by now, with him as your vice president. The power you could have wielded with a Templar Knight under your control! Until he met with an untimely and accidental death, of course. But we both know that assignment was royally botched."

Richard fought the rage that had him fantasizing about pushing the old man off a nearby cliff and into the ocean, where frenzied sharks waited to rip him to bloody shreds. "We've been over this a thousand times! How could I have known he was wise to us all along, just playing me and colluding with that fucking angel to set me up? But he got what he deserved, didn't he?"

"He did, but his younger brother is still breathing. Your instructions were to eliminate the whole family."

"How was I to know the kid was sick at home? It couldn't be helped."

"And what about his cousin, the laird? Have you made any progress there?"

Richard had no intention of telling his father about the failed manticore attack and adding to his vast arsenal of his son's shortcomings. "I've delegated that assignment to a very capable agent. I'm confident he will resolve the problem in short order."

President Zyro pulled to a stop at the next hole. The look he sent his son was cold and calculating, with no trace of warmth. "It had better be. I've heard whispers. Nothing official yet, but you would be wise to heed the warning. Your rise to power was prophesied by the witch Ravena—first the presidency, then the Counsel of Brethren. She foretold that you would be the one to purge the world of the Kincaid bloodline and reclaim our family honor. But nothing is immutable. If you don't finish the job and take those knights off the chessboard? The Brethren may decide to...replace you."

"*No!*" Richard's vision clouded, and his pulse pounded in his ears. "I proved myself worthy. I made the sacrifice the Dark Lord demanded of me. I put a gun to her head and pulled the trigger. I loved her, and I did it anyway! *For him!*"

"Love? Oh, boo-hoo. That ginger slut was nothing but a good lay—youth and hormones." President Zyro sent his son a look of utter disdain. "Sometimes I wonder if the paternity test was wrong, and your mother cuckolded me."

Rage made Richard's blood boil, and the only thing that held him back from wrapping his hands around his father's throat and strangling the life out of pompous old fuck was the legion of secret service that would stop him. "I *will* sit in the Oval Office and on the Counsel of Brethren," he ground out through clenched teeth. "I will! It's my destiny!"

"Then get rid of the Kincaids! But keep your hands clean. If you compromise yourself, you're no good to our master. No one is indispensable."

The bridal suite at the Cornelius Rose Hotel was a large, three-story round turret that projected from the southeast corner of the Victorian building. Lace-curtained windows encircled the tower and offered an unobstructed view of both sunrise and sunset. As they entered, Chase squinted against the bright rays of the setting sun that poured through the windows.

He smiled. Emma would freakin' love this place. White wicker furniture with green and white striped cushions faced a fancy white fireplace. Wall-to-wall carpeting covered the floors; the sage-green background had a subtle pattern of pink roses climbing a white trellis, creating the illusion of a garden. Even the fancy white-metal dining table for two looked like it belonged on a terrace.

Benji headed for the spiral staircase. "Eli died in bed. Must be upstairs."

Chase followed him. They emerged into a sunlit bedroom that boasted a king-size, white-iron-and-brass bed. The new-looking mattress was stripped of linens and tagged for removal and replacement.

Benji set the small duffle bag he carried on the dresser. "I know you like working it old-school, but Emma bought us a few new toys. Oh, and she asked that we use a phone to record the GPS coordinates directly over the bed, as close as possible to where they found Eli's body, which, according to the coroner's report, was in the middle of the bed. She wants to map out exactly where each vic died, to see if there's a pattern. Close the blinds, will you?"

While Chase noted the coordinates for Emma and pulled down the shades on all the windows, his cousin unpacked the bag and set stuff on the dresser. Chase's tasks completed, he returned to where Benji stood. "Two cameras? Why two?"

"Different functions. One's a full-spectrum camera. It sees more kinds of light than a regular camera. All the visible light and light beyond what our eyes can see. Infrared, ultraviolet. The other one is a thermal camera, a FLIR. Picks up variations in temperature. Cold spots, hot spots. The higher an object's temperature, the lighter the color on the camera's screen." Benji handed the FLIR camera to him. "Check it out."

Chase pointed the camera at Benji and continued slowly around the room. "Yeah, seen this on cop shows. Awesome." He paused when it was pointed at the bed. "Whoa, whoa, *whoa*. Dude, look at this."

Benji hurried over to look at the camera's LCD screen. In pale yellow, as clear as if were spray painted on the mattress, was the shape of a man's body. Chase gave a shaky laugh. "I take it that ain't pee."

"It's a heat signature. But how? Eli died over a week ago." Benji reached over and hit the record button on the FLIR. He leaned over the bed and examined the mattress. "Nothing visible to the naked eye." He took out his EMF detector and ran it over and around the bed. "No trace of EMF." He hurried to the dresser, retrieved the full-spectrum camera, returned to the bed, and took a dozen pictures from different angles. "We should check with Burrows; make sure no one could have been in this room in the last few hours. The room was locked, but maybe an employee with a master key was in here earlier and took a nap on the mattress. Could be residual body heat. Unlikely—and really sick, considering—but you never know."

Chase headed for the door. "I'll go ask him."

Ten minutes later, Chase returned to the bridal suite to find his cousin sitting downstairs on one of the cheerful wicker sofas. Benji wore an odd expression, like he'd stuck his foot in his shoe and found something cold and wet but didn't want to look. "What?" Chase asked.

Benji said nothing; he just held up the full-spectrum camera.

He took it and looked at the digital image displayed on the four-inch LCD screen. He peered closer. "Am I trippin', or does that look like an old-school film negative of a photo of Eli?"

"That's my take."

"This one of the shots you took of the mattress?"

"Yeah."

"Huh. Well, this is new."

"Vast understatement. What'd Burrows say?"

"He checked his computer. Until we opened it, the digital lock on this door hadn't been unlocked in over forty-eight hours."

"Come on, let's finish this and get back to our room. I want to download these pics on my laptop so we can see them bigger, and I want to get everything to Emma right away so she can get to work. Whatever killed Eli and took his soul left a lasting heat signature *and* a monochrome negative on the fabric of the mattress in a light spectrum beyond human perception. This isn't like anything we've ever seen before. I don't have a clue what we're dealing with. Hope our little resident genius can get a handle on this."

"Slow your roll, Benji. Reality check. Can't say we haven't seen this before, 'cause we never had these cameras before, right? So let's not panic."

With a sigh, Ben let his head fall back against the cushion. "You're right. I don't know if that makes me feel better or worse."

"A lasting heat signature. Hmmm. Radiation maybe?"

Benji jerked his head up, his eyes wide. "Nice. Yeah, could be. I'll get the Geiger counter out of the trunk."

Chase plopped down on the sofa to wait. "We got a Geiger counter? Awesome."

Benji came back quickly with the radiation meter. He also carried a pair of pliers and the lead-lined and warded wooden box they kept on hand for cursed objects. They hurried up to the bedroom, and sure enough, when they held the meter over the mattress, it clicked rapidly.

Uh-oh. Chase covered his junk with his hands and stepped back. "This dangerous?"

Benji glanced at him and laughed as he set the meter down and pulled a boxcutter from his pocket. "Well, I wouldn't suggest a nap on here, but this amount of radiation for this short amount of time won't hurt us. Like getting a dental x-ray." He used the blade to cut a dinner-plate-sized piece of the mattress cover and used the pliers to pick it up and put it in the lead-lined box. He closed and locked the box. "I want Ash to see this, too. With his angelic powers, he might be able to shed some light on what's going on here."

Chase nodded. "Agreed. Get this box back in Chimera's trunk. Right now, this is our best evidence, and with a fire-starting poltergeist around, I'll feel better knowing it's protected. I'm gonna hit up Burrows again.

Forgot to ask how many people are gonna be here tonight. Be better if we don't have to worry about civilians gettin' hurt."

When Chase returned to their room after speaking with the hotel's manager, Benji looked up from where he lay on the floor, doing abdominal crunches. "What'd Burrows say?"

Chase crossed his arms and stared down at his huffing cousin. "Dude, really? Can't skip one freakin' day?"

"Few minutes to kill. Healthy body, healthy mind."

"What's that say about me?"

"My point exactly."

Chase grinned. "Bite me. Fifty says I outlive you."

"You're on."

Chase dropped onto the sofa as Benji continued his crunches. "Burrows said he'd be gone by eight, and he gave the staff the night off. We'll have the place to ourselves until nine tomorrow morning. From what he told me, this thing likes to play tricks. Mean tricks. Like turning someone's shower to boiling or pulling out someone's chair just as they're sitting down. Since we're gonna be the only targets here tonight, I figure we wait for it to make its move and blast it with rock salt mixed with agrimony. I brought some just in case, so we're good. According to Emma, if it's a poltergeist like we think it is, that should pin it down, but it's gotta be a direct hit."

Chase reached into his jeans pocket and came up with a folded piece of paper. "She found this spell. Supposedly sends a poltergeist packing, and it don't come back. Might even kill it, or maybe sends it into the light? Who knows? Once we pin it down with the salt and herb combo, we say the words while we burn a new—and it's gotta be new, never lit before—pure white candle with the wick dipped in holy oil. Assuming it actually works, that should do it. Problem solved and case closed."

Benji rolled to his feet. "Wow. I'm impressed. She's a serious asset."

"For sure, but don't get used to it." The coffee maker on the granite counter of the kitchenette caught Chase's eye. "That a Keurig? Love those things. Fresh cuppa joe every time. We should bring the citadel into the twenty-first century and get one."

"What the heck do you think I'm doing with the computerized inventory?"

"Yeah, well, there's important, and then there's *important*."

He opened the cabinets and found an assortment of K-cups. "Coffee, tea, hot cocoa, even apple cider. You name it, they got it. Oh, man, they got French roast. Love French roast." He grabbed a stoneware mug and made a cup of coffee. He looked at his watch and timed it. "Less than thirty seconds, start to finish. Awesome."

"Done, mister coffee? We've got other things to worry about."

"Caffeine is a necessary job tool." Chase lifted his full cup and sniffed deeply. "That's what I'm talking about." He carried his coffee to the table and was just about to sit down when the mug shattered like a bullet struck it. Hot liquid and shards of stoneware exploded. Chase cursed as hot coffee spattered over his hands and chest. *Shit!* Stung like hell. He hurried to the sink and splashed cold water on the scalds.

Benji rushed over to check on him. "You all right?"

"Yeah, yeah, I'm fine."

"Think it was the spirit?"

"What else? You ever had a cup of coffee explode before? Oh, this bitch is so going down. Let's get the shotguns primed and ready. Sooner we blast this thing, the better."

"Okay, assuming the ghost shattered your mug, I didn't see or hear anything when it manifested. You?"

"Nope."

"How are we going to know where to aim?"

"Once again, Emma's got it covered."

Chase retrieved his duffle bag from the bedroom, put it on the sofa, and dug around inside the bag. He came up with a baseball-sized, silvery-white metallic crystal. "Germanium crystal. Emma says it's supposed to lure spirits in like bait. You sprinkle ground wormwood plant on it, and if a spook touches it, you can see little sparks flare up on the surface where you sprinkled the herb. But it's gotta be dark in the room to see."

"Bait crystal? Well, no wonder we've got company. Wait. You're not planning to shoot the thing in here, are you? You know what kind of damage a shotgun, even one only loaded with rock salt, is gonna do to this room?"

"What, am I stupid? I wanna come back for vacay, so I don't wanna piss 'em off. They got a basement. We'll set up down there, bait the hook, and reel him in." Chase squirmed in his seat and stood. "Guess two Big Gulps was pushing it. You set up. Agrimony's in my duffle. Two parts salt to one part herb."

No sooner did Ben set the bullet press on the table when a toilet flush morphed into an explosive splash, and Chase bellowed, "*Sonofabitch!*"

Ben dropped what he was doing and ran for the bathroom. Just as he got there, the door opened. Chase stood on wet tile, soaked from head to toe, a muscle twitching in his cheek, trying hard to keep his cool.

Ben's nose wrinkled. "Uh, is that…?"

Cringing, Chase dragged his sleeve over his dripping face. "This little spook is gonna rue the day. 'Cause now? *It's personal.*"

Benji's body shook with laughter he seemed trying to hold back.

"Go ahead and yuk it up. You could be next." Chase shook his fist in the air as he glared around the sitting room. "Oh, it's on now! Mess with the bull; you get the freakin' horns." He pointed at Ben. "Take that damn crystal and put it in the trunk until we're ready. I gotta take a shower."

Chapter Twenty-Seven

Emma stepped into her room, flipped on the light, and stopped short. "What in the world?" A long garment bag and a shoebox lay on her bed, with a pink note card and a white long-stemmed rose on top of it. She picked up the flower and held it to her nose, closing her eyes as she breathed in the heavenly fragrance. Her mother's face smiled in her memory. Mama always smelled like roses. She read the note.

> *My dear Miss Borello, please do me the great honor of joining me for our dance recital in the Great Hall at nine o'clock this evening.*
>
> *Ashriel.*

She laughed, hugged the card to her heart, and did a graceful twirl. She put the note on her pillow and opened the shoebox, gasping as she found a pair of transparent acrylic dancing pumps embellished with blue crystal bows on the toes. "Oh, they're beautiful!" Her eyes settled on the garment bag.

She bit her lip as she unzipped the bag. Her mouth fell open with a cry of delight as she gazed down at a sky-blue satin ballgown fit for a princess. It was the most beautiful thing she'd ever seen!

She lifted the gown out of the bag and held it up against her, turning to look at her reflection in the cheval mirror. She trailed her fingertips over the diamond-like crystals that adorned the sweetheart neckline and tiny puffed sleeves.

A blue ballgown and glass slippers.

Her lower lip trembled, and her eyes filled with tears. "Oh, Ash."

Chase sat on a wooden workbench in the pitch-dark basement of the Cornelius Rose Hotel, swinging his legs and getting more pissed off by the minute. He couldn't see his cousin. Hell, he couldn't even see his hand in front of his face, but Benji was sitting on a chair not ten feet away. They both held shotguns aimed at the table where they'd set up the bait crystal.

"I tell ya, the little bastard's doing this on purpose."

"Maybe."

"Sure we set everything up right?"

"Yeah, everything Emma told us to do, right down to the letter."

Chase took out his phone and hit the button to activate the display. Although dim, the sudden light seemed like a flood lamp after the pitch dark. Squinting, he peered at the screen. "Two freakin' hours, man. My ass is numb from sitting on this stupid bench." He squirmed. "Think I picked up a damn splinter. You sure there ain't any more chairs down here?"

"Not that I could find. Go upstairs and get one. Know what? Just take this one. I gotta hit the head. I'll bring one down." Benji activated his phone's flashlight and headed for the stairs.

As his cousin clomped up the wooden basement steps, Chase took his place on the rickety old dining room chair. "Make me wait all you want, you little bastard. Don't care if it takes all night. Or all damn week. You're going down."

A heavy thud on the floor above his head made him flinch. The door slammed shut, sending the basement into complete darkness. Then Benji's muffled voice shouted, "Chase! Chase, help!"

"Coming!" Chase turned on his phone's flashlight, then ran across the basement and up the stairs. The door was jammed and wouldn't budge. He flipped the switch to turn on the dim basement light, pocketed his phone, and rammed his shoulder against the door again and again. "Benji!" Things banged, crashed, bumped, and shattered in the hotel's kitchen on the other side of the door.

But his cousin didn't answer him.

"*Benji!*" Still no answer. His heart pounding, Chase ran down the stairs and back up as fast as he could, hoping the running start would give him the extra force he needed to get the door open. But just as he got to the top of the stairs and hurled himself at the door, it opened all by itself. He careened into the kitchen, blinded by the sudden bright light, stumbling over pots and pans and broken plates strewn across the floor.

The forward momentum sent him crashing into the stainless-steel commercial prep island, and he slammed his forehead against the upper spice shelf. Pain stole his breath and had him seeing stars; his ears rang like church bells. He slid to the floor as tins, bottles, and jars tumbled over him. It took a few seconds for his mind and vision to clear.

Benji was plastered to the wall, arms spread wide, suspended about two feet off the floor. "Little help," he squeaked.

His left ear still ringing, Chase hauled himself up and staggered over to help his cousin. He pulled and yanked on his arms, his legs, and his clothes, but couldn't pry even a single finger away from the wall. "Dude, it's like you're glued up there." He stiffened as a soft whirring sound came from behind him.

He slowly turned to find an energy orb, about two feet in diameter, floating several yards away. What the hell? An orb visible to the naked eye? And in bright light yet? Usually, orbs were only visible in photographs or video. *Huh.* This was another one for the books.

In his panic to get to Benji, he'd neglected to bring a shotgun upstairs. Well, he'd try intimidation first. Clenching his fists, he took a menacing step toward it. "Let him go! *Now!*"

The orb bobbled.

Chase got the distinct feeling that the damn thing was laughing at him.

He didn't like being laughed at.

"Be right back, Benji." Chase stomped to the basement door and kicked it off its hinges. The door fell to the floor with a bang. He hurried down to the basement, grabbed a shotgun, and took the stairs three at a stride back up to the kitchen. The orb was exactly where he'd left it. Hovering. Perfectly still.

He released the safety on the Remington 1100 and took aim. "I'm bull. We met earlier, remember? Had coffee together? Meet horns." He pulled the trigger. *Kaboom!*

It was a clean, right-on-target, perfect shot.

That did absolutely nothing.

The orb was still in the same spot.

Bobbling.

With a growl of frustration, Chase reset the gun's safety and laid it on the counter. He rubbed his throbbing forehead where an egg-sized lump was rising from his head butt with the spice shelf. "*Son of a bitch!* What in the fuck are you?" He reached into his pocket for his phone.

Wearing only a white lace bra and panties, Emma stood before her dresser mirror, wrapping a section of her hair around a hot roller. She barely recognized the face that looked back at her. She was so glad that among the many items she'd ordered on a whim weeks ago—items that, according to Glamour magazine's online blog, were every woman's beauty essentials—was a complete makeup kit that had just been sitting in her drawer, untouched until now.

It had taken her over an hour to complete her makeup. She'd messed up the mascara twice and had to start over, but she thought she'd done a decent job. She took a deep breath as a wave of nervous excitement made her heart pound.

It wasn't just her face that she barely recognized. The Victoria's Secret matching bra and panty set she wore were also new. For years, she'd avoided looking at her scarred and mangled body, but now? Now, she gazed at herself, thrilled by what she saw, because what she saw was an attractive and sexy woman.

The fashion-forward bra displayed her full breasts to advantage, creating an astonishing amount of cleavage. French-cut bikini panties showed off her toned thighs and derriere. She turned from side to side, admiring the stylish cut and how the ornate lace applique on the front looked so pretty displayed across her flat tummy.

Her gaze flicked to the ballgown hanging on the back of her door. It was so beautiful! She wanted to touch it again. As she walked across the room, she imagined she moved differently in the sexy lingerie, somehow more flowing, more graceful...more feline.

She trailed her fingertips over the gown, admiring the soft, smooth texture of the silken fabric and the way the material glistened in the lamplight. But she needed to finish getting ready.

She'd wrapped the last section of hair onto a roller and reached for a curler clip as her cellphone rang. She clipped the roller in place and then hurried across the room to her nightstand to get her phone. Her eyebrows rose when she checked the caller ID. Well, this was a first. "Hi, Chase."

"Shot it with the salt and agrimony, but no effect. It ain't like any ghost or specter I've ever seen. It's a freakin' orb. And it's got Benji pinned up on the wall like a butterfly specimen. What the hell is this thing?"

With a small gasp, she pressed a hand against her chest. "Is Ben hurt?"

"He's okay, just stuck."

She sat on the edge of the bed. "If salt didn't hurt it, then it can't be a poltergeist or a ghost. Tell me what you know."

"Little bastard likes to play tricks. Mean tricks. It's a real wiseass. Swear to God, Emma, the damn thing's laughing at me."

"I think you're dealing with a kobold."

"A *what?*"

"A kobold. It's rare. Mostly in Europe." She closed her eyes, reading from memory. "The lore says, 'The kobold is a comparatively weak but very mischievous little spirit, playing tricks on humans and doing things to upset whoever is occupying its space. Although not considered malevolent, once a kobold lays claim to a place, it will not leave unless forced to. A kobold may materialize in different forms, such as an orb, an animal, or an element, such as air, fire, or water. Of note, unlike its more powerful ghost cousins, a kobold cannot phase through solid matter'."

"How do I take it down?"

"Hang on." She was still reading in her head. "Okay, while chanting in the name of all that is holy, I command you to depart into the light, mix mint with salt and human blood, and then you say the same chant when you throw the mixture on the kobold, and then keep chanting until it's gone. There's no recipe, so I don't know the ratio for the ingredients. Best guess? Equal measures; the more, the better. That should put the spirit to rest. Do you have mint? I don't remember packing any for you."

"Not on me. Maybe in Chimera's trunk. But I don't wanna leave Benji in here alone with that thing!"

"Search the hotel's kitchen. I can't imagine their chef won't have mint. Look for a spice jar with little green serrated leaves. Or they might keep fresh mint in the fridge. Make sure you crush the leaves up as much as you can to release the essential oil." She cringed at a loud crash, followed by Chase cursing. "What happened?"

"Bastard threw a pot at me."

"Do you need help? I could send Ash, or we could both come."

"No! You don't leave the citadel and consider that an order. No telling what kinda monster your curse would draw, and I got enough on my plate with this little pain-in-the-ass spook."

"Okay, good point. But what about Ash?"

"Sweetheart, the day I need an angel to help me take down a little ghost is the day I hang it up and take a job stocking shelves at Walmart. Don't worry; now that I know what this sucker is and how to handle it, we got this. And thanks, Em."

"No problem. Good luck."

On his hands and knees, Chase rifled through the wreckage of the prep island, searching for mint. It seemed like a hundred spice jars and tins littered the floor. He'd already searched the fridge, and there were no little leaves. He glanced up at his cousin, still hanging on the wall. "You okay up there, Spidey?"

Benji rolled his eyes, still unable to move. "Peachy," he rasped, panting shallow breaths and glaring at the kobold still hovering nearby.

"Hang in there, dude. Won't be long now." Finally, Chase found mint. He shoved the jar in his pocket and pushed himself up off the floor. He grabbed a stainless-steel mixing bowl and a box of salt off a shelf and put them on the countertop. He chanted, "In the name of all that is holy, I command you to depart into the light. In the name of all..." Continuing to chant as he worked, he dumped the leaves into the bowl and used the bottom of the jar to crush them. A movement out of the corner of his eye made him glance up.

The orb was spinning like a top.

Chase chuckled. "Gotcha worried now, don't I? In the name of all that is holy, I command you to depart into the light..." He poured salt over the crushed mint leaves, pulled his boot knife, slashed his palm, and let his blood flow into the bowl. He milked his hand, getting a good amount of blood, then pulled a rag out of his jacket pocket and bound it tightly around his palm to stem the bleeding. As he continued to chant and stir the ingredients with a spoon, he looked again at the kobold.

Still as a statue.

He flinched as it shot across the kitchen like a bullet and disappeared through the doorway that led to the basement stairs. Benji fell off the wall and dropped to his hands and knees, gulping air.

The lights went out.

Pitch black.

Ashriel raised a hand, and the Great Hall lights dimmed. He frowned. It was still too bright. Too harsh. Too...yellow. With a flick of his wrist, all the lights went out.

He undid the button of his tuxedo jacket and raised his arms toward the ceiling. He splayed his hands and slowly turned in a complete circle as hundreds of sparkling bubbles of light floated from his glowing palms up to the ceiling and hung there, like twinkling stars in a night sky, illuminating the Great Hall with a soft, magical radiance.

Smiling, he nodded in satisfaction.

He flexed his neck, straightened the black bow tie that matched his classic tuxedo, and buttoned his jacket. He surveyed the room, making sure that everything was ready and perfect.

It had to be perfect.

He'd put the long reading tables and chairs upstairs in a storage room, so they would have room to dance. The vintage record player sat on a side table next to a stack of Emma's favorite dance music records. A bottle of champagne chilled in a silver ice bucket on the coffee table, with two etched-crystal flutes sparkling beside it.

Smiling in anticipation, he stood there. Waiting for her.

He understood now what the term *butterflies in your stomach* meant.

Like a vision, she appeared under the stone arch, pausing as their eyes met.

Ashriel's breath caught.

In all his centuries, he'd never beheld such beauty. She wore the ballgown he'd selected for her. The angel stars sparkled like blue diamonds on her gown, flickered like flames on her fiery hair, and turned her eyes the color of honey kissed by morning sunlight.

The dress fit her body perfectly, hugging her slim waist and flaring into a graceful silhouette of shimmering satin. The form-fitting bodice enhanced her breasts, and the sweetheart neckline revealed deep cleavage and twin mounds of creamy flesh that made his heart skip a beat then pound.

She'd done something wonderful with her hair, so that it cascaded over her bare shoulders in fat curls of silken mahogany. And her pretty face—always so lovely. But tonight, her eyes seemed wider and deeper somehow, and her cheeks were pink, as if something had made her blush, and her skin seemed to glow. Her lips were the color of a ripe pomegranate and glistened in the soft light.

Entranced, he could only stare.

Emma couldn't take her eyes off of him. Ashriel was breathtakingly handsome in the crisp, black tuxedo, his eyes sparkling like blue sapphires and his white-blond hair shining. He could have been a prince in a royal castle or the leading man in a glitzy Hollywood movie.

Cary Grant's Dudley had nothing on her angel.

Trembling, her heart beating like hummingbird wings, she memorized every tiny detail. She wanted to remember him exactly the way he looked tonight. Of the hundreds of photographs she kept of him in her memory—priceless treasures, each one—this was the special portrait she would emblazon across her heart, the one she would see whenever she closed her eyes.

She started toward him, but with a gasp, she stopped, her gaze drawn to the ceiling. How beautiful! Laughing with delight, she gave a slow twirl, the full skirt of her gown billowing into a bell as she admired his angel stars. She glided across the room to him, stopped a few feet away, and executed a perfect curtsy. "Good evening, Prince Charming."

Ashriel smiled. "I knew you'd figure it out." He reached for her hand, raised it to his lips, and bowed to her. "Good evening, Cinderella."

"Tell me, Your Grace. Does the spell wear off at the stroke of midnight?"

"If it does, be sure to leave a glass slipper behind so I can find you."

She touched his cheek. "I'll leave them both."

He strode to the record player and set the needle on the record, waiting on the turntable. As the lilting strains of Johann Strauss' "The Blue Danube Waltz" filled the Great Hall, he stepped into the center of the room and extended his hand toward her. "May I have this dance?"

She joined him and placed her hand in his. Her smile was teasing. "Ash, this is supposed to be a recital. Where is our audience?"

With a charming grin, he pulled her close into the classic dance embrace. "Oh, they're here. Jaq and Gus are hiding under the coffee table. Lucifer the cat has been very naughty lately."

She giggled as he swept her into the beginning steps of the waltz. "With a name like that, how could he not be?"

Chase and Ben crept down the basement stairs of the Cornelius Rose Hotel, guided by the powerful beam of a Maglite they'd found on a shelf in the kitchen. They'd split the batch of mint, blood, and salt into two bowls, with each cousin holding one. While Benji methodically swept the basement with the flashlight, Chase waited at the bottom of the stairs, ready in case the kobold charged him.

Benji ducked under a low wooden beam and brushed cobwebs from his face and hair. "Think it left?"

"No, it's gotta be here. Emma says they only leave if they're forced to go. They can't pass through walls or floors, so it would have to go up the stairs. Keep looking." Chase watched as his cousin searched the basement again, walked back, and shrugged.

"Nothing. It must have escaped."

"No! It's here, dammit! I know it is. We'll wait; it'll show itself." Head pounding, he unclenched his tight jaw and flexed his neck, then dropped onto the old dining room chair, stretched out his legs, and crossed them at the ankles. He rubbed his throbbing shoulder and gingerly touched the egg-sized and painful lump on his forehead, wishing he had some Advil. Or, better yet, a bottle of scotch. "And when it shows, it's fucking toast."

Benji blew out a sigh and hopped up onto the workbench.

Emma selected an album from the stack of her favorites. She set the needle on the record and smiled when pops and hisses gave way to a bittersweet melody and a woman's sultry voice steeped in yearning and heartache.

It was the kind of music that belonged in a black-and-white movie from the 1940s. The kind of movie with a femme fatale songbird who seduced with a sweeping length of platinum-blonde hair falling over one eye, tempted in a long slinky gown that accentuated every dangerous curve, and teased with a sexy little mole painted next to blood-red lips as she belted out a song about love gone wrong through an elegant nightclub's smoky haze.

She turned, and she found him watching her.

A delicious, shivery ripple of desire made her breath quicken as something hot and wild and a little dangerous sparked cobalt in his eyes. He smiled at her, and just like the first time—just like every time—her heart swelled with emotion.

Keeping her eyes on his, she walked back to him on legs that were just a little wobbly. She twirled into his embrace, her gown swirling around their legs in a shining azure cloud.

The languorous, seductive music called for a slow dance.

She rested a hand on his shoulder, and with the other, she traced his jawline with her fingertips. She slid her hand around to his nape, her fingers threading into his silky curls. With a soft, blissful sigh, she laid her head on his chest and breathed deeply of the heady, spicy scent of his aftershave, stirred by her touch.

He wrapped her in his arms and rested his cheek against her hair.

And they danced.

They swept her away—the music and her beloved angel. She closed her eyes and let the magic seep into her—the flowing, liquid notes of the melody, the stir of emotions, the sexual pull—until there was nothing but music and movement and Ashriel and the sweet, aching pleasure of being held in his arms.

She drifted along to the gentle current of the lazy rhythm, dipping down into the low, bluesy throb of the bass and rising with the high, wailing sobs of the sax.

It was music to dream to.

When the song ended, they stayed that way, holding each other and swaying to the rhythmic scratch of the needle at the end of the record. Ashriel raised a finger, and the needle reset itself on the vinyl.

And the song began again.

Benji checked his phone. "It's been over two hours!" He picked up a soup can of nails sitting on the workbench and hurled it across the basement. "Chase! I'm telling you, *it's not here!*"

Chase gritted his teeth. He really, *really* wanted to get the little bastard! But Benji had the patience of a saint. Maybe he was going off the rails with this thing. "Okay. One more sweep, and then we'll call it a night down here. Maybe you're right, and somehow it got past us. We'll try upstairs."

Benji grabbed the Maglite and searched again. "Nothing. Just a mangy old cat hiding under the workbench. The kobold must have sneaked past us."

A cat? Suspicious, Chase grabbed the flashlight from Benji, handed him his bowl, and cautiously approached the workbench. He was allergic as hell to cats. So why wasn't he sneezing his fool head off? He crouched and pointed the light under the workbench. Huh. Yeah, it was a cat all right—an ugly, ratty-looking thing that hissed at him. It'd been a long time since he'd been near a cat. Not since that witch's familiar in Chicago. Maybe he wasn't allergic anymore?

But then he noticed something weird.

He played with the light, shining it in the cat's face. He stood and backed away. He took out his phone and typed *Got him! No eyeshine. That ain't no cat. On my mark*. He held the phone up for his cousin to read.

Benji's eyes widened as he read the text. He nodded and gripped a bowl in each hand. Humming nonchalantly, Chase meandered over to the workbench and gripped the lipped plywood top. He nodded at Benji and then flipped the workbench over, exposing the cat.

As Chase chanted, "In the name of all that is holy..." Benji threw the contents of the bowls at the cat, but the kobold was quick, and only a small amount hit its tail as it bolted. The cat howled and morphed into a ball of fire.

It ricocheted around the basement like a blazing pinball.

Benji ducked as the fireball whizzed past him. Chase dove for cover behind an old dresser as the kobold seemed to aim right for him.

The flaming kobold zoomed up the stairs and into the kitchen. The basement door—the same door Chase had kicked off its hinges—slammed back into place. The cousins ran up the stairs, but no matter how hard they tried, they couldn't get that door open.

"Stand back, Chase. I'm gonna try a karate kick Emma taught me. Packs a wallop. Hard to do on stairs, but I'll give it a shot."

Chase trotted down the stairs. "Let's see whatcha got, Bruce Lee."

Benji landed a solid—and impressive—kick on the door. Again. Again. And again.

The door didn't budge.

A faint acrid odor raised the hairs on the back of Chase's neck. "Benji?"

Benji limped down the stairs, favoring his right foot. "Yeah?"

"Smell smoke?"

Looking over Chase's head, Benji froze at the bottom of the stairs and slowly nodded, his horrified expression making Chase whirl to look behind him.

"Oh, *fuck me!*" The unmistakable flickering-orange glow of fire came from behind a tall wooden shelving unit. They ran to check it out. A dozen old roll-away beds stacked in a corner of the basement were on fire, tall flames licking the wooden floorboards and joists overhead.

Chase assessed the situation: door sealed by spectral whammy; no water; flames too big to beat out with their coats. He reached for his phone to call for help and found its glass face cracked and hazed. He tried to swipe and pushed the side buttons, but it was dead. He must have broken it during his dive for cover. "Gimme your phone."

Benji reached into his jacket. His eyes widened as he patted his pockets. "Guess I lost it when that thing threw me around in the kitchen."

Chase grabbed Benji's shotgun and ran up the stairs.

"You think rock salt is gonna go through wood?"

"Not really, but worth a try. Unless you got a better idea?" He took aim, turned his face away, and shot the door. All it did was blast some paint off and raise some splinters. He shot again—just more splinters. "*Shit!* Time to call in the cavalry. Pray for Ash like you ain't ever prayed before." Chase ran down the stairs, dropped to his knees, folded his hands, and prayed with all his might, but got no answer.

Benji seemed to do the same.

Nothing.

Panicking now, they yelled and screamed for Ashriel, but to no avail.

"Where is he?" Benji raked his fingers through his hair, his eyes wild. "What the hell is going on?"

"No clue, but we gotta get outta here fast!"

Coughing and wheezing from the smoke that rapidly filled the basement, they searched frantically, but they could find no way out. The basement had no windows and no accessory door to the outside. They found a few basic hand tools in a small box, but nothing that could aid their escape.

By now, the wooden floorboards above the burning mattresses were ablaze, and embers were drifting. Chase tore up the stairs and pounded on the door, yelling over and over, "Help! Fire! Help!"

A smoke alarm screamed in the kitchen, but no one was there to hear it.

"Chase! Get down here! It's an old-fashioned coal delivery chute. This should open to the outside."

Chase stumbled down the steps, nearly falling, his head spinning. *Idiot!* Stupid mistake, born of panic. Standing at the top of the stairs had exposed him to the worst of the fumes produced from the chemicals in the burning mattresses.

The deadly toxins took their toll.

By the time he made it to where Benji stood, Chase's gut roiled with nausea, and he swayed drunkenly on his feet. Benji used a screwdriver to pry the rusted coal-chute door open. The last thing Chase saw were Benji's bloodshot green eyes coming toward him, and the world went black.

Ben caught Chase as he passed out and then pushed him head-first through the coal door. It was a tight squeeze, and his cousin would likely have bruises and scrapes from the harsh treatment, but he shoved Chase all the way through the thick stone foundation wall to the outside.

Chase landed in a crumpled pile on the grass. He didn't move.

Coughing and choking, his eyes tearing from the stinging smoke, Ben tried to squeeze himself through the coal-chute door, but his muscle-bound shoulders were too wide. Even in a diving position—with his arms stretched out in front of him—it was no use. He shoved and pushed and pulled and twisted and kicked with all his considerable might, but there was no way he was going through that coal door.

His heart pounded with fear and oxygen deprivation. He needed air! He sank to his knees and stuck his head in the chute, but not much fresh air came in. He prayed for Ashriel, then for Michael, out of sheer desperation, but the room started spinning. Smoke clogged his lungs, and he coughed uncontrollably, gasping for air as embers rained down on him in little bursts of searing pain. His back and scalp crawled with the excruciating sting of a million tiny biting insects.

His clothes and his hair were burning!

He rolled to put out his clothes, then lurched to his feet and beat on his head with his hands to put out the fire, his palms blistering, and the pain excruciating! Gasping for air, his legs gave out, and he fell hard on his back. Lost in searing pain, he stared up at the ceiling with blurry, stinging eyes—the ceiling that was nothing now but a rippling red and orange carpet of flames.

Chapter Twenty-Eight

Ashriel had planned a surprise for the last dance of their special evening. He retrieved the bright-blue record album titled *Disney Classics-Magic Philharmonic Disney Orchestra* from where he'd hidden it on a shelf. He'd purchased the pristine antique record as a gift for Emma.

Careful not to let her see the album's cover, he hurried to the record player, slipped the shiny black disc from its sleeve, and placed it carefully on the turntable. Smiling in anticipation, he gently set the needle into the first groove of the spinning vinyl. He whirled, so he could see her face when the song began.

Emma recognized the music immediately, just from the first few magical plucks of the harp. Her eyes filled with tears as the lilting flutes, the ethereal, fluid notes of the violin and the cello, and the spirited piano added their lyrical voices to the timeless classic from the movie *Cinderella*, "A Dream Is a Wish Your Heart Makes."

The romance of that beloved song wrapped shining ribbons of joy around her heart. The music was steeped in sweet memories of childhood innocence and bright, cherished dreams of enchanted castles, handsome princes, and true love. Countless times, she had watched that movie and listened to that song as a little girl.

Through the haze of tears, as the simple yet hauntingly beautiful notes of the melody were tapped out on the xylophone, she watched her angel return to her.

Ashriel gently smoothed away the tears from her cheeks. "I didn't mean to make you cry."

She smiled up at him. "They're happy tears."

"All right, then." He drew her into his arms and led her into the graceful, whirling steps of the Viennese waltz.

———— ⌘ ————

Ben stared at the ceiling as the world faded away, until there was no more pain or fear, until the acrid stench of burning hair and melting plastic disappeared from his memory, and the terrible last thoughts of regret for things left undone and unsaid slipped from his mind...until there was only silence and the dancing, mesmerizing beauty of yellow and orange flames.

Time held no meaning, but eventually the peaceful silence gave way to a soft tickle of music that gently nudged him, like a mother's whisper and a soft touch on his shoulder. *Time to wake up, sleepyhead.* The music grew louder. It was...Christmas music. His mother's favorite Christmas song. Nat King Cole singing about chestnuts roasting and Jack Frost nipping noses.

Benji stood at the fireplace, warming his chilled hands as a cheerful fire blazed, and Christmas music and the heady aromas of gingerbread and pine filled the Great Hall with holiday cheer.

He couldn't wait for Jamie and Dad to see the awesome snowman he'd built! And Ash had made snow angels with him. How cool was that? Snow angels made by an actual angel. He bit his lower lip as a mischievous impulse beckoned. He checked over his shoulder to make sure he was still alone before he stood on his tiptoes and reached for the fire coin on the mantel. *Yes!* A thrill of pride hitched his breath as he grasped the ancient coin.

"Benjamin Franklin Kincaid."

Uh-oh. Mom used his whole name? He was in trouble! He spun around, hiding the coin in his fist. His mother stood in the doorway, holding a ceramic Santa mug and a small red plate.

"Put it back, young man."

"But, Mom, if I'm man enough to reach it, then why can't I use it? Jamie gets to!"

"Jamie is twenty and a grown man. You may be as tall as an oak already, but you're only nine. Not until you're thirteen. You know the rules. It was the same for Jamie, and it will be the same for Chase."

Frowning, he put the coin back in its place atop the mantel. Jamie got to do *everything*.

"And don't pout, young man. Men don't pout, and neither do knights." Mom held up the mug with a coaxing smile as she crossed the room. "Fresh gingerbread men and hot chocolate, just the way you like it, with mini-marshmallows and a peppermint stick."

Marshmallows? He forgot about the coin and headed for the mug.

"Careful, honey," she said as she handed it to him. "It's hot."

"Okay. Think Dad and Jamie and Grandpa are really gonna bag that buck?"

Mom snorted and glanced at the wall clock as she headed to the sofa. "Well, you heard your dad." She set the plate of cookies on the coffee table and propped her hands on her hips. She said in a deep voice, "*We're gonna have venison on our Christmas table, mark my words, or my name isn't Douglas Aaron Kincaid.* But they've been slogging through the snow for nearly five hours now, and it's gonna be getting dark soon. So, I'd say the odds are slim. Your dad may need to change his name."

They shared a laugh as she plopped down on the sofa and patted the seat next to her. "But don't worry, we'll have plenty to eat either way. Did you see the size of the turkey Aunt Sarah bought? The thing looks like it came from Jurassic Park!"

With a giggle, Benji sat next to his mother. He sipped his hot chocolate and wolfed down two cookies. Happiness, contentment, and excitement enveloped him like a warm hug. There it was—that special Christmas feeling. Would Santa bring him the guitar and the telescope he'd put at the top of his list? He hoped so. He'd been really good this year.

His gaze wandered around the Great Hall, from the twinkling lights and evergreen garland tied up with big red bows that wrapped around every column to the lineup of nine Christmas stockings hung from the fireplace mantel, and finally to the ornament boxes stacked by the fresh Frasier fir that soared toward the ceiling. "Isn't my little buddy gonna help with the tree?"

"He was, but Aunt Sarah put Chase down for a nap. Poor little guy kept eating raw gingerbread behind her back while they were making the cookies and got himself a bellyache. Uncle George is keeping an eye on him."

Benji huffed. "Well, that was a dumbass thing to do."

His mother frowned and gently combed her fingers through his thick red hair, rumpled from wearing a wool hat while he played in the snow earlier. "Benji," she said softly. "That isn't nice, young man. He's only four, after all."

"I know. Sorry. It's just...stuffs more fun when he's around. Why can't Ash just fix him up?"

"How will you boys ever learn if an angel swoops in to fix it every time something goes wrong? A knight must rely on himself and not become dependent on his guardian angel. Aunt Sarah told Chase not to eat the raw dough, but he did it anyway. He needs to learn responsibility and that there are consequences to his actions. A little tummy ache isn't serious, but I'll bet he won't soon disobey his mother again."

"I guess. But he'll be upset to miss out. I don't want him to cry."

"Well, it's a really big tree. How about we leave the bottom part for you and Chase to decorate together when he's feeling better?"

"Yeah, that's good. He can't reach any higher than that, anyway. Thanks, Mom. And remember, Jamie puts the star on top."

"Yes, your brother always does the star."

Emma held her champagne flute as Ashriel poured the pale-beige sparkling wine. She'd never had champagne before. She peered into the glass as streams of tiny bubbles rose to the surface and light reflected in the delicate flowers etched into the crystal.

So pretty, so elegant.

Everything was perfect.

She glanced at the clock that sat on a bookshelf. Only one minute until the stroke of midnight. She half expected her beautiful gown to transform into rags and the elegant ballroom Ashriel had created in the Great Hall to turn into a pumpkin.

Of course, she was being silly.

Ashriel slipped the champagne bottle back into the ice bucket and raised his glass to hers. "To a wonderful evening and a wonderful memory. For both of us."

"Thank you, Ash. I'll treasure the memory of this night forever. Cinderella was always my favorite story, but now? It means so much more."

"I'm glad."

They clinked their glasses together and sipped. "Mmm," Emma said. "Delicious. And the bubbles tickle my nose."

Ashriel winced and grabbed his head, his eyes going wide.

"What's wrong?" Emma asked.

"Michael, I didn't hear any prayers! *Ben!*"

He touched her, and they vanished.

The crystal flutes fell to the hardwood floor and shattered.

Ashriel and Emma appeared on the side lawn of the Cornelius Rose Hotel. Flames danced in the hotel's windows and through a hole in the roof, illuminating the night with a flickering orange glow. Chase lay on the grass a few yards away, crumpled and motionless, next to an opening in the basement wall where black smoke billowed and rose into the sky.

"Chase!" Emma hiked up her ballgown skirt and ran to him, falling to her knees beside him. But Ashriel was already there, one hand on Chase's chest. Chase came to and sat up with a huge gasp, and Ashriel vanished.

"Chase, where's Ben?"

"He's not out here? Oh, God! He must still be inside!" Chase struggled to his feet and helped her up. "Ben! *Benji!*" They both ran back and forth, trying to find some way to get in, but there was no entry point that wasn't blocked by a wall of flame.

Embers drifted down, carried aloft on the vortex of air from the rising heat. Emma whimpered and slapped at her upper arm. Chase feared the danger to her bare arms and shoulders and her voluminous curls that could so easily catch fire, not to mention the ridiculous dress she wore. "Emma, get back! Ash will find him." When she didn't move, he pulled her away from the burning building. Away from the heat produced by the fire, it was chilly. He took off his jacket and put it on her, lifting her limp arms and guiding them through the sleeves as if she were a child.

Crying helplessly, she stared at the flames.

He pulled her against him. "Don't worry, sweetheart. He'll be okay. Ash will get him." Was he trying to convince her or himself? Where the hell was Ash? It was taking too damn long!

The icy hand of fear slid down his back, making his knees shake and his ears ring. Their Templar brands hid them and kept them safe from the dark angels who were in league with Lucifer and the Illuminati, but it hid them from *all* angels.

Including Ash.

Unless Benji was conscious and praying, Ashriel was looking for a needle in a burning haystack.

Oh, God. What if Benji died? If his soul left his body and got sucked into the veil before Ash could find him? If his reaper took him to Heaven? Benji would be gone. Forever. *No, dammit! Don't go off the deep end, Kincaid. Have some freakin' faith.* He had to believe that wouldn't happen. He had to!

A window shattered from the heat, glass exploding outward, and shards propelled through the air like tiny glass knives. Shielding Emma with his body, Chase pulled her even farther away from the house, but the sudden, loud blast sent her over the edge into hysteria. She yanked out of his grasp and ran back, screaming for Ben.

He ran after her, picked her up, and carried her away from the house. Screaming, she fought him, kicking, pummeling him, and trying to twist out of his arms, but her ballgown restricted her movements. "No! Ben! *Ben!*"

He set her down but kept a firm grip on her arms. He gave her a shake. "Emma, *stop!* You can't help, sweetheart. You'll only make it worse if you get hurt."

With a shuddering sob, she sagged against him.

Another window shattered, and another. And another. It sounded like bombs detonating.

Smoke rose high into the night sky, painting grim ribbons of black across the enormous face of the full moon as the distorted, muffled warble of a melting smoke alarm drifted from the house.

But no sign of Ben. Or Ashriel.

Emma sank to her knees in the grass and rocked back and forth, crying so hard she could hardly take a breath.

"Chase!"

Ashriel's voice. Chase whirled and spotted Ashriel a dozen yards from the house with Benji's body in his arms. He only assumed it was Benji. He couldn't tell for sure, but he hoped it wasn't—hoped the charred, blistered, smoking body Ashriel placed on the grass wasn't his cousin.

But in his heart, he knew it was.

Oh, God. No. My fault, all my fault. His cousin's blood was on his hands. Benji hadn't wanted to do this stupid job, had just wanted to go home, but he'd insisted because he was weak and didn't trust himself around Emma, and he'd made them stay in that deathtrap basement out of some childish vendetta against that little spirit.

He'd killed his own cousin!

His best friend.

The last of his family.

Pain, guilt, and horror wrapped him in heavy barbed chains that squeezed tighter with every second. He couldn't breathe, couldn't think, couldn't move.

Then Emma cried out behind him, a terrible, keening, heart-wrenching cry. He whirled toward her. She stared at Benji's body, her hand covering her mouth, her eyes wide, slowly shaking her head. She'd gone white as a sheet and trembled so violently that Chase thought it was a wonder she was standing. He ran the few steps to her and pressed her face against his chest as he turned her away from the horrific sight. "Don't look, baby. Don't look." He held her as she screamed, tears blurring his eyes as Ashriel tried to save his cousin.

Ashriel kneeled on the lawn beside Ben with both hands on his friend's smoking, charred, blistered chest, but it was too late to heal him. Ben was dead, and his soul had departed his body.

But if his soul was still in the veil—if his reaper hadn't taken him yet—there was still a chance. But he'd have to move fast. He concentrated, focused his power, and traveled deep, merging his coruscentia into the spatial-temporal plane of human existence that spanned the metaphysical bridge between life and death.

Ashriel sought and located his target. Tracking the unique frequency waves of Ben's soul, he followed the same path. He rocketed through the helical tunnel between dimensions, his wake agitating the space-time continuum. Quantum gravity exerted deadly shear forces that unbalanced the vertical pressure, and threatened to disrupt his spectral signature, and sent him barrel rolling and pulsating as he recklessly pushed the limits of his speed and endurance.

He ignored the danger.

With an ultrasonic explosion, he burst through the rippling-blue flash-line sequence of the harmonic universe and entered the veil—that Earthly parallel dimension where human souls awaited their transport to either Heaven or Hell, and reapers collected their charges.

Mom stood on a ladder next to the Christmas tree and hooked a shiny green ball ornament over a branch. "I think a red one now. Something fancy, since this one is plain."

"How about this one?" Benji held up a blown glass ornament in the shape of a cardinal.

"Perfect. Careful, sweetie. That one's really old. It was my grandmother's."

Holding the glass bird as if it might explode, he held it up for her to take and watched as she arranged the ornament just so. "Very nice," she said, nodding. "Let me have the baby's first Christmas ornaments now. They're in that blue box," she said, pointing. "I'll put them up, and then you can take over for a while." She pressed a fist against the small of her back and, holding the top of the ladder, stretched backward. "My back is cramping up."

"Sure, Mom." He opened the blue box and picked up a flat, round silver ornament with a picture of a raven-haired baby with gray eyes and the name *James* inscribed on it. "Here's Jamie's." He held it up to her. Next came a puppy in a Christmas stocking with Chase's photo and name on it.

Mom smiled at the ornament and then hung it on a branch. "All you boys were such adorable babies. Of course, I'm totally unbiased," she added with a wink.

He handed her his ornament, a snowman with his baby picture in the middle section and *Benji* written on the bottom. A mess of red hair on top of a Charlie Brown head, big green eyes, a toothless grin, and dimples. He was kinda cute. "Hey, Mom? Why do I look like you, but Jamie and Chase look like Dad and Uncle George?"

"Genetics. You'll learn about it soon. Parents pass down certain characteristics to their children. Actually, red hair and green eyes run on both sides of the family."

There was another ornament in the box. Curious, he picked it up. *Huh?* It was a picture of two babies, one wrapped in a blue blanket and the other in a pink one. The top of the ornament said *Twins*, and the bottom had two names: *Logan and Keira*. He held it up. "Mom, who are these babies?"

With a small cry of distress, she pressed a hand against her neck. "Oh, no, I didn't...I didn't think of that. Oh, shoot."

Benji's ears buzzed, and the room seemed to tilt for a moment. He stared at the ornament, and the hand that held it changed from a boy's hand to that of a grown man.

His hand.

Keira and Logan. His cousins lost long ago. But not even born when he was nine. What the hell was going on here? "What is all this? Not real. This...this is a memory?"

"Yes, it is," Mom said. "One of my favorites. But I goofed with the ornaments."

He watched warily as she climbed down off the ladder and moved toward him. He stepped back and tried to ignore the stab of guilt as sadness came into her eyes. "Don't come near me!"

Chapter Twenty-Nine

WHAT CRUEL TRICK WAS this? A doppelganger? Thought projection? Hologram? Shape shifter? Ben stared at the *thing* that looked exactly like his mother. It even smelled like her! "Who, or should I say, what, are you?"

"Benji, please believe me. I'm your mother."

"My mother died a long time ago! You could be a demon, for all I know. This could be some kind of Illuminati scam or a witch's spell." He widened his stance and looked wildly around the room, searching for danger.

"It's really me. I promise."

"Yeah? Prove it. Tell me something only my mother would know about me."

"Oh, gosh. I don't know." She tugged on the thick braid of red hair that fell over her shoulder. "You weighed fifteen pounds at birth. I was in labor for twenty-seven hours to push your gigantic head out."

"Not good enough. Anyone could find that out. Or guess."

She thought for a moment, then arched a brow and propped her hands on her hips. "Okay, how's this? There was that time when you were eleven, and I was changing your sheets and found that skin mag hidden under the mattress."

Ben threw his hand up as his face heated. "Okay, I believe you."

"Good."

Realization hit like a cannon ball to his solar plexus, leaving him breathless and reeling. "I'm dead."

She nodded. "For the moment, anyway."

He staggered the two steps back to the sofa and sank weak-kneed onto the cushion. His mother sat beside him and held his hand as he digested the truth. He gazed at the delightful holiday scene and then at his mother's beloved face. He should probably be upset—after all, he was dead—but he felt peaceful. And light. Feather light. And happy. Like the weight of the world had been lifted from his shoulders. What a wonderful feeling! Well, if this was death, it was okay with him.

"Mom." He kissed her cheek and hugged her, nearly overcome with emotion. "*Mom*. I can't believe it."

"I know, honey. I feel the same way."

After a few moments, he let her go and leaned back. "But what happened? I don't remember dying."

"Most don't. It's a blessing."

"Wait. What did you mean, for the moment?"

"It's not your time, son."

"Apparently, it is."

"No, you have work to do. You need to go back."

"No!" Ben jumped up from the sofa and strode to the twinkling tree, planting his feet squarely on the hardwood. He crossed his arms, feeling like the stubborn nine-year-old he'd just been. "No. I want to stay here in Heaven. With you! And I want to see Dad and Jamie. See everyone!"

"This isn't Heaven, sweetheart. It's...Heaven adjacent. Like a preview. We're in the veil. But we'll all be together again one day, you and me, and Dad and Jamie and Grandpa and Uncle George." A ghost of a smile curved her mouth. "And you'll see Aunt Sarah and Logan and Keira again, too. I promise. But you have very important work to do first."

"What? No, what are you talking about? Chase is laird, not me. I'm not the important one."

She jumped to her feet and went to where he stood. She reached up and gently cupped the sides of his face. "You couldn't be more wrong." Her words thickened with such intensity of emotion that they gave him goosebumps. "You're every bit as important as Chase. Everything that needs to happen depends on *you*. Go back." Her voice dropped to a strangled whisper, her eyes glittering with tears. "Be the hero you were born to be."

Every word felt like a boulder pressing down on his chest. His mouth went dry, the lingering flavors of chocolate and gingerbread turning bitter on his tongue. *Hero?* He was no hero! He did the job, banked his pay, and longed for the day when he could leave it all behind.

And they'd just found each other again! How could she want to send him away? The sting of rejection was like a thousand pinpricks in his heart. He pulled her hands from his face and turned away, staring at the twinkling multicolor lights of the Christmas tree, lights that blurred through a haze of tears he desperately blinked back. He wrenched away when she laid a gentle hand on his shoulder.

"Benji. Please don't be upset. I would give anything to keep you with me. But I can't be that selfish. You don't know what's at stake."

He whirled toward her, throwing his arms wide. "So, tell me!"

Sadly shaking her head, she shrugged. "I can't." She touched her forehead. "You wouldn't remember in here." Then she laid her hand over her heart. "But you'd remember it here. And that might sway your judgment." She shrugged helplessly as a tear rolled down her cheek. "If you have to hate me, so be it."

He couldn't take seeing her like that. Knowing he caused it. He pulled her into a tight hug. "I could never hate you, Mom. I love you. I've missed you so damn much."

"I love you too, my Benji."

After a long moment, his mother drew back and, wiping her eyes on her sleeve, gazed up at him. "Look how my little boy has grown. So big and strong and handsome. It's amazing. You're the very image of my father." She glanced toward the fireplace with a sigh of relief. "Good. He's almost here. It's about damn time!"

"Who?"

Ashriel materialized near the fireplace. Mom whirled and marched toward him, hands on her hips, eyes blazing. "You have one fucking job, Ash! *Just one!* To protect the Kincaids of Orion Citadel!" She pointed toward Ben. "And here is the not-so-living proof that you fucked up!"

Wow. Ben had never heard his mother yell that loudly or use such language. And he'd forgotten how tall she was. She stood nose-to-nose with Ashriel, who looked like the quintessential startled deer frozen in headlights.

His mother resembled a furious Valkyrie. He was impressed.

Grimacing, Ashriel took a step back, throwing his hands up beseechingly. "Bevan, I didn't—"

"Obviously!"

"Please, let me explain."

"Talk, and it better be good!"

Ashriel looked toward him. "I'm so sorry, Ben. I didn't know you were in trouble. I didn't hear any prayers. Michael alerted me."

A frisson of alarm skittered down Ben's spine. "Again? I prayed when the manticore stung me, and I couldn't move. At the time, I figured it was because your power was tapped out on Emma. But now? That can't be a coincidence."

"I agree," Ashriel said.

"Are Chase and Emma all right?" Ben asked.

"Physically, yes, but they're grieving for you. Even here, in a different dimension, I feel Emma's pain. Will you come back with me?"

"You're asking?" Hope blossomed inside his chest. "Wait. You mean, I have a choice?"

Mom grabbed his arm, and her voice was panicked. "No, you have to go! Ash, take him now before—"

"No, Bevan. I cannot force him to return. You know this. The choice is yours, Ben. But surely you understand the cost if you remain."

Ben's heart pounded. He wanted to stay. But what about Chase and Emma? How could he take his ease in this wonderful place and leave them behind to fight their enemies alone? The heavy iron yoke of responsibility crashed down over his shoulders.

Before Ben could respond, an elderly man dressed in a plain black suit, looking like a cover model for *Morticians' Monthly*, appeared. What else could he be but a reaper angel?

"Ashriel?" The reaper sounded surprised. And annoyed. "What are you doing here?"

Ash moved to stand between the reaper and Ben, who protectively ushered his mother behind him. He didn't know the rules in this place, and in his book, strange angels were enemies until he knew otherwise.

"It's not his time, Zophiel," Ashriel said. "Benjamin Kincaid still has important work on Earth."

Zophiel looked down his nose at Ash. "And why should I listen to you?" He gave a derisive laugh. "How the mighty have fallen. The great Ashriel, once the stuff of legend, is now an outcast banned from Heaven. You're a disgrace."

What? Ash was banned from Heaven? Wow! Michael was really, *really* pissed.

Ashriel shrugged. "Actually, I didn't know that. But it matters not."

"Wait." Zophiel's eyes narrowed, and he drew his sword. "Last I heard, you had succumbed to a witch's spell. When and how did you get these new feathers?"

Ashriel hesitated and then blew out a sigh. "I don't know."

"Well, isn't that interesting? I should kill you here and now."

Ash jerked his arm. His sword fell from the sleeve of his tuxedo into his hand. He held the weapon at the ready, his jaw set, a warrior prepared to fight. "You're welcome to try. I'm a soldier, Zophiel—a veteran of the Xenohari war—fought long before you were even created. You are but a glorified crossing guard. You will not take him."

Both the insult and the threat hit home. "Fine. But I'm reporting this and those new wings."

Ash shrugged. "What's the expression? Oh, yes. You can kiss my feathery ass."

With a last look of utter disdain, Zophiel vanished.

Ashriel put his hand on Ben's shoulder. "Will you go back? Do you want to live?"

"Well, you just ditched my ride, so I guess I have to."

"The decision is yours. Another reaper will come if you choose to remain."

Ben looked longingly at his mother, who stood next to him, wringing her hands, her face scrunched with worry. He'd missed her so much over the years, every day since he was twelve years old. The thought of leaving her nearly drove him to his knees. Blinking back tears, he wrapped her in his arms again and drank in maternal comfort as she hugged him back. But Chase and Emma...

The little boy inside him cried and clung to his mother.

But the man let her go.

And did the right thing.

On the grass at the Cornelius Rose Hotel, Ashriel leaned over Ben with his hands still on his chest, and the blisters and burns regressed, healed, and vanished. All but his hair and clothes were restored to normal. He was naked, and what little was left of his formerly thick red mane was short and singed and stuck out in little charred tufts. His lash-less eyes opened under a forehead devoid of eyebrows, and he gasped as he sat up, then gulped air like a marathoner. Ashriel shrugged out of his coat and tossed it over his lap.

"Benji!" Chase ran toward him, with Emma right behind him.

"Chase? Ash, what's going on?" Disoriented and confused, he tried to get his legs under him to stand, but Ashriel put a restraining hand on his shoulder.

"Take it easy, Ben. Just stay there for a bit."

Chase fell to his knees and grabbed him in a hug that nearly cracked his ribs, as Emma, sobbing, kneeled behind him and wrapped her arms around his waist.

"I'm sorry, Benji. I'm so damn sorry."

Chase's voice sounded choked, like he was crying too. "Okay. For what? Emma? Chase, why's she so upset?"

Chase sat back on his heels, shaking his head and wiping his eyes with his sleeves.

Chase couldn't speak? What the hell happened? Ben patted Emma's arm, which curled around his middle. "Emma? Come here, honey." She crawled the few feet around him and threw herself into his arms. He held her for a few minutes, rocking and patting her back as she sobbed. Tears stung his eyes to know how much she cared for him. "It's okay. Don't know what happened, but we're all here, and we're all okay. That's all that matters."

Nodding, she got a hold of herself and stopped crying. "You're right." But her eyes filled with tears again, and she whimpered as she ran her hand over his head. "Oh, Ben. All your beautiful hair."

He raised his hand and touched his head, then swiped his palm over his scalp as a bolt of shock stole his breath. Cringing, he let out a horrified gasp. All that was left were stiff little tufts and bare scalp! He didn't remember exactly what happened, but he remembered that the basement had caught fire, and since the hotel was going up in smoke, it didn't take a rocket scientist to figure it out. "Well, Em, you told me to get a haircut."

She gave a watery laugh. "Oh, silly." She kissed his cheek and hugged him.

Chase pushed himself up, walked straight to Ashriel, gave him a hug, and clapped him on the back. "Thanks, Ash. Don't know what we'd do without you, man."

Ben shivered in the chill air, and he realized that except for Ashriel's coat slung haphazardly over him, he was naked. And Emma was sitting on his lap. That was...awkward. "Chase, can you grab my backup clothes from the trunk?"

While he dressed, Emma, Chase, and Ashriel turned their backs to him and watched the old house go up in flames. Over the snapping and crackling of the fire, the distant sound of sirens reached their ears.

"Oh, crap," Chase said. "Decent yet, Benji?"

"Yeah."

"Good. Let's get the hell outta Dodge."

Emma giggled, but Ben sighed and rolled his eyes as he buttoned his jeans. "You were waiting to drop that line. I bet you had it planned all along."

But Chase's grin faded as the sound of sirens quickly grew louder. "Only one way in and out. They're gonna see us if we drive out, and they'll have too many questions we can't answer. Ash, can you zap us outta here?"

Chimera materialized in the middle of freakin' nowhere. Breathing deeply, fighting the nausea from teleporting, and trying to ignore the loud ringing in his left ear, Chase evaluated their position. But everywhere he looked, all he saw was an ocean of flat prairie grassland that seemed to go on forever under the light of the enormous full moon. "Where in the hell are we?"

Ashriel sat shotgun. "Exactly ten miles east of where we were. You didn't specify a destination."

Drumming his fingers on the steering wheel, Chase sighed. "No, I guess I didn't." He added under his breath, "But a road woulda been nice." He looked in the rearview mirror. Emma sat in the back with Ben, plastered up against him with his arm around her. It would be a while before she'd want to let Benji out of her sight. He knew the feeling. "You guys okay back there?"

Benji nodded, and Emma smiled.

Chase hung his arm over the back of the seat and twisted to face her. "Okay, now that we're all alive and well, I just gotta ask. What's with the Ken and Barbie routine?"

She gave a little shake of her head. "Huh?"

His gaze flicked for a second to the swell of her breasts visible above the neckline of his way-too-big jacket. "Not that you don't look amazing in that prom dress, but what gives? And the angel in the penguin suit? It ain't Halloween." *Oh, great.* Now she was frowning at him. Jeez, would he ever learn to keep his big, fat mouth shut?

"Not Ken and Barbie. Cinderella and Prince Charming."

He waited for the punchline, but she just glared at him. Shit, she was serious? "Oh. Sorry. My bad." Rolling his eyes as he turned back to face the front, he decided he didn't want to know. She wanted to play dress-up and tea party? Better Ash than him. He reached for his phone before he remembered that he'd broken it. He opened the glove compartment, intending to retrieve one of their secondary burner phones, but the compartment was empty. "Benji, where's the other phones?"

"On their chargers in our hotel room, which means they're piles of melted plastic right about now."

"Ash, got your phone?" Chase asked.

"No."

Sighing, Chase let his chin drop to his chest. *Note to self: buy Superglue.* "Can you tell me where the road is?"

Ashriel pointed. "Highway fifty is one mile that way."

Chase didn't want to teleport again, but he was already close to puking, and the new mufflers he'd installed on Chimera a few months ago were pricy. "This terrain is gonna beat the hell out of the suspension and the undercarriage. Can you zap us there?"

Ashriel sighed. "I've spent a considerable amount of energy tonight. Teleporting from the citadel with Emma, healing you when you were so close to death, shielding myself while searching through an inferno, bringing Ben back from the veil and then healing him, and now teleporting three people and your four-thousand-five-hundred-and-eighty-six-pound car *and* several hundred pounds of weapons and ammunition? My power is low, and this is not a critical situation. I'm afraid you'll have to rough it. I suggest you switch to a more appropriate vehicle and drive slowly."

Chase stared. "Did...did you say near death?"

"You were suffering from severe toxic smoke inhalation. A few more minutes..." Ashriel shrugged.

Emma leaned over the seat backs and pointed at something through the windshield. "Guys? What's that?" In the distance, a cloud of dust billowed over the plain, clearly visible in the bright moonlight.

Chase peered through the windshield. "Good question." He got out to stand in front of the car, trying to figure out what he was looking at. The others joined him. The ground trembled, and a monotonous rumble rode the breeze. "What the hell?" Chase squinted, but it was too far to make out. "Looks like it's coming our way. Stampede, maybe? Could be cattle or horses. Maybe wild mustangs broke loose from Flint Hills sanctuary?"

Ben ran to the trunk and came back with a pair of binoculars. He raised them to his eyes. "Definitely alive, but it doesn't look like livestock. What the heck is that?"

Chase took the binoculars and looked for himself. "Got no clue what I'm looking at."

Emma held her hand out. "Let me see, Chase?" He handed her the binoculars. She looked for a few moments and then gave a weird, nervous laugh that sent a chill through him.

"No, it can't be," she said. "It can't! Oh, God. But it is. Akhenaten locusts. Giant locusts, and I mean giant, Chase. Like five feet long, giant."

"*What?*" Chase took the binoculars back from her and stared at the rapidly approaching horde. "Talk to me, Emma."

"According to the lore, they were a plague sent by the Egyptian goddess Isis to punish the pharaoh Akhenaten for abandoning the old gods and demanding all of Egypt worship only the sun god Aten. They decimated the Nile crescent. Ninety percent of the human population died. They hibernate for three hundred years, emerge, mate, eat everything in sight, and then lay their eggs. Apparently, they can migrate, too. Then they die off, and the cycle repeats. But they're not due to emerge again for over a hundred years."

She gasped and grabbed his arm. "It's me! It must be. My curse must have awakened them early. They're homing in on me!"

Chase hauled her up against his side. "It ain't your fault, sweetheart. Ash, recon. Tell me how many."

The angel disappeared, but he was back in a few seconds. "Sixty-four. They move quickly."

"Wings?"

"Yes, but they're only hopping; a few are crawling."

"Can you smite 'em all?"

"Perhaps a few, but not all."

"Crap!" Chase rubbed the throbbing bump on his forehead, trying to think clearly over the nausea and painful distraction.

"Em, anything about how to kill them?" Benji asked.

"No. Best guess? Maybe fire? Or a gigantic flyswatter."

"Take Emma home, Ash," Chase said. "Now. And stay there, you hear me? We got this."

But Emma stepped back as Ashriel reached for her. "Wait!" She grabbed Chase's shoulders. "Be careful! They'll be able to fly soon after they eat. And they don't just eat plants. They eat meat, too. And they can see heat. All living things radiate infrared heat, and that includes us. They'll eat people if given the chance."

She stepped back, and she and Ashriel disappeared.

"We got this, Chase?" Benji gave a mirthless laugh and went to bury his hands in his hair, cringing when he touched scalp instead of hair. "Seriously? A freakin' swarm of giant, man-eating locusts?"

"Emma had to go, and Ash had to take her! Or did you wanna add flame-throwing rattlesnakes to the mix? God only knows what else could be out here and come after her because of that fucking curse. We got this because we gotta got this. No choice."

"But why can't Ash come back and help?"

"A plague sent by a goddess? For all we know, those things can kill angels. And you heard him. He's weak, running on fumes. What if all three of us buy it out here? Who's gonna take care of Emma?"

Benji blew out a sigh. "Good point. What's the plan?"

"For starters, I'm thinking flee."

"That'd be my choice."

Chapter Thirty

Chase ran to Chimera's trunk. He tossed a shotgun to Benji. "Get in! There's a reason they call it riding shotgun." The cloud grew closer, and the ground trembled like a herd of buffaloes was stampeding. Shivering in the chill, Chase grabbed his spare jacket out of the trunk and yanked it on. He lost precious seconds rooting around in his arsenal, but he came up triumphant.

He lifted the handheld rocket-propelled grenade launcher they'd snagged from the Illuminati during their mission in Africa. "Hello, gorgeous." He gave the double-barrel RPG a smacking kiss, tucked it under his arm, and grabbed a few boxes of shotgun ammo. He slid behind the wheel as he tossed the ammo on the seat and shoved the launcher at Ben. "Hold this."

"Think it'll work?"

"Who the fuck knows? Only got the two grenades already loaded. Never thought we'd use this thing on home turf. Let's switch to the Jeep." Chase turned the head of the gearshift to the right, then to the left. The cap popped open, exposing the moonstone embedded in the head.

But it wasn't glowing.

"Uh-oh," Chase said. "That can't be good." He placed his right thumb on the moonstone. "Jeep Wrangler, four by four." Nothing happened. "What the hell?"

"Oh, no!" Ben said. "Must be too far from the sword to summon the magic."

"Well, that sucks!" He blew out a sigh. "It's a hail Mary."

"So, the usual."

"Yup." Chase put Chimera in drive and hit the gas, but the untamed prairie grassland hit back with ruts, bumps, and craters, making it impossible to maintain any real speed without ripping out the undercarriage of the Challenger.

"Still loving the Old West authenticity?"

"We live through this; remind me to kick your ass. Better yet, I'll sic Emma on you."

"Rather take my chances with the locusts."

"Assuming we actually do live through this, your first assignment is ramping up the magic signal, so this won't happen again. Gotta be able to depend on Chimera no matter where we go."

"No argument here."

Chase swore as the car bottomed out on a particularly high ridge. The unmistakable sound of metal twisting and crushing made his gut twist. "There go the freakin' glasspacks." He crooned to the car, "Sorry, Chimera."

Benji swiveled in his seat and looked behind them. "Forget the damn mufflers. They're closing in!"

"Can't go any faster. Break an axle, we're screwed. Got plenty of ammo. Start shooting as soon as they're in range. Doubt you're gonna hurt 'em, but I just need you to slow 'em down a little bit. I see the highway up ahead."

The paved highway was less than a mile away.

It seemed like twenty.

They finally turned onto the smooth pavement of the highway, but the Challenger's ride was off. Something was wrong, which wasn't surprising, considering, but he couldn't stop and check it out, not with a herd of man-eating locusts on their ass.

Hanging out of the passenger-side window, Benji fired round after round at the locusts, which kept them at bay, but it was time to bring out the big gun. Literally.

Chase hit the gas and soon had a decent lead on the locusts, although the wobble he felt through the steering wheel had him holding his breath between gasps for air. "Take the wheel." As soon as his cousin had the wheel in his hand, Chase grabbed the RPG and flung himself into the backseat.

The Challenger jerked back and forth a few times as Benji maneuvered himself, with some difficulty, into the driver's seat. "What in the hell are you doing?"

"Gotta get on the roof. Can't shoot this bitch in here. She belches fire, remember?"

"Yeah, but what about hanging out the side windows?"

"Only get one shot at this. Gotta make it count, straight and true." He grabbed the crowbar he kept under the back seat. "Watch your eyes." Turning his face away, he slammed the crowbar into the back windshield, sending tiny chunks of safety glass flying. He slung the RPG's strap around his neck and shoulder. "Keep the speed and keep her straight and smooth. I don't wanna miss, and I really, *really* don't wanna be bug chow."

He crawled out of the hole where the windshield had been and made it safely onto the roof of the car, and then slowly did a one-eighty on his belly, careful not to let the wind get under him. If that happened, he'd be flipped like a pancake, and he figured that wouldn't end well. His feet hung over the windshield, so he angled himself so he wouldn't block Benji's view.

He was setting the grenade launcher into position when Benji shouted, "Chase, hold on!"

He just had to laugh. *Hold on?* Hold on to what?

Ben adjusted his grip on the steering wheel, and with his eyes wide and his breath coming hard and fast, he leaned on the horn as a black Longhorn steer meandered onto the road in front of them. *Rock and a hard place—pick one.* If he swerved to miss the animal, Chase would no doubt tumble off the roof, and at the speed they were going, most likely he would break his neck. And if not, he'd still wind up in a locust's gullet.

If he didn't swerve and the car hit the massive steer, it would be like hitting a brick wall. They'd probably both be killed.

With his heart in his throat, he kept the Challenger straight. He'd died once already today, and it hadn't stuck, but maybe it was meant to be. He'd figured lately that when the curtain came down, he and Chase would take their bows together.

If this was the day, so be it.

Obviously annoyed by the sound of the blaring horn, the Longhorn flicked his long tail and broke into a trot, making it into the other lane just in time. Chimera hit only the steer's tail as it lashed out in agitation, but the car's bumper hit with enough force to break bones. With a bellow of outrage, the animal took off at a gallop, but it wasn't fast enough to outrun the terrible fate that awaited it.

After they'd passed the steer, Chase stared in horrified fascination as the locusts attacked and devoured the enormous animal, bones and all, in only seconds. Only the Longhorn's rack, which he figured was about six feet long, remained. Even over the drone of engine and tires and the wind rushing by his ears, the sickening sound of their powerful beaks ripping and tearing flesh and breaking bones made him shudder. *Holy Crap! At least it'll be quick.* He remembered what Emma had said.

They'd eaten.

Soon, they'd be able to fly.

Flying, they could go anywhere!

Crunch time, Kincaid. With a deep, steadying breath, he aimed the launcher, peered through the scope, drew his bead, and waited.

The locusts resumed their pursuit of the Challenger. Still, Chase waited. After the distraction of their snack, the swarm was a little too far behind for the RPG's ideal range. *Patience, dude. Only get one shot at this.*

"Chase, you okay up there?"

"Yeah. Breezy. Not loving the view, though."

"They're getting close. You gonna shoot already?"

"Wait for it..."

"Chase?"

"Wait for it..."

"Chase!"

"Wait for it..."

"*Goddammit, Chase!*"

Chase eased his finger into contact with the trigger. "Eat this, motherfuckers." He pulled the trigger, the blast of the percussion cap that powered the ignition system deafening. The launcher sent a backlash of flames blazing behind it. The grenades ran straight and true and found their target, exploding in the midst of the locust swarm, but the powerful recoil knocked Chase off the roof of the car.

He tumbled head over heels through the air, and as concrete and almost certain death came rushing up to meet him, something yanked him hard around the middle. With a dizzying rush that swamped him in a sea of nausea, he found himself in the Challenger's backseat, sitting on Ashriel's lap.

Awkward. So awkward.

He flung himself onto the other seat. "It work, Benji?"

"Don't see any."

"Ash, go check. Anything moves, smite it."

With a flutter of wings, he was gone. Two seconds later, he was back. "Nothing left but bits and pieces."

Chase gave a fist pump. "Yes! Up yours, Orkin man." Wait. *What the fuck?* "I told you to stay home! What in the hell are you doing here?"

In the front seat, Benji gasped and glared at him in the rearview mirror. "Saving your damn ass again!"

"I'm sorry, Laird. Emma was worried and insisted—loudly—that I return and help."

Chase tried to be angry because he expected his orders to be carried out. But he couldn't be angry. Not today, since both he and Benji would be dead if not for Ash.

And Emma. Knowing she made Ashriel come help and that she was worried about them made Chase feel all warm and fuzzy inside. That she cared about them, worried about them, like she did?

It was a good feeling.

No, it was an amazing feeling.

It would feel even better if he wasn't close to hurling up his guts.

"Well, since you saved Benji the trouble of having to squeegee me off the road, I'll just say thanks, Ash. Good timing. Awesome freakin' timing. Both me and Benji in one day. Me, twice. New record, ain't it?"

"My honor and duty to help."

"Got enough power to get home, or you riding with us?"

"I can teleport myself home."

"Okay. We're good now, so go tell our girl we're fine and coming home."

With a nod, Ashriel was gone.

Chase gagged as his stomach rebelled. "Pull over. Quick."

"Wanna drive?"

"Yeah, right after I puke, and we gotta figure out what's causing that wobble."

"Wobble? I don't feel anything."

"Don't know her like I do."

"It's your imagination."

"Wanna bet?"

A few minutes later, they stood on the side of the road, Chase wiping his chin and pointing to a sidewall bubble on the rear passenger-side tire. "That look imaginary?"

Benji frowned and blew out a sigh.

"Have fun changing the tire. Oh, and use lots of tape on the tarp for the back window. Don't want it flying off on the way home." Chase opened the trunk. With a wiseass grin, he handed his cousin an old ball cap. "And cover that ugly melon, will ya, Deadpool?"

Benji slapped the hat on his head and gave him a hand gesture that sure didn't mean *I love you*.

Laughing, he handed Benji the jack and tossed the tire iron, a tarp, and a roll of duct tape on the ground. He opened the cooler and grabbed a Coke. "Yeah, I'm just gonna kick back and have me a cold one. Oh, and by the way, you owe me fifty bucks."

"How you figure?"

"You died today. I outlived you. We didn't say nothing about staying dead. No worries, you can pay me when we get home."

With a disgusted sigh, Benji turned back to his task. "You suck ass."

"Maybe, but I suck ass fifty bucks richer." Chase shot his cousin a cocky grin then took another can of Coke out of the cooler for Benji, sat it on the roof of the car, and put the cooler on the ground. He sat down on it with a hearty groan, popped the top of his drink, and guzzled it down.

But his good mood after taking out the locusts tanked as the events of the night replayed in his mind. Benji had died; Emma was traumatized, and it was *his* fault. Yeah, Ash brought Benji back, but that didn't change the facts. He'd been selfish and irresponsible, and what was that other word? Negligent.

And Benji had paid the ultimate price.

Chase shuddered. *Holy crap*, he'd burned to death! Unless he'd passed out from the fumes first. He didn't really want to know the answer, but he had to ask. With his heart thudding against his ribs, he said, "Benji?"

"Yeah?"

"Do you...do you remember it?"

Wiping his dirty hands on his jeans, his cousin walked around the car and picked up his Coke. He leaned back against the car door and thought for a moment before popping the top. "You mean, do I remember dying?"

"Yeah."

"No. Last thing I remember, I was coughing up a lung and shoving you through the coal chute. Then, nothing. But when I first came to after Ash fixed me up, there was something. Something on the periphery I couldn't quite grasp. Ever wake up and you know you've been dreaming, and you don't want to let it go, but when you try to remember, it just gets further and further away, until there's nothing?"

Chase nodded, relieved beyond words that his cousin didn't remember suffering.

"That's all I've got. I know there was *something*. It wasn't just blackout city, but we know that. And the weird thing is, I feel peaceful about it. Don't know why since I can't remember it. But I do."

"I'm glad."

"Me, too. I thought about asking Ash what happened on the other side, but we both know he can't tell us anything."

"Nope. They'd take away his grappling hook and decoder ring, and then we'd really be screwed."

Ben laughed and walked away, but stopped when Chase spoke again.

"Wait. Listen, I fucked up big time. I'm sorry, Benji. I played fast and loose with your safety and mine. You were right. I was using this whole thing to avoid being around Emma."

Benji crouched next to him. When Chase couldn't look him in the eye, Benji lightly punched him on the arm. "It happened. But it's over. Learn from it and let it go. Yeah, we were wasting time sitting in that basement, but you couldn't have known the kobold would turn into a flaming ping-pong ball and set the place on fire. And in time, I'm sure you'll figure out your path with Emma."

"Are you? Wish I was. I'm in way over my head here."

Lowering himself to sit cross-legged on the ground, Benji yanked at a few blades of grass. "After what Holly did, it's only natural that you'd be scared to get serious with a woman again."

Chase bristled. "Don't—"

"No! You don't! I can't listen to you defend that woman again. I won't! *She was young and scared, blah, blah, blah.* She was twenty, Chase. And all three of us warned her of the dangers, gave her the rules. It wasn't your fault. *She* made the stupid decision to leave the citadel alone after she'd been warned time and again. Then you make a Hell-deal to save her, and while you're enduring what I can't even imagine, she dumps you and walks away?

"It's been four goddamn *years*, and not so much as a text or email to see what happened to you!" Growling, his face red and twisted, Benji yanked a plump tussock of prairie grass from the soil and ripped it to shreds. Then he blew out a sigh, tossed the mangled bits away, and brushed the dirt off his hands. "Huh. Felt good to get that off my chest. Long time in coming. But let's put the feels aside for a minute and look at this logically. Let's say, for the sake of argument, that my ass wound up in serious trouble, for whatever reason. Somebody was holding me somewhere, my life on the line. What do you think Emma would do?"

What would she do? Was he kidding? "She'd do everything and anything to get you back. She'd storm the gates, guns blazing, kicking ass and taking names."

"Damn right, she would. She wouldn't rest until I was home and safe, and she'd do the same for any of us." He grinned. "And then she'd probably bake my favorite oatmeal-raisin cookies."

Chase couldn't help but smile. Benji hit the nail on the head. But he was way off base in thinking he was scared Emma would hurt him. Sure, it had crossed his mind a few times—more of a reflex than anything else.

Once you've been kicked in the teeth by an easily spooked horse, you were smart to keep your guard up.

But his real fear was that *he* would hurt her.

For a second, he thought about telling Benji about his nightmare, but he couldn't. He couldn't bear the thought that his cousin might look at him differently if he knew the terrible thing he was afraid he'd done. "Just let it go, please? That's enough soul-baring for one night. Appreciate the armchair psychology, but the facts remain. Everything that happened tonight *was* my fault."

"Hey, look at it this way. We've got some clues now about the missing souls case, right? And thanks to Emma's curse, people a hundred years from now won't have to deal with a swarm of giant locusts coming out of hibernation. We may have just saved thousands of people, maybe more."

Chase sighed, but looking at things that way did make him feel better. "You're lettin' me off way too easy. Should at least punch me in the face or something."

Benji faked a punch toward his nose. "Nah. Don't think that crooked beak of yours could stand another round."

Chase laughed, grabbed Benji's shoulder, and gave it a squeeze. "I'll finish up the repairs."

"No, you won't." Benji stood and headed back to the rear of the car. "A bet's a bet, and I lost."

"Hang on. One more thing."

"What's that?"

"Tomorrow, or whenever you're up to it, think you can find out online about the hotel's insurance situation? That place burning down is my fault, too. The owner shouldn't have to lose money over it. Whatever the deductible, I'll pay it."

"Okay, but don't forget, the kobold was already starting fires around the place. From the looks of things and what the manager said, they were close to going out of business as it was. Might have only been a matter of time, anyway. The owner might actually owe you his thanks. Now, he gets to pocket the insurance money instead of boarding up the windows and taking the loss. So don't beat yourself up about it too much. But yeah, I can do that."

Chase watched Benji change the tire and cover the broken window. He enjoyed a crisp and now-tranquil night illuminated by a full moon so close and big and bright that they needed no flashlight, but his thoughts remained troubled. Benji tended to look on the bright side, but Chase didn't kid himself. Life was dicey at best, and he'd been damn lucky tonight—luckier than he deserved.

Had fate dealt him a different hand, he might be preparing to bury his cousin. In fact, he might be dead himself. But for once, fate had been kind. She'd given him a chance to become a better cousin, a better friend, and a better laird.

A better man.

He vowed not to waste the opportunity.

In the distance, a lone coyote howled.

He could picture the scene in his mind—a gray coyote standing on a ridge, looking up at that magical moon, calling to its mate.

Damn, it was so freakin' good just to be alive! To be alive, have Benji by his side, and know Emma was at home waiting for them.

Once the repairs were done and they'd pulled back onto the highway, Chase switched on the stereo. Southern rock exploded out of the speakers, the dashboard vibrating to the ass-kicking drum beat and the warbling scream of an electric guitar. Chase blew on his finger like it was the smoking barrel of a gun and nodded. *Oh, yeah.* Drumming the steering wheel with the heels of his hands, he shot a cocky grin at his cousin.

Benji joined in with a mean air guitar, and they belted out the song at the top of their lungs.

The track ended. Chase hit replay and let his steel horse take the bit between her teeth and run. As they streaked across the moonlit plains, Chase's yelled "*Yeeeeee haaaaaa!*" echoed over the land.

Chapter Thirty-One

THE BRIGHT-YELLOW FACE OF the morning sun winked through the trees as Chase negotiated the twists and turns of the switchback road leading up the mountain. He heaved a sigh of relief as he pulled Chimera into the garage. *Ahhh, home, sweet home.* He and Benji trudged up the stairs, hung up their coats, took off their boots, and put them in the corner. They shared a smile as they put on the slippers that waited for them near the door. All was quiet.

Benji headed down the hallway. "Gotta hit the head."

Chase continued on to the Great Hall and came to a surprised halt. *What the heck?* Ash sat on an awesome sectional couch and was watching a monster-size flat-screen TV. He had the volume turned down low because Emma was asleep and cuddled up against him. Chase gestured to the couch. "Where did this come from?" he whispered.

Ash smiled down at Emma. "She wanted to surprise you and Ben."

Chase had to swallow the lump in his throat before he could speak. "She did all this for us?"

Ashriel nodded. "She's physically and emotionally exhausted, and she fell asleep only a couple of hours ago, but she made me promise to wake her when you arrived home."

"Let me." She wore only a long, thin cotton nightgown. "Ash, it's cool in here. Shouldn't she have a robe or blanket?"

"She's warm. She's under my wing."

He took a moment to absorb that and to choke back the jealousy. As long as she was okay. He sank to his knees and brushed his knuckles over her soft cheek. "Hey, sleeping beauty. We're home."

Emma opened her eyes and smiled. "Hi, Chase."

His heart rolled in his chest as she blinked sleepily at him for a few seconds. But she lost her smile and pushed up against something with her hand, which he figured was Ash's wing, and then sat up abruptly. "Where's Ben?"

"Right here, Em." Benji smiled as he hurried across the Great Hall toward them. He kneeled next to him, and she nearly knocked Benji over when she threw herself into his arms and burst into tears. He patted her back as he held her. "Aww, honey, it's okay. I'm all right. Good as new, except for the hair, and that'll grow back." His suddenly alarmed gaze flew to Ashriel. "It will grow back, won't it?"

"Yes. I healed the burned follicles, so it will grow back, but since the hair outside your scalp is technically dead, I can't restore that."

The word *dead* had her crying even harder.

As Benji continued to comfort her, Chase caught Ashriel's eye and gave him a slow nod full of meaning. Ash could erase that terrible memory—erase the sight of Benji's body burned beyond recognition. There was no need for her to remember that horror.

Ash leaned forward and laid his hand on Emma's heaving back. "I can erase that terrible memory from your mind if you want me to."

She turned tear-filled but hopeful eyes toward him. "How?" she asked between hitching sobs.

"I simply place my hand on your head, locate the memory, and erase it."

She twisted toward Ashriel, grabbed his hand, and slapped it onto her head. "Yes, *please*."

"I'm sorry to ask it of you, but the memory eradication will be far more precise and effective if you concentrate one last time on the image."

Nodding, she closed her eyes. A whimper tore from her throat, but she fell silent as Ashriel's blue eyes and his hand glowed with unearthly light, veiling her head in an iridescent blue halo. After a moment, he removed his hand, and the light dissipated. "How do you feel, Emma?"

She opened her eyes and used the hem of her nightgown to mop her wet face. "Better, I think." She took a deep breath and closed her eyes.

Chase held his breath and hoped. She was testing; he knew. But with her copy-machine brain, would Ash's angelic mojo do the trick? Or would she be saddled forever with that horrible sight embedded in her mind—like it certainly would be in his? But he let out a sigh of relief when her eyes flew open and a smile as big as Texas wreathed her face.

"It's gone! I know what happened. But I can't see it anymore!"

An hour later, she was sleeping peacefully in her bed, thanks to Ash's angelic sleep inducement, another offer she gratefully accepted. Chase lounged with Benji and Ash on the new sofa, enjoying orange juice and the platter of sausage and egg sandwiches Emma had made in anticipation of their return home before she'd conked out on the sofa earlier.

Ash rose and stood in front of the fireplace. "We need to talk, and I know you're both exhausted, but since Emma is asleep, this is a good time."

"Okay," Chase said reluctantly, hoping it wasn't anything serious. He'd hit the wall hard, and his bed was screaming his name.

"We have three matters to discuss," Ashriel said. "Along with our investigation into the missing souls, I suggest we turn our efforts to the most pressing matter at hand, which is that your prayers to me are being blocked. Until we rectify that situation, I strongly recommend neither of you leave the citadel unless I'm with you."

Chase couldn't argue with that and gave his nod of approval. After what happened in Dodge City, they couldn't take the chance.

"Also, during my visit to the prison in New York, I discovered a good man imprisoned there, an innocent man. I promised him that I would assist in bringing the guilty party to justice as soon as possible and so gain his release. I'll attempt to handle the matter myself, but I will be dealing with humans, so I would appreciate your assistance in this matter if the need arises."

Chase pointed to the Kincaid coat of arms that hung over the fireplace. "Sign says we defend justice, don't it? Count us in."

"Thank you, Laird." Ash drew his cellphone out of his pocket. "Lastly, I already told you I found something odd about Emma's ancestry." He accessed his picture gallery and handed the phone to him.

Peering at the small screen, Chase rubbed his tired, blurry eyes and looked again. *Huh?* "Dude, what am I even looking at here?"

"Gravestones. I took these at Emma's mother's gravesite. All those photos are her mother's relatives' headstones."

He looked again at the screen. *What?* He drew a sharp breath and scrolled through picture after picture. "Holy crap! Are you freakin' kidding me?"

"What?" Benji snatched the phone from his hand and looked for himself. "I don't believe it. *Sinclair?* Her mother's maiden name is Sinclair?" He turned wide-eyed to Ashriel. "As in Henry Sinclair?"

"I don't know. I'm not omniscient. It could be, or it could be an unrelated family lineage. But I'm sure you'll agree that it bears investigation."

"Yeah, it does," Benji said. "We knew she carried Templar blood when she commanded the fire coin, but I never imagined this. Still, let's not jump to conclusions. Sinclair isn't that uncommon a name." He headed for the arch. "I'll get my laptop. I'll start with the Templar genealogy records and cross-reference with modern public records. With all the genealogy websites there are, I should be able to trace her family history."

With a bitter laugh, Chase fell back against the cushions, the crush of disappointment tightening his chest and making his head pound. He pressed his fingers against his stinging eyes to stop the flow. "Why bother? Of course, it's gonna be him. Well, this is the last domino, the final nail in the coffin, ain't it? Benji was right all along. She's Chosen. She ain't gettin' out and having the normal life she wants. She's screwed."

"We don't know that."

Chase jerked upright and shot the angel a scornful glare. "Yeah, sure. Pull your head outta your ass and shove your fool optimism right up there." He stalked to the liquor cabinet to pour himself a drink, but instead took an unopened fifth of whiskey back to the couch and drank straight from the bottle.

Several hours later—one bottle of Jack Daniel's and two pots of coffee later—Benji had printed the evidence and hidden it in a drawer in his bedroom. Emma Borello was indeed a direct descendant of legendary Templar Knight Henry Sinclair, the father of the Knights Templar Order in America. Moreover, she was his last living descendant. What that meant was anybody's guess.

They agreed not to tell her yet and that they should wait until the turmoil of her curse was over. She had enough on her plate without the addition of yet another freaky coincidence. That's what Benji and Ash said aloud to each other, but Chase could tell that neither believed it was a coincidence at all.

And Chase? He hadn't uttered a word since he took the whiskey bottle back to the couch and proceeded to empty it.

A few hours later, Ashriel looked up from the mystery novel he was reading. Frowning, he put the book down and made himself invisible as the door to Emma's bedroom quietly opened.

Chase paused in the doorway for a moment, then walked into the room and stood there, gazing down at Emma as she slept by the light of a small lamp. His heart constricted, and tears stung his eyes. She looked so beautiful, curled on her side and asleep with her hair spread out over the pillow.

He was pretty much shitfaced, but he could hold his liquor with the best of 'em. Had lots of practice. Although he knew she wouldn't wake up for hours after Ash's dose of angelic Ambien, he spoke softly and a bit slurred. "I'm so sorry, sweetheart. You want a normal life, and I'm trying to get it for you. But this? This Chosen crap is out of my hands. Benji tried to warn me, but I wouldn't listen. Shocker, right? Tried to deny it, tried to convince myself you weren't cursed with this, too. But now? Can't deny it anymore."

Tears welled up and spilled over. He wiped his eyes with his sleeves, sank to his knees, and sat back on his heels. "I dunno. Maybe we're wrong. Maybe it'll be okay. Maybe you only see angels 'cause your soul was inside Ash, and maybe it's just a coincidence that you're related to Henry Sinclair. Possible, I guess. Hope to God it is. Just don't know what's coming down the road for you.

"But whatever it is, I'll be there for you. I got your back, no matter what. We all do. And there's something I gotta tell you, sweetheart. I get what you were saying in the kitchen about your mom and Indy. When you said you needed to say the words, but you never got the chance. Well, I need to say these, so they won't be stuck inside me forever. You taught me that."

He knee-walked closer to the bed, braced his elbows on the mattress, and gazed at her face. "My whole life, something was missing inside me. There was this empty place nothin' ever filled. At first, I figured it was 'cause I was a dumbass kid, trying to live up to what my dad and grandpa expected of me. But how could I ever live up to that?" He huffed a laugh. "I still can't.

"Then I blamed it on losing Mom and the twins, and then I blamed it on losing Dad. Then I blamed it on Hell and the terrible things they did to me." He looked heavenward, then ducked his head and covered his face with his hands. "And there's something I think I've done. A terrible thing. An unforgivable thing. You don't know this, but I was a demon for a little while. Don't remember much about that time because I wasn't...me anymore."

He lowered his hands to wipe his eyes and runny nose on his sleeve. "It was like wearing a virtual reality helmet with a dirty face shield, and the sound muted. Everything was all warped and hazy. I had no normal feelings at all, just this...awful hunger and rage. But I think...I think I might've murdered someone." He choked on a sob. "I dream about her all the time. Not every night anymore since you came, but I still do. She's scared, and she's screaming. And I'm holding a bloody knife. She haunts me. Maybe that's my punishment."

He held his hands up and stared at them, seeing them splattered with blood—gripping a bloody knife. His gaze moved to Emma's face. "But I knew the first time you touched me in that alley. I knew what was really missing was you. With you here, I'm as whole as I can be. I'm so sorry I'm pushing you away, sweetheart. I don't want to, believe me. But I'm trying to do the right thing. And the truth is...I don't deserve you. Thorne's right. I'm damaged goods. Tainted, marked with evil, reborn under an unlucky star. So I'm trying to get you that normal life you want so much. The normal life *you deserve*. But now? Just don't know if it's gonna happen."

He took a ragged breath. "But I'm gonna keep trying to get it for you. Because I love you, Emma. With all my heart and whatever's left of my soul." He stayed there for a few minutes, his heart aching, simply looking at her. He could look at her face for a thousand lifetimes and never get enough. With a shuddering sigh, he wiped his face with his sleeves, gently kissed her cheek, and pushed himself up. He left the room, closing the door quietly behind him.

Two days later, as Emma ate breakfast with Ben at the kitchen table, a smiling Chase walked into the room. She glanced at the clock. Only a few minutes after seven, and he was up? And from the glistening wet sheen of his ebony hair, he'd already showered, and he was dressed for the day.

"Good morning," he said cheerfully.

"Good morning," she and Ben said in unison. Ben leaned toward her and whispered, "We in a time warp or something?"

She kicked him under the table and smiled at Chase. "You're up early."

"Seize the day, am I right?"

"Absolutely." Huh. Maybe Ben was right, and they'd slipped into an alternate universe.

Chase dropped a thick stack of paper on the table with a resounding thud. "Eat hearty, kids, 'cause we got work to do. Hades sent me the list of missing-soul victims. Good info, actually." He headed for his new Keurig and continued as he grabbed a mug and made his coffee. "Names, birth dates, date of demise, home addresses, place of death, next of kin, place of employment." He paused and gave a quick shake of his head. "Even medical records. Guess privacy laws don't extend to Hell. But in this case, it's helpful, so whatever."

Emma couldn't help but notice that he added only cream to his coffee. *No sugar?* Ben must have noticed, too, because he exchanged an amused glance with her.

Crossing his arms, Ben quirked a brow. "Okay, who are you, and what have you done with my cousin?"

Chase ignored him. He lifted the lid on a skillet of Denver-style scrambled eggs that sat on the stove. "Mind if I take some of these, Em?"

"Help yourself." Her startled gaze went back to Ben, who shrugged. "But you know those green and red chunks are veggies, right?"

"Yup." Chase threw a wink at her as he loaded up his plate.

"And there's bacon in the oven keeping warm and fruit salad in the fridge."

"Smells great, sweetheart."

Ben snorted. "What, we run out of frozen waffles and Count Chocula?"

She had to stifle a giggle, and she kicked him again. Harder this time.

"Nope. Sugar's the new smoking, right? So I'm eating healthier from now on. Gonna cut back on the drinking, too." He carried his plate to the table and joined them. "Let's set up a dedicated workstation in the war room. I'm thinking we should start by setting up a map with those little red pins for where each of the vics died. See if there's any pattern there. Then maybe some kind of spreadsheet system with the rest of the deets, so we can see what else they have in common. If anything. What's that word? Oh, yeah, so we can cross-reference the data." He picked up his fork and dug into his eggs.

Gaping, Ben stared at Chase as if he'd just spoken in tongues. She reached over and nudged his mouth closed. "That's a great plan," she said. "We'll get started right after breakfast."

"Awesome. Oh, and I wanna start a weightlifting program. Benji, if you'd be willing to coach me, I'd appreciate it."

"Uh, sure. No problem. But we usually hit the gym around five-thirty. A.M. That means *morning*, Chase."

"Sign me up."

An alarm pinged. Emma reached for her phone that sat on the table and turned it off. "Laundry should be dry by now." She carried her plate and mug to the sink and then left the kitchen.

Although Ben was happy that Chase wanted to join him in the gym, he was curious as to why the change of heart. He sat back and stared at his cousin for a moment. "Why the about-face?"

"What d'ya mean?"

"The gym? Weightlifting? I've offered a bunch of times, but you always blow me off."

"Let's just say I'm lookin' at things a little differently now."

"Meaning what?"

"Been doing a lotta thinking the last few days, and I realized I was taking something my dad and Grandpa taught me wrong. When they told me I had to always be strong and never show weakness to anyone…I included you in that. And that was a mistake. Yeah, you're bigger than me, stronger than me, but that's okay. I've always known that.

"I can't compete with you, especially in the gym. Always felt like I'd be showing weakness if I even tried. Don't get me wrong. Watching you lift? Man, it's freakin' intimidating. But we're partners in this. It ain't a competition. Your strength *is* my strength. My ego was gettin' in the way of me being the strongest man—the strongest knight—I can be, and that's gotta stop." He inclined his head. "So I bow to the master. Teach me, Yoda."

Ben was speechless for a moment. "I didn't know you felt that way. I'm happy to coach you. Hey, believe me, I get it. Ash spots me when I lift heavy. There I am at the point of muscle failure, and he uses like two fingers to set the bar back in the rack, like he's lifting a toothpick. But you know, you got me beat with gun and blade."

Chase grinned. "Yeah, I do. Well, guess what? We're gonna work on that, too. Michael didn't leave us with a training schedule, but I'm puttin' one in place. Dude, the top of our game just got loads higher, so get ready to climb."

Chase went back to finishing his breakfast. Although Ben was glad to see Chase maturing and stepping further into his role as laird, it felt as if a thousand tons of pressure had just been strapped to his back. *But we're partners in this.* Yes, for now, but he didn't intend to be there forever!

But this would work in his favor. The stronger Chase became, the more skilled in every area, the easier he would be able to cope when the day came when he had to fight alone with only Ash by his side. Ben knew a pang of guilt, but he pushed it away. He wouldn't leave until his oath to Uncle George was fulfilled, but eventually, he would leave.

Although he'd sworn fealty to Michael, he wasn't a slave. God granted humans free will. He was well within his rights to move on if he so chose. A man had a right to pursue the life he truly wanted.

Didn't he?

Chapter Thirty-Two

EMMA SURREPTITIOUSLY WATCHED CHASE as he sat at the other end of the rectangular table in the war room. His laptop was open in front of him, and the stack of paperwork from Hades was neatly arranged next to it. He'd borrowed her Kindle eReader, and she'd shown him how to buy and download an eBook he'd chosen, *Excel for Dummies*. He looked so serious—and so damn cute—as he painstakingly typed using one finger, first squinting at his computer screen where he had a new Excel spreadsheet open, and then squinting at the Kindle, then squinting at the first sheet of paperwork.

Squint. Peck, peck. Squint. Peck. Squint.

Maybe he needed reading glasses.

She was proud of him. It was clear that he'd turned over a new leaf after the disaster at Dodge City, and along with his new personal goals, he'd turned his full focus to the case of the missing souls.

A zing of anxiety made her heart patter. This assignment was so much more important than the cataloging and translating she'd been doing. People had lost their lives, their souls had been stolen, and more people could be at risk. She wanted to do a good job.

No, a great job.

She wanted Chase to be impressed. To be proud of her.

"Ready to go again, Em?" Ben sat next to her at the conference table with his laptop. Displayed on the largest monitor in the room was a virtual map of the United States with a scattering of bright red dots—location pins where each of the missing soul victims had died. "I've got the next batch loaded. The first one is simple typography."

"Okee dokey." She set her water bottle down and rose, but she paused for a moment next to Ben's chair. He looked a bit under the weather. Was he getting sick? "You okay, sweetie?" She pressed her palm against his forehead. Good, no fever.

"Sure, why you ask?"

"You look tired, and our workout this morning was...lackluster." She ran a gentle hand over his velvety stubble of red hair. It was growing back nicely.

He smiled. "No worries, kiddo. Not sleeping great lately. I've decided to cut out all caffeine after four."

"Good idea." She went to stand in front of the monitor, looking for patterns of the red pins within the natural landscape features: mountains, plains, deserts, high elevation or near-sea level, proximity to bodies of water. She didn't see any. "Nothing here. Ready to superimpose the other maps?"

"Yeah, there's a list on the monitor to the right. Which one do you want first?"

"Doesn't matter."

"Here's plate tectonics."

They spent the next few hours working, with Chase creating a data spreadsheet while Emma and Ben evaluated maps for any patterns linked to the red pins, including road, street, and highway maps; electrical grids; crime statistics; recent earthquakes; other natural disasters; volcanic hazards; geologic maps detailing known deposits of precious metals, gemstones, and quartz crystals; oil and gas deposits; underground water tables; and even localized weather maps to determine whether there were any weather anomalies present on the day each victim died.

"Not a dang thing I can see." Emma rubbed out a kink in her neck from looking up at the monitor screen.

Chase's cellphone chimed. He checked the caller ID. "Sorry, gotta take this." He hurried from the room.

Emma rubbed the small of her back, then groaned as she leaned down to touch her toes. The stretch felt sooooo good! She straightened up and returned her attention to the map. "How many do we have left?"

"Just two," Ben said. "Human pop—"

They froze at the shriek of a smoke alarm.

"My muffins!" Emma jumped up and ran for the door, glancing at the wall clock. She'd put blueberry muffins in the oven before they'd begun working over three hours ago! She must have forgotten to set the timer. She ran into the kitchen, where smoke billowed from the oven door. Holding her breath, she hurried to turn off the oven and grab the tin of smoldering black pucks out of the oven.

Ben ran to open the windows and then yanked the ear-piercing smoke alarm off the ceiling and removed the battery. "Don't worry. Between the windows and the ventilation system, it'll clear out fast."

Her eyes stung, and she coughed from the acrid stench of smoke that filled her nose and sinuses. A picture burst into her mind—a terrifying, gut-wrenching, nightmarish picture of Ben lying on the grass, his body lobster-red and blistered, his handsome face warped, deformed, and unrecognizable. The vision was fuzzy and blurred and cracked around the edges, but clear enough that she had to choke back a sob.

The memory Ash had erased. *Returned?*

Damn her freak memory! Even an angel couldn't erase it? Tears rolled down her face, but it was easy to blame them on the smoke and her embarrassment at forgetting to set the alarm. She didn't tell Ben that her memory had returned. She didn't want her knights to feel sorry for her. Especially Ash. He'd feel like he'd failed her. No, she'd do what she'd always had to do with memories she wanted to forget: bury them behind the wall. And make damn sure to avoid smelling smoke.

At her suggestion, she and Ben took a ten-minute break on the tower terrace to get some fresh air and enjoy the stunning views. By the time they went back to the war room, she'd blocked the terrible picture and was ready to work.

She took her place in front of the monitor. "Where were we?"

"Human population concentration and ley lines. Which one you want up?"

"Well, I don't see how population could be a factor. Ley lines first."

As Ben changed the overlay, Emma closed her eyes and reviewed what she'd read about ley lines:

> Although not widely accepted by mainstream science, ley lines—straight lines that connect three or more prehistoric or ancient sites—are said to be imbued with paranormal and mystical qualities and are purported to be invisible lines of vertical energy fields, possibly powered by extinct volcanic deposits within the Earth's crust. It is believed that early pagan societies recognized this power and erected standing stones all around the Earth to concentrate and focus this energy, the best examples of which are Stonehenge in England and the Carnac Stones, an ancient, 100-acre megalithic complex in France with over 3,000 standing stones arranged in lines. In England and Scotland in particular, many ancient churches, burial sites, and other holy shrines and stone circles

> are purported to be located along ley lines. One line in particular, known as the St. Michael's line, supposedly links many monasteries and historic churches across the British Isles, Europe, and the Middle East that have a connection to the archangel Michael.

The archangel Michael? That was interesting. Coincidence? Or perhaps a clue?

As soon as Ben changed the overlay map, Emma sucked in a breath. A pattern!

"What? I don't see anything."

The pattern was obvious. How could he not see it? "Delete the map and just leave the pins and the ley lines overlay." Sure enough, every one of the red location pins lay along one of the green ley lines, like strands of red Christmas lights.

"That's it," Ben said. "We've got it!"

Chase hung up from his FaceTime call with Olivia and crossed the driveway to where Ashriel stood, looking out over the sun-drenched valley. "Okay, she's expecting you. She said no guarantees, but hopefully she'll be able to tell if you're witch-hexed. If you are, ask her if she knows how to reverse the spell so you can hear our prayers again."

"I heard her." Ash's voice was growly, and he wore a disgruntled expression on his face.

"Look, I know gettin' anywhere near a witch rubs you the wrong way, and I'm right there with ya, believe me. But the usual tests don't work on you, Ash, and we need to know. So drop the attitude, please. She's a Wiccan, not a dark witch, and an old friend. And it wasn't easy to talk her into this. She's freaked out about meeting an angel. So be nice to her, hear me?"

"As you wish, Laird. However, is there not some other way? I'd prefer not to leave Emma—"

"Dude! Don't be a helicopter angel. She's fine, and you won't be gone long. Both me and Benji are here, and the place is locked up tight, so hit the road. Air. Whatever. Got your phone?"

Ashriel slipped his hand into the pocket of his coat, first on one side, then on the other. "No."

Chase slapped a hand on his forehead. "I swear to God."

"Wait." Ashriel patted the front of his coat. "Here it is, in the inside pocket."

"Good. Keep me posted."

Ashriel disappeared, and Chase hurried back inside, locked the door, and headed back to the war room. He hadn't gotten halfway across the Great Hall when Emma shouted his name. He froze for a second, numb with disbelief, then broke into a run, his heart pounding. *What the hell is happening now?* And just when he sent Ash away?

She came careening through the archway and nearly slammed into him. He pulled her against him and turned, yanking his gun from its holster and putting himself in a defensive position between Emma and the arch, assuming something terrible was coming after her, but...wait.

She was laughing?

Relief swept through him, but he went rigid as a new danger reared its head. His heart still pounded, but now it was for a far different reason. He held her tightly, full breasts pressed against him, the sweet scent of roses igniting a flare of desire. Her hands resting on his shoulders, she gazed up at him, smiling, her eyes sparkling with excitement.

A memory of pink lace and cleavage taunted him. And her lips were so close...

It took all his willpower not to lower his head and kiss her. He let her go as if her touch burned, but she didn't seem to notice.

"We found it!" She grabbed his hand and pulled him toward the arch.

Ashriel stood on the cobblestone street in front of Olivia Rydell's Tallahassee, Florida, home. He wasn't sure what he'd expected of a witch's house—something dark and dank, with a cast-iron cauldron bubbling in the back room, perhaps—but surely not this.

The charming Mission-style cottage was sage green with white trim, nestled on an equally charming tree-lined street among neighboring vintage homes of various styles. Towering pin oaks provided shade from the hot Florida sun, as did the welcoming front porch, where potted plants and flowers grew in abundance and white wicker chairs with floral cushions extended their hospitality.

He double-checked the address. It was the correct location. He stepped up onto the porch and rang the bell. The woman who answered the door was as much a surprise as her home. Although he'd had many dealings with dark witches—and they ran the gamut from aged hag to stunning young beauty, the latter usually achieved by a magical spell—he'd never met a Wiccan before.

Olivia Rydell was naturally beautiful—a tall, willowy blonde in her mid-twenties with intelligent blue eyes the shade of a robin's egg. She wore a peach-colored sundress, and her narrow feet were bare, although she wore a multitude of rings on her toes.

"Hello, Ashriel." Her expression was wary, but she opened the door wide. "I'm Olivia. Please come in."

She led him to an airy room where sunlight shone through two stained glass windows that flanked the fireplace. She sat on the sofa and motioned for him to sit on the wingback chair across from her. On the coffee table between them sat a porcelain tea set on a silver tray, along with a plate of cookies. Steam wafted from the teapot's spout. "Would you care for a cup of tea? It's organic and fair trade."

Ashriel didn't particularly enjoy tea, and he was there for information, not as a social call, but Chase had instructed him to be nice, so he nodded. "Thank you. Just cream."

Her brow furrowed, and a shadow of fear crossed her face. "I'm sorry, but I don't have cream. I'm a vegan." She lifted the creamer with a trembling hand. "Is almond milk all right?"

Almond milk? He didn't know what that was, but it sounded dreadful. "Just black, please. You needn't fear me, Miss Rydell. Please be at ease. I won't harm you."

She gave him a slight smile. "I'm not easily frightened, but meeting an angel and having heard stories from Chase about the power you wield is more than a little intimidating, to say the least."

"I'm here at Chase's request, and you are his friend. Surely, you know that he would never place you in danger. Also, angels are forbidden to harm humans except under extraordinary circumstances. I cannot imagine the circumstances that would make me want to harm such a lovely lady as yourself, so please be at ease."

She gave him a genuine smile. "Thank you. I see that charm is not a trait limited to humans."

He glanced around the room as she prepared his tea. It was, in fact, a library. The furniture was arranged in the center of the space, and floor-to-ceiling bookshelves lined the walls, overstuffed with books of every size and conceivable color, as well as crystals, geodes, jars of dried herbs, plants, and flowers. "You have quite an impressive book collection."

"Thank you. I inherited many of them. What you see here is just the tip of the iceberg. I have a climate-controlled storage locker filled with crates that I haven't opened yet. My mother was an avid reader and a professional writer. As am I." She handed him a cup of tea. "I'm sure you have important things to do, so I won't keep you long. Yes, I'm sorry to say, but it's quite obvious that you've been marked by a spell."

She motioned with graceful hands in a series of circles in front of his body. "Your aura is amazing. So powerful and bright white. It's quite stunning. But there are stains—black and dark brown. They're like parasites embedded in your energy."

He wasn't surprised. He'd surmised as much. What else but a dark magic spell could block his charges' prayers to him? "This is not surprising. Do you know how to break the spell?"

Her eyes widened in surprise. "*Me?* Didn't Chase tell you I'm Wiccan? We don't mess around with that kind of magic. All my life, I've had the natural ability to see auras, but it's not magic; it's a gift. I don't cast evil spells or do anything to harm others, so I have no idea how to reverse such a thing. Our main tenant, as Wiccans, is that we hurt no one. *An it harm none, do what ye will*. We practice rituals to align ourselves with the natural rhythms of Mother Earth and her sister, the moon. We seek to live in harmony with nature and honor a greater power than our own, the creative power of the universe."

"The creative power of the universe is God."

"Well, now that I've met a member of your species, I guess I'll have to consider that." She raised her teacup with an elegant hand, the light sparkling on the rings she wore on each finger. "Tell me, is He as legend would have us believe? An old man sitting on a throne and looking down at us from Heaven, passing judgment on our every thought and deed? Have you met Him?"

She'd taken him by surprise by asking such a volatile question, especially after her earlier unease. Most humans were not so direct, but this woman seemed to have no guile. He couldn't answer her first question without violating the Angelic Code, but he could be honest about his personal experience. "I've never met Him."

"Hmm. That's interesting." She sipped her tea, smiled, and raised a brow. "You avoided my first question."

"I cannot answer it. Belief in God and His word is a matter of faith. Faith is a choice of the heart and must be given freely, without supernatural manipulation or persuasion. I believe He exists, although I've never seen

Him with my own eyes. The evidence is everywhere. The fact that you and I are here, living, breathing, and communicating, is proof, isn't it?"

"I suppose it is, so let's not argue. Whether God is an individual entity, as you believe, or a universal creative force, as I believe, the result is the same. Something—or someone—created everything from nothing. Shone light where there was only darkness, gathered up stardust and formed the first creature, and so set the first heart beating. Is God not then in every rock, tree, and butterfly? In the vast oceans, the sun, the moon, and the stars? In every good person's heart? So, are we really different in what we venerate?"

She gave him a soft smile. "A rose by any other name would smell as sweet." She laughed and set her cup on the table with a gentle *clink*. "Willie Shakespeare could turn a phrase, couldn't he?"

"I suppose. But even an instruction manual would sound literary in Elizabethan English and iambic pentameter."

Her face lit up with surprise and amusement. "How astute of you. Perhaps I should stop comparing my writing to the old masters, then. I consistently come up short. You're quite interesting, Ashriel."

"And you are an interesting woman."

"Thank you." Her brow furrowed, and her eyes flickered with regret. "I'm truly sorry. I wish I could do more to help."

"I understand. Thank you for meeting with me." Disappointed, Ashriel set his cup down and was about to leave when she spoke.

"Wait, please. I have a friend, a fellow Wiccan, whose sister was a dark witch. Thank goodness she saw the light and turned away from that life. She's now one of us. But it wasn't easy for her to break those heavy chains. I can't speak for her, but if she's willing, she may provide guidance to you in finding a counterspell."

The glimmer of hope made Ashriel smile. "Thank you." Although his purpose in visiting her was complete and he wanted to return to Emma's side, he was curious about this enigmatic woman. "May I ask you a personal question?"

"Go ahead. I may or may not answer, depending on the question."

"Understood. How did you and Chase meet?"

"Halo three."

He frowned and rolled his eyes up toward his own halo, glowing brightly. "Three halos?"

She laughed. "No, it's a video game. When Chase and I were, oh, about twelve years old, we met online while playing a multiplayer video game. The players can talk to each other using headsets, you know? Well, we hit it off, eventually shared our real names and pictures, and started emailing, texting, and had a few phone calls over the years. Nothing really came of it other than friendship."

"It's hard for me to imagine that Chase wasn't attracted to you."

"Oh, he was. And that attraction was mutual. He's a beautiful man. We met up a time or two when we came of age, but I couldn't let myself go there with him. It turned out that our auras weren't a good match, and getting romantically involved with him would have only ended in heartbreak.

"And there was something unique about his aura that concerned me—an aspect that wasn't conveyed through electronic screens. I couldn't see it until we met in person. His energy, although positive, was...closed off to me. Encapsulated. I suspect he's energetically bound to someone else already, even if they haven't met yet. Most likely his soulmate. But we've stayed friends over the years. He's a good man."

"Yes, he is." She'd surprised him again. Greatly. "You've met literal soulmates? That is extremely rare. How did you know?"

"Well, I don't know for sure that's what it was, but I can't imagine what else it could have been. It was my maternal grandparents. They were happily married for over sixty years before Grandfather passed. Their auras were an exact match, and when they stood close together, their auras would mesh and become one. That only happens with soulmates, as far as I know."

Ashriel knew a moment of disquiet. His and Ben's agreement to keep Chase and Emma's soulmate status a secret could be at risk of exposure. But the chances of Olivia being in the same place as both Chase and Emma were extremely small. "I must be going. Thank you for your assistance."

"You're quite welcome." She walked him to the front door. "It was a distinct pleasure to meet you, Ashriel the angel. Blessed be."

Chapter Thirty-Three

CHASE SAUNTERED INTO THE kitchen. His cousin sat at the kitchen table, staring into space, with an untouched sandwich and a full cup of coffee in front of him. The only sound was the ticking of the clock on the wall. He snagged a beer from the fridge. Still no movement from Benji. He stared at his zoned-out cousin for a few seconds and noticed the dark circles and the haunted look. "Dude, you okay?"

Benji flinched. "Oh, hey. What?"

"I said, are you okay?"

"Yeah. No." He scrubbed his hands over his face. "I don't know."

"Cleared that right up." Chase took his drink to the table and sat across from his cousin. "Talk to me. What gives?" He leaned over and punched him lightly on the arm. "You worried about the spell on Ash? We're making headway, so cheer up. Olivia's friend agreed to meet with us next week."

"No, that's not it."

"Worried about the missing souls, then? Gotta admit, me too. Emma picked up on the ley line pattern, which is a great start, but we still got no idea what it means. Yet. Just that and the data from Hades, a few freaky pics, and a slice of Posturepedic that glows in the dark—not even Ash knows why. But we ain't done yet. Still lots of data to crunch. Medical records up next."

"Maybe it's that. I'm not sure. I mean, I'm not happy we're going nowhere fast since Emma spotted that pattern—which I didn't see, by the way. Never would have caught that without her. But I don't think that's it. I've had this uneasy feeling—this pit in my stomach—since before that, and it's getting worse every day. I can't eat, I hardly sleep. It's killing me."

"Emma? Time's almost up. Just a couple days until Russo bites the dust."

"Yeah, maybe. Probably." Benji blew out a harsh breath and sat back, throwing his hands up. "There's just so damn much up in the air! Not just whether her curse will end. What will she think when she finds out she's descended from a Templar Knight, and not just *any* Templar Knight, but Henry Sinclair himself? Will she be pissed at us because we kept it from her?"

"Don't know, don't care. Newsflash, Benji—we ain't telling her. If she finds out and she's pissed, then she's pissed. I'll take the rap. Blame it on me, my orders."

"What? We're not gonna tell her? Are you serious?"

"Damn right, I'm serious." Chase took a pull of his beer and then leaned toward his cousin. "We were taught from the cradle that honesty is the best policy, and I believe that. Usually. I hate the thought of lying to her. I do! But just how damn much is that woman supposed to take? Almost lost her down the rabbit hole that first day, and I'm not about to risk that again. Just so my conscience can be clear because I didn't lie to her? How fucking selfish would that be?"

"Who says it means anything, anyway? Yeah, it freaked me out at first, but I've had time to think about it. Most folks don't know who the hell they're descended from after a few generations. It's not like a heralding angel descended from Heaven and presented her family tree on a damn scroll. Ash just stumbled over it."

"I hate lying, too." Benji drew in a long breath and pressed a hand to his chest as he let it out. "But that's better. I'm relieved we're not gonna tell her. Maybe that's what's been bothering me. Worrying how she might react—that she might freak out or something. I have to admit, you're not wrong. I mean, what if you discovered out of the blue that you were a descendant of, I don't know, Jack the Ripper? Wouldn't make any difference in your life."

No, I'd fit right into the family. "Exactly. Best-case scenario? Her curse ends, she dances off to her shiny new life, and all's well that ends well." When Benji didn't agree with him, didn't say anything, and just stared at the sandwich going to shit on his plate, Chase got a weird feeling in his gut, and it pissed him off. "What, you don't agree with that?"

"No, no, of course I do." He gave a half-hearted shrug and sighed defeatedly. "I guess. It's just so damn hard to imagine this place, our lives, without her now." He choked up, his eyes brimming. A tear rolled down his face he quickly dashed away with his sleeve.

Chase's breath caught. He couldn't remember the last time he saw Benji cry. Probably not since he buried his parents and brother.

"How do we do it, Chase? How do we go back to the way it was before her?"

Rubbing the tension knot in the back of his neck, he pictured Emma, suitcases in hand, walking out the door and out of their lives. Forever. And it made him want to curl up on the floor and cry, too.

"I don't know, Benji. Maybe you're right, and she might be safer here with us, but we don't know that for sure. Let's assume that the best-case scenario happens—the Russos are history and her curse ends. She'd be as safe as anyone else out there—safer, really—with her defensive skills. And I can't forget how that fucking manticore got in here!"

"Yeah, but we updated the tech security, and I revamped the warding spells to account for every creature in the records, living or extinct. We're as protected as I can make us."

"I know, but hell, we don't know anything for sure. God knows, I don't want her to leave! But we gotta do what's best for *her*."

"But who are we to decide what's best for her? Russo took away her choices for a long time, but now she's free. She's a grown woman, and she deserves to make her own decisions. Look, if she wants to go—it'll kill me—but I won't say a word. But what if she wants to stay here with us? Don't you think we should at least give her the option?"

"What she wants is a normal life. You know that. *You* told me that! But you know her. If we ask her to stay, she might stay just to make us happy, even if that's not what she really wants. She'd do that; you know she would."

"Yeah, you're right. She would." Benji took his coffee cup to the sink, poured it out, and got himself a beer instead. But as he sat back down at the table, he sucked in a breath. "Then maybe after dinner tonight, we ask her a different question."

Emma stacked the last dinner plate in the dishwasher, dropped a soap pod into the dispenser, and closed the door. She rinsed her hands at the sink as the machine hummed. She dried her hands and held them out in front of her. They were shaking.

Her whole body was shaking.

This was it—the moment she'd been dreading.

Chase and Ben asked her to meet with them in the Great Hall after dinner. They needed to talk to her, they'd said. Her sixty days were almost up. God, it had gone so fast! The happiest days of her life, and now they were over.

She slid her hand into her jeans pocket and made sure the folded paper was still there. If it didn't work, how long would they give her until she had to leave? If her curse ended, she'd have to rent an apartment. She had money, and she'd use one of her fake identities to rent one. But it broke her heart to think about leaving her castle and her knights.

Still, hadn't she known all along that they were only hers temporarily? So why did it hurt so damn much?

And if her curse didn't end?

She pressed a hand to her belly as nausea born of fear rose. She'd have to go back to her old life. Running. Hiding. Isolation. Ashriel—loyal, kind Ashriel—might want to stay with her to to protect her, but she wasn't going to let him waste his time and angelic powers protecting a hopeless case. A lost cause.

A burden.

She loved him far too much. She'd rather die. The door in her mind that led to Ashriel was strong, and it was shut tight. She thought she could control herself to keep that door locked. And with her warding tattoo, even if she prayed to him, unless she told him exactly where she was, he wouldn't be able to find her.

Ashriel. A sob bubbled in her chest at the thought of losing him, of never seeing him again, of never hearing his voice again. For a second, she almost opened the door and called him to her, longing to throw herself into his arms and beg him never to leave her.

It was a brutal fight, but she forced the pain down. She took ten deep breaths to calm herself. And she went to the Great Hall to discover her fate.

They were waiting for her, all three of her handsome knights, seated on one side of a reading table, while a chair waited for her on the other side.

It looked as if she were going to a sentencing hearing.

In a way, she was.

Ben gestured to the empty chair. "Have a seat, kiddo."

Emma sat with her hands clasped tightly together in her lap. She wanted to look at Ashriel to seek his comfort, but she forced herself to look only at Ben and Chase. If she looked at Ashriel, she'd burst into tears. She at least wanted to hold on to her dignity.

Chase slid an open beer across the table to her. "You okay, sweetheart?"

She nodded but didn't touch the beer. Her hands shook too badly to grip the bottle.

"Emma," Ben said, "Your talents have been a huge asset, and now with your options expanding in a couple of days, we want to offer you a permanent job—"

"Stop, Benji." Chase smacked his beer bottle down on the table. "Just stop. I know what we said, but forget it. I just can't do it. This ain't about work, and I'm not gonna pretend it is. It's about family."

Chase angled his silver gaze at her. "And you are family, Emma. This pile of rock is a home again, a real home, and you did that. Not just by what you do for us, but just by being who you are. We want you to stay. Cook or don't cook, work or don't work, we don't care. Not that you aren't an awesome cook, and what Benji said is true. With you on the team, with your smarts and research skills, it's a big advantage for us."

He leaned toward her. "But it's *your* choice, sweetheart. If you wanna go, then go. And don't look back. We'll understand. If you wanna go out there and have a normal life, we'll help you in any way we can. We should want that for you, and maybe we'll burn just for asking, selfish bastards that we are. We're asking you to live here with us. But don't do it just to make us happy. If you stay, do it because it's what you want."

Emma's head reeled as she went from abject misery to joyful delirium in less than a minute. *They wanted her!* She'd have a home. A job.

A family.

Smiling so big that her cheeks hurt, she reached into her pocket for the folded sheet of paper, unfolded it, and put it on the table in front of Chase. "This is a list of all the reasons I was going to give you when I begged you to let me stay." Her vision was blurred with happy tears. "Screw normal! I get to live in a castle with three knights in shining armor!"

His handsome face made even more handsome with a grin, Chase jumped up and grasped her hand. "Come with me." He led her to the fireplace, pulled a pocketknife from his jeans, opened the blade, and handed it to her. He pointed to his and Ben's initials that were carved into the wood. "Your turn, sweetheart. Make it official."

She wiped her tears on her sleeve, held the knife in a trembling hand, and cut EB into the wood, right next to the CK and BK that were already there. Her heart full to bursting with emotion, she returned the knife to Chase's waiting hand. He smiled at her, gently kissed her cheek, and then held the knife out to Ashriel. "Your turn."

Ashriel's eyes went round. "What? Chase, I don't—"

"He's right, Ash," Ben said. "You belong here, too."

Chase nodded. "Do it, Ash. This is our family tree. It ain't complete without you."

Ashriel went poker-faced, but his eyes were glassy as he carved an A next to Emma's initials.

After they went back to the table, Ben dropped a key on the table in front of Emma. The key was attached to a plastic chef's hat keychain with Emma's name written in pink. "You can't use it until your curse is lifted, and even then, it's probably best if one of us is with you, and it's not warded yet, either—but here's something from Chase and me. We were gonna give it to you anyway, even if you decided to leave, but I'm glad it's a welcome home gift."

Emma picked up the key, her brow puckering in confusion. "Love the keychain, but I thought the entry door only operated by incantation."

"It does," Chase said. "That, sweetheart, is the key to your new car. Well, it's not new, but I think you'll like it anyway. Cute little white number in the garage, top comes off. I hear you already tried it on."

With a squeal of delight, she hugged Ben and then Chase. She grabbed Ashriel's hand and pulled him to the garage to look at her new car.

As Emma and Ash disappeared through the arch, Chase's grin faded, and his heart plummeted ten stories and hit rock bottom. Just because she was staying didn't mean she would be his. All he'd done to keep her at arm's length, and now she was staying anyway. Well, wasn't that the story of his life? Thinking he was doing the right thing for all the right reasons, and then having it blow up in his face.

But she was finally home, and that was the most important thing. She was safe in the citadel—as safe as she could be—and he could keep an eye on her. And there was time.

Maybe it wasn't too late. Maybe he still had a chance with her.

Hours later, Ben looked for the umpteenth time at his alarm clock. 2:43 a.m. *God Almighty!*

He sat up and ripped his headphones off, cursing when a few strands of short hair caught on the hinges. He rubbed his scalp and cursed. Ironically, that never happened when he had long hair. The headphones were annoying to wear, especially when lying down. Where in the heck had he left his earbuds? He'd order a pair tomorrow, but that did him no good right now.

It was far too late to play music on the Echo Dot that sat on his bureau. He fluffed and adjusted his pillow and sat back against the headboard. Music wasn't working anyway. He'd tried classical, rock, jazz, pop, and country music, but tonight it all jangled his nerves. He'd tried to read earlier, but after reading the same paragraph five times and not remembering a word, he'd given up.

His initial relief at Chase's order not to tell Emma about her heritage—and his cousin's change of heart in asking her to live with them at the citadel—had faded. As a last-ditch effort, he'd been prepared to tell Chase that Emma was his soulmate—*anything* to get her to stay!

But now she was staying.

So why did he still feel jittery and apprehensive?

He'd gotten what he wanted, hadn't he? It was just a matter of time before Chase would come around and give in to his attraction to Emma. Just a matter of time before Chase's happiness would be assured and a new generation of the Kincaid clan came into the world.

Just a matter of time before his oath was fulfilled, and he could leave the citadel to create the life he wanted.

So why still the pit in his stomach, the ache in his chest, and the sense of dread? It didn't make any sense! Maybe the problem really was too much caffeine. He'd cut himself off at four in the afternoon lately, but his consumption of the stimulant still bordered on addiction. Bordered? *Please.* He wore a monkey on his back, and it was chugging a giant-sized espresso. Okay, he was going to quit coffee altogether.

Maybe that would help. Or kill him. Either way, problem solved.

He had to do something, or else he was going to wind up in a straitjacket. He had to get some sleep. He turned off the lamp, scooted back down, and closed his eyes.

"Alexa. Play sleep sounds, box fan sound."

"Okay, here's Sleep Sounds, Box Fan sound." The humming, monotonous, static-like sound filled the room. Using yoga meditation techniques, Ben tried to empty his mind and concentrated on taking deep, even breaths...

It didn't help. His mind galloped on, and pinches of anxiety made him tense and jittery. "Alexa. Discontinue." The room fell silent. Once again, he stared at the coffered ceiling, the crisscross pattern of oak beams barely visible in the gentle starlight that shone through his windows.

Unbidden—and unwanted—thoughts of Miranda filled his mind. He often thought about her, even more so now that Emma had entered their lives. He tried to fight the impulse to check her social media, and he hadn't succumbed lately. But a post a few months earlier had ripped open those old wounds—Miranda and her war-hero husband Alex recently welcomed their third child, this time a son to join his two sisters.

Ben and Chase had rescued Alex from certain death, and in doing so, Ben had lost the woman he loved. How could he have guessed that among the small group of military prisoners held captive in Iran by Illuminati scum operating under the guise of Al-Qaeda terrorists was Miranda's presumed-dead husband?

The irony still rankled.

Had she shown up to meet him at the appointed time at the Denver duck pond, where they'd first met? Had she chosen him instead of her back-from-the-grave husband? He would never know. At the last minute, he hadn't gone, and so he had taken the choice out of her hands. But looking at those happy family photos on Facebook, he couldn't help but think, as much as it hurt, that he made the right choice.

But he also couldn't help but think she could have been his wife. Those could have been his children. *His son*.

His legacy.

A jumble of emotions made his heart pound and his throat tighten. Unable to lie in bed for one more second without screaming, he put on his robe and slippers and hurried to the Great Hall. He poured two fingers of scotch and tossed it back. Still, his chest tightened, the walls closing in, even in that large space. Maybe some fresh air would help him relax enough to sleep. He retrieved his coat, poured another scotch, and took the glass with him as he headed up the circular stairs.

He emerged from the warmth of the turret into a frosty Colorado night lit up by a trillion stars. He stepped onto the battlement that encircled the tower and the uppermost part of the citadel and smiled. Emma had brought up a couple of old lawn chairs and set them on the widest part of the battlement that overlooked the most spectacular view of the forest, river, and mountain. But those chairs would soon be buried in snow. He drew several deep, calming breaths of fresh, cold air that relieved the tension in his chest and made clouds of fog that dissipated along with his anxiety as he exhaled.

Standing at the crenellated wall, he sipped his drink and gazed out over the forest. The graceful, naked limbs of cottonwood and aspen gleamed silver-blue in the soft light, their outstretched hands reaching longingly toward the winking crescent of the new moon. An owl hooted twice nearby, then fell silent.

He'd spent countless hours in those woods, playing and exploring as a boy, learning to hunt with Jamie, Dad, and Grandpa, then hunting alone as an adult, since Chase had no interest in hunting game animals. Chase's attitude was a bit hypocritical. He'd eat venison with no issue, but when

Ben had invited him to go hunting, he'd said, 'Look, you wanna hunt werewolves, vamps, or any other evil piece of shit? Target practice on rats at the dump? Count me in. But I ain't blowing a hole in Bambi's mom.'

Chase hadn't wanted to hear how culling the herd resulted in healthier, easier lives for the rest of the deer population. No matter. Ben didn't mind going alone. Often, he'd take his rifle and simply walk through the woods, using the guise of hunting as an excuse to get out of the citadel. The quiet and solitude were a good place to be alone with his thoughts.

He was alone with his thoughts now—the kind of thoughts he'd stifled for the last five years.

A stir of excitement swirled in his gut as he imagined getting on a plane and striking out on his own. New York, Chicago, or maybe Seattle. Somewhere with an incredible skyline, with skyscrapers and bridges spanning great rivers. Streets bustling with people in a hurry to get where they were going, lined with elegant shops and restaurants serving varied cuisines from around the world, with classy bars and clubs where people enjoyed good conversation, and on any given day, one could choose from a plethora of intellectually stimulating activities and special events.

Events that had absolutely nothing to do with angels, demons, preternatural creatures, or the Illuminati.

He could pull his degrees out of mothballs and land a job—maybe even work in an office at the top of one of those skyscrapers. Buy an apartment with an amazing view. And then maybe he could meet a fine woman and have a good life to offer her—a safe life, a normal life.

For the first time in a long while, that out-of-reach dream seemed to lie mere inches from his grasp!

The cold penetrated his coat and thin pajamas, and he shivered. He threw back the last sip of scotch and headed back to his room, feeling better for the drink and the fresh air that cleared his head, his heart lighter with the renewal of a dream he'd long ago given up as a lost cause.

But ten minutes later, he jerked upright in bed, his eyes wild, his breath coming in huge, panicked gulps.

Chapter Thirty-Four

Chase had no problem falling asleep. He felt better than he had in years now that Emma was staying. Still, it was hard to let go. Hard to give up and accept that he couldn't give her that normal life she'd wanted so much. But she really wanted to stay, and the list she'd made proved it.

His little warrior fairy was home.

He'd fallen asleep with a smile on his face.

Hours later, he lay on his belly, a puddle of drool on the pillow. But even asleep, Chase had reflexes like a cat, and when his bedroom door flew open, he'd palmed the gun he kept under his pillow and pointed it at the door in two seconds flat. Benji stood there, staring with frantic eyes into the barrel of his gun, sucking air like he'd just run a marathon.

"Idiot, I coulda shot—"

"Emma's in big trouble!"

Chase and Ben hurried into the dungeon and closed the door. Yawning and rubbing his bleary, sleep-encrusted eyes, Chase leaned against the wall. "Okay, Benji. Explain it to me. Like I'm six. Like I'm six and stupid. And drunk. I'm a stupid, drunk, six-year-old. Make me understand."

"Wake the hell up! This isn't rocket science. A vampire tried to turn her. He forced her to drink his blood—his *infected* blood. The only thing that stopped her from turning into a vampire was her curse. What do you think is gonna happen when her curse is lifted?"

Chase held up a hand. "Whoa, whoa, *whoa*. Just hold on a minute. Refresh my memory, professor. Only thing I paid attention to was how to ice the sons of bitches. Ain't it a virus? Wouldn't her resurrection procedure, with all that power and radiation, have fixed that?"

"Anything's possible, but I doubt it. That's the thing! Vampirism isn't just a regular virus; it's like mad cow disease. The vampiric virus triggers a cellular cascade that forms prions in the infected person. It causes abnormally misfolded proteins throughout the body—especially in the brain."

He reached for his phone and accessed the internet. "According to the University of Utah, 'Prions cannot be destroyed by boiling, alcohol, acid, standard autoclaving methods, or radiation. In fact, infected brains that have been sitting in formaldehyde for decades can still transmit spongiform disease.' Here's another one. According to MDPI.com, 'Common sterilization methods used for bacteria and viruses, such as high-pressure steam sterilization, ultraviolet irradiation, formalin fixation, *and gamma irradiation*, are insufficient to eliminate prions.' Chase, we have to assume the worst. She's probably gonna turn."

Chase's scalp crawled, and his ears rang. He dug his fingers into his hair as an uncontrollable shudder went through him. *No! This couldn't be happening!*

Trembling like a neurotic chihuahua, Benji covered his face with his hands. "It was right there. I don't know how I missed it. She said it plain as day. All this time! *How did I miss it?*"

Chase paced, his mind reeling, numb with fear, as close to sheer panic as he'd been since he'd come home and found Holly missing. But Dad's voice yelled in his head, pulling him back from the edge. *Tears won't kill the enemy, son! Pick up your damn weapon and fight!* "Don't blame yourself. We all missed it. At least we know now. We still got time."

Benji gave a bitter laugh. "Time? Not even two full days?"

"Better than nothing!"

"For months, we wanted nothing more than for her curse to be over, and now that's the very last thing we want. If only we knew for sure if her curse will end when Russo's time runs out. Maybe it won't, and we're panicking for nothing."

Chase banged his hands against the sides of his head, trying to knock out the remaining cobwebs of deep sleep. "Okay, let's stay calm and go at this like we would any other mission. Figure out exactly what we're up against, consider the options, and decide on a plan. The assumption is that Emma's curse is the only thing keeping her from turning into a vampire. If she turns, we need to give her the Babylonian Transfiguration Spell cure. For that, we need the heart of the vamp that tried to turn her, but Emma said my dad wiped out the whole den, so we can't get..."

The terrible reality of it hit him.

Without that heart, there was no cure. No magic that could save her.

He had no weapon.

The world crumbled beneath his feet. He stumbled to the wall and rested his cheek against the cold concrete. "That vamp bit the dust years ago. There's no cure, Benji! What are we gonna do? *What the hell are we gonna do?*"

"I don't know!"

"No!" Chase punched the wall as a bulldozer of guilt flattened him. "*It's my fault!* I did it again. Thorne's right. I'm the fucking kiss of death, a jinx. We shoulda let her die. She'd be in Heaven, but now she's gonna turn into a fucking monster!" He punched the wall again and again, the pain all that kept him standing.

Ben grabbed his arm and pulled him away from the wall. "Stop! Get a grip! You going off the deep end won't help Emma. Let's text Ash. Maybe he can help."

"No! He can't help."

"How do you know? We didn't even ask."

Chase turned to face his cousin, blood dripping from his mangled knuckles. "How do I know? I know because not even an archangel can cure a vampire. I never told you this, but years back in Oregon, when Michael and I were on the trail of that he-witch who left you for dead, we stumbled across a vampire den. We took 'em out, but one of them was a little girl, Benji. Just a little thing, not fully turned yet, with big blue eyes and a headful of blonde curls, and I begged Michael to save her, to make her human again. This was before you came across that scroll about the cure. The answer was no, and it wasn't just him being a heartless dick. He said he didn't have that power, and I believed him."

"Even if Ash can't help, we still have to tell him. You can't just shut him out because you're—"

"What?" Chase took a menacing step toward his cousin. "I'm what?"

"Jealous! Stow your crap and get a hold of yourself. She needs all of us now."

Chase dragged his sleeve over his face. "Okay, you're right." He took a few deep breaths to get control. Panic led to mistakes, as he'd learned in Dodge City. No time for emotion, only time for clear and logical thinking. "You're right. Text Ash. First thing we gotta do is find out for sure if her curse will end at midnight. If it don't, we're in the clear."

"How do we do that? We've been wondering about that for two months. Wouldn't we have done it by now if we knew how to get that information?"

"No. Sure, we wanted her curse to end, but it wasn't life or death. Now it is. And here's where it gets complicated and dangerous. To get the answer, we gotta go straight to the horse's mouth. Or demon's mouth, to be more specific."

It was unusually warm for late autumn in the backwoods of Montana. A soft breeze rustled pine needles and sent the remaining scatter of gold and crimson maple leaves fluttering, and the sun shone brightly in a cloudless, cerulean-blue sky.

Ben noticed none of it.

He stood in the center where two dirt roads crossed, his eyes bloodshot and heavy-lidded with fatigue. Sighing, he flexed his aching neck and mopped sweat from his brow with his forearm. Sleep was a distant memory, and every cell in his body screamed for rest, but the heart-pounding fear that drove him was like a powerhouse, producing more than enough adrenaline to keep him alert and moving.

His attention returned to the task at hand. He brushed the remaining fallen leaves aside and dipped a paintbrush into the bucket of lamb's blood he held, stooped over once again, ignored the burning pain in his lower back, and painted the bare ground with a circle about six feet in diameter—a ring of protection to shield him against the evil he meant to call into his presence.

Nearby was a larger circle on the ground, spray-painted in black, marked with a pentagram and occult symbols.

The task complete, he set the bucket of blood behind a tree. He stood in the center of the blood circle and raised his arms to the sky. His voice was sandpaper gruff as he uttered the prayer—a dozen words in Latin that drifted away on the breeze.

But he was heard.

The lamb's blood burst into flame and slowly burned away, leaving no detectable trace on the soil. He brushed the fallen leaves back over the ground to conceal the ring.

Returning to the copse of trees, he grabbed a different bucket that contained chicken bones, herbs, and the last of the graveyard dirt and picked up the shovel that waited on the grass. *Please, God, let this be the last time.* He dug a hole in the center of the pentagram, dropped a handful from the bucket into the hole, covered it with dirt, and tossed the shovel aside.

"Heads up," he whispered. "Here we go again." He stood within the ring of protection and said as loudly as possible, his voice as creaky as a rusty gate, "Daemon hoc bivio praecipio tibi vidiri!" He crossed his tired, aching arms and waited.

It didn't take long.

In less than a minute, he got the response he expected from the soul-trader demon.

"What human dares summon me, and for what purpose?"

A male demon, eyes ink-black with no trace of white before they changed into normal brown human eyes, stood mere feet from him in the center of the pentagram. The demon looked like he stepped out of the pages of *GQ* magazine instead of the smoke and fire of Hell. Hades liked his minions to look sharp, or, in the case of female demons, *Playboy* sexy, as they wheeled and dealed for human souls.

The acrid stench of brimstone stung Ben's eyes and nose, but he found a smile at the amazing stupidity of most demons. How many times over the centuries had Templar Knights captured the evil sons of bitches this way? And yet, the greedy morons didn't ever learn to recon before popping in.

Just plain stupid.

Ben jerked his chin up a notch in a smug gesture of contempt. "Shut up, dickhead."

Ashriel materialized behind the demon and wrapped arms like steel bands around it. The demon struggled, but he was powerless against the angel.

"You can't do this!" he snarled.

Ben snorted a laugh as he slapped a pair of iron handcuffs engraved with Templar spellwork on the enraged demon's wrists. "Call a cop." He checked to make sure the cuffs were secure. "Let's go, Ash."

The trio disappeared, and peace returned to the forest.

In a dilapidated, fire-damaged house on an abandoned farm, the soultrader demon, bruised and bleeding, sat handcuffed and chained to a chair. His eyes darted again and again to four demon corpses stacked like grisly firewood in a corner.

Ben and Ashriel watched as Chase—his gunmetal eyes as hard and cold as the terror that gripped his heart—slashed across the demon's chest with the Aegis of Solomon. The demon screamed in agony as the deceptively blunt dragon's tooth rent his flesh in a shower of sparks and blood. "Talk, you filthy hell-spawn sonofabitch!"

"I don't know!"

Benji hissed a shaky breath. "It isn't working, Chase. This is the fifth one, and *they don't know!*"

Chase threw a hard look at his cousin. "Shut up! Demons lie. It's what they do!"

Ashriel stepped forward, his blue eyes filled with anguish, his usually calm and stoic expression replaced with a mask of terror that bordered on sheer panic. "Ben's right. We can't keep doing this. Time is running out. We must try something else!"

Chase glared at the angel, his chest so tight he wouldn't have been surprised to keel over from a heart attack. "You think I don't know time's running out? You think I don't hear every fucking minute tick by like a gunshot in my head? You got a suggestion, Ash? Then spit it out, or shut the fuck up!"

Ash turned away, but Chase saw the fear and the frustration in his eyes before he did. He knew a zing of guilt for being so short with him. Even with all his angelic powers, Ash was powerless in this situation. That had to be a bitch. But right now, he didn't have time to care.

On an overturned barrel stood a silver flask. He grabbed the flask and splashed holy water on the demon's face. The consecrated water burned his flesh like sulfuric acid. As the demon screamed, Chase ruthlessly plunged the Aegis into its thigh and twisted.

The demon screamed again and begged as its flesh burned and sparked. "Stop! Please, stop!"

Chase yanked the Aegis out, cupped a hand to his ear, and leaned toward the demon. "Words. The right words. *Now!*"

"I don't know! I swear to Satan. I've never heard of a deal like that—someone selling their soul just to curse someone. People want wealth, or youth, or beauty, or fame, or they want someone healed or killed, but they want it *now*. Humans have no patience."

With a malicious smile, Chase nodded. "Well, you're right about that." His lips curling into a snarl, he grabbed the demon's hair and yanked its head back. He thrust the dragon's tooth into its shoulder and twisted it viciously. While the demon howled in pain, Chase, teetering on full-blown panic, screamed into its face, "*Tell me! Tell me!*"

"Chase!" Ben grabbed his arm and dragged him away from the demon. "Take a knee. Let me try."

Chase jerked out of his cousin's grasp. "Get your fucking hands off me!"

"Fine! But calm down. Look, if you kill it, even if it knows something, it won't be talking."

Pressing the heels of his hands against his eyes, Chase nodded. Ben was right. He was going off the rails again. Way off. He took a couple of deep breaths. "Okay. Okay, I'm good." He went back to where the demon waited. "One more time. Listen carefully. It's such a simple question. Does a curse that's part of a soul deal end when the hellhound plays fetch?"

"I've told you a thousand times! I don't know! *I don't fucking know!*"

Chase raised the Aegis yet again and plunged it into the demon's shoulder. The demon screamed. "Stop! Just kill me. I know you will anyway. And I can't go back to Hell after allowing myself to be captured by *knights*." He practically spat the word. "What Hades would do to me is far worse than death. You'll be doing me a favor."

After exchanging a look with Ben, Ashriel grabbed Chase before he realized what was happening and pulled him back, holding him there as he struggled in vain to break free. "Let me go, dammit!" He nearly cried out as Ben wrenched the Aegis of Solomon from his swollen, busted hand.

"Enough is enough!" Ben said. "He doesn't know anything. You're wasting precious time. It's over!" He turned and sank the weapon into the demon's chest. The demon jerked as it lit up from within and flickered red, its bones visible as if by x-ray, then went limp. The twisted soul oozed out of its mouth, nose, and ears, slowly collecting into a puddle of lumpy black goo on the wooden floor.

Ben, his eyes glistening with tears, turned back to face him. "It's over, Chase. Let's just go home and be with her."

"No!" Chase shoved away from Ashriel. "It ain't over! It ain't over until *I say it is!*" But the terror that Ben was right had him hyperventilating. Dizzy, he stumbled to a window and leaned on the sill as he glared through sooty, cracked glass at the orange ball of the late-afternoon sun shining over rolling white hills of farmland. It had snowed while they were questioning the demons.

He clenched his mangled fists and welcomed the searing pain. The Christmas card landscape was obscene! How could everything look clean and white and fresh, when everything was filthy and hopeless and black? But the pain pushed away the terror, and his thoughts cleared as he stared at the sparkling path of diamonds cast by sunlight on the snow.

Wait. Wait a damn minute...

He had an idea.

The kind of idea that should get him forced into a straitjacket and thrown into a padded cell for life.

It was a hail Mary, for sure. But it could work.

He whirled toward his team, his heart pounding with renewed determination and a crapload of fear he fought to ignore. "Benji, drive Chimera home." He threw up a hand when Ben opened his mouth with questions Chase had no intention of answering. "No time. We'll meet up later. Ash, take me home, pronto."

Ashriel looked aghast at him. "*Teleport you?* All that way?"

"You heard me. Assuming I survive, I give you permission to heal me. And fix my hands, too."

Chase swallowed his pride.

It sure as hell didn't go down easy.

But he had no time to waste on puking or pride. And he couldn't afford to show any sign of weakness when he faced his enemy.

He held out his arm for Ash to touch and braced himself for the worst. "Beam me up, Scotty."

Emma stood at the kitchen island, making a cup of tea. She was taking a snack break while watching a marathon of one of her favorite old shows on Netflix to distract herself from worrying about what would happen at midnight, worrying about whether her curse would end or not, and exactly how they would determine the outcome. She couldn't figure out how to test it, not without placing herself in danger, and no way would her knights or her angel allow her to do that.

Her attempt at self-distraction wasn't working—she alternated between heady excitement and crushing anxiety—but she put on a brave face for Ashriel's benefit. "Sure you don't want some tea, Ash? I can put fresh ground pepper in it for you."

No response.

She watched him as she dunked the tea bag in the hot water. He sat slumped at the table with his face in his hands. Her poor angel looked so sad—so distressed. It made her heart ache to see him like that. She couldn't take it anymore. She knew something was going on, and it wasn't just a headache.

When Ash and Chase had arrived home earlier, Chase had changed clothes and immediately gone out again, with no explanation, and Ashriel had become more and more despondent as the minutes ticked past. And she had no idea where Ben was, only that 'he'd be home soon' according to Chase.

She left her tea and went to sit beside Ashriel at the table. She smoothed her hand over his hair. "I know you're worried about whether my curse will end. But somehow, I don't think that's all that's bothering you. Tell me what's wrong, sweetie. And don't tell me again that you have a headache, because you're lying, and you, my dear angel, truly suck at it. That's why you always lose at poker."

But her teasing smile disappeared when he looked up, and a tear trailed down his tortured face. He pulled her into his arms and held onto her as if he were afraid she would disappear into thin air. Trembling, he choked back a sob.

Stark terror stole her breath and made her face and hands go numb. *Oh, God, oh, God, oh, God...*

"I'm so sorry, little one. I thought I could protect you from anything."

Seated at an isolated table in the back of a sports bar, Chase didn't spare even a passing glance for the cleavage masquerading as a cocktail waitress who brought their drinks.

He eyed Hades's drink, a blood-red cocktail served in a martini glass with slices of jalapeño floating on top and decorated with a plastic pitchfork stirrer. "What in the hell is that?"

"This delightful concoction is called a brimstone kiss."

"A little on the nose, don't ya think?"

Hades chuckled and took a small sip of his drink.

Chase tossed back his shot of Jack and downed half his beer in one long, gulping swig.

"So, Chase. You said when you called me that this wasn't related to the missing souls, and from the *I want to kill someone* expression on your unshaven face and the copious amount of liquid courage you're imbibing, I assume this is not a social call. Are you just going to sit here and bask in the magnificence of my being, or are you going to tell me why I'm here?"

Chase peered into his beer glass, his heart in his throat. Was he doing the right thing? What choice did he have? He'd left no stone unturned. He'd called in every marker he had, spoken to Olivia in Tallahassee, and tried to get in touch with Malachi—*Gone fishing. Leave a message*—even contacted a voodoo priestess in New Orleans, and nothing. The clock was running out, and he'd run out of options. He forced himself to look Hades in the eye. "Is it within your power to cure a vampire?"

Hades smirked. "Has Benjamin recently sprouted fangs, then?"

Chase fought for control. He couldn't blow this. "No, it's someone else. Just answer the question. Please."

"No. However, under just the right circumstances, I can render the poor unfortunate creature human again for a finite period of years."

"You're talking about a soul deal."

"Those are the circumstances of which I speak."

Chase had been afraid of this. Terrified, in fact. His greatest fear was staring him in the face, but he found that he was calm. Steady. All he had to do was picture his little warrior fairy, and he had all the courage in the world.

But what if Hades tried to screw him over with the same crap deal Thorne had forced down his throat? What if he had to give up the ghost right away? What if—

He slammed on the mental brakes. *What if's* were a waste of time. When he'd made the deal to save Holly, he'd figured that Michael would haul him out eventually, but he couldn't count on Michael or Ash to drag him out this time. Ash would be signing his own death warrant, and Michael would most likely throw his hands up in disgust and cut his losses. But if Hades tried to get cute, Chase had some leverage this time, and he'd play hardball.

Hades wanted the missing souls case solved? Well, he couldn't do that with his ass roasting over a spit in Hell, now could he? He'd do this thing, and he and Benji would have thirteen years to find another way to help her, and maybe, if they were lucky, find a way to keep his ass from winding up back in the pit, too. "Deal. The standard deal, you got me? You get my soul in thirteen years, in exchange for thirteen human years for her."

Hades's eyes widened, and he gaped. "*Her*? Chase Kincaid, throwing himself on his sword for a girl yet again? Must be a very special lady, or you have a peculiar form of psychosis. I vote for the latter. Unfortunately, for this kind of spell, only the victim's soul will work." At Chase's stunned look, Hades shrugged. "Not that I wouldn't love to have you back in the fold, but even I can't bend this rule. Only way the magic happens, I'm afraid."

"No *fucking* way! Okay, truly desperate times call for truly desperate measures." Chase knocked back the rest of his beer and took a deep breath. "The truth."

Chapter Thirty-Five

A VAMPIRE? EMMA STARED at Ashriel and shuddered as fear trailed an icy finger down her neck. She could turn into a vampire at midnight?

It couldn't be true!

But...it was.

They tried to turn me into one of them, but it didn't work. The curse stopped it.

She'd suppressed the memory and packed it away behind the wall again. *Stupid, stupid, stupid!*

Part of her had expected something like this all along. Her beloved Ashriel. Ben, Chase, the citadel. Her knights, her castle, dangled like glittering gems in front of her, allowed to rest in her hands for a few precious moments, and then brutally yanked away.

"Ben and Chase are still out there, looking for a way." Ashriel's voice cracked with emotion. "But we don't know what else to do. I'm so sorry. I've failed you. It's my fault. I should have let you go, should have let you die in the hospital and let your reaper take your soul. You would be in Heaven now."

She took his face in her hands. "No, you haven't failed me, Ash. You gave me the most wonderful gift. Truly, I wouldn't change it, wouldn't trade a moment of the time we had together for anything. Being with you and Ben and Chase, being here? These have been the happiest days of my life."

How long did she have left? She glanced at the wall clock. Less than two hours. Indy's training kicked into gear. No time for fear, no time to grieve.

Only time for clear thinking and action.

She had to be calm, had to think, had to decide what to do. She kissed Ashriel's cheek and then paced the length of the kitchen. No way to accurately figure the odds. She didn't have enough data. Okay, she'd go with fifty-fifty. Equal chances that at midnight, she'd either be fine or she'd transform into a vampire.

Indy's voice came into her head. *Hope for the best but prepare for the worst.* What were the ramifications if she turned? Would she turn immediately? Or would she follow the usual course of a newborn vampire, with extreme sensitivity to light and sound, weakness and disorientation? No way to know if they would have that opportunity to get her under lockdown.

The virus that caused vampiric prions had been in her body for years, presumably held in check only by the spell of her curse. Was it a latent virus, dormant and lying in wait but with no active viral reproduction? In that case, it would be days before the prions spread and the illness manifested symptoms.

Or was she riddled with prions, and the curse only masked the symptoms? In that case, she could go full-on vampire in the blink of an eye. If that happened, with her karate skills combined with a vampire's strength and fangs, she'd be lethal, nearly unstoppable, except for a well-aimed machete or Ashriel's smiting power.

But would her angel be able to bring himself to hurt her, even after she morphed into a monster? She didn't know, so she couldn't count on him to stop her.

Even if she retained part of her humanity in her freak memory, even if she could maintain some control, eventually the bloodlust would drive her to feed.

Feed.

She would kill people.

No! Ben and Chase! Because it was her, they would hesitate before they swung their blades. And hesitation could mean their deaths.

Lockdown.

They'd have to put her on lockdown in the dungeon before midnight. Iron shackles and chains would hold her for a while, at least. But then what?

She'd already read all the Templar files on vampires. The only treatment she'd come across was the Babylonian Transfiguration Cure spell. But that spell required the heart of the vampire who tried to turn her, the one that forced-fed her his infected blood all those years ago.

But Indy killed every vampire in the den.

There would be no cure.

Only a slow, agonizing death by blood starvation or a machete with her name on it. And when she died? A new terror filled her heart. If she died while a vampire, her soul wouldn't go to Heaven. She would go to Hell.

The lowest level of Hell, where monster souls preyed upon each other for eternity.

No peace, no rest. Ever.

The dealer was done. She had to play the cards in her hand. She had only two choices. Hold 'em or fold 'em.

Hold? She could wait for midnight and leave it up to Lady Luck. Take the chance that her curse might not end, or if it did, she wouldn't turn. A huge risk.

Fold? She could be proactive and assume she held a losing hand. Take appropriate action to mitigate her losses. If she died before midnight, she would die human. But taking her own life? She wasn't so distraught that she didn't know what she was doing. It would be a calculated maneuver. If she took her own life, there was no guarantee her soul would go to Heaven. She could still wind up in Hell. Another tremendous risk.

Fifty-fifty.

Hold or fold.

Win or lose.

Life or death.

Heaven or Hell.

Indy's voice cautioned her, a memory from when he taught her how to play poker. *Never gamble what you can't afford to lose.* She turned to Ashriel, who sat at the table watching her, his face ravaged with worry and fear.

Wait. Suicide wasn't a sure thing, but what if Ashriel took her life? But how could she ask him to do that?

She couldn't.

Her heart sank, but then soared. She had an ace up her sleeve, after all. In fact, she had all four of them.

Chase figured he was about to bite the dust as he stared into the glowing red eyes of the seriously pissed-off overlord of Hell. Luckily, a raucous burst of laughter from the other side of the bar reminded Hades that they were in a public place, and his eyes turned back to their normal blue color, although his voice vibrated with anger.

"I'm outraged that you and that haloed hemorrhoid dared to interfere with my business. You could have ruined an investment that took only *seven years* to mature. Yes, the curse will end when the contract is fulfilled.

Will the girl turn into a vampire? I don't know. She was supposed to be dead! But I'd say the odds are not in her favor.

"So, the way I see it, you have two choices. One, do nothing and take your chances. Or two, I can continue the curse for the rest of her natural life. She'll still be bait for all things creepy, crawly, fanged, and clawed, but at least she'll be human. However, it's going to cost you a very pretty penny."

Chase's gut roiled, even as his heart dared to hope. But it sounded way too good to be true. Hades, being helpful? Not fucking likely. He was being set up, but again, what choice did he have? "Lemme guess. A pretty penny meaning my soul, and hers, and Ben's to boot?"

Chase could almost hear the gears turning in Hades's clever, evil mind. A slow smile crawled across his face as he held up the pitchfork stirrer from his drink and carefully examined it. "No. No, I want something much, much better."

Ashriel stared at the double image of Emma that wavered in front of him, afraid he was going to pass out. He swallowed convulsively as nausea brought a sour, metallic taste to his mouth, and tiny black dots swam in front of his eyes. No, he couldn't have heard her correctly. He shook his head, trying to get rid of the buzzing noise. "What did you say?"

"I want you to kill me. Don't you see? It's the only way."

She dropped to her knees in front of him and took his hands in hers. "Will you do it, Ash? Will you kill me and take my soul into your body again?" She gave him a tremulous smile and laid her hand on his chest. "The two of us, together—the way we were before. I remember, Ash. I remember how amazing it was. We could be together like that forever." But when he didn't answer her immediately, her eyes welled up. "Unless…you don't want me?"

With a gasp of dismay, he pulled her against him and held her tightly. "Of course I want you. There's nothing I want more than to have you with me forever. But you deserve to live your life. Please, give me a minute. Let me think."

Ashriel's head spun. There was no way he would take the chance that her gentle soul would go to Hell. The month he'd spent there, sentenced to penance in the lowest level of Hell by Michael after disobeying the archangel to rescue Chase, endlessly running, hiding, fighting demons and every other kind of monster—just picturing her in that hopeless, dark, blood-soaked place struck a new level of terror into his heart.

And she was right. They couldn't risk the gamble of waiting until midnight—waiting to see if her curse would end. It was far too great a risk.

But what she wanted wasn't risk-free, either.

He released her so he could see her face. "Emma, you know angels can die. If I took your soul into this body with me and somehow I was killed? Your soul would be destroyed, as well."

She laid a rock-steady hand on his cheek. "I know."

He covered her hand with his and gazed into her eyes, and in that moment, he felt their bond stronger than ever. He would do anything for her. *Anything*. But this?

Did he have it in him to take her life, even to save her from a worse fate, even knowing that afterward they would be together?

Could he plunge a blade into her or put his hand on her head and smite her? Every fiber of his being cried out in agony at the very thought. But he worried that if he refused, as a last resort, she'd take her own life out of fear that she'd hurt Chase, Ben, or some other innocent person. He couldn't let her kill herself and take the chance that her soul might still go to Hell.

At least if he took her life, she would feel no pain. He would make her sleep first. And when it was over? He closed his eyes as an unexpected wave of joy passed through him. When it was over, he would have her with him again. She would be his, only his. They would be together, always, for as long as he lived, which could be until the end of time.

But she had another option, and honor demanded that he tell her. "If that's what you want? Yes, of course I'll do it. But you have another option. I could kill you, stand back, and let your reaper take your soul to Heaven."

"No!" Her voice was frantic, and she wrapped her arms tightly around him. "No! Please, Ash, promise me you won't do that. Please don't send me away to another strange place!" She leaned back so she could see his face. "I want to stay with you."

Closing his eyes against the rush of emotion that swamped him, he leaned his forehead against hers. "If that's what you truly want."

"It is what I want! It is." She heaved a sigh of obvious relief, and then kissed his cheek and hugged him tightly. "Thank you, my angel. Thank you."

He stayed where he was as she went to stand at the kitchen window. She moved the curtain aside and gazed up at the crescent moon. After a while, she spoke softly, more to herself than to him, it seemed. "Guess I always knew it was too good to be true. But I was so lucky to have the time I did." She stared up at the moon for a few more minutes, then let the curtain fall back into place.

She left the window and walked to the stove, reverently touching the control knobs and then her gleaming copper teakettle that sat on a burner. She reached for the pair of antique Popeye and Olive Oyl salt and pepper shakers she'd found tucked away in a cabinet, which now sat in pride of place on the range's built-in shelf. "I did the research on these. They're rare and *really* old, like around a hundred years old. Must have belonged to—" Her voice broke, but she swallowed hard and then continued. "Must have belonged to their grandmother. Please make sure the guys take good care of them." She pressed them to her cheeks before placing them carefully back on the shelf.

"I will." Ashriel's heart broke for her—broke for them all—even as anger had him clenching his fists. Why did God let such terrible things happen to good people?

She walked along the island, trailing her fingers lovingly over the countertop tile as she returned to stand in front of him. But she smiled as she combed her fingers gently through his curls and gazed into his eyes. "We still have some time, Ash. Do I get a last wish, a final request?"

Anything. He'd fly to the ends of the earth to bring her whatever she wanted! "Just tell me what you want, and I'll get it for you."

She opened her mouth to speak but hesitated, and her cheeks grew pink. When she spoke, her voice was barely a whisper. "I don't want to die without knowing what it's like to make love." Her gaze slid down to his mouth. She touched her fingertip to his upper lip, right in the middle, and slowly traced the outline of his lips, making him shiver even as his body seemed to burst into flames. "I want you."

Under the sleepy eye of a crescent moon that shone oblivious to the menacing bank of storm clouds gathering on the horizon, a midnight blue Porsche rocketed along a lonely rural road.

Chase punished the car, pushing the limits of road and machine as if death itself were chasing him.

It was.

His eyes were wild like a cornered animal, his jaw like granite, and his knuckles white on the wheel.

He slammed his foot on the brakes and left a long serpentine trail of burned rubber as he brought the Porsche to a screeching, fishtailing halt on the side of the road next to an open field.

He flung open the car door and bailed, running like a madman for the field. He stumbled and lurched over row after row of cold-hardened, plowed soil to the middle of the fallow wheat field and stopped. He yelled up at the sky. "God! God, it's Chase Kincaid. God, if you can hear me, I need your help. Please! I been there every time you needed me. You owe me, and I'm calling in my marker. I need your help! None of this is her fault. Please, don't let this terrible thing happen to her! Don't let her pay for my mistakes! Put it on me, instead. She don't deserve to suffer."

An hour later, Chase remained in the middle of that frigid, barren wheat field and looked to the night sky, where billowing storm clouds partly obscured the moon. He fell to his knees on the cement-like dirt and clasped his numb hands in front of him in prayer.

His throat was raw from yelling for so long: his voice was reduced to a hoarse whisper. "I'm on my knees. I'm begging, and Chase Kincaid don't beg. I can't let this terrible thing happen to her! And I just found her. I can't lose her; I can't! But how can I do what Hades wants me to do? *How can I do that?* Tell me what to do. I don't know what to do. Please, help me. I'll do anything you ask for the rest of my life. Anything. *Please!*"

He waited.

And watched.

Nothing.

He pounded his fists on the ground and then sat back on his heels, hanging his head as his body shook with sobs.

Anxiety and tension had Emma's heart pounding as she stepped out of the shower. She wrapped a towel around her body and closed her eyes, taking a few minutes to build a wall in her mind. It was thin and weak, but she only needed it temporarily. She pushed the anxiety, fear, and sadness out of her conscious mind and shut it away.

Smiling now, thinking only of Ashriel waiting for her on the other side of the door, she slipped into the new pink satin robe she'd been saving for this very event. She toweled the shower fog from the bathroom mirror and then unpinned her hair from the top of her head. As she ran a brush through her hair, her body hummed with delicious excitement—she was finally going to experience making love! How many times had she imagined this? Although, until recently, in her fantasies, it had always been Chase.

No. It wasn't meant to be. She firmly pushed those memories behind the wall, too. She had no more hopes, no more maybes, and no more dreams of what tomorrow might bring.

All she had left was now.

She opened the bathroom door, gasping softly as she stepped into her room.

Again, Ashriel made magic for her.

A trio of white and pink candles lit the room, the air caressed by the scents of strawberry and vanilla. He'd scattered white and pink rose petals across the bed, and achingly beautiful music whispered.

He stood in that soft, flickering light, waiting for her.

Her heart swelled at the sight of her angel. How was it even possible for her to feel so much when, for such a long time, she'd felt so little?

She was dazzled by the way the candlelight glinted on his pale hair, shimmered on his snow-white wings, and turned his eyes to sparkling sapphires.

He'd left several buttons of his white shirt open at the throat, revealing a deep vee of smooth skin. His expression was intense, the passion that burned cobalt in his eyes taking her breath away.

She hurried across the room on legs that seemed to float across the hardwood. Her hands slid up to his shoulders and into his hair as his arms enfolded her. He took her mouth in a deep, soul-stirring kiss that made her heart soar and her body tingle with delicious, silky desire.

It was tempting to pull him to the bed to satisfy this aching need—this craving. But they had only a short time left for physical love, and she wanted to savor every moment. She wanted to unwrap every touch, every emotion, every sensation, and every new experience like the precious gift it was.

Her eyes on his, she slowly unbuttoned his shirt, drew it off, and let it drop to the floor. She smoothed her hands over his chest, trembling as a heated wave of passion crashed over her. He was beautiful. Lean and muscular but not too muscular. Not overdone. It seemed to her as if God had breathed life into some ancient artist's marble sculpture of the perfect male specimen.

She reached up to stroke his wings. It struck her anew, because she'd grown used to his wings, how incredible it was that she could see them and touch them yet they existed apart from everything else. His clothes, the furniture, Ben, and Chase. Everything and everyone but her. His wings simply passed through them, unseen and unfelt, like a ghost.

Amazing.

And so beautiful.

And all hers.

Heart racing, she trailed her fingertips over the leading edge of a folded wing. She looked to him for consent, and when he nodded, she stepped behind him. She smoothed her hands up and down his back and between and around his wings. She marveled at the anatomy—at muscles as hard as steel, at the way his wings projected from his back, amazed at the size of them, even folded.

Ashriel looked back at her and smiled. "Step back." His powerful muscles flexed as he spread his wings. Feathers rustled, air wafted, and shuddering candlelight cast a dramatic double-arched shadow on the wall.

Awe overtook her face when his wingspan stretched from wall to wall, and even then, they weren't completely extended, and the wingtips were bent over on themselves. *Magnificent.* She reached out and ran her fingers through layers of soft, downy feathers. When his head fell back and a husky moan rumbled in his throat, she hesitated.

"Please don't stop. That feels amazing."

She combed her fingers through the bright plumes. "Tell me what you want."

"Deeper. Harder. You can't hurt me."

She dug her fingers into the layers and increased the pressure as she stroked, combed, massaged, and pulled. Under her hands, wings ruffled, and feathers twitched. He moaned in obvious pleasure, his eyes squeezed shut, and his breath came hard and fast.

"Stop, Emma. *Now.*"

Gasping, she stepped back. Had she done something wrong? "Why?"

He took a shaky breath. "Because I want to be gentle with you, and you're driving me wild."

She had done that? A gratifying surge of satisfaction brought a coquettish smile to her face.

He folded his wings and almost slammed them closed. The gust of air made her long hair billow and her satin robe ripple, making the candle flames dance and the burning wax crackle and snap.

She wanted to touch him. To see. To explore. To know all of him. Commit even the smallest detail to memory so they could relive these precious moments together whenever they wanted, after he'd taken her soul back into his body and they were reunited.

She'd never touched a man before—not like this.

She'd imagined it, of course, many times. Sleeping with a man. Having sex. She'd read about it in books, and watched it in movies and on TV, but this? This was so much more.

Touching Ashriel was magic.

She caressed the smooth, warm skin of his chest, his arms, and his shoulders, his muscles bunching and quivering beneath her fingers. She lingered over the place where his heart thundered under her palm. She pressed a soft kiss to the spot and laid her cheek there as her hands roamed along the ridges of muscle that ran across his abdomen.

He fascinated her as much as he excited her. So strong, so hard.

So thrillingly male.

She stretched up on her toes, her body leaning against his, and pressed her mouth to his neck, at the line where his stubble began, at the place where the heady contrast of coarse and smooth beckoned to her, where his pulse beat hard and fast.

She licked his skin, moaning at the salty, spicy taste of him. She nibbled and lapped her way down his neck and over his chest. Emboldened by the way his breaths quickened and how he trembled under her touch, she reached for his belt. Her fingers were weak and shaky; she couldn't work the buckle. "I can't."

Ashriel stayed her hands. With a tender kiss to calm her, in seconds, he'd tossed his clothes aside and stood naked before her.

Her gaze dropped to his erection. She shivered as sweet tendrils of desire swirled low in her belly and warmth spread over her skin like a kiss of sunshine. She drew in a long, shaky breath as she tentatively reached for him. She gently wrapped her hand around him and found his warm, velvety flesh to be as hard as stone.

Chapter Thirty-Six

Ashriel burned with hunger. Raw, howling, desperate hunger. He wanted to devour her. He wanted to carry her to the bed, throw her down, mount her, and pound himself into her until the clawing need that tormented him was satisfied.

Until she was his, only his, forever branded by his possession.

He shuddered, shaken by such intense and primal urges—feelings that were completely foreign to him. But his love for her and his passion for her had taken him to new heights and depths of emotion. Breathing deeply, he took control of his desire and waited for her to take the lead.

It was her first time.

Her *only* time.

He wanted it to be perfect for her.

He moaned when her hand closed around him. As she glided her hand over the length of him, her touch as light as a breeze, he growled—a raw, throaty, primal sound he barely recognized as himself. Although he didn't want her to stop—he *never* wanted her to stop—after only a few moments of the thrilling, erotic pleasure, he gently drew her hand away, afraid he would spill himself where he stood.

Trying to maintain a grip on the last slippery thread of his self-control, he stood still, his eyes squeezed shut, and concentrated on taking deep, even breaths.

"Are you all right?"

He could only nod. In her innocence, she didn't understand. The reminder of her virginity was like a splash of ice-cold water, and just what he needed to regain control.

With a soft whimper, she hid her face against his chest. His expression softened as a wave of tenderness struck him. He drew her head up and held her face in his hands. "My sweet Emma," he whispered. He kissed her softly and sweetly at first, then went deep and deeper still as he pressed her against him, his tongue delving into her mouth to slide against hers, stirring flames of passion into wildfires he fought to bank. *No! Gently. Go gently with her.*

He ended the kiss and smiled at her dreamy, bemused expression. Her eyes widened as he raised a hand and slipped the robe from her shoulders. He watched it glide to the floor, a cloud of pink satin at their feet.

He looked up and sucked in a breath.

She wore nothing underneath.

Candlelight turned her ivory skin to warm honey and her amber eyes to burnished gold. His hands skimmed down the length of her long, silky hair, glints of bronze shining in the candle glow, his touch sending wisps of her sweet fragrance into the air. He gathered up her hair and pressed it to his face, loving the soft, smooth sensation against his skin and the intoxicating scent of her perfume.

She enchanted him.

She inflamed him.

He let go of her hair, watching as it cascaded over her shoulders and down to her waist—a curtain of shimmering spun copper. He cupped her full, rose-tipped breasts in trembling hands, acutely aware of the immense strength those hands wielded. He squeezed ever so gently before rubbing his thumbs over her nipples until they were hard and erect, and her breath came in shallow gasps. He kneeled and worshipped her, drawing first one taut bud and then the other into his mouth, gently flicking her nipples with his tongue.

Emma moaned as he set her body on fire. Shocks of exquisite pleasure raced from her nipples to her feminine core. A hot pulse throbbed between her legs and burned there. Her head fell back, and her hands fisted in his hair as he teased, swirled, and sucked, until she cried out at the overwhelming sensations.

Her head spun as he swept her into his arms, carried her to the bed, and laid her down as gently as a sigh. He kneeled on the floor beside her and smoothed his hand over her skin.

Lying there completely exposed, she tensed, suddenly becoming self-conscious, the memory of her scarred, ugly body still clear in her mind. But her insecurity soon melted away as his fiery eyes wandered over her, and he seemed to drink her in, his gaze roaming over every line, every curve, every dip and rise, as if she were flawless. Desirable. Perfect.

"You're so beautiful."

Her heart soared at his words. He made her feel beautiful.

He made her feel *everything*.

Wanting his mouth, she pulled his head down for a mind-drugging kiss as he explored her body. He glided his hand over her breasts, her ribs, and her belly, smiling against her curved lips when he unintentionally tickled her, making her giggle and quiver.

He continued further, lightly trailing his fingers through the auburn curls between her legs and further still, to the soft, sensitive flesh that swelled at his gentle caresses.

She moaned into his mouth, simmering in the pleasure—in the heat and in the thrill of his touch. But soon, it wasn't enough. Her hips moved restlessly. Whimpering, she bent her legs and bucked against his hand, needing *more*.

Trailing kisses over her flushed skin, he moved down her body, angling himself up onto the foot of the bed. Smoothing his hands over her thighs, he gently spread her legs. With a husky, eager groan that excited her as much as his touch, he lowered his head and pleasured her with his mouth.

He sent her flying, high and fast—a startling, immediate rush that had her grabbing hold of the sheet as a lifeline. Never had she known such incredible pleasure! His hot, clever tongue swirled and fluttered, the feeling so wild and so intense that she thought for a moment she would faint.

The climax happened so quickly that she could do nothing but hold on and ride it out as wave after wave of stunning ecstasy washed over her, until she lay boneless, helpless to do anything but drag air into her lungs.

Ashriel gave her a few minutes, his heart pounding and his muscles quivering. Her sweet feminine scent, intoxicating taste, and wildly passionate cries of release had pushed him to the brink.

He was desperate to have her.

He eased a finger inside her and found her wet and ready for him. But it was her first time, and he knew he had to go slow. "I need you," he whispered.

She opened eyes clouded with passion. "Then have me."

He rose over her, and although he'd never wanted anything, had never needed anything, as much as he needed to be inside her at that moment, he forced himself to wait. "Are you sure? I'll stop if you ask me to." *Please, please, don't ask.*

She stroked his cheek with a trembling hand. "Love me, Ashriel. I've waited so long for this."

Their mouths met in a smoldering kiss. As her soft hands wandered over his chest and shoulders, he positioned himself between her legs. Gasping at the incredible sensation, he slid slowly into the tight, slick heat of her body.

He met the tight resistance of her virginity and stopped. Needing to move but unwilling to hurt her, he raised his hand to her forehead to spare her the pain of his invasion.

She grabbed his hand. "No, don't. I want to feel it."

Deeply moved, he lowered his forehead to hers for a few seconds, but just for a few seconds. He could wait no longer. He surged forward and buried himself up to the hilt.

Her whimper cut him to the core. "I'm sorry, little one."

"Don't be sorry. Just a twinge. Nothing, really."

Panting, his muscles screaming for movement, and his heart pounding as if it would burst from his chest, he forced himself to be still to give her body a chance to accept him.

She'd felt his possession as she'd wanted, and that was enough. He refused to hurt her any more than that. He pulled out and healed her. Kissing her tenderly, he guided his throbbing shaft back inside her, groaning at the exquisite pleasure of her tight, hot, wet body. He began to move with long, slow strokes, and her moans and soft sighs told him there was no more pain.

Only pleasure—so much pleasure—for them both.

As her soft hands roamed over his back and wings, he gazed at her lovely, flushed face, her stunning eyes heavy-lidded with passion, her lips swollen from his kisses, and all he could think was *Mine. My sweet Emma, all mine.*

His heart was satisfied, but his body demanded more.

Her breaths quickened along with his as he thrust faster and harder, giving himself over to the hunger, to the fever, and to the thrill, sending them both hurtling toward that magnificent edge. And when she arched and shuddered beneath him as she tumbled over, her cries of ecstasy echoing in his ears, he buried his face in her glorious hair and fell with her.

Ben had caught a second wind while driving home along miles of snow-blanketed farmland and forest. An amazing sunset against a cornflower-blue sky and an extra-large Styrofoam cup of strong gas station coffee had helped, too. He'd realized that Chase was right. He couldn't simply give up, go home, and possibly witness the woman he loved as a sister transform into one of the hideous creatures she loathed and feared.

He didn't allow himself to think about what would need to be done if that happened.

He didn't know what his cousin had planned—Chase wasn't answering his phone—but he couldn't assume that Chase would be successful, so he was going to hedge their bets. Instead of driving straight home as instructed, he'd taken a detour. He'd had everything he needed already in the truck, except for a handful of graveyard dirt, but he figured that would be easy to find.

He was wrong.

He'd stopped the truck alongside the road and found directions to the nearest cemetery on his phone. From where he'd been in the middle of nowhere, it was a two-hour drive. Darkness had fallen by the time he'd arrived at the cemetery, but luckily, it was across the highway from a gas station that also sold sandwiches and strong hot coffee.

Unluckily, the ground was frozen solid, and it took him another hour to chisel off enough for the spell.

Now he stood at yet another crossroads, the sixth time in two days he'd performed this ritual. His aching back would never be the same. He couldn't say he wasn't afraid. He had no expectation that Michael would rescue him, and surely Ash wouldn't be so foolish as to risk the archangel's wrath again just for him. After all, he wasn't a laird. He was expendable. But thirteen years is a long time. Long enough to figure out a way to circumvent the execution of the contract.

Surely, there was a loophole in there somewhere, and he'd happily spend every last dime of his considerable savings and sell off his investments to hire a dream team of lawyers to find it.

But what he'd just heard was a hard punch in the gut. He stared in shocked disbelief at the gorgeous soultrader demon who stood before him.

The demon, impervious to the freezing temperature, wore a black-leather miniskirt, crop top, and man-killer heels. Smacking a wad of gum, she tossed her blonde hair over her shoulder and shrugged. "Really wish I could help, sugar pie, believe me. To bag a Kincaid, a freakin' Templar Knight? That would be the high point in my career, lemme tell you."

Ben rubbed his aching forehead and prayed for patience. How he hated demons! Especially dumb blondes with southern accents thick as molasses who just killed his last glimmer of hope. "No? What do you mean, no? Why not?"

"Not just any soul will do for the kinda deal you're talking about." She tilted her head and smiled an evil little smile. "My, my, my. Well, this is funny as all get-out, but you got gumption, I'll give you that. I take it Cousin Chase don't know you're fixin' to do this?"

"What? No. What do you care?"

She toyed with a lock of her hair. "I don't. Just loving the symmetry, that's all. Or is it irony?" She giggled. "I always mix those two words up."

Ben blew out an aggravated sigh. "Okay, hang on a minute. You lost me. Why won't my soul work?"

"I don't make the rules, sugar. But reversing vampirism? Big magic like that requires the victim's soul. That's what it says in the handbook, but don't ask me why. I'm in sales and acquisitions, not management. Now, why don't you run along and get her, and then we can—"

"No! No fucking way!"

"Okay, hold your horses, big boy. Long as we're here, surely there's something else ya want. Wealth? Fame? Knock fifteen years off your age? Oh, I know! How about an Oscar or a Grammy? Just name it, handsome."

But Ben was already walking away.

He'd be damned if he'd let a demon see him cry.

Emma lay with her head pillowed on Ashriel's shoulder and her arm resting on his heaving chest. He lifted her hand, pressed a gentle kiss to her palm, then put it back over his pounding heart. They'd wound up on the floor, and although she was naked, she was warm on top of his wing. A fierce blush heated her face, and a slow, sultry smile curved her lips as she thought about how they'd ended up on the floor.

Her angel was insatiable. But so gentle, so careful with her. Her heart did a long, slow tumble. But her smile faded as reality crashed down on her. She'd blocked it out, living only in the moment, but now?

Now, she would have given anything to make time stand still. But the minutes continued their relentless march, and as their breathing settled, it became quiet in her room, the only sound being the ticking of the clock.

Her little wind-up alarm clock sounded like Big Ben tolling. *Ask not for whom the bell tolls; it tolls for thee.*

The time had gone by so fast. So very fast. The ticking reminded her she needed to tell Ashriel something. "It's almost time. Please don't let Ben and Chase see my body here. I don't want them to remember me here at home like that. Take my body somewhere else—after—and call them there. Somewhere, they wouldn't normally go or drive past. It'll be easier for them that way."

He nodded.

"They'll probably want to give me a Templar funeral, and that's fine. I'd like that. And I'd like to be buried near Indy if Chase will permit it." When he didn't say anything or even offer a nod, she angled herself up on her elbow so she could see his face.

Tears shimmered in his eyes, and his chin quivered.

There was nothing she could say that would make him feel better, so she didn't even try. She understood why this was so much harder for him than for her. She was simply going to go to sleep, but he had to kill her. She wished she could spare him that pain, but there was no other way, and he'd be all right once they were reunited inside his body.

She tenderly kissed him and wiped away the tears that trailed down his temples, and then she got up and gathered her clothes. Ben and Chase would surely be home soon, and she wanted it all to be over before then.

They wouldn't understand. They might try to stop her, and although Ashriel could seal her door, she didn't want to put any of them through that ordeal.

It was better this way.

When she'd dressed, brushed her hair, and tidied her room, she pocketed her phone and went into her bathroom to brush her teeth. As she looked in the mirror and enjoyed the cool, minty feeling of the toothpaste in her mouth, it stunned her to realize that she had just done all those things for the last time. She was brushing her teeth for the very last time...

Her hand stilled, and a ribbon of foamy white drool ran down her chin.

Was she doing the right thing?

She imagined herself as a vampire—corpse-pale skin; filthy, matted hair; lifeless black eyes, her pupils fully dilated in a living death; jagged fangs dripping saliva, or worse, human blood. And the smell...God, how she hated the reeking stench of vampires!

She shuddered. Of course, she was doing the right thing. Just a case of cold feet, that was all. Nothing had changed. She rinsed her mouth and sat on the bathroom floor with her phone. She made a tearful video recording, a goodbye message, and an explanation for Ben and Chase, so they would have to accept that this was her idea, her choice, and her decision. She didn't want them to be angry with Ashriel.

She splashed her face with cold water and hurried to Chase's bedroom. She'd never been in his room before. Even if she hadn't known it was Chase's room, she would have recognized that it was from the framed pictures on the wall of classic muscle cars and paintings of cowboys on horseback and wild horses running free. A Stetson hat hung on the wall alongside a pair of spurs. An old dream came into her mind of Chase wearing that Stetson and skipping stones on a sparkling lake while a pretty paint horse grazed nearby, saddled up and ready. And it made her smile.

She left her phone on his dresser. He'd spot it immediately and find the message. As she turned to leave, a photo on his nightstand caught her eye, and her breath caught in her throat. It was a picture of her in the kitchen, laughing. When had he taken it? And why?

His bed was unmade and dirty clothes were tossed on the floor. He'd been in a mad rush to leave earlier. She hadn't known why at the time. *It was for her.* He was still out there, along with Ben, trying to find a way to save her. Such good men! They'd do the same for any innocent person in need. Her eyes brimmed. She'd never see them again! Ben, the brother of her heart, and Chase, the man of her dreams. Would more time have made any difference in his feelings toward her? Could they one day have had a future together?

Tears trickled down her cheeks as she ran her fingertips over his pillow, over the indentation where he lay his head. A chest-tightening wave of sadness for what might have been raised a lump in her throat.

But none of it mattered now.

As she walked down the hall to her room, each step brought her closer to the end of her physical life, and a cold numbness wrapped around her like an invisible shroud of ice. By the time she walked through her bedroom door, she didn't feel anything.

Ashriel drew her into his arms and held her tight. "Are you sure this is what you want?"

She nodded, unable to speak. It wasn't what she wanted; she wanted to live her life. But it wasn't in the cards, and it was time to cash out. She stepped out of his arms, and with one last, long look in his beautiful angel eyes, she lay on the bed and forced a smile for him. In that moment, she knew no fear. No doubt. There was peace in knowing that she had no other choice. "I'm ready."

He nodded and sat on the edge of the bed. She put her hand over his heart. "Pah deh rah," she whispered. The words were Enochian, the language of angels, meaning *always and forever.* "Thank you, my angel. Thank you for saving me."

All Ashriel could do was close his eyes against the torrent of raging emotions that battered him. He put his hand over hers on his chest and laid his other hand over her heart. "Pah deh rah, little one."

With a sob lodged in his throat, but with a smile on his face—because she'd told him the last thing she wanted to see with her own eyes was his smile—he eased her into a deep unconscious state.

She looked so lovely. So peaceful.

How could he do it?

Never gaze upon her sweet face again? Never hear her laugh, her eyes sparkling with happiness? Never hear her sing again? Never kiss her lips or hold her beautiful body against him again, except in a memory?

He rested his forehead against hers and wept as he stroked her silky hair. He gathered it up, pressed the gleaming auburn tresses to his face, and breathed in her lovely fragrance before letting the strands slowly slip through his fingers. He pressed tender kisses on her eyelids. Her forehead. Her cheeks. The tip of her nose. With a shuddering breath, he kissed her soft lips one last time.

He had to do it.

He'd given her his word.

She was counting on him to save her, counting on him to be her hero.

Sobbing, his body shaking, and his heart breaking, he raised his sword high over her chest.

With a scream like that of a wounded animal, he plunged it into her heart.

Ben's cellphone trilled. He glanced at the caller ID and groaned. It was Chase. He braced himself, expecting a reprimand for disobeying orders. He should have been home hours ago. Keeping his eyes on the dark, rain-swept highway, he activated the hands-free mode. "Yeah."

"Where the hell are you?"

"About ten minutes from home. Just passed through the stoplight at Baker and Route Four. Look, I'm sorry, but—"

"Whatever. Come and get me. The Porsche broke down. I'm at that burned-out, cinderblock gas station with all the stacks of old tires in the yard."

"On my way." Ben continued past the turn that would take him to the citadel. Within minutes, he spotted Ash's midnight blue Porsche parked under the derelict gas station's rusty, swayback awning. He pulled in alongside the car. Chase strode for the rain-beaded truck before Ben even came to a complete stop and wrenched the driver's side door out of his hand as he opened it.

"I'm driving," Chase said.

Ben moved over into the passenger seat. "Where we going?"

"Gotta meet up with Ash." Chase pulled the truck onto the road, tires screeching. "Keep an eye out for Manning Road. It'll be a right turn in about half a mile after we turn onto the old logging camp access road."

Chase's stormy expression was as harsh as the weather, and his clipped tone didn't invite conversation, so Ben was silent. But he did a double take when he noticed, even in the dim light of the dashboard and the sporadic streetlights, that Chase was trembling.

Not just his hands on the wheel.

His entire body.

"You okay? You're shaking like an aspen leaf."

Chase shifted in his seat and adjusted his grip on the steering wheel. "Forgot to eat."

Fat snowflakes joined the freezing rain that fell from the pitch-dark sky and pelted the Ram's windshield as they drove at a snail's pace along a treacherous, winding road. The windshield wipers had a hard time keeping up with the frosty mess.

Ben peered out the window, keeping an eye out for their turn. Their destination was close to the citadel, but he didn't think he'd ever been down this narrow road before. They passed several boarded-up industrial buildings, relics of a bygone age when the logging industry boomed in the area.

Chase let up on the gas as the truck skidded and fishtailed on the icy road. "*Dammit!* Even with four-wheel drive, we're playing slip and slide."

Ben pointed in front of them at a street sign barely visible in the storm. "There's the turn."

"I see it."

As they negotiated the slippery corner, the truck slid again on a patch of ice. Ben braced his feet against the floor and his hand against the dash. He heaved a sigh of relief as Chase regained control. He glanced at his cousin's face again. Looked like he'd been carved from granite. But he had to ask; the suspense was killing him! "Well? You gonna tell me what's going on?"

"Ash called and said he found a way to protect Emma, to meet him immediately. Gave me the address and hung up. You know Ash. Phone etiquette ain't his strong suit."

Ben grinned as a wave of relief moved through him. "Well, why the heck didn't you tell me? That's great! Leave it to Ash to come through in the eleventh hour. Man, I was losing it today. Shaking every tree, looking under every rock for something, *anything*. I swear, I've aged a good fifteen years."

"Put me down for thirty. And counting."

What did that cryptic remark mean? Before he could ask, Chase pulled the Ram into the pothole-ridden parking lot of a run-down warehouse that had a *For Rent* sign hanging lopsidedly on the facade. Light shone through dirty, cracked windows. Ben arched a doubtful brow. "Sure this is the place?"

"Must be. Lights are on." Chase held his hand up to the dashboard light so he could double-check the address he'd written on his palm. "Yeah, this is it." They hiked up the collars on their coats and dashed through the icy storm to the rickety entry porch. With his hand on the doorknob, Chase turned and paused, looking out into the tempest.

"Chase?"

"Just give me a goddamn *fucking* second!"

Ben's throat tightened. What the hell was wrong with him? "Hey, I'm relieved, too, but we can get falling-down-on-our-asses drunk later and work off the emo. Let's go hear what Ash has to say."

Chase took a deep breath and nodded curtly. He opened the door, and they stepped inside.

Chapter Thirty-Seven

Ashriel stood waiting for them in the middle of the empty warehouse. The angel said nothing as the cousins crossed to him, their footfalls on the concrete floor echoing in the large, vacant building.

Ben grinned at Ashriel. Emma would be safe, and it was all because of him. "Hey, Ash."

Ashriel nodded in greeting.

Chase walked right up to Ash and put his hand on his shoulder. "Ash, I know you'd do anything to help Emma."

"Yes, of course. Anything."

Ben caught a flash of light out of the corner of his eye. In Chase's hand, the shimmering facets of a crystalline bident reflected the harsh overhead lights.

Before Ben could process what was happening, Chase plunged the bident into Ashriel's belly with a powerful upswing. The sharply pronged weapon cut through the leather anchetoch like a hot knife through butter. Ashriel's face was twisted with shock and pain. Beams of blue light exploded from his eyes and mouth with a sonic boom that rattled the building, shattering windows and blowing dust and debris into the air.

As Ashriel crumpled to the floor, the bident slipped from Chase's hand and fell to the concrete, the crystal ringing with its clarion death knell. "I'm so sorry, Ash," he whispered brokenly. "Please, *please*, forgive me."

Ben took two staggering steps back, not believing what he just saw. He finally found his voice. "*No! Ash!*"

The angel lay on his back, arms spread wide, unmoving.

As Chase turned away, his face a mask of grief, Ben rushed forward and fell to his knees beside Ashriel. He clutched the lapels of the angel's leather coat. "Ash!" He yanked on the lapels, shaking his friend, but there was no movement. "Ash! No, no, no, this can't be happening." Tears running down his face, Ben lurched to his feet and turned to his cousin, his mind reeling in shock and disbelief. "Chase? What have you done?" When Chase didn't answer, didn't even look at him, Ben's gut twisted with horror and rage. "*What the hell have you done?*"

Hades materialized in a cloud of sulfur dust and stood looking dispassionately down at Ashriel's body. "What he's done, Benjamin, is keep his end of our bargain. The angel's life for the girl's." He reached toward his scepter, and the bident obediently levitated into his hand. Hades's gaze shifted to Chase, and he gave a little laugh of disbelief. "Well, I'll be damned. Again. You actually did it. Killed your pet angel. Color me surprised. I owe Thorne a hundred souls. I guess love really changes a man." He nudged Ashriel's inert body with the toe of his shoe. "So glad I never suffered the affliction myself."

Chase glared at Hades, his face contorted with unconcealed hatred. "You got what you wanted, you fucking son of a bitch! Now make the curse on Emma permanent. And remember the rest of our deal. You never harm or have anyone else harm Emma or Ben. Ever!"

"You earned it." Hades raised his scepter, producing a sound wave that rang like a wet finger running around the edge of a crystal goblet. "Done and done, and so it shall be."

Trying to hold back the sobs that shook him, Ben stared at Ashriel's body in disbelief. It was surreal, a nightmare. Oh, God. Emma! How could he tell Emma her beloved angel was dead? And that *Chase* killed him? And Michael! What would he do? *Please, please, God, let me wake up. Please, let this be a nightmare.* He pinched his forearm hard, hoping the pain would wake him up. Only the stench of sulfur that always accompanied Hades anchored the horror in reality. "Why, Hades? Why kill Ash?"

With a grin, Hades shrugged. "It's always a good day to kill an angel." But his expression hardened, and his amused tone turned bitter and laced with hatred. "Revenge truly is a dish best served cold, and tonight my appetite is well sated. I've been biding my time ever since that feathered sod cheated me out of my prize. You, Chase. A Templar Knight, a laird no less, turned demon by my own clever manipulation. What a feather in my cap! I'd accomplished what they said couldn't be done. But Ashriel stole you from me. Foiled by a mere seraph—not even an archangel! He made me a laughingstock. My own demons laughing behind my back. No one makes a fool of Hades and gets away with it. *No one!*"

Chase pulled the Aegis of Solomon and pointed it at the Overlord of Hell. "You just won a spot on my kill list. The next time you see me—"

"Let me guess. You'll be there to kill me." Hades inspected his perfectly manicured fingernails. "I look forward to that, don't you?" His gaze shifted to Chase, and his eyes glinted with satisfaction. "However, you're missing the punchline. You, and by extension, your gargantuan cousin, just became my most loyal bodyguards. I die, and your girlfriend's curse dies with me. And don't forget that bit of information you want on the Illuminati demon who killed your father."

Smirking, Hades watched as it sank in and the color drained out of Chase's face. "Ahh, sweet victory, thy name is Hades. Oh, and boys? I'll expect a daily update from now on regarding the case of the missing souls. For the moment, no need for personal delivery. Just text me." Hades vanished, his evil laugh echoing.

His head pounding and his chest so tight he could barely draw breath, Ben kneeled again at Ashriel's side, looking down at his old friend, the angel who had protected him since birth. A memory squeezed his heart—Ash making snow angels with him on a sparkling, long-ago winter's day. *How could this be happening?*

He looked up at his cousin, still not believing the man he'd grown up with—the man he loved and trusted—could be capable of such a heinous thing. Had Hell changed him that much? "All he did for our family, for centuries. All he did for us. And for Emma. How could you?"

With sadness clouding his features, Chase stepped forward. "Benji, I—" But then he stepped back, his expression hardening. "I did what I had to do to protect her!"

Lurching to his feet, Ben gave a bitter laugh. "You think she's gonna *thank* you? She loves him. She'd have chosen to die before this. It'll be a miracle if she doesn't kill you. That's part of this, isn't it? You were so damn jealous of Ash, you let Hades manipulate you!" His ears rang and black spots danced in front of his eyes, and he couldn't get enough air into his lungs. He grabbed his head, knowing he was close to hysteria but powerless to stop it. "*You've ruined everything!*"

In a heartbeat, Ashriel's body shimmered and morphed into Malachi. He raised his head and grinned. "Hey, easy there, big guy. You're gonna hurt yourself."

Ben scrambled backward, stumbled, and fell hard on his ass. "*Malachi?*" He dropped his face into his hands, as overwhelming relief made him even more lightheaded. "Oh, thank God!"

"No, man." Malachi stood. "You should thank Chase. This was all his idea. So, guys, do I die good or what?" He punched the air with a quick succession of left and right jabs and jumped a good two feet into the air. "*What a rush!* That was a fucking blast! Who else can we punk?" He morphed into Ryan Reynolds, then Shaquille O'Neal, Bruce Springsteen,

Kim Kardashian, and finally back to his usual self, his dark-brown eyes twinkling. "I'm really versatile."

Laughing, Chase turned his gaze to Ben. And stopped laughing.

Ben remained on the floor, not sure his legs could support him yet. His emotions ricocheted wildly between intense relief and rage at being had. His face must have reflected his anger, because Chase's expression turned serious.

"I'm so damn sorry, Benji. You gotta know I hated doing that to you, but Hades had to choke it down, hook, line, and sinker, and you're no actor. Your honest reaction was the clincher." He shrugged and then jutted his chin to the side. "C'mon." He tapped his jaw. "One free punch, as hard as you want. I deserve it."

But Ben's anger disappeared as the full situation sank in. A bit of emotional torture was a small price to pay for Emma's safety. "No. I'd have done the same thing. We're good."

"Figured you'd see it that way." Chase's gaze swung back to Malachi. "You sure he's gone?"

Malachi shrugged. "Think so. Don't feel him anymore. *Holy shit*, that dude is scary powerful. Energy rolls off him in waves." He touched Ashriel's torc that hung around his neck. "And this thing's even worse. Plugging into this was like being strapped to a rocket and blasted into space. Thought my damn head was gonna explode."

"Thanks, man." Chase shook Malachi's hand, but then pulled him into a quick hug and clapped him on the back. "I owe you, dude. Big time, the biggest."

"No problem." He smiled and winked. "Can't be a bad thing to have a Templar Knight—and a freakin' angel—owe you a favor."

"Wait, guys," Ben said. "How did you know Hades wouldn't see through the ruse?" Chase and Malachi exchanged a look that raised the hairs on the back of Ben's neck. "You didn't know, did you?"

"Nope," Chase said. "Ash thought his torc might give enough cover, but he wasn't sure."

Ben gaped at Malachi. "Okay, I get Chase taking a chance like that for Emma every day of the week. But you? Do you have any idea what could've happened if Hades hadn't been fooled?"

Again, Malachi shrugged. "He's the King of Hell, so I got some inkling. But hey, if you won't take a risk to help a friend save the woman he loves, what kinda shit are you?"

Ben struggled to swallow a pterodactyl-sized portion of crow. He rose to his feet and extended his hand. "Emma's the sister I never had, so let me give you my thanks."

Mal gripped his hand and gave it a good shake.

"And my apology," Ben continued. "I didn't think too highly of you, and I've said as much to Chase. But he stood up for you. I see now that he was right."

Malachi nodded. "Thanks, man. Appreciate that."

"Oh, shit." Chase pulled his phone from his pocket and made a call. "Coast is clear, Ash. Come and get it." He pointed to Ashriel's torc that still hung around Malachi's neck. "He needs that back."

Ben gestured toward the torc. "How'd you even get it over your head in the first place? There's no catch on that thing."

Malachi smiled, and like a living version of a Stretch Armstrong toy, he morphed his head into a long cylinder. He lifted the torc up and over his head with ease before morphing back. "Nothing to it."

Ben had seen a multitude of strange things in his lifetime, but this was a new one. "Now I think I understand how Emma must have felt that first day when she woke up in the citadel."

Laughing, Chase clapped Malachi on the back as he handed him Ash's torc. "Now I understand why the ladies love you. Despite your ugly mug."

"Shapeshifting has its perks."

"I'll bet."

With a flap of wings that sent debris scattering, Ashriel appeared and nodded to Malachi. "Thank you for your assistance, Malachi."

"No sweat. Glad to help." But he took a step back, warily eyeing the angel.

"Okay, Ash," Chase said as he handed him his torc. "Get to it and fix our girl up. We'll be home real soon." Ashriel disappeared.

"Well," Malachi said, "if we're done here, I'll see ya on the flip side. Heading back up the road toward Alaska. I'll leave the angel's threads in my garage."

"Have a good fishing trip."

Malachi grinned. "Thanks. Got me a powerful hunger." But his grin faded, and he got a serious look. "Take real good care of her, man. That's a special girl you got there."

"I know."

"Ya know, I don't think you really do." He winked and sauntered across the warehouse toward the back exit, whistling as he went, his thick ponytail of brown spirals glinting under the lights and the clomping of Ashriel's black leather boots echoing through the space.

Ben's hands fisted. The knot that had been in his belly reformed. *Dammit!* Could Malachi tell that Emma was Chase's soulmate? Would he tell him? Or was it something else?

Malachi disappeared through the door, and it creaked closed behind him.

"I know he just helped pull Emma out of the fire," Ben said. "So why do I suddenly want to punch that guy in the face?"

"Just let it go. One epic problem at a time, please." Chase flexed his neck and rubbed his eyes. "Man, I'm deep-fried. Let's pick up the Porsche and go home."

"Thought it broke down."

"It didn't—" Chase shook his head, rolled his eyes heavenward, and headed for the exit. "Dude, try to keep up."

Chase and Ben trudged up the stairs from the garage. Emma ran into the room as they were taking off their wet boots. She got to Ben first, and he scooped her up and twirled her around and around, both laughing.

Chase dropped his boots in a corner, put on his slippers, and waited, grinning as her hair flew by him like a banner. "Okay, okay. My turn."

As soon as her feet hit the floor, Chase gathered Emma into his arms. He didn't lift her or twirl her; he just held her close to his heart. She hugged him hard, and he stood there with her pressed tightly against him, tears stinging his eyes, overwhelmed by so much emotion that he didn't think there was a word big enough to describe it.

"Thank you, Chase," she whispered. "Thank you so very much."

He nodded, unable to speak. He couldn't get the picture out of his mind of her lying on her bed, lifeless, with an angel sword sticking out of her blood-soaked chest—couldn't forget the sight of Ashriel, that stoic, self-controlled angel, on his knees next to her, sobbing his heart out.

They continued to hold each other tightly as the seconds passed.

That amazing feeling he got whenever they touched swirled through him like a warm, healing balm, smoothing out the raw, jagged edges. He would have stayed holding her like that forever, but finally, she eased back. She brushed a lock of hair from his forehead, then stroked a gentle hand down his face. She smiled softly up at him, and for a second, the look in her eyes took his breath away. Was that...could that possibly be...love?

Get a grip, Kincaid. He was kidding himself, seeing what he wanted to see. She was grateful, nothing more. "So glad you're okay, sweetheart." She nodded and gave him another quick hug, but when he glanced up, the look on Ashriel's face sent a chill down his spine. The angel looked like he wanted to pound him into dust.

His attention turned back to Emma as she patted his chest. "I can't even imagine what you went through. Why don't you and Ben go have a drink and relax? Tonight, I want to celebrate, and that means food, music, and booze." She gave her head a little shake. "Lots of booze." She headed for the kitchen with Ashriel following her, but he glared at Chase as he passed.

Chase pushed back hard against the frustration and jealously that had him clenching his fists. He couldn't blame Ash. He'd done it to himself, hadn't he? Planted his own ass firmly in the friend zone. He'd walked off the field and given Ash the right of way, free and clear.

What was it that Mal had said? *Take real good care of her, man. That's a special girl you got there*. Yeah, he'd take care of her, for sure. With everything he had until his last breath. But she wasn't so much his, not by a long shot.

Ash was clearly staking his claim.

Was that what Emma wanted? He had no clue.

He had some serious thinking to do.

But not tonight. He hadn't slept or eaten in days and could barely put two thoughts together. "C'mon, Benji. Bar's open, and I'm buying if you're pouring."

"Works for me."

Benji followed him to the Great Hall. Chase dropped onto the sofa, fell back against the cushions, and closed his dry, itchy eyes. The left side of his head pounded, and every damn bone in his body hurt. "I'm seriously thinking about a career change."

Benji snorted as he crossed the room to the liquor cabinet. "No, you're not."

"A vacation, then. A real vacation—the kind when you pack a bag and get on a plane and go hang out on a beach somewhere, gettin' sunburned and drinking rum from a coconut."

"Again, works for me. Head's up." Benji tossed him a can of Beer Nuts. "Better put something in your stomach or you'll pass out before the food is ready. Pretend it's airline peanuts and you're mid-flight on your way to the Caribbean."

"Thanks." Chase flipped the lid off the can as his stomach growled loudly. He gave his cousin a cocky grin. "Makes you my stewardess, don't it?"

"That's flight attendant, you Neanderthal, and I'm too tall to make the cut. Out of rum, but want whiskey?"

"Hell, yeah," he mumbled around a mouthful of peanuts. "A double. For starters."

What could she make that was fast and yummy? Emma peered into the refrigerator, making a mental list of the ingredients she had on hand and cross-referencing them with the hundreds of recipes stored in her memory. She already had a batch of cooked meatballs in the freezer and a jar of her homemade garlic, fennel, and basil pasta sauce in the cabinet. She had romaine lettuce and a loaf of French bread. Maybe spaghetti and meatballs with garlic bread and a Caesar salad? Not very challenging, but the guys would love it.

Especially Chase.

She wanted to do something nice for him, even if it was just making one of his favorite meals. He deserved so much more. Because of him and his friend she'd never met, she had a chance to live her life. They'd risked their lives for her!

Her heart constricted with emotion. Chase had tears in his eyes when she'd ended their hug. In truth, she hadn't wanted it to end, but the intense feelings she'd experienced in Chase's arms were confusing and disconcerting. All those feelings she'd harbored for years—when she'd truly believed that he was her meant-to-be love—had come rushing back, along with a heart-pounding dose of desire.

How could she still feel so strongly about Chase after what she'd just shared with Ashriel?

Still, she wished she'd allowed that hug to go on a while longer.

With a sigh, she shut the fridge door. Not the only door that closed for her that day.

Her curse was permanent.

Forever.

There would be no carefree drives in her new convertible under the incomparable Colorado sky, no getting in touch with Heather, or Rachel and Clayton, maybe going to visit them, meeting their adorable children.

But she was alive, and she was home.

She had no right to complain.

"Emma?" Ashriel stood with his arms crossed, a hip propped against the table. "I must leave for a while."

"Now? Where are you going?"

"It's near midnight. I'm going to Russo's home. I need to make certain things go according to plan. It's the only way to know you're safe."

"Is it dangerous for you to go? Can the hellhound hurt you?"

"No. There's no need for you to worry."

Not worry? Her heart pounded with anxiety. He would be in the same room with two monsters—Octavio Russo and a hellhound! What if Russo had armed himself with another spell from that damn book he'd bought? What if he'd somehow gotten his hands on something powerful that could kill the hellhound and maybe use it to hurt Ashriel? Not likely, and he didn't know Ashriel would come, but what if somehow he did? What if the hellhound—

She clamped down on her racing thoughts. She was overreacting, sliding down the slippery slope toward hysteria. She took a deep breath to calm herself and gain control of her emotions, but her voice trembled. "Please, hurry back."

"I will." He stepped toward the doorway.

"Ash, wait!" She clapped a hand over her mouth, regretting the outburst even as she reached for him.

He made it across the kitchen to her in only two long strides.

Ben poured two glasses of whiskey, handed Chase his drink, and headed for the kitchen.

"Where you going?"

"Ice."

Ben returned to the Great Hall in less than a minute. Without ice. He picked up his drink, tossed it back, and poured another.

"Thought you wanted rocks."

"We're out." In truth, Ben had no idea if they had ice or not. He hadn't gotten that far. He'd frozen in the doorway to the kitchen when he saw something that made his heart sink. Ash had Emma backed up against the fridge in a passionate kiss, and from the sexy little sounds she was making and the way her arms were wrapped around him, it was clear the attraction was mutual.

Ben's gut burned like fire as the alcohol landed in his empty, stress-irritated stomach, but he didn't care.

Disappointment burned far hotter.

His worst suspicions were confirmed, and it seemed that his hope of seeing Chase married to his soulmate and living happily ever after was doomed—and in turn, so was his own dream of leaving the citadel.

But...then again, was it? Yeah, it was a serious kiss, but still just a kiss, and emotions were running high for all of them after the overwhelming events of the day. Also, he had no proof that Ash and Emma's relationship had progressed any further than that kiss.

But he also had no proof that it hadn't.

But how could he find out?

And in either case, what could he do about it?

And there was something else that also had him worried. Had Chase realized it as well? If not, he had to tell him. He took his drink and sat across from Chase on the other side of the sofa, pulled the lever, and leaned back in the recliner seat. "Something's bothering me."

Chase sighed and gave him a baleful look. "There's a shocker."

"Seriously. You stabbed Malachi with Hades's scepter, a weapon that's supposed to kill anything. *Anything*. So why is he still breathing?"

Chase set the nut can on the coffee table and picked up his drink. "If I'd really been gunning to take him out, and he hadn't seen me coming, it woulda killed him. I assume. But he expected the blow, so he morphed his body around the prongs as I sunk it into him."

Ben's gut churned and his heart pounded as a wave of anxiety moved through him. "That's both the coolest thing I've ever heard of—like Marvel Superhero cool—and one of the scariest damn things I've *ever* heard of. How do you fight something like that?"

"As long as we're on the same side, it's the coolest. That ever changes? It goes back to scary. I ain't worried. As you saw tonight, he's a good guy. But you know what they say about keeping your friends close and your enemies closer. I figure that's so you get real familiar with their strengths. And their weaknesses. Good to know no matter what side of the fence you're on, ain't it?"

"For sure. So fill me in. My damn head's spinning. How'd this all go down?"

"That's right, you weren't in the room when we hashed out the plan." Chase grimaced and pressed his fist against the side of his head.

"Headache?"

"Yeah. Not surprising, I guess. Anyway, when we got nothing outta the demons, I got the idea to go to Hades, make another Hell-deal. I was out of my freakin' mind desperate, and it was the only card left to play. Called him to meet me, but I burned up the phone lines on the way, looking for something else. But nobody could help. Got Mal's voicemail, said he'd left for Alaska, so I left a message, just SOS, and sent a text with the same. So, not having any other damn choice, I went through with it. Asked Hades for help. Thought maybe he might have the power to just outright cure her, but he didn't. So I offered him up my soul in exchange for keeping Emma's curse activated to keep her safe from turning. But, apparently, only the—"

"Only the victim's soul will work."

"Yeah." Chase looked at him suspiciously. "How'd you know that?"

"Because I tried the same thing."

"Benji! What the fu—?"

"*Hey!* I love her, too!"

Chase's expression softened. "I know you do." He tossed back the rest of his drink. "Gotta give him credit. Hades came up with the ultimate torture. Force a man to choose between two people he loves, make him hold their lives in his hands...and only one gets to walk away."

As Chase stared at the flickering flames in the fireplace, Ben's mind reeled at the concept. He put himself in Chase's shoes, his heart pounding. The mental anguish his cousin must have suffered!

After a few minutes, Chase spoke, his voice reduced to a strangled whisper. "He broke me, Benji. I ain't proud of it, and I'd never admit this to anybody but you, but he did. Broke me in a way they never did in Hell. I was on my knees in this empty field, having prayed my damn heart out for God's help, and nothin'." He took a shuddering breath and turned to face him again. "It was just too fucking much. Something inside me...just...crumbled. I lost it. Put the Beretta to my head, and I was seriously thinkin' about pulling the trigger."

A rush of horror sent an icy chill down Ben's spine that made him shudder. "God Almighty," he whispered.

"Pray you never gotta face an impossible choice like that. Pray I don't have to, either." Chase stared at the fire for a few more minutes, then turned back to face him, eyes glittering with tears, although a slight smile curved his mouth. "But I think maybe God heard me, after all, 'cause just at that moment—" He paused and put a finger gun against his temple. "Just at that exact moment, with the gun muzzle against my head, Mal called me back. He'd been driving through that dead zone up between Fort Collins and Cheyenne. Somehow he'd got my text, although a call wouldn't go through, but he'd turned around and was hauling ass back here. Called me as soon as he had bars again. And while I'm telling him what's going on, outta the blue, I got the idea of pulling a fast one, having Mal pretend to be Ash and make Hades think he got what he wanted. My dad always said, if you can't beat 'em—"

"Trick 'em."

"Exactly. Mal agreed to do it, God bless him. He was about a half hour out, so I went home and found Ash crying over—" He broke off and swallowed convulsively, scrubbing his sleeve over his eyes as he took a shuddering breath. "Over Emma's dead body. She'd asked Ash to kill her, to save her. He'd taken her soul inside him again, so it wasn't too late if we could pull it off. Mal got there soon after, and we decided on the logistics. Ash showed him how to access his torc's power, gave him clothes. You hadn't shown up yet, but Chimera's tracker showed you were close, and we figured if you didn't know what was really going down, it would help fool Hades. So I called you to meet me at that gas station, while Mal headed over to the warehouse to wait for us. And the rest is history."

Having dismissed his staff, Octavio Russo was utterly alone in his twelve-thousand-square-foot Sagaponack, Long Island mansion. He sat in his study, the elegant room lit only by the flickering light provided by a gas-fed hearth, as he waited for midnight, and for his life to end. Puffing on a $750 Gurkha cigar, he sat among his most prized possessions and sipped Dom Perignon Rose Gold 1996 as opera played on a stereo system that cost more than most peoples' cars.

That single bottle of champagne cost $49,000.

His first wife and both his sons were dead, and his second and third wives had divorced him on grounds of mental and physical cruelty. He had no other children, no grandchildren, no siblings, no real friends.

He stared into the carved-marble fireplace, stiffening when a sudden gust of air made the fire dance. His heart stuttered, and he glanced at the mantel clock. Not yet midnight. He turned and saw someone standing across the room. "Who in the hell are you?"

The figure smiled. It wasn't a pleasant smile. "I'm an angel."

Octavio gave him the once-over and snorted. "An angel, my ass. You look like an undercover IRS agent. And I should know. Get the hell out! You can deal with my lawyers after I'm gone."

The supposed angel's eyes narrowed, and with a crash of thunder, a flash of lightning filled the room, casting an impressive shadow of outstretched wings on the wall.

Sudden hope lit Octavio's face. "Are you here to save me?"

His expression rock hard, his eyes frigid-blue glacier ice, the angel strode to where Octavio sat. He braced a hand on each arm of the eighteenth-century Georgian wingback chair and leaned over him. Octavio cowered back against the chair's back.

"*Save you?* You sentenced an innocent young girl to a lifetime of pain and terror and loneliness. I'm an avenging angel here to witness justice on her behalf. I'm here to watch the hellhound rip your black soul from your body and drag it back to the pit where it belongs. And then I'm going to burn down everything you've ever held dear, until nothing is left but ashes, including your mortal remains. I'm going to salt them and cast them into the four winds, so that nothing of you remains to sully the world. Oh, and on a personal note? I'm going to enjoy every second. Just as I enjoyed sending your misbegotten, murdering son to his just reward."

The mantel clock struck the first chime of midnight.

There was a thunderous, rumbling growl and sharp, heavy claws raked down the study door, accompanied by deep, dark, vicious barking.

As Octavio began to sob and shake, his eyes bugging out in terror, the angel went to stand in a corner near the fireplace. "That door is very sturdy, and I don't have all night. I have family waiting for me, so let's move this along."

And with a flick of his wrist, he opened the door.

Chapter Thirty-Eight

Ben leaned back in his chair, his stomach full and his mind at ease for the first time in months, thanks at least in part to the amount of alcohol he'd downed. He sat in the Great Hall with his family around one of the reading tables Emma had transformed into a dining room table, complete with a linen tablecloth and china dishes he hadn't seen since his childhood.

Music played on the stereo, and Emma's spur-of-the-moment feast had been consumed down to the last crumb, but the alcohol was still flowing, all but Ashriel in some state of drunkenness. Although he was drinking too, it would have taken the entire inventory of a good-sized liquor store to inebriate the angel.

Ben bit his lip as Emma tossed back her second shot of Jack Daniel's. There was already a line of hard apple cider bottles lined up in front of her plate.

Empty bottles.

He was glad she was having a good time, but she didn't usually drink much, and if she kept it up, she was going to make herself sick.

"Honest to God," she said, her words understandably slurred. "Never had a drink before I met you guys. Indy said not to, 'cause it dulled the senses, so I didn't. Hard apple cider is delicious." She held up her empty shot glass. "Even this stuff's not too bad once you get used to it."

Chase leaned over and took the glass from her. "I think you've had more than enough, sweetheart."

She hiccupped and raised a coy brow. "Maybe I have, and maybe I haven't."

"You have," Chase said firmly. "Bar's closed."

Pouting, she picked up two empty beer bottles, laid them on their sides on the table, and made them spin, her eyes rolling in circles.

Ben chuckled. "Poor Emma. Hangovers suck. Especially your first one. Still remember mine. Thought I was gonna puke forever."

Yawning, Chase scratched his beard. "Yeah. Me, too. Right up there with the first time I got shot." He looked over at Ashriel. "Maybe you can do something about that for her later?"

"Certainly."

"Well," Ben said, "Emma's safe; a hellhound is picking Russo's black soul out of his teeth as we speak, and Hades believes Ash is dead, which pretty much makes him our secret weapon. As much of a bitch as it was, I'd still call that a good day."

"Yeah, but downside. Until we find another way, you and me gotta make sure Hades keeps breathing. Not that I'm real worried about that. Not even sure the Aegis could take him down."

Ben sighed. "Great. Now, we're Hades's bitches." But his eyes settled on Emma, and he shrugged. Family defended family, no matter what. She got a little too enthusiastic about her spinning, and one bottle careened into a full glass of water, knocking it over.

"Oh, crap!" She dragged herself up and staggered around the table, snatching up napkins and slapping them down into the spill.

Ben got up to help her, but she didn't see him behind her, and she backed up against him. Startled, she lurched forward, tripped over her own feet, and landed sideways in a surprised Chase's lap. Her head dropped to his shoulder. Groaning, she closed her eyes. "Why is the damn room spinning?"

Laughing along with Ben, Chase wrapped his arms around her when she almost slid off and onto the floor. "Okay, I gotcha, sweetheart."

The look of adoration on Chase's face as he gazed down at her made Ben's heart warm. There was no doubt in his mind that his cousin was in love with her. Chase pressed a kiss to the top of her head, but when he glanced up, he recoiled. Ben followed his gaze and was shocked at the furious scowl that hardened Ashriel's face.

What the hell? Chase couldn't even be affectionate with her now without Ash getting angry.

But Chase's jaw tightened. His eyes narrowed, and he held her closer to him.

For a long, tense moment that had Ben's heart racing, steel-gray eyes locked with angry blue.

Until Emma moaned. "Sick."

Ashriel was by her side in an instant. "Come on, let's get you to bed." He touched her, and they were gone.

Even though Ben had witnessed that kiss between Ash and Emma in the kitchen, the intense look on Ashriel's face still shocked him.

His eyes wide, Chase looked over at him. "Dude, see his face?"

"Oh, yeah." Ben dropped back into his chair. He'd decided not to tell Chase about that kiss, but it was time to poke the tiger. "Looks like he's got it bad. What about you?"

"I want her. God knows I want her."

Ben slapped his hands down on the table. "You *want* her? What does that even mean?"

"You gonna make me say it? Fine! I'll say it!" Chase scrubbed his hands over his cheeks and then sighed, dropping his hands into his lap in a defeated gesture. Both his expression and his voice softened. "Benji, I'm crazy in love with that girl. But she ain't ever gonna look at me the way she looks at him."

"You don't know that. You get that this isn't about special powers or physical strength, right? It's about winning her heart."

Chase gave a half-hearted shrug. "But what if it's too late?"

"But what if it isn't? You gotta be in it to win it." Ben leaned forward, lowering his voice. "I know what you did to save us from the manticore."

"How the hell—"

"You left the transference spell open on the computer."

"Oh." He blew out a sigh. "*Fuck me.*"

"Chase. An entire year of your life?"

"No choice. Don't tell Emma. That's an order. Unless I suddenly disappear at the dinner table or something, and you have to."

Ben nodded. "I'm so damn proud of you."

"You're drunk."

"And Uncle George would be, too. I'm honored to call you my laird."

Chase's pained and confused expression was almost comical, if not for the silvery glitter of tears he furiously blinked back. "Don't! *Don't do that.* I can't fill his shoes!"

"You already have. We'd all be dead if not for your bravery and your leadership. Emma, twice over."

With a sigh, Chase reached for the scotch bottle. "What nonsense are you spouting now?"

"I figured it out. She was done for after her resurrection. Her curse was blocking Ash's healing power, just like it's blocking the vampire sickness. His healing power only worked *after* you transferred her curse onto you to lure the manticore. The only reason she's still alive is because you sacrificed a year of your life, and I'd have been that manticore's dinner. And tonight? You were the one who tricked Hades, and that cleverness saved her life yet again. Ash killed her, and I don't hold that against him. It was what she wanted—her decision. She couldn't see another way out. Your actions are why she's still with us."

"With Malachi's help. Couldn't have done it without him."

"And now you owe a skinwalker a favor—as he clearly pointed out. Not a position I'd want to be in."

"Yeah, but it's Mal. I ain't worried."

"I hope you're right. Look, Malachi earned my gratitude and respect tonight. What he did—what you both did—took balls of steel. And I'll never forget that maybe you're sitting here because of him. But I can't say he earned my trust—not my complete trust. Not by a long shot."

"I know. And I get what you're saying. You're right. I don't trust him the way I trust you or Ash, but I don't not trust him, either." He swirled the scotch around in his glass, then raised it in salute. "Hey, you wanna see the real hero in all of this? Look in the mirror."

Hero? He was no hero! An unsettling moment of déjà vu made his head swim. "*Me?* What are you talking about?"

"Benji, if it weren't for you, we'd have been caught swimming naked and toasting marshmallows on the beach when the tsunami rolled in. You're the only one who put two and two together and warned us in time. And don't forget, you're the one who found the counterspell to that fucking love potion and cut me loose from Santana. That was all you, buddy. Sounds like hero to me."

Ben squirmed in his chair, and his ears grew warm. He was beyond glad that he'd helped. But pointing out at the last minute what should have been obvious from the start about the danger Emma was in didn't add up to hero in his book. "Yeah, well, back to Emma. You love her, man. Well, fight for her! But it's the bottom of the ninth, Chase, and the bases are loaded in his favor. You've been warming the bench, but if you're gonna get in the game, you better step up to the plate, and after the way you've been avoiding her? You better bring your A-game, and you better hit it out of the park."

Chase leaned forward, his eyes filled with frustration. "You know me. When I play, I play to win. But get real. Any other guy, I'd be swinging hard. But he's a freakin' angel! What chance do I got?"

"That's the thing! He's an angel. You're a man, and she's a woman."

"Don't matter to her. Ash hung the moon as far as she's concerned."

Ben couldn't argue with that, and if Chase wasn't willing to fight for her, the game was already over. Unless...

Unless he pulled out the big gun.

Maybe it was time to tell Chase that Emma was his soulmate. Now that he'd admitted he was in love with her, maybe he would look past the Chase-the-Muppet-with-God's-hand-up-his-ass concept of soulmates. Maybe it would give him the confidence to fight for her.

But just as Ben would have opened his mouth to speak, Chase's jaw tightened, and he flexed his neck and squared his shoulders. The gray eyes that met Ben's now blazed with steely determination. Chase raised his beer in a toast. "Game on, and screw the odds. Sometimes the long shot wins and wins big. Here's to your future cousin-in-law. If she'll have me."

Relief coursing through him, Ben grinned and clinked his bottle to Chase's. "Now you're talking."

Ashriel came back to the table, sat down, and picked up his beer.

"She okay?" Chase asked, his voice clipped.

"Sleeping peacefully. She'll wake with no hangover."

"Good. Thanks."

Hoping to defuse the tension, Ben raised his beer bottle again. "Here's to the cutest little drunk ever. To keeping her safe, and happy, and here with us, where she belongs." Three bottles clanged together.

Ashriel pulled an ancient, leather-bound book out of his coat pocket and handed it to Chase. "I took the liberty of removing this from Octavio Russo's home. This is the book of spells Russo purchased."

Ben's heart soared, and Chase's face lit up. Maybe the counter-spell to Emma's curse was in that book! But Ashriel shook his head. "I already checked. Unfortunately, only the summoning spell to call the soultrader demon is in there. There's nothing on a possible counter-spell written within those pages."

Ben's heart sank. *Dammit!* Why couldn't anything ever be easy?

Eyeing the spell book, Ashriel's lip curled in revulsion. "That tome reeks of evil magic. I'm sure you recognize the sigil on the cover."

Ben nodded, grimacing. "The Sigil of Satan."

"Yes. And the leather? It's human skin."

Chase gasped and dropped the book onto the table. "*Dammit*, Ash! Couldn't tell me that *before* I touched the fucking thing?"

"Simply touching the book will not harm you."

"Tell that to my future shrink." Chase jumped up and headed for the arch.

"Chase, wait," Ben said. "You should store that thing away in the Laird's Library. Inside a cursed-objects box, just to make sure."

"Way ahead of you, Benji. Be right back." After a moment, Chase returned with a pair of kitchen tongs. He picked up the book with the tongs and carried it to one of the built-in bookshelves. He reached up and twisted a pewter statuette of an owl that sat on the shelf and murmured a few words in Latin. Soundlessly, the bookshelf swung open to reveal a secret room lined floor to ceiling with glass-covered bookcases loaded with books, scrolls, boxes, and artifacts.

Selecting a burled-wood box covered with occult symbols from a shelf, he dropped the book inside, closed the box, and put it inside a glass case. Then he left the hidden library, twisted the owl to face forward, and the bookshelf swung shut, once again concealing the room. He headed back toward the arch. "I'm gonna throw these tongs in the trash and then scrub the hell outta my hands."

After Chase returned, they sat in silence for a few minutes until Ben took a deep breath and blew it out with a long *whoosh* to release the tension that had built up inside him. "Something big is coming, guys. Like, cosmically big. I can feel it."

Chase swirled the rest of his beer and studied the amber liquid as if the answers he sought were trapped in the bottle. "Yeah, me too. Felt it for a while now. Dammit."

"Think it has anything to do with Emma?" Ben asked.

"Something's definitely going on with her, but I don't feel like this is it." Chase eyed Ashriel. "You?"

"No. But the issue of the missing souls is an anomaly we cannot ignore. Hades is correct. Energy of that enormity cannot simply disappear. Something took them. Or someone. And whoever or whatever it was is incredibly powerful."

Ben poured himself a last shot of whiskey. He really needed to cut back on the alcohol. But not tonight. "And all we need to do is figure out who or what took them, and where. And why. And if we can get them back. And how." He tossed back the shot and gave a sarcastic snort. "Hey, nothing to it. Of course, a solid lead other than some dots on a map might be helpful."

"Something's gonna turn up, Benji. So far, forty-three people dead, their souls Bermuda-triangled? Gotta be more evidence somewhere, or they got something in common, and we're missing it." Chase grinned, tossed back a shot, guzzled down the rest of his beer, and grabbed another. "And after I get over my own impending hangover, we'll get right on that."

They drank in companionable silence for a while. Then Chase, just a bit wobbly, got to work cleaning up. He wasn't gonna leave the mess for Emma to deal with in the morning. He smiled as he gingerly placed another china plate on the stack he'd just scraped. He loved that Emma had brought out his mother's fancy dishes to use. Mom woulda liked that, too. They'd been sitting unused in a cabinet for sixteen years.

"This sucks," Ben said. "She's gonna figure it out when she has time to think."

Chase threw a questioning glance at his cousin. "Figure out what?"

"The reality of her situation. She's been so happy here with us. Now she has to live with the fact that Hades holds her fate in his hands. Any time he wants, he could lift her curse, and she could turn into a vampire. It'll wreck her."

Chase hadn't thought of that. His mellow mood crashed and burned. He slammed his fist on the table. "*No!* This is on us. We made decisions for her—decisions that got her into this mess in the first place. Now it's up to us to get her out. Look, Hades may be a dick, but he keeps his agreements. Unless he finds out Ash is still kicking, we're golden."

"No, we're not," Ben said. "Don't you see? You didn't make a soul deal. This is just a deal. The rules don't apply. With a soul deal, if he doesn't keep up his end of the bargain, he doesn't get the soul. That's God's rule, and even Hades can't break it. But what's he got to lose if he defaults on your agreement? Did you get it in writing?"

"No. What good would that do? Not like we could take him to court."

"Exactly! So, basically, all we've got here is his word. *His word?* We can't trust that douchebag."

Chase blew out a harsh sigh, propped his elbow on the table, and dropped his head into his hand. "Son of a bitch, you're right." After a moment, he looked up. "But he's got us by the balls, and he knows it. He wants the missing souls case solved, and we're his best shot. And now we're his lackeys. Jump when he says jump, and we gotta ask how high. He's got us exactly where he wants us. He won't wanna screw that up. But that can't last forever, or I'll stick a knife in my own throat."

A knot formed in his gut as he imagined Emma's face when they told her, or when she figured it out, her chin trembling and her eyes filled with tears. Benji was right. It would wreck her.

Memories flickered through his mind—Emma in the kitchen, singing along to the radio as she kneaded bread dough while a pot of beef soup simmered on the stove; seated at a table in the Great Hall, her brow furrowed as she painstakingly translated an ancient scroll into English; sitting on the sofa, her feet propped on the edge of the coffee table as she painted her toenails and watched TV; laughing and congratulating Benji in the dojo after he drove her to the mat for the first time.

Safe and happy.

After the hell she'd been through, how could he take that away from her?

What good would it do for her to know?

None at all.

And he knew just how to fix it.

"You're right, Benji. We gotta find a way to get her out of this—and we will, or I'll die trying—but you're right. Emma shouldn't have to deal." He cocked his head toward Ashriel. "And she don't have to."

Understanding dawned on Ben's face. "She doesn't have to know. Ash could erase her memory of it."

"Bingo. She could go right back to Happy Town, population one, while we take care of business and set things right."

Ben nodded, but doubt crept over his face. "It's lying to her. Again."

"Yeah, it is. But same holds true. This gonna be our burden? Or hers? You in willingly, or do I gotta make it an order?"

"In. For sure. But what do we tell her? What about the missing time?"

Ashriel was lost in whirling, desperate thoughts. *Erase it?* They wanted him to wipe her memory of all of it! And along with it, erase all that had passed between Emma and him?

The priceless treasure he'd held so briefly in his arms. Gone? *No!* No, he wouldn't do it! But his throat was constricted with shame. He was being incredibly selfish. Ben and Chase were right. Emma shouldn't have to suffer, and she would suffer. She'd figure it out in no time, and she'd live in fear that she could turn into a vampire without warning and hurt someone.

Kill someone.

She would never know a moment's peace, a moment's happiness.

Although it was unlikely that Hades would discover they had tricked him, it was a real possibility, and if he did, Ashriel had no doubt that the cruel ruler of Hell would begin his revenge by lifting Emma's curse. Her situation was different now, anyway. The immediate danger was past. His mating with her directly resulted from her desperation and her decision to die rather than risk becoming a vampire. He never would have touched her otherwise!

Not that he wasn't culpable. He could have refused.

Yet...he couldn't. His own desire for her aside, how could he have denied Emma her last request?

But now she was alive and well.

Because of Chase.

He remembered the way she'd looked after Chase kissed her in the garage. She'd stood there, her fingers pressed to her lips, staring at the garage door long after they'd gone. And that hug tonight that went on far longer than a simple thank-you hug should have.

As deeply as it hurt, it was clear she had feelings for Chase.

Chase, who also loved her.

Chase—her soulmate.

After overhearing his drunken admissions to Emma, he understood why Chase had avoided her and denied his attraction. He hadn't been rejecting her; he didn't believe himself worthy. It had shocked him to his core to hear that Chase might have murdered an innocent. But he knew Chase Kincaid very well; he had known him since his first newborn breath, and he didn't believe such an honorable man was capable of such a terrible act, not for a second.

But maybe he was wrong. Chase had been a demon at the time and was not in his right mind. It was possible. There had to be a way to discover the truth, and he vowed to find it.

He pictured Emma hugging Chase again. His breathing sped up, and his wings violently twitched as shame and regret warred with jealousy and sank vicious claws into his heart. He'd come close to physical violence earlier. Just a hug, and yet he'd come close to harming his friend, his charge, the current laird of the family he was duty-bound to protect!

What had he become?

He had to find the strength to put his own feelings aside and do what was best for Emma and for Chase. She'd become too dependent on her guardian angel. And he'd allowed it—encouraged it. Selfishly. He saw that now. It was time to step back and give Chase and Emma time and space to find each other. He hadn't lied to Ben; the concept of soulmates was a divine mystery. Were Chase and Emma meant to be together? He didn't know. But they deserved the chance to find out.

By wiping her memory, not only could he save her from needless worry and suffering, but he could also give her back the freedom to choose her own path and her own destiny.

To freely choose her mate.

It's what an honorable angel would do.

What a hero would do.

He flinched when Chase waved a hand in front of his face. "Ash! You having a stroke or something?"

"No. What?"

"What was she doing right before you clued her in on what was going down?"

"She was in the kitchen making a cup of tea."

"Before that?"

"Sitting on the sofa, watching TV."

"Good, that's good. She conks out on the couch all the time. Wipe her memory back to that point. We'll tell her she fell asleep again watching TV, and you gave her a dose of angelic Ambien again, so she'd just stay asleep through it all, so she wouldn't make herself sick with worry about whether her curse would be over or not at midnight."

Ben leaned back in his chair. "That's a good plan. But what about when she wakes up tomorrow? I mean, we three know her curse didn't end, but she's gonna want to know. You know Emma and her experiments. She'll want to test it."

Chase nodded. "Yeah, you're right. Obviously, we're not gonna let her dangle herself out there like a worm on a hook to see if she attracts a monster." His brows drew together as he drummed his fingers on the table. After a moment, he slapped his palm down and grinned. "What we need is a ringer. A friendly monster who'd go along with us in setting up a safe, controlled experiment."

Ben gave a disbelieving laugh. "A friendly monster? Just where are we supposed to get a friendly monster? Oh, wait. Gavin?"

Grinning, Chase nodded. "Yep. Gavin. Our own peace-loving, bong-banging, hippy werewolf. He can put himself in lockdown, and when her curse makes him wolf-out, we can get her out of there fast." Chase stood, fished his phone out of his jeans, and scrolled through his contacts list. "Been a while, but I still got him in here somewhere."

Ashriel stood next to Emma's bed, gazing down at her. Earlier, he'd extracted the alcohol from her body and healed the alcohol-induced inflammation, and with no ill effects remaining, she slept comfortably.

She lay on her back, one arm flung behind her head, her hair cascading over the pillow, her lovely face rosy from sleep.

He touched her forehead and eased her into a deep sleep, then raised his trembling hand and held it poised above her head. This was almost worse than having to kill her. At least afterward, she'd have been with him forever.

He was losing her.

No! He couldn't allow himself to think of it that way. He was putting things right. He would be her friend and her protector. Her guardian angel.

But he would remember those precious hours when she loved him. Even when she didn't.

His grieving heart shattered into a million pieces; each piece she owned, she would always own. He knew—just as surely as he knew the sun would rise—that he would never love another.

The pain all but destroyed him. His hand, still poised above her head, shook. But he lowered his hand and erased the memories.

To be continued…

BOOK TWO JUST RELEASED!

KNIGHTS OF ORION CITADEL

Nightmare of Consequence

I hope you enjoyed spending time at Orion Citadel and plan to join us for the next adventure.

Please consider leaving a review; it only takes a few seconds to leave a starred review, but I'd love to know your thoughts in a written review. If you're on an eReader, click the EZ link below to leave a review on Amazon.

https://www.amazon.com/review/create-review?&asin=B0CH5T9YKK

Reviews are critical for an author's success, especially for independent authors like me.

If you would consider leaving a review on Goodreads, too, that would be greatly appreciated!

Sign up for announcements and special offers at **www.Avalon-Writes.com.** (Just the good stuff, like new release announcements and discount offers. No spam or monthly newsletter to clog your inbox.)

Thank you!